Red Star Tales

RED STAR TALES

A CENTURY

OF RUSSIAN AND SOVIET

SCIENCE FICTION

YVONNE HOWELL, EDITOR

ANNE O. FISHER, TRANSLATION EDITOR

RUSSIAN LIFE BOOKS

Cover design: Taisiya Kulygina

Video Editor: Victoria Savchenko
Rights Researcher: Aigul Yangalina

ISBN 978-1-880100-38-7

Library of Congress Control Number: 2015953223

RIS Publications
PO Box 567
Montpelier, VT 05601-0567
www.russianlife.com
orders@russianlife.com
phone 802-223-4955

Contents

INTRODUCTION

Red Star Tales: A Century of Russian and Soviet Science Fiction. For most Anglophone readers, the title itself suggests something intriguingly exotic, otherworldly, and as thought-provoking as any trip to an entirely different place. What kind of science fiction was produced in the Soviet Union, which began as a radical experiment in social change, and ended seven decades later in sudden, unplanned political and social dissolution? Why haven't we heard more about Russian science fiction (in translation) before? After all, one of the most salient features of Soviet society was the overvaluation of literature – and the genre of science fiction was no exception – as nearly the only forum for discussion about individual values and the organization of society, as well as about the possible paths society might take in the future.

From 1917 until 1990, the Soviet Union's single political party (Communist) upheld an officially uncontested state ideology (Marxism-Leninism). In this arrangement, there could be no airing of debates about public policy, economic goals, or cultural institutions in the platforms of competing political parties and factions (since there were none), nor would debates about the future of Soviet socialism play out in official newsprint and other state-controlled media. Yet the lack of an outlet for civic debate and the limited possibility of voicing alternate viewpoints in non-fictional forums did not mean that there was no such discussion at all. Instead, it meant that literature retained the heightened importance it had won in Russia already under the tsars: writers of Russian literature were considered to be Russia's "second government," with an obligation to articulate "the conscience of the people." Literary works were read not just for entertainment, and often not even primarily for entertainment, but for what they could convey to their readers about the state of the collective national consciousness. Throughout the twentieth century, one of the most "exotic" things about Russian literature, from the perspective of most Western societies, was that people read a lot of it, and they read it *as if it really mattered*. Science fiction mattered.

Science fiction itself is a genre that is characterized by two basic principles: *extrapolation* of a rational, plausible scientific premise (*what if* we had this knowledge or technology?) and *estrangement* (*how different* things would seem to be). By virtue of the genre itself, we are already prepared to confront visions of the outside world, or of our inner selves, that are in some way at odds with known reality. Yet science fiction is not fantasy or fairy tale: the motive for the altered reality depicted – or even just hinted at – in these stories is never supernatural, or magical, or nostalgically nestled in a golden age of pre-industrial folk pastorals. On the contrary, science fiction is a genre that arose in response to the completely unprecedented power of new knowledge paradigms, beginning in the latter half of the nineteenth century. As has been endlessly pointed out (because it's so easy to forget), for the great duration of human history, people have lived, as it were, by candlelight and on horseback. The planet-altering discoveries of our geological era – which many people now consider to be the Anthropocene[1] – are startlingly recent. It wasn't until the beginning

---

1. The Anthropocene is a proposed term for the geological epoch in the late Holocene (which followed the Pleistocene), during which the impact of human activities begins to significantly shape planetary ecosystems. The Russian geochemist Vladimir Vernadsky first coined the term "noosphere" in the 1920s to describe a geological era in which human cognition begins to fundamentally transform the biosphere. In recent years, the term Anthropocene has been popularized by the Dutch atmospheric scientist Paul Crutzen.

of the twentieth century that the widespread use of electricity, radio, automobiles, airplanes, and radiation technology allowed societies in the more developed parts of the world to not only compress unfathomable distances in time and space, but also to control and manipulate the natural and social environment with unprecedented technologies. No wonder the genre of science fiction grew up so quickly in the 1920s, and dominated so much of our cultural imagination during the nuclear build-up and space race of the Cold War; no wonder we now think of a lot of our daily experience with self-guiding vehicles and knowing computational devices as vaguely "science fictional."

But wait a minute! Why would science fiction emerge so early, and so strongly, in late nineteenth-century Russia, of all places? Paradoxically, the precocious flowering of a futuristic genre whose imaginary worlds were not only *estranged* from the present, but also rigorously extrapolated from *cognitive* (plausibly scientific) premises happened in a society that lagged noticeably in almost all indicators of social, economic, and technological development. In other words, science fiction grew most vigorously in a place where one might least expect it: a backward agricultural empire at the outermost margins of Europe. The Russian Empire under the last tsars was only belatedly beginning to industrialize along Western European models, and the vast majority of the Empire's population still toiled in rural landscapes that seemed almost untouched by modernity. The peasants were religious, superstitious, and illiterate. To be sure, a small but influential cohort of educated urban intellectuals was intensely interested in new scientific developments and their potential to transform existing society. As evidenced by the stories presented in the first part of this anthology, the insights of Russian artists, scientists, and intellectuals at the turn of the century derive from an extraordinary vantage point. Russia was at the margins of the industrialized world, belatedly undergoing a process that Leon Trotsky famously diagnosed as "combined and uneven" development. There was something inherently science fictional about this situation: during the Revolutionary decades before and after the Bolshevik coup in 1917, one detects a desire to jump from behind, over the present, directly into a radically more advanced future. Thus, in the waning decades of the Russian Empire, many of the most renowned artists and intellectuals of the time produced works of fiction that consciously probed a revolutionary new premise: what if the unprecedented pace of scientific and technological discovery is consciously harnessed to utopian ideas of social and even spiritual advancement, so that age-old dreams of peace, plenty, and even immortality are no longer the stuff of fairy tales, but the impetus for rational blueprints to shape the future? It might be a short step from science fiction to Soviet *sputnik*.

PART I: RED STAR RISING
SCIENCE FICTION FROM THE REVOLUTIONARY ERA

One can confidently make the claim that the Soviet space program was born not in the throes of military-technological competition between the U.S. and U.S.S.R., but in the seminal philosophical writings of Nikolai Fyodorov (1829-1903), and in the aerodynamic experiments of his legendary pupil, Konstantin Tsiolkovsky (1857-1935).[2] We include two short pieces by these Russian visionaries, in order to give the reader a sense of the erudition and audacity of Fyodorov's thought, and the degree to which Tsiolkovsky's precocious feats of aeronautical engineering were also exercises in "applied futurism."

Nikolai Fyodorov's 1892 essay, on the "meteorurge" who would use science to orchestrate global weather patterns, rather then just predict them as the meteorologist does, illustrates the expectation of spiritual salvation that was indivisible from the Russian thinker's scientific rationalism. The essence of Christianity itself, according to Fyodorov, is to join all human beings in the common cause of resolving

---

2. Michael Holquist, "The Philosophical Bases of Soviet Space Exploration." In *The Key Reporter* 51:2 (Winter 1985-6). Tsiolkovsky was the first person to figure out most of the things necessary to make, launch and sustain life in rockets. Working alone, mostly deaf since childhood, he wrote hundreds of reports on, among other things, designs for rockets with steering thrusters, multistage boosters, airlocks for exiting a spaceship, how much fuel is needed to overcome the Earth's gravitational pull, etc.

the *meaning* of the "interdependence between sentient beings and the blind, unfeeling forces of nature." We leave it to each reader to contemplate the powerful oddness and appeal of Fyodorov's vision, as well as the wry commentary on things that remain the same across eras and cultures: in his story, government representatives veto funds that would have supported research to prevent famine-causing droughts, but with a stroke of the same pen, they pour money into a proposal to increase spending on a "zeppelin, capable of carrying enough passengers and explosives to blow up all the fortifications or personnel of the greatest military powers."

Tsiolkovsky's short story "On the Moon" – written in 1893 – is almost devoid of fictional grace or plot tension, although he clearly enjoyed describing (quite accurately!) the physical sensations of weightlessness, low boiling temperatures, disorienting diurnal rhythms, and other things that a human being would encounter during a sojourn on the moon. One anonymous Russian blogger summed up the value of this story over a century later with the quip: "a tiny baby step for Russian literature, but a giant leap towards humanity's era of cosmic exploration."

The story "One Evening in 2217" was written by an almost unknown Nikolai Fyodorov (not related to the first). It stands out as one of the earliest dystopias of its kind. It is remarkable to find most of the essential themes of Evgeny Zamyatin's brilliant dystopian novel *WE* (1924) already present in this under-acknowledged harbinger, written in 1906. The two sketches by Valery Bryusov, a renowned poet and member of the mystical-aesthetic Symbolist movement, were written a few years later, in a time of almost apocalyptic anticipation, just before the onset of WWI and the Russian Revolution. For many Russian intellectuals, the approaching upheaval was not so much a political matter as an expression of a deep shift in the relationship between human beings and the natural and spiritual world. Bryusov's fantasies about machines that suddenly acquire a perverse will (to rebel), and human beings grown so sedentary that doctors issue warnings about muscular atrophy, were meant as cautionary tales, but today they no longer seem so far from current realities.

Throughout the 1920s, citizens of the young Soviet State read science fiction and clamored for more. One of Lenin's earliest priorities was to "liquidate illiteracy" in a vast population that remained uneducated in tsarist times. "Without literacy," Lenin declared, "there can be no politics – there can only be rumors, gossip, and prejudice."[3] A massive educational campaign rapidly increased rates of literacy, especially in growing urban populations. Moreover, the relatively limber market that resulted from Lenin's New Economic Policy strategy in the 1920s allowed for a burgeoning publishing industry that was quite responsive to consumers' desires. While Party ideologues and literary critics fretted over quality control, the newly literate masses devoured "rumor, gossip, and prejudice" in the form of adventure stories, detective fiction, and fantastic tales about mad scientists, technological wonders, and daring cosmic voyages.[4] One of the most beloved Soviet science fiction writers was Alexander Belyaev, whose exciting yet heartfelt tales of liminal existences (an anguished living head severed from its body; an extraordinary yet sad Amphibian Man) remain popular to this day. Belyaev's 1926 story "Professor Dowell's Head" was the first to use the genre term "science fiction" (*nauchnaya fantastika*) explicitly in its subtitle, and to defend the value of the genre on the shifting terrain of Soviet cultural politics. An editor's introduction pointed out that Belyaev's story is based on the kind of scientific advancement (a head transplant!) that is not yet a reality, but current Soviet experiments in the field might make such advancements possible in the future. Meanwhile, "Professor Dowell's Head" was an instant success – who doesn't like snappy writing, a taut plot full of devious intrigue, fantastic scientific horizons, and a terrible ethical conundrum that must be solved?[5]

---

3. Joseph Slabey Roucek, *The Challenge of Science Education* (U.S.A.: Philosophical Library, 1971).
4. Matthias Schwartz, "How *Nauchnaia Fantastika* Was Made: The Debates about the Genre of Science Fiction from NEP to High Stalinism" in *Slavic Review*, Vol. 72, No. 2 (SUMMER 2013), pp. 224-246.
5. An earlier English language translation of "Professor Dowell's Head" by Antonina Bouis (NY:

PART II. RED STAR IN RETROGRADE?
SCIENCE FICTION IN STALIN'S TIME

Under Stalin, the horizons of scientific discovery were circumscribed by the regime's ideological biases; aesthetic norms were dictated from above; and in a perverse travesty of "communist ideals," ethical discussions were driven out of the public sphere (officially, in public, Soviet society was the freest, happiest, and most moral in the world) into the often heroic, often tortured private spaces of individuals coming to terms with an era of widespread terror, suffering, and – paradoxically – grandiose national accomplishments. Stalinist cultural policy mandated a function for all the arts: to provide inspiring, yet realistically portrayed visions of soon-to-be-perfected Soviet socialism. The key features of the immanent society to be depicted in art were full industrialization, palpable leaps in life expectancy and education, and genuine enthusiasm for a collective future that is *a priori* worth the sacrifices made on its behalf. In practice, these Stalinist literary strictures constrained the range of science fiction to the rather un-science-fictional "near goals" of the "near future." Was Cold War scholarship justified in writing off two decades of Soviet "near" science fiction as worthless? Our Stalin-era selections suggest that the situation was more complicated.

Yuri Dolgushin's novel *Generator of Miracles* was completed in 1938 and published in its entirety in 1939 and 1940, in serial installments of the journal *Technology-Youth*. Oddly enough, the journal publications were never interrupted, despite a ban on the negative portrayal of Germans that went into effect with the Molotov-Ribbentrop Pact, a Soviet-Nazi non-aggression treaty that was signed in August 1939 (and abruptly violated when the Nazi Army invaded the Soviet Union on June 22, 1941). Dolgushin noticeably reworked his novel for a book publication in 1958, during the post-Stalinist period of reform. The chapter translated in our volume is from this later book version,

<hr>

Macmillan, 1980) is based on Belyaev's much-expanded and altered 1938 book-length version of the original story. We are grateful to Matthias Schwartz for providing an authenticated copy of the 1926 source text.

which allows for a suggestion of psychological complexity in the villain Vikling. Dolgushin's 504-page scientific-thriller (in either version) does not stand out for its artistic merits; yet it has stood the test of time (and readability) to a much greater extent than other patriotic literary productions from the same period. Dolgushin wanted to fill his novel with lightly fictionalized, but genuinely exciting information about new discoveries in the biological and physical sciences. He spiced things up with a melodramatic plot involving a nefarious Nazi double-agent, the (implied) rape and murder of an innocent Russian maiden, and the ineluctable moral triumph of both Soviet science and true love. Yet the novel's preoccupation with wireless communication across great distances, and (in the chapter below) medical reversal of death suggests a profoundly ambiguous commentary on the historical moment in which it was written. Dolgushin released *Generator of Miracles* at the height of Stalin's terror (Soviet citizens disappeared into the Gulag in waves of arrests that peaked between 1936-1939), and on the eve of a catastrophic World War, in which the USSR would lose an estimated 25 million people. In this context, something eludes the clichés: the idea that the dead or disappeared might be able to convey their thoughts to their loved ones telepathically through space, as well as Nikolai's aching desire to see Anna literally come back to life.

Alexander Kazantsev's "Explosion" was an instant sensation in 1946. It gave new legs to the theory that the very real – but never fully explained – explosion over the Tunguska area of Siberia on June 30, 1908, could only be the result of an alien visitation. Kazantsev went on to have a long and less-than-admirable career as a cultural conservative and Party hard-liner who pushed back against literary innovations and artistic freedom in the 1960s. Ironically, "Explosion" would have fit easily into the realm of U.S. science fiction in the 1940s. As a Communist Party stalwart, Kazantsev wrote a macho, fun-to-read, mystery-catastrophe in which the figure of the dangerous alien is easily summed up in two words: "female" and "black."

On the other hand, "The Nur-i-Desht Observatory" (1944) highlights some of the most interesting features of the best of Soviet science fiction: the attractive female protagonist is an interesting person, not a highly sexualized or completely de-sexualized alien. The story unfolds in the recognizable present, in the middle of World War II, and only the vague mystery surrounding an archeological dig in remote Soviet Central Asia allows an opening for the fantastic to creep in. In the end, what seems to be fantastical – the extraordinary sense of vitality and well-being the protagonists experience in the environs of the strangely beautiful ruins of an ancient observatory – is accounted for with an explanation that is not only scientific, it is also quite patriotic (Soviet scientists are working on radium cures!). Nevertheless, "The Nur-i-Desht Observatory" strikes a hauntingly beautiful chord of ambiguity in its resolution, since its underlying premise is primarily philosophical. What causes human beings to experience joy? If we discover that our feeling of joyful well-being is due to some external, material stimulus rather than an internal state of harmony, how does this discovery affect us?

The story is explicitly set in late July 1942, at the outset of the Battle of Stalingrad, one of the bloodiest battles in human history.[6] The protagonist will experience nothing of this, since he has already been wounded and removed far from the front, to recuperate in a Central Asian sanatorium. The entire story of the magical archeological dig seems to take place outside of time, yet our awareness of the historical events that are unfolding in the devastated background make a difference. It is against this background that we see the beginnings of Yefremov's belief in the positive pull of cosmic evolution, which will ultimately lead human beings towards communion with other intelligent life. In Yefremov's groundbreaking 1957 space epic *Andromeda Nebula*,[7] utopian science fictional optimism about this

---

6. An estimated two million combatants and civilians were killed in this single battle, which halted the German advance into the Soviet Union and turned the tide of World War II in favor of the Allied Forces.

7. *Andromeda Nebula* changed the face of Soviet science fiction, and brought its author international fame. In an epic sweep that would characterize Western science fiction of this period as well, Yefremov imagined a completely transformed universe of the far-future. In this universe, inhabitants of the planet Earth have long since transcended the problems of the twentieth century – racism, gender inequity, material deprivation, the diseases of old age, and so forth are all distant

communion is conveyed in complicated plots and intricately drawn far-future protagonists and technologies; in this story, it is condensed into a single transcendent moment, when two human beings look up and see "piercing the glistening shroud of the Milky Way, [shining] Cygnus the Swan, stretching its long neck out in eternal flight towards the future."

PART III. RED STAR RISES HIGHER, UNTIL.... FROM REFORM TO FANTASY

The Soviet Union after Stalin's death in 1953 was an entirely different place than it had been under his iron rule. The new Party boss, Nikita Khrushchev, was a reformer who openly repudiated the "excesses" of the past and openly (if inconsistently) advocated liberalization. A decade after the end of a devastating war on Soviet soil, the economy was on a rebound, the standard of living for ordinary citizens was going up, the atmosphere of terror was lifted, and for the first and last time, a generation of thoroughly educated Soviet citizens was seized with genuine enthusiasm for the idea that the worthy promises of socialism – enlightenment, education, equality – could be realized. In particular, people placed their hope in science. In the 1950s, a repudiation of the irrational goals and mystical terror that defined Stalin's "cult of personality" was accompanied by a newfound belief in the humane goals of mathematics, cybernetics, physics, and the other exact sciences. It seemed that these objective disciplines, rather than grotesque ideological excesses, would finally usher in the communist future: thanks to science, there would be efficient agriculture, abundant energy sources, a rationalized economy, and even – yes! already in 1957! – a man-made Soviet satellite orbiting outer space.

At this propitious moment, the undisputed kings of Soviet science fiction – Arkady and Boris Strugatsky – made their writing debut. The Strugatsky brothers went on to dominate Russian science fiction,

---

historical issues that have been overcome – and the action driving future history has to do with the struggle to connect across vast cosmic distances with our fellow advanced civilizations throughout the galaxy.

and in some sense late Soviet fiction in general (most of their novels were what today would be called "cross-over best sellers"), for the next three decades. They became internationally famous and their major works were translated into over two dozen languages, including English. Therefore, in this volume we present only one of their earliest stories in an new translation,[8] and an excerpt of one of their previously un-translated novels from the last phase of their career. The 1958 story "Spontaneous Reflex" exhibits the combination of intellectual curiosity and deftly-drawn, humorous characterization that made the Strugatskys' early science fiction seem refreshingly intelligent and engaging, setting a new tone for a new generation of Soviet readers. The excerpt from *Those Burdened by Evil* (1988), on the other hand, reflects the authors' difficult reckoning with their own assumptions about the power of rational enlightenment and humanistic ideals. *Burdened* is not canonical Strugatsky fare. There are no swashbuckling heroes ready to bring decency and democracy to cruelly oppressed peoples on other planets; there are no wisecracking biophysicists ready to take the "para-" out of parapsychology in a top-secret Soviet research institute; there is no golden wishing ball at the end of a Stalker's long quest through the unfathomably weird Zone.[9] Instead, our readers will encounter the Demiurge, a brooding deity who answers to every name in the world's mythologies for "the Maker, he who fashions the material universe," and his servant Ahasuerus, the Wandering Jew. After enduring many deaths "worse than that primitive crucifixion" on multiple worlds, the returning Christ, the would-be spiritual savior of mankind, is back on Earth again for a visit. What will he do with the realization that "nothing has changed…"? The excerpt only raises the question, which is gradually explored in the course of the Strugatskys' darkly compelling final work.

---

8. "Spontaneous Reflex" was translated into English in 1959 and again in 1960, in the first wave of post-*sputnik* American fascination with Soviet science fiction. Both previous translations feature unauthorized additions, omissions, mistakes, and, in one case, an introductory frame with the question "Do the actions of a wild-running Communist robot reflect the thinking of a Communist master?"

9. *Hard To Be a God* (1964), *Monday Begins on Saturday* (1965), and *Roadside Picnic* (1972), respectively, to mention just three of the Strugatskys' most popular novels.

Michael Ancharov is entirely unknown in the West. "Soda-Sun" (1961) captures a persistent theme in the vast ocean of Soviet science fiction that was produced and read by millions of readers during the last Soviet decades. The narrator of "Soda-Sun" is concerned above all with the phenomenon of genius: where do the Mozarts and Einsteins and Leonardo da Vincis come from? If creative genius springs up occasionally among us normal mortals, why doesn't it spring up more often? Can we change something within ourselves, or within the structure of our societies, in order to bring forth the untapped capacity of human genius? Vladimir Savchenko's "Mixed Up" (1980) can also be interpreted as an extension of this theme. If the brain gets "mixed up" and begins to *hear* colors and shapes, and to *see* sound, how much will our comprehension of the universe around us expand and deepen? Even Sergei Drugal's far-future eco-parable "The Exam" includes a prominent digression on the nature of inventive genius. Drugal (1927-2011) himself was the author of several patented inventions in the realm of railroad engineering. He held prominent positions in rail transportation research and development throughout his life; writing science fiction was a hobby he pursued mainly in the 1970s and 1980s. "The Exam" is one story in a much larger cycle that Drugal devoted to the "Institute for the Restoration of Nature." In this cycle, a far more advanced race of humans resides mostly on other planets, having once upon a time carelessly destroyed the flora and fauna of our home planet. Gradually, the earth is being repopulated with secondary nature and biogenetically engineered animals, many of which are whimsical creations of our imagination. Nevertheless, in Drugal's far-future world, people have learned their lesson, and only the most stringently qualified moral and creative personalities are granted the honor of teaching a new generation of children.

When the great Russian modernist Andrei Platonov wrote "Lunar Bomb" in the late 1920s, he forced the language of peasants to confront the language of the future, so that in Platonov one finds the heart of a sad man "becoming overgrown with the fat of forgetting," even as a Special Committee puts him in charge of a project that will rocket a manmade sphere ("bomb") to the lunar periphery and back, part of the kind of technological advancement the sad man hopes will "open up new virgin sources of sustenance for life on earth, run[ning] hoses from these sources to the earth, [to] swallow up the meanness and the burdened, cramped feeling of human life."

Platonov's plot may be science fictional, but his language forces us right to the brink of the absurd, or of what the post-war European existentialists would identify as the abyss of meaningless. Platonov's ambiguous depiction of machine-driven progress did not fit the spirit of Stalinist times, nor did it characterize the generally upbeat attitude towards scientific enlightenment that animated mainstream Soviet science fiction until the late 1980s.

The last stories in *Red Star Tales* were written in the immediate aftermath of the Soviet Union's abrupt collapse. Everything had changed: when government censorship of literature was suspended, artistic innovation was no longer propelled by the need to "write around" possible censorship. Instead, artistic choices would now be measured against consumer demand, since for the first time, Russian readers would decide what sells. As it turns out, science fiction would not sell for long. When the official myth that promoted scientific rationalism as a kind of social panacea turned out to be exhausted, other long-suppressed expressions of "how to cope" rushed into the void: a resurgence of interest in religion, money-making self-help schemes, parapsychology and magic, alternative national and folk histories, and a fascination with power for power's sake.

Dalia Truskinovskaya's "Doorinda" charmed readers with its humorous depiction of a working mom's exasperation with notorious Soviet (and post-Soviet) consumer product deficits. In 1990, though, the literary solution is not longer a technological marvel – it's fantasy and magic. Sergei Lukyanenko's 1992 story "My Papa's an Antibiotic" anticipates the tough-guy, weapons-and-morality fantasy genre that has propelled subsequent Lukyanenko novels to blockbuster status in print and on film.[10] In this story, as well as in all subsequent Lukyanenko productions, the central dilemma concerns the hero's ability to remain strong without losing his essential decency and humanity.

It's a tough dilemma.

Yvonne Howell
Summer 2015

AKNOWLEDGEMENTS

This volume started as a small brainstorming session among a few colleagues. The editor wants to give a special thanks to Anindita Banerjee, Sibelan Forrester, and Sofya Khagi, who advocated for new collection of Russian and Soviet science fiction to "delight and inform" all kinds of readers and fans. Muireann Maguire and Kevin Reese also generously contributed their knowledge and their translations. Our favorite ex officio consultant, Matthias Schwartz (Zentrum für Literatur- und Kulturforschung) responded with great insight to every query. The marvelous Annie Fisher made editing seem like fun. Our publisher Paul Richardson did what great publishers do best: he combined enthusiastic vision with the ability to keep things in line and on time.

---

10. Lukyanenko's breakout novel *Night Watch* (Nochnoi dozor, 1998) is the first of a series that chronicles the eternal battle of the "Others," an ancient race of humans divided between the forces of Dark and Light. The novels have been translated into English by Andrew Bromfield.

AUTHORS

MIKHAIL ANCHAROV (1923-1990) was a writer, poet, and one of the first Soviet bards to pioneer the country's singer-songwriting genre. After completing his studies in oriental languages at the Military Academy of the Red Army, he was sent to the Far Eastern front during World War II to serve as a Chinese translator. In the latter half of his life Ancharov became a prolific screenwriter, writing the screenplay for the first Soviet television serial, *Day After Day*.

ALEXANDER BELYAEV (1884-1942) was a leading figure in Soviet science fiction whose works from the 1920s and 1930s earned him the title of "Russia's Jules Verne." Belyaev wrote dozens of stories and 13 novels, including *Professor Dowell's Head* and the well-known *Amphibian Man*, which were both later turned into films. He died of starvation in the occupied town of Pushkin, after refusing to evacuate while he was recovering from an operation.

VALERY BRYUSOV (1873-1924) was a Russian poet, prose writer, and literary critic who was influential in shaping artistic culture.

He was an ardent disciple of the French Decadence movement, translating Mallarmé, Rimbaud and others into Russian. He became a leading member of the fin de siècle Russian Symbolist movement, and did as much as anyone to endow poets and the art of poetry with mystical significance and cult-like status in pre-Revolutionary Russia. His prose fiction includes historical novels in a decadent mode, depicting the decline of past civilizations and future histories in a science fictional mode.

KIR BULYCHEV (1934-2003) was the pen name of Igor Mozheiko, a prolific Soviet science fiction writer who wrote for adults and children alike. He spent his professional career as an expert on Burmese history at the Institute of Oriental Studies in Moscow, penning hundreds of novels and short stories on the side. The author of more than 20 scripts, Bulychev is the Russian science fiction author who has been most widely adapted to film.

YURY DOLGUSHIN (1896-1989) was a Georgian writer and journalist. His longest and most significant work is *The Generator of Miracles*, excerpted in this volume, which he wrote before the war, and then reworked again in the 1950s.

SERGEI DRUGAL (1927-2011) was born in Kazakhstan and trained as a railway engineer. It wasn't until age 50 that he began to publish his first stories, combining his interests in ecology and pedagogy to create a series about a futuristic institute that perfects nature using the advancements of science. A recipient of the Aelita Prize for the best Russian work in the science fiction genre, Drugal has been translated into Polish, German and Hungarian. His story "Every Tree Has Its Bird" appears in the English-language anthology of Russian fantastical fiction *Tower of Birds*, published in 1989.

NIKOLAI F. FYODOROV (1828-1903) was the most important progenitor of Russian "cosmism," a version of non-secular transhumanism. An omnivorous reader and charismatic polymath, for most of his life he worked as a librarian in Moscow's Rumyantsev

Library. His philosophy of Orthodox Christianity incorporated modern science on the path to transcendence and preaches the necessity of controlling natural processes so that human beings can become literally immortal. His intellectual influence on a succession of important thinkers, including the writer Dostoyevsky and the rocketry engineer Tsiolkovsky, had a profound impact on Russian culture.

NIKOLAI FYODOROV ("the other Fyodorov"), author of "One Evening in 2217" – the seminal anti-utopian text that prefigures many others to come – has a mostly untraceable biography. In the preface to the volume containing "One Evening in 2217" (St. P: Gerold, 1906), the author is described as a Christian anti-socialist.

ALEXANDER KAZANTSEV (1906-2002) was trained as a mechanical engineer. He rose to a fairly high rank as a military engineer during WWII. Descriptions of the nuclear explosions over Hiroshima and Nagasaki caught his attention in 1945 and reminded him of the unsolved mystery of the 1908 explosion in the Tunguska region of Siberia. His story devoted to this subject is published here. For the most part, Kazantsev's writing in the post-war years is associated with the notorious Stalinist decree that science fiction should depict the "near goals" of Soviet industry.

SERGEI LUKYANENKO was born in Kazakhstan in 1968 and educated as a psychiatrist. He began writing science fiction in the 1980s and has published over 25 books. Today, owing to the spectacular success of his *Night Watch* series, he is one of the most visible and popular SF-fantasy authors in Russia. The *Watch* series of novels have sold over two million copies worldwide and have been translated into 28 languages.

ANDREI PLATONOV (1899-1951) was born in Voronezh. He was a passionate supporter of the 1917 Revolution and remained sympathetic to the dream that gave birth to it, yet few people have written more searingly of its catastrophic consequences. His position within the Soviet literary world was equally fraught with contradictions. Some of his works were published – and immediately subjected to fierce criticism; others were accepted for publication – yet never in fact published.

VLADIMIR SAVCHENKO (1933-2005) was a Soviet Ukrainian science fiction writer and engineer. He studied electronics engineering and worked in the Institute of Cybernetics in Kiev. He began his writing career in 1955, and became a leading figure in Soviet science fiction in the 1960s, especially after the publication of his award-winning novel *Self-Discovery* (1967), which explores the ethical problems that arise as we computerize consciousness.

ARKADY (1925-1991) AND BORIS (1933-2012) STRUGATSKY are perhaps the most celebrated names in Soviet science fiction. Their collaborative works became immensely popular in the 1960s and 1970s for their rejection of Stalin-era totalitarianism and their use of rich, colloquial language. One of the Strugatskys' most famous novels, *Piknik na Obochine* (*Roadside Picnic*), was turned into the movie *Stalker*, directed by Andrei Tarkovsky.

DALIA TRUSKINOVSKAYA was born in Riga in 1951 and studied philology at the University of Latvia. Since the publication of her book of short stories, *The Smell of Amber*, in 1984, she has gone on to publish nearly a dozen novels and short story collections in the science fiction genre. She continues to live and work in Riga as a journalist and Russian-language author whose books enjoy great success in Russia.

KONSTANTIN TSIOLKOVSKY (1857-1935) was one of the founding fathers of modern rocketry and aeronautical engineering. Largely self-educated, he spent most of his life as a semi-recluse in the provincial town of Kaluga, where he built an aerodynamics laboratory to conduct experiments, and wrote over 400 papers on the theory and practice of space travel. His discoveries led directly to later twentieth-century successes in space exploration. Tsiolkovsky was greatly influenced by his early tutor and mentor, the cosmist philosopher Nikolai Fyodorov. From the books of Stanislaw Lem and William

Gibson, to the games of Assassin's Creed, world science fiction contains many allusions to Tsiolkovsky's name and legacy.

IVAN YEFREMOV (1908-1972) was a Soviet paleontologist, science fiction writer, and social thinker. He is credited with resetting the generic horizons of Soviet science fiction after the Stalin years. His 1957 blockbuster *Andromeda Nebula* signaled the return of epic cosmic plots and the depiction of a far-future universe populated by galactic man under conditions of near-perfect communism. His earlier science fiction stories are less well known, and reveal another side of his deep imagination.

TRANSLATORS

ANINDITA BANERJEE is Associate Professor of Comparative Literature at Cornell University. She is a specialist in the literature and cultures of Russia, Eurasia, and the Indian subcontinent, with a particular interest in the relationship between techno-science and global modernities. She is the author of a prize-winning book, *We Modern People: Science Fiction and the Making of Russian Modernity* (Wesleyan University Press, 2013).

KEITH BLASING became infatuated with Russian literature as a student at the University of Tennessee and pursued this infatuation to the PhD level at the University of Wisconsin. He wrote his dissertation on the works of Andrei Platonov and continues to be interested in the history and culture of the early Soviet period. He has translated a number of works by Platonov and other authors and works as a translator and editor based in Lexington, Kentucky.

LIV BLISS lives in the White Mountains of Arizona with her husband, Jim, and an assortment of far wilder creatures. She translates the Taylor & Francis quarterlies *Russian Studies in Literature* and *Russian Studies in History*. Her most recent long-fiction translation, Dmitry Chen's

The Pet Hawk of the House of Abbas, was published by Edward & Dee Books in 2013.

NORA SELIGMAN FAVOROV has been translating Russian into English professionally for more than 25 years. Most of her translation work these days – including her regular task of translating **Russian Life** magazine's Calendar feature – centers around her favorite subject, Russian history. Her most recent book translation is *Stalin: New Biography of a Dictator* by Oleg V. Khlevniuk (Yale: 2015). She is associate editor of *SlavFile*, a newsletter for Slavic translators and interpreters.

ANNE O. FISHER has translated fiction by Ilf and Petrov, Ksenia Buksha, and Margarita Meklina, as well as – with husband and co-translator Derek Mong – the poetry of Maxim Amelin. These translations have appeared (or are forthcoming) in *Chtenia: Readings from Russia, Flash Fiction International, InTranslation, Two Lines*, and elsewhere. She has a PhD from the University of Michigan and lives in Portland, Oregon with her family.

SIBELAN FORRESTER is Professor of Russian Language and Literature at Swarthmore College. She specializes in Russian and Balkan literatures and is an experienced translator. She recently published a new translation of Vladimir Propp's classic study *The Russian Folktale* (Wayne State Univeristy Press, 2012), and she won the 2006 Heldt Prize for Best Translation, for her translation of Dubravka Oraić-Tolić: *American Scream/Palindrome Apocalypse*.

YVONNE HOWELL is Professor of Russian and International Studies at the University of Richmond. She is the author of *Apocalyptic Realism: The Science Fiction of Arkady and Boris Strugatsky* (1994), as well as numerous articles on the relationship between scientific progress and humanistic thought in comparative international contexts. She teaches and translates Russian and Czech literature.

MUIREANN MAGUIRE is Lecturer in Russian at the University of Exeter. Her most recent translations include *Red Spectres: Russian Twentieth Century Gothic Tales* (London: 2012 and New York: 2013), a collection of previously untranslated short stories by Bulgakov, Grin, Krzhizhanovskii and others; and *Before I Croak* (Glas 2013), a novel by the Debut Prize-winning author Anna Babiashkina. She has also published *Stalin's Ghosts: Gothic Themes in Early Soviet Literature* (Peter Lang 2012). She is currently working on depictions of maternity in Russian literature.

KEVIN REESE is a lecturer in Russian language and literature at the University of North Carolina – Chapel Hill. He is currently working on a book about the role of astronomy and cosmology in the works of the Strugatsky brothers.

J.M. SIDOROVA is a Russian-born American biomedical scientist and author of speculative fiction. Her debut novel, *The Age of Ice* (Scribner/ Simon & Schuster), was published in 2013, and her short stories appeared in *Clarkesworld*, *Asimov's*, *Abyss* and *Apex*, and other venues. She is a graduate of the prestigious Clarion West workshop for writers.

JAMES VON GELDERN is Professor of International Studies and Russian at Macalester College, where he teaches courses on Soviet culture and international law. He is author of *Bolshevik Festivals, 1917-1920*, co-author of *Mass Culture in Soviet Russia: Tales, Poems, Songs, Movies, Plays and Folklore, 1917-1953* (1995) and *Entertaining Tsarist Russia: Urban Entertainments, 1798-1917* (1998, and co-developer of the website Seventeen Moments in Soviet History (soviethistory. macalester.edu). He is also a practicing attorney, representing asylum seekers pro bono in collaboration with the Advocates for Human Rights, of Minneapolis, Minnesota.

RED STAR

RISING

NIKOLAI F. FYODOROV
1892

KARAZIN:
METEOROLOGIST OR METEORURGE?

In this essay we will talk about Karazin, a man of many talents, not as a meteor*ologist* but as a meteor-*urge*. The difference between a meteorologist and a meteorurge may be defined as follows: the ultimate objective of the first is to predict famine, and the second takes as his task – and incidentally, only as the *first step* of the task – *salvation from famine*. Unfortunately, the word *urge* was corrupted by mystics and acquired the connotation of *witchcraft* – arcane, supernatural acts, unseen influences of spirits – and not the clear, open, comprehensive exercise of reason on the blind forces of nature.

While attempting to manufacture saltpeter, an idea occurred to Karazin: potassium nitrate could be made with electricity captured from the atmosphere's highest strata by specially constructed balloons, which would be anchored to the earth with metallic cables. On the 9th of April, 1814, Karazin wrote about this to Arakcheyev, residing in Paris at that time. Among other matters, he mentioned: "If the experiment, as I hope, conclusively confirms my hypothesis about extracting electricity from the stratosphere, it will signal the invention of a *new*, unprecedented weapon in the hands of humankind. Water, air, fire, muscles of living beings, tension, and expansion of certain bodies are still considered to be regulated by natural forces, some of which we have managed to harness and replicate in machines. Consider, your excellency, the consequences of mastering the massive amount of electrical energy scattered throughout the atmosphere and bending it to our will." Subsequently Karazin expresses hope that through the medium of electricity, humans *will attain the ability to determine the state of the atmosphere, producing rain at will.*" Intrigued, "Arakcheyev showed Karazin's letter to the renowned chemist Chaptal, an expert in the production of saltpeter, who unconditionally approved its contents." This opinion was echoed by the committee that Prince Gorchakov, head of the Ministry of Defense, appointed in 1815 in order to review Karazin's proposal of creating condensed explosives and saltpeter for military purposes. Professor Scherer, a chemist and member of the Imperial Academy of Sciences, responded to the committee that "according to his own observations, which he intended to publish, he saw no other explanation for the creation of potassium nitrate, even in the usual course of producing saltpeter, than the effect of atmospheric electricity. Finally, Karazin managed to get the attention of His Majesty Alexander Pavlovich himself, to whom Karazin conveyed a note about meteorology during the latter's tour through Kharkov in September 1817. His Royal Highness was particularly taken by the following words in the note: "The implementation of electricity from higher atmospheric strata for the benefit of humankind. The important invention presented herewith could be applied only at a small scale due to the inadequacy of resources. It accords with our age and Russia's glorious position within it. As a patriot, it would be a pity for me to see a foreigner stumble upon this very same idea." In response to the sovereign's request for further elaboration, Karazin submitted a new document in which he proposed – based on the fact that the higher one ascends in the atmosphere, the higher the concentration of electricity – that the highest strata of the atmosphere "consist of a perpetual upheaval, like a sea in stormy weather, from the arriving and departing oscillations of electric currents.… Why is it impossible to think that humanity can tame electric power as it has tamed animals, water, wind, and fire? It all depends on reaching the source of the power and creating a channel for directing it for this or that purpose, according to our will. But the source in this case is the farthest height of the atmosphere; metallic cables may serve as the channels, and balloons as anchors for holding down the ends of the cables at a constant height." Recalling the salient chemical properties of electricity, Karazin warns that "the largest electric machine, clad in strips of metal foil and sailing through the heights of the atmosphere, will be a child's toy vis-à-vis a mid-sized zeppelin, comparable with a miniature model sailboat set against an English battleship on its course. Man in all his ingenuousness can never replicate the immeasurable scale of nature. He can only hope to discover the best ways to implement her resources." That is to say, humanity is not meant to compete with nature, but only to regulate her. "Experiments conducted with the proposed equipment will undoubtedly be astounding. The results may include the following. 1) The most accurate information about the factors of changing atmospheric conditions. This data, combined with general meteorological observations, would open the way for transforming meteorology into an exact science, i.e., a science as capable of calculating and predicting the weather in given places at given times as astronomy is accurate in predicting eclipses.… Our country has a distinct advantage in realizing this vision.… No other kingdom is endowed with such breadth and variety of landscapes for conducting such experiments as our Russia. 2) The achievements of chemistry and technology... In the north, manufacturing and industry will be powered naturally by harnessing the sun's energy. 3) Benefits of land management." This proposal was forwarded to the academy of sciences, where Nikolai Fuss interpreted its contents at the members' conference. Fuss concluded that quite a few methods already existed for harnessing electricity in amounts sufficient "for fulfilling all technical demands," and that "most, if not all, of Karazin's supposed predictions were nothing more than hypotheses without any proof." Therefore the 20,000 rubles Karazin had deemed necessary for conducting his experiments "would be spent in vain," Fuss concluded. Although precisely this conclusion was marked by an anonymous penciled comment – "Russia won't go very far on Fusses like these" – nevertheless Fuss' opinion prevailed, and Karazin's project, which would have provided humanity with real power to eradicate suffering, remained untested. Incidentally, "a project for manufacturing an acid to power Leppikh's zeppelin, capable of carrying enough passengers and explosives to blow up all the fortifications or personnel of the greatest military powers" was awarded 40,000 rubles.

Thus "the representatives of Russian science conclusively rejected the Karazin proposal; they did not notice what was original and productive about it." It is worth noting that Karazin's thoughts stood so far out of the mainstream that they may even be inaccessible to our contemporaries. Theories and projects pertaining to Karazin's areas of interest are viewed suspiciously by, and elicit scant response from, the worldly trade and industrial sectors that hold the public captive and condition it to such an extent that people cannot conceive of a common task to rally around; they are in fact repelled by any task that requires collective effort; after all, Karazin's plans would have required exactly such a collective effort involving everyone, all of humanity from all walks of life.

Considering that the military has recently begun to incorporate aircraft, it would be easy to attach the equipment proposed by Karazin to the existing infrastructure to carry out experiments. But I doubt if we will have the patience to await the results; in order to eliminate errors and arrive at the correct conclusions in projects such as Karazin's, it is first necessary to apprehend the genuine importance of its subject matter. Alas, in Karazin's own words, "the relevance of the subject may not be fully comprehensible to ordinary citizens and bevies of magazine critics," i.e. neither to those who are expected to make reasonable judgments nor to those who, living in cities and captives in the rhythms of urban life, have lost the ability to understand the meaning of *the interdependence between sentient beings and the blind, unfeeling forces of nature*. And this interdependence – which we are compelled to acknowledge as unavoidable, preordained, superseding all the achievements and vanities of modern man – is the primal riddle that humanity, whether consciously or unconsciously, has been attempting to solve. In antiquity, the awareness of the *meaning* of this interdependence was encoded in the myth of the Sphinx, which asked passers-by to solve riddles; the wrong answer would cost the human interlocutor his life, while the Sphinx would die if the riddle was solved. As the whole of humankind is about to face the Sphinx, it is consequently obliged to work towards a solution to the riddle, i.e. to marshal all its current resources and seek additional ones in order to resolve its differences with the blind, intractable forces of nature that herald nothing but death in all its different manifestations. Intractable nature, precisely because it is intractable, is an agent of death; ignorance is the gravest sin, punishable by death. However, as darkness and gloom melt away before light, this blind force will disappear when light floods *each and every* human life emerging on earth – instead of remaining limited to a small minority, where it loses its innate properties and appears as a mere gleam. As long as one social group commands some knowledge without possessing any power, and the other wields some power but remains largely ignorant, the knowledge of the former will not be genuinely capable of regulating power, while the blind actions of the latter will necessarily be ineffective and repetitive despite all humankind's pride at possessing so-called cognition, which hardly deserves its name. A spark from the electrical generator may have all the properties of a lightning bolt, its crackle may possess the characteristics of thunder, but producing this tiny discharge does not make us Jupiters or free us from that deity's power. Even Karazin's brand of redirecting thunder, when it becomes ubiquitous and is carried out according to plan, will only be a step, the first step, towards the regulation of blind meteorological processes of the planet.

Humanity is faced with two choices. Acknowledge that life is evil and aim towards self-destruction (Buddhism), or, if life is good, then within this acknowledgment lies the motivation for restoring it, which is exactly the same as the Christian tenet of resurrection; surely the goal of transforming the blind forces of famine, plague, and death into life-affirming ones should unite all of us. To consider destruction good (as Count L. N. Tolstoy preaches) is the same as believing that there is no good; it is equivalent to Buddhism, which considers life evil; this means renouncing Christianity, which only the most ignorant would confuse with Buddhism.

The very forces of nature ask to be regulated by humans, and show them where to begin this task. As long as maritime powers, originating in countries with temperate climates and nurturing skies, dominated world history, the question of regulating meteorological phenomena could remain on the margins; but from the moment when land-based powers with extreme climates that fluctuate suddenly between drought and cloudbursts entered the scene, this question began to demand a solution. And if in Russia it had not emerged at the center of attention until now, this was only because we lived under the epistemological yoke of countries for which it was not urgent. Moreover, the solution demands methods and approaches that are not available to our role models. It is necessary to change the very foundations of producing knowledge and make the new paradigms universal, omnipresent, and eternal, to unify all experimental knowledge into one. Fortunately, while blind nature, afraid of its own extinction, begs for the unification of all rational forces – and rational forces, armed with weapons of mass destruction, unwillingly consider both the imperative of disarmament and its impossibility – the opportunity arises to remake the greatest evil into the greatest good. People who can band together to fight in the army, i.e., as a unified mass according to a given plan, can easily fulfill the primary criteria of a great common task: ubiquity and universality. The only remaining step is to bring meteorological observations into the sphere of peaceable military exercises, to test not only the

American method of creating rain with explosives, but also Karazin's project, and all the other ways of acting on nature *that will emerge as soon as they receive the close, intensive attention long due to them.*

First published in Russian: 1892
Translation by Anindita Banerjee

KONSTANTIN TSIOLKOVSKY

1893

ON THE MOON

I

I woke up and, still lying in bed, pondered the dream I'd just had: I was swimming, and since it's winter now it felt especially pleasant to imagine summer swimming.

Time to get up!

I stretched, lifted myself up a bit… So easy! It was easy to sit, easy to stand. What was going on? Could I still be dreaming? I felt especially light, as if I were standing in water up to my neck: my feet barely touched the floor.

But where was the water? I didn't see any. I waved my hands, and I sensed no resistance.

Was I still asleep? I rubbed my eyes, but everything stayed the same. Strange!

Nonetheless, I had to get dressed.

I moved the chairs, opened the cupboards, got out my clothes, picked up various things, and – nothing made any sense!

Have I gotten stronger? Why is everything so weightless? Why could I pick up objects I couldn't even budge before?

No! These were not my legs, not my arms, not my body!

Usually they were so heavy, and everything took them so much effort…

Where had I acquired such might in my arms and legs?

Or maybe some kind of power was pulling me and everything else upward, and making my work easier that way? But if so, what a strong pull! Just a little more, it seemed to me, and I'd float up to the ceiling.

Why was it I leapt instead of walking? Something was pulling me in the opposite direction to gravity; it tensed my muscles, forced me to take a jump.

I couldn't resist the temptation – I jumped…

It seemed that I rose up fairly slowly and landed just as slowly.

I jumped harder and took a look around the room from a fair distance up… Ouch! Hit my head on the ceiling… The rooms are high, I hadn't expected to hit it. I'd have to be more careful.

My shout woke up my roommate, though: I saw him start tossing and turning, and after a little while he jumped out of bed. I won't describe his amazement, just like my own. I observed the same kind of spectacle I had acted out myself, without noticing it, a few minutes before. It gave me great pleasure to see my friend's eyes bugging out, his funny poses and the unnatural liveliness of his movements. His strange exclamations, very like my own, amused me.

I waited for my friend the physicist to recover from his surprise, then I asked him to resolve my question: what on earth had happened – had our strength increased, or did our weight decrease?

Both suggestions were equally astounding, but there's nothing a person won't start to view with indifference once he gets used to it. My friend and I hadn't gotten that far yet, but we already felt a desire to figure out the answer.

My friend, who was accustomed to analysis, soon made sense of the mass of phenomena that had overwhelmed and confused my mind.

"We can test our muscle strength on the dynamometer, with the spring weights," he said, "and find out whether it has increased or not. Here, I'll press my feet against the wall and pull on the lower hook of the spring. See – five poods:[1] my strength hasn't increased. You can do the same, and prove to yourself that you haven't turned into a fairy-tale hero like Ilya Muromets."

"It's hard to agree," I objected. "The facts contradict you. How is it that I can lift the edge of this bookcase, which has to weigh at least fifty poods? At first I thought it must be empty, but I opened it and saw that every book was still in place… Can you explain, by the way, how it is that I can jump twenty arshins high!?"[2]

"You aren't lifting heavy weights, jumping high and feeling light because your own strength increased – we've already disproved that hypothesis with the dynamometer – but because gravity is lower, and you can prove that to yourself with the same spring weights. We can even find out how much lower it is…"

With these words he lifted the first weight he found, a twelve-pounder, and hung it on the dynamometer.

"Look!" he continued, pointing at the scale. "A twelve-pound weight turns out to weigh two pounds. That means gravity has weakened by a factor of six."

After thinking for a minute, he continued, "That's just the gravity on the surface of the Moon, due to its small volume and the low density of its composition."

"So are we on the Moon now?" I laughed.

"If we are on the Moon," the physicist laughed, in the same joking tone, "that's not a huge misfortune, since we can repeat a miracle like that, given that it's possible, in the opposite direction – that is, we'll be able to go back where we came from."

"Wait, enough playing games… But what if we weigh something on an ordinary cross-beam scale! Will we see a reduction in weight?"

---

1. pood – a pre-Revolutionary Russian measure, approximately 16.4 kilograms to one pood.
2. arshin – a pre-Revolutionary Russian measure, approximately 71 centimeters.

"No, because the weight of the thing will be reduced by the same amount as the weight you put in the other cup of the scales, since balance is not violated, regardless of the decrease in gravity."

"Yes, I see."

Nevertheless I still tried to snap a stick, hoping to discover an increase in my strength. I didn't succeed, by the way, though the stick wasn't thick and I had already bent it yesterday.

"You're so stubborn! Give it up!" said my friend the physicist. "Instead, think about how the whole world must be disturbed by these changes…"

"You're right," I said, throwing down the stick. "I had forgotten about everything. I forgot about the existence of humanity, with which I feel a passionate desire to share my thoughts, just as you do…"

"Has anything happened to our friends? Have there been any other major changes?"

I opened my mouth and yanked aside the curtain (they were all drawn at night to block the moonlight that kept us from sleeping), to exchange a few words with our neighbor, but I jumped back on the double. Oh horror! The sky was blacker than the blackest ink!

Where was the city? Where were all the people?

It was some kind of wild, unimaginable, brightly sunlit place!

Could we really have been taken away to some desert planet?

All that stayed in my thoughts. I couldn't say anything, I just mooed something incoherently.

My friend was about to rush over to me, thinking that I must be sick, but I gestured towards the window. He leaned to look out and also fell silent.

If we didn't fall down in a faint, it was only thanks to the low gravity, which kept too much blood from flowing to our hearts.

We looked at each other.

The curtains on the windows were still drawn; the thing that had struck us wasn't visible to our eyes. The ordinary look of the room and the familiar things in it calmed us down even more.

We drew together with a certain timidity and lifted only the edge of the little curtain first, then lifted the whole thing and then, finally, made up our minds to go out of the house to observe the sky, black as mourning, and our surroundings.

Even though our thoughts were preoccupied by the stroll we were about to take, we were still noticing certain things. So, as we walked through the spacious and high-ceilinged rooms, we had to move our large muscles with extreme care, otherwise our soles would slide uselessly on the floor – without the risk of falling, however, the way there is on wet snow or on frozen ground. When we did this our bodies jumped noticeably. When we wanted to put ourselves into rapid horizontal motion, to start moving we had to lean forward noticeably, the way a horse leans to pull an overloaded wagon. But it only seemed that way – in fact all our movements were extremely light… Going downstairs from one step to the next – how boring! Moving step by step – how slow! Soon we got rid of all those ceremonious habits, which suited the Earth but were ridiculous here. We learned to move by leaping; we started going up and down stairs ten or more at a time, like the most reckless schoolboys; or sometimes we'd jump the whole length of the staircase or right out the window. In a word, circumstances forced us to turn into leaping animals like grasshoppers or frogs.

Thus, after running around the house a bit, we jumped outside and galloped off towards one of the nearest mountains.

The Sun was blinding and looked a bit bluish. Shading our eyes with our hands against the Sun and the brilliant reflected light from the surroundings, we could see the stars and planets, also for the most part bluish. None of them were twinkling, which made them look like silver-headed nails hammered into the black firmament.

Ah, and there was the Moon – in its last quarter! Well, it couldn't fail to surprise us, since its width seemed three or four times greater than the diameter of the Moon we had seen before. And it shone brighter than by day on Earth, when the Moon shows up like a white puff of cloud. Silence… clear weather… a cloudless sky… There were no plants and no animals.. A desert with a black sky and a blue, dead

Sun. No lake, no stream, and not a drop of water! Even the horizon wasn't any paler – that would have indicated the presence of vapors, but it was just as dark as the zenith!

There was none of the wind that rustles the grass and tosses the tops of the trees on Earth… There was no chirping of crickets… No sign of any birds, or colorful butterflies! Just mountains and more mountains, horrible, high mountains, whose peaks didn't gleam with snow. Not a flake of snow anywhere! There were the valleys, plains, plateaus… How many rocks were scattered there… Black and white, large and small, but all sharp, shining, not rounded, not softened by a wave, since no sea ever rolled here, ever played with them with a cheerful sound, ever labored over them!

But there was a completely smooth place, though rippled: you couldn't see a single pebble, only black cracks crawling in all directions, like snakes… Hard ground – stony... No soft black soil: no sand and no clay.

A gloomy picture! Even the mountains were bare, shamelessly unclothed, since we didn't see the light veil, the transparent bluish smoke that the air casts over earthly mountains and distant objects… Severe, strikingly precise landscapes! And the shadows! Oh, what dark shadows! And what sharp transitions from shade to light! There were none of the soft tones that we're so used to and that can be produced only by an atmosphere. Even the Sahara – even that would seem a paradise in comparison with what we saw here. We missed its scorpions, the locusts, the hot sand lifted by the dry wind, not to mention the occasional sparse vegetation and groves of fig trees… We had to think about returning. The ground was cold and exuded cold, so that our feet were chilling, while the Sun baked us. Overall, we felt an unpleasant sensation of cold. It was like when a person comes in from the cold to warm up in front of a blazing fireplace and can't get warm, because it's too cold in the room: his skin feels pleasant waves of warmth that can't overcome the chill.

On the way back we warmed ourselves by leaping as lightly as deer over piles of stones two sazhens high…[3] There was granite, porphyry, syenite, quartz crystals and various pieces of transparent and opaque quartz and flint, all of igneous origin. Later, though, we noticed traces of neptunic activity.

We were back in the house!

Inside you feel good: the temperature's more even. That put us in the mood to start trying new experiments and to discuss everything we had seen and noticed. Clearly, we were on some other planet. This planet had no air, nor any other kind of atmosphere.

If there had been gas, then the stars would have twinkled; if there had been air, the sky would have been blue and there would have been a blue veil on the distant mountains. But how was it that we could breathe and hear each other? We couldn't understand it. A multitude of phenomena made it clear to us that there was no air or any kind of gas at all: for example, we couldn't light a cigar and in our haste we spoiled a lot of matches. We could also compress a sealed rubber bag without the slightest force, which wouldn't have been the case if there had been any kind of gas inside it. Scientists have indicated this lack of gasses on the Moon.

"Could it be that we're on the Moon?"

"Have you noticed that from here the Sun doesn't seem any bigger or any smaller than from the Earth? Such a phenomenon can be observed only from the Earth or from its satellite, since these heavenly bodies are located almost the same distance from the Sun. From other planets the Sun must appear either smaller or larger: so, from Jupiter the visible diameter of the Sun is five times smaller, and from Mars, one and a half times smaller, but from Venus, on the other hand, one and a half times greater. On Venus the Sun burns twice as brightly, but on Mars, only half as brightly. And that's just the difference from the two planets closest to the Earth! On Jupiter, for example, the Sun gives twenty-five times less heat than on the Earth. We see nothing

---

3. sazhen – a pre-Revolutionary Russian measure, approximately 2.13 meters.

like that difference here, even though measuring it would be entirely possible thanks to the store of instruments for measuring carbon and other things."

"Yes, we're on the Moon: everything points to that!"

"Even the size of the clouded moon we saw suggests that – it's obviously the planet we left, not of our own volition. Too bad we can't examine its spots now and definitively define our own location. We'll wait for night time…"

"How can you say that Earth and the Moon are at the same distance from the Sun?" I objected to my friend. "I thought the difference was quite significant! Why, as far as I know, they are three hundred sixty thousand versts apart!"

"I'm saying they're *almost* at the same distance, since those three hundred sixty thousand versts comprise only one four-hundredth of the entire distance to the Sun," objected the physicist. "A four-hundredth can be disregarded."

II

How tired I was, and not so much physically as mentally! I felt irresistibly drawn to sleep… What did the clock say? We got up at six, now it was five… eleven hours had passed. At the same time, judging by the shadows, the Sun had hardly moved: there the shadow from the steep mountain had barely moved towards the house, and even now it didn't quite reach, while over there the shadow from the weathervane was still touching the same stone…

This was one more proof that we were on the Moon.

In fact, its rotation around its axis is so slow… Here a day should last around fifteen of our days, or three hundred and sixty hours, and a night should last just as long. It's not entirely comfortable… The sun would interfere with your sleep! I remember, I experienced the same thing when I had to live several weeks in the summer in polar countries: the Sun never set on the horizon, and it got really tiresome! Here the Sun moves slowly, but in the same order; there it moves quickly, and every twenty-four hours it makes a circle low above the horizon…

Here and there you could use one and the same solution: close the shutters.

But was the clock right? Why was there such a disagreement between my wristwatch and the clock on the wall? My wristwatch said five, but the one on the wall showed just ten… Which one was right? Why was the wall clock's pendulum swinging so lazily?

Obviously, that clock was slow!

My wristwatch couldn't be wrong, since it didn't have a pendulum swung by weight, but the tension of a steel spring, which was the same on the Moon as it was on Earth.

You could check that by measuring your pulse. Mine was seventy beats per minute… Now it was seventy-five. A bit faster, but that could be due to the nervous excitement from the unusual setting and strong impressions.

Anyway, there was still one more way to check the time: at night we would see the Earth, which turns once every twenty-four hours. That's the best, the least erroneous clock!

Regardless of the sleepiness that had overcome both of us, my physicist couldn't bear not to fix the wall clock. I saw him lifting the long pendulum, measuring it exactly and shortening it to one sixth or thereabouts. The honorable clock turned into a little tick-tock. But here it wasn't a tick-tock, for the shortened pendulum behaved gravely, though not so gravely as the long one had. Thanks to this metamorphosis the wall clock started to agree with my wristwatch.

At last we went to bed and covered up with our light blankets, which seemed weightless here.

We hardly needed to use our pillows and mattresses. Here, it seemed, you could sleep even on bare boards.

I couldn't get rid of the thought that it was still too early to go to bed. Oh, this Sun! This time! You were both standing still, like all time on the Moon!

My comrade stopped answering me, and I fell asleep too.

A jolly waking… cheerfulness and a wolf's appetite… Until now our excitement had displaced our usual appetite.

I was thirsty! I pulled out the cork… But what's this – the water was boiling! Only slightly, but it was boiling. I touched the decanter with my hand. I didn't want to burn myself… No, the water was merely warm. It was unpleasant to drink water like that!

"What do you say, my physicist?"

"There's a complete vacuum here, that's why the water's boiling, it's not prevented by the pressure of Earth's atmosphere. Let it boil a bit more: don't close the stopper! In a vacuum boiling ends up by freezing….But we won't let it get to freezing… That's enough! Pour some water in the glass, and put the stopper in, otherwise a lot will boil away."

Liquid poured slowly on the Moon!

The water calmed down in the decanter, but in the glass it continued its lifeless boiling – though the longer it went on, the more weakly.

The water left in the glass turned into ice, but the ice still evaporated and shrank in mass.

How would we have lunch now?

We could eat the bread and other more or less solid food freely, though it quickly dried up in a box that wasn't hermetically sealed: the bread turned into rock, the fruits shrank and also got pretty hard. On the other hand, their skins still retained some moisture.

"Oh, this habit of eating something hot! How can we manage it? You can't make a fire here: there's no wood, no coal, even the matches don't burn!"

"Can't we use the Sun for this? You know, they bake eggs in the hot sand of the Sahara!"

We fixed our pots and pans and other vessels so that their lids closed tightly and firmly. We filled everything with what was needed, according to the rules of the culinary arts, and put it all in a pile in the sun. Then we gathered all the mirrors in the house and set them up so they reflected the Sun's light onto the pots and pans.

Before even an hour had passed, we could dine on foods that were well boiled and fried.

And what can I say! Have you heard of Mouchot?[4] His perfected solar delicacies were far behind ours! Boasting and bragging? Call it that if you like… You can blame these self-satisfied words on our ravenous appetites, which would have made any kind of vile stuff seem delightful.

Only one thing was bad: we had to hurry. I admit it, we stuffed ourselves and choked. You'll understand this if I say that the soup boiled and got cold not only in the bowls, but even in our mouths, our throats and digestive tracts; the moment we got distracted – look, instead of soup there was a lump of ice…

It's a wonder our digestive systems stayed in one piece! The pressure of the steam stretched them out a great deal…

In any case, we were satisfied and fairly calm. We didn't understand how it was we could live without air, and how it was we ourselves, our house, garden, and the stores of food and drink in the pantries and cellars had been transferred from Earth to the Moon. We were even struck by doubt, and we thought: isn't this a dream, a daydream or a demonic delusion? And along with all that we got used to our situation and related to it partly with curiosity, partly with indifference: what we couldn't explain didn't surprise us, and the danger of dying of hunger, alone and miserable, didn't even enter our minds.

You'll learn the reason for our impossible optimism at the end of our adventures.

We wanted to take a stroll after eating… I didn't dare sleep a lot: I was afraid of suffering a stroke.

I distracted my friend, too.

We were in a spacious yard, with gymnastics equipment in its center, and on its sides a fence and outbuildings.

Why was this rock here? A person could trip and fall on it. In the yard the ground was ordinary earthly soil, soft. Out with it, over the fence! Be confident! Don't be frightened by the size! And there we lifted a stone of sixty poods by our mutual efforts and tossed it over

---

4. Augustin Mouchot (1825-1911), French inventor of a boiler that used solar power to heat water to produce energy.

the fence. We heard it land with a dull thud on the stony ground of the Moon. The sound reached us not by way of the air, but under the ground: the blow was carried by the ground's vibration, then by our bodies into the fine bones of our ears. By this path we could often hear the blows we had struck.

"Could that be the way we hear each other?"

"Hardly! The sound couldn't resonate the way it would in the air."

The ease of our movements awakened a most powerful desire to climb and jump.

The sweet time of childhood! I remember how I would get up on the roof and trees, just like the cats or birds. That was pleasant…

And the competitive leaps across the tape and over ditches! And running for prizes! I loved that passionately…

Shouldn't I remember the old days? I had little strength, especially in my arms. I jumped and ran fairly well, but I had trouble climbing a rope or a pole.

I used to dream of great physical strength: I would pay back my enemies and reward my friends! A child and a wild savage are the same Now those dreams of muscular strength seemed funny to me… All the same my desires, so ardent in my childhood, had become real here: it was as if my powers were increased sixfold thanks to the Moon's puny gravity.

Besides that, here I didn't need to overcome the weight of my own body, which increased the effects of my strength even more. What was a fence for me here? No more than a threshold or a footstool that I could step over on Earth. And there, as if to prove this thought, we sailed upward and we flew over the fence without a running start. Then we jumped up and even leapt over the shed, but for that we needed a running start. And how pleasant it was to run: you didn't feel your legs beneath you. Off we went… who could beat the other? At a gallop!

Every time our heels hit the ground we flew a few sazhens, especially horizontally. Wait! The whole yard, five hundred sazhens, in one minute: the speed of a race horse…

Your "giant steps" don't allow you to make such leaps!

We made measurements: at a gallop, even a fairly gentle one, we rose about four arshins above the ground; we moved along the ground five sazhens or more, depending on the speed of our pace.

"Time for some gymnastics!"

Hardly tensing our muscles, and even, for our own amusement, using only our left hands, we climbed up the rope to the platform.

Strange: four sazhens above the ground! It kept seeming as if we were on the clumsy Earth! Our heads were spinning…

With a sinking heart I was the first to dare to jump down. I'm flying… Ouch! I hurt my heel a bit!

I should have warned my friend about that, but I slyly encouraged him to jump. I lifted my head and shouted to him, "Jump, it's easy – you won't hurt yourself!"

"You're urging me for nothing: I know very well that jumping from here is the same as a two-arshin jump on the Earth. Of course you'll feel it a bit in your heels!"

My friend flew down too. A slow flight… especially at first. The whole thing lasted about five seconds.

In that much time you can think of a lot of things.

"So what do you think, my physicist?"

"My heart is beating – that's all."

"To the garden! To climb the trees, to run through the alleys!"

"Why haven't the leaves dried out there?"

Fresh green… protection from the Sun. Tall lindens and birches! Like squirrels, we leapt and climbed on the slender branches, and they didn't break. But of course – here we weren't any heavier than fat turkeys!

We glided above the shrubbery and between the trees, and our movements recalled flight. Oh, it was fun! How easy it was to keep your balance here! If you tipped on a branch, ready to fall, the pull downwards was so weak, the tip off balance so slow, that the slightest movement of an arm or leg was enough to restore it.

To the open spaces! The huge yard and garden seemed like a cage… At first we ran over the flat area. We came upon shallow trenches, up to ten sazhens across. We flew across them at a run, like birds. But the climb had started; at first it was gradual, then steeper and steeper. What an incline! I was afraid I'd run out of breath.

There was no need to fear: we went upward freely, with broad and rapid strides up the slope. The mountain was high – even the easy Moon exhausted us. We sat down. Why was it so soft here? Had the stones been softened?

I picked up a big rock and struck it against another; sparks scattered.

"We're rested. Time to go back…"

"How far is the house?"

"Not far now, about two hundred sazhens."

"Can you throw a rock that far?"

"I don't know, I'll try!"

We each picked up a medium-sized sharp-cornered stone… Who could throw it farther? My stone went over our residence. And a good thing. Following its trajectory, I was afraid it would break a window.

"And yours? Yours went even farther!"

Shooting here would be interesting: bullets and cannonballs ought to fly for hundreds of versts horizontally and vertically.

"But would gunpowder work here?"

"Explosive materials in a vacuum ought to express themselves with even greater force than in an atmosphere, since the air only interferes with their expansion. As far as oxygen is concerned, they don't need it, because they already contain the necessary amount."

III

We came home.

"I'll sprinkle some gunpowder on the windowsill in the light of the Sun," I said. "Use a magnifying glass to focus light on it… See – fire… an explosion, even though it's a silent one." The familiar scent, which dissipated in a moment.

"You can fire a shot. Just don't forget to put on a firing cap: the magnifying glass and the Sun will replace the blow of the hammer."

"Let's set the rifle up vertically, so we can look for the bullet somewhere nearby after the shot…"

Fire, a faint sound, a slight shaking of the ground.

"Where's the wad?" I exclaimed. "It should be right here, somewhere nearby, though it won't be smoking."

"The wad flew away with the bullet and will hardly have fallen behind it, since it's only the atmosphere on Earth that prevents it from flying off after the lead. Here even eiderdown would fall or fly upward as fast as a rock… You take that piece of fluff sticking out of the pillow, and I'll take an iron ball bearing: you can throw your fluff and you'll hit your mark, even if it's far away, just as easily as I can with the ball bearing. I can throw a ball of this size about two hundred sazhens; you can throw a piece of fluff the same distance. True, you won't kill anyone with it, and as you throw it you won't even feel that you're throwing anything. Let's throw our projectiles with all our strength, which is about the same for both of us, and aim at the same target: that red granite over there…"

We watched the piece of fluff move slightly ahead of the iron ball, as if drawn by a strong whirlwind…

"But what's this: three minutes have passed since we shot, but the bullet hasn't come back?"

"Wait two more minutes, and it will surely come back," the physicist answered.

In fact, after about the amount of time he said, we felt a light shaking of the ground and saw the casing jump not far away.

"Where's the bullet? It can't be the shred of oakum that made the ground shake?" I asked in surprise.

"Probably it was heated to the melting point by the blow and spattered in tiny drops in every direction."

We looked around and in fact we did find a few miniscule drops that were apparently the remaining fragments of the bullet.

"The bullet flew for so long! What sort of height could it have reached?" I asked.

"About seventy versts up. That height is due to the low gravity and the absence of atmospheric interference."

My mind and body were exhausted and demanded a rest. The Moon was all very well, but the outsized leaps were making themselves felt. As a result of the long distance of our flights we didn't always land on our feet as they ended, and we got some bruises. During four or six seconds of flight we could not only examine our surroundings from a fair height, but also complete certain movements with our arms and legs; however, we didn't manage to tumble at will in space. Then we learned to give our bodies the initial and the tumbling movements simultaneously; in those cases we could flip over in space up to three times. It is curious to experience that movement, interesting also to see it from the side. Thus, for a long time I watched the movement of my physicist, who carried out a lot of movement experiments with no support, without the ground under his feet. It would take a whole book to describe them.

We slept about eight hours.

It was getting warmer. The Sun had risen higher and was baking more weakly, covering a smaller area of the body, but the ground had warmed up and no longer gave off such cold; in general, the effect of the Sun and the ground was warm, almost hot.

It was time, however, to take steps to protect ourselves, since it had already become clear to us that even before midday arrived we would be burnt to a crisp.

What could we do?

We had various plans.

"We could live for a few days in the cellar, but I can't guarantee that in the evening, about two hundred and fifty hours from now, the heat won't penetrate there, since the cellar isn't that deep. Besides, we'll get bored in the absence of any kind of comfort and in the enclosed space."

Let's say that suffering boredom and discomfort is easier than being cooked.

But wouldn't it be better to choose one of the deeper crevices? We'd creep into it and spend the rest of the day and part of the night there in pleasant coolness.

That would be much more cheerful and poetic. Or else – a cellar!

Necessity will drive a person into such places!

And so, the crevice. The stronger the Sun burned, the deeper we would go down. By the way, a depth of several sazhens is sufficient.

We would take along umbrellas, provisions in sealed boxes and casks; we would put on fur coats, since they could come in handy in either excessive heat or excessive cold; besides, here they wouldn't weigh on our shoulders.

A few more hours passed, during which we managed to eat something, take a rest and talk a bit more about gymnastics on the Moon and what kinds of wonders earthly acrobats could perform here. We couldn't linger any more: it was hellishly hot. In any case, outside, in the well-lit places, the stony ground was heated to the point where we had to strap thick wooden boards to the soles of our shoes.

In our haste we dropped some glass and clay vessels, but they didn't break – the gravity was so weak.

I almost forgot to mention the fate of our horse, who had been carried here along with us. When we wanted to harness the unfortunate animal to the wagon, he somehow broke loose from our hands and at first raced off faster than the wind, bucking and running into things; then, unaware of the power of inertia and unable to avoid a rocky mass in his way, he shattered against it. The meat and blood froze at first and then dried out.

And I should mention the flies. They couldn't fly, but only jumped, at least half an arshin…

And so, we took along everything essential, with immense loads on our shoulders, which amused us considerably, because everything we were carrying felt empty and thin. We closed the doors, windows and shutters of the house, so they would heat up less and would suffer less from the high temperature, and we set off to look for a suitable crevice or cave.

While we were searching we were struck by the sharp transitions in temperature: places that the Sun had been heating for a long time exuded the heat of a red-hot oven, so we tried to pass them as quickly as possible. We rested and freshened up somewhere in the shade cast by a boulder or a cliff – and we cooled down so well that if we had lingered we could have made good use of our fur coats. But these places couldn't be depended on either: the Sun would move to the other side and light up the place where now there was shadow and cold. We knew this and searched for a crevice where the Sun would cast its light, but only for a short time that would not heat up the stones.

There was a crevice with walls almost plumb-straight. We could see only the beginning of the walls – it was black and appeared bottomless. We went around the narrow part and found there a gentle slope, which led, apparently, to hell itself. We took a few steps without mishap, but the dark thickened, and nothing could be seen ahead of us; going farther seemed terrifying, and also risky… We remembered that we had brought along an electric flashlight: candles and torches were impossible here… The light turned on and in an instant lit up a crevice about twenty sazhens deep; the slope turned out to be comfortable.

So that's your bottomless crevice, that's your hell! We were disappointed by such pettiness.

Its darkness was explained, in the first place, by the fact that it lay in the shade, and because of its narrowness and depth the rays reflected by the illuminated surroundings and high mountains did not penetrate there; in the second place, by the fact that it was not illuminated from above by the atmosphere, as it would have been on Earth, where for that reason you can't find such thick darkness down any well.

In proportion to how far down we went, sometimes grabbing the walls, the temperature went down, but it wasn't less than fifteen degrees Celsius. Apparently that was the average temperature of the latitude where we were. We choose a comfortable, even spot, spread out our fur coats and arranged ourselves comfortably.

But what was this? Had night come? Covering the lamp with one hand, we looked at the scrap of dark sky and the multitude of stars, shining fairly brightly above our heads.

However, the chronometer showed that not much time had passed, and the Sun couldn't have set unexpectedly.

Oh no! An awkward movement broke the flashlight bulb, although the carbon filament continued to glow even brighter: if we were on Earth, it would have gone dull immediately, burnt out in the air.

I touched it curiously; it broke – and everything was cast into darkness. We couldn't see each other, our outlines were only barely noticeable at the height of the opening of the crevice, and the long narrow stripe of the black sky lit up with an even greater quantity of stars.

I couldn't believe it was midday. I couldn't bear it: with difficulty I found the extra flashlight, turned on its electric current and went upward… It was lighter and warmer… The light blinded me; it was as if the electric lamp had burned out.

Yes, it was daytime, and the Sun and shadows were just where they were before.

It was hot! Back as quickly as possible.

IV

We slept like logs from having nothing to do. Our lair didn't get warm.

Sometimes we came out of it, searched out a shady spot, and observed the movements of the Sun, stars, planets, and of our big Moon, which, if you compared its size to your pathetic Moon, was just like an apple compared to a cherry.

The Sun moved almost at the same rate as the stars and lagged behind them hardly noticeably, which you can notice from the Earth as well.

The moon stood entirely motionless and wasn't visible from our crevice, which we very much regretted, since from the darkness we could have observed it with as much success as at night, which was still far away. We should have chosen another crevice, from which we could have seen the moon, but it was too late now!

Midday was approaching; the shadows stopped growing shorter; the moon had the form of a narrow sickle, paler and paler, in proportion as the Sun moved closer to it.

The Moon is an apple, the Sun a cherry; if the cherry didn't ever cross paths with the apple there wouldn't be a solar eclipse.

On the Moon this comprises a frequent and grandiose phenomenon, while on Earth it is rare and nothing much: a little spot of shadow, the size of a pinhead (albeit sometimes several versts long, but what is that, if not a pinhead compared with Earth's magnitude?). It traces a stripe on the planet, moving if one is fortunate from city to city and lingering in each of them for several minutes. Here the shadow covers either the whole Moon, or in the majority of cases a significant part of its surface, so that the complete darkness lasts for several hours…

The sickle grew even narrower and barely visible alongside the Sun…

The sickle became completely invisible.

We crawled out of our crevice and looked at the Sun through a dark glass…

Now it looked as though someone had squashed an invisible gigantic finger into the star's shining mass from one side.

Now only half the Sun was visible.

Finally its last particle vanished, and everything was cast into gloom. An enormous shadow ran over and covered us.

But the blindness quickly lifted: we could see the moon and a multitude of stars.

This wasn't that other moon like a sickle; this one had the form of a dark circle, surrounded by a magnificent scarlet glow, especially bright, but paler on the side where the remnant of the Sun had just disappeared.

Yes, I saw the colors of sunset, which we used to admire from the Earth.

And our surroundings were bathed in scarlet, as if in blood…

Thousands of people were looking at us with their naked eyes and through telescopes, observing the total lunar eclipse…

Familiar eyes! Could you see us?

While we were grieving here, the red wreath grew more even and beautiful. Now it lay evenly around the whole circle of the moon; this was the midpoint of the eclipse. Now one side, opposite to where the Sun had disappeared, was getting paler and lighter… Now it was getting brighter and brighter and taking on the look of a diamond set in a red ring…

The diamond turned into a bit of Sun – and the ring became invisible… Night passed over into day – and our blindness passed: the former picture appeared before our eyes… We started talking animatedly.

I said earlier, "We picked a shady spot and made observations," but you, my reader, might well ask: "How could you observe the Sun from a shady spot?"

I would answer, "Not all the shady spots are cold and not all the lit spots are red-hot. In fact, the temperature of the ground depends mainly on how long the Sun has been heating that place. There are expanses that have only been lit by the Sun for a few hours, but were in shadow until then. Understandably, their temperature not only can't be high, it's even extremely low. Where cliffs and steep mountains cast shadows, there you find expanses that are still cold, though they're lit up, so that you can see the Sun from them. It's true that sometimes they're not close by, and before you can get to them you get pretty heated up – even an umbrella doesn't help."

We noticed the multitude of rocks in our crevice and so, for our own comfort and in part for the exercise, we decided to haul those that hadn't yet warmed up in sufficient quantity to the surface, so as to cover the space that was open from all sides with rocks and thus protect our bodies from the heat.

No sooner said than done…

That way, we could always go out onto the surface and, resting in the middle of the mass of stones, triumphantly make our observations.

Let the rocks get heated through!

We can haul out new ones, since there are so many down below; we have at our disposal plenty of strength, increased sixfold thanks to the Moon.

We executed this plan after the solar eclipse, which we had not even been certain would take place.

Besides this job, right after the eclipse we set to work establishing the latitude of our location on the Moon. This was not hard to do, keeping in mind the epoch of the solstice (which we could determine thanks to the eclipse that had taken place) and the height of the Sun. The latitude of our location turned out to be forty degrees north, meaning that we were not located on the equator of the Moon.

And so, midday passed – seven Earth days after the rising of the Sun, which we had not witnessed. In actual fact, the chronometer showed that the time of our stay on the Moon was so far equal to five Earth days. Therefore, we had appeared on the Moon early in the Moon's morning, some time after its forty-seventh hour. That explains why, when we woke up, we found the ground very cold: it hadn't had time to heat up, and it was terribly chilled by the previous extended fifteen-day night.

We slept and woke, and every time we saw more and more new stars above us. They were always in the same pattern, familiar from the Earth, always the same stars: only the narrow hole in which we were settled didn't allow us to see a great quantity of them at once, and they didn't twinkle against the black field, but passed by twenty-eight times more slowly.

There was Jupiter; here its satellites were visible to the naked eye, and we observed their eclipses. Jupiter disappeared. The North Star rolled out. Poor thing! It played no important role here. Only the Moon alone would never glance into our crevice, even if we waited a thousand years for it. It wouldn't come out, because it was eternally immobile. It could be animated only by the movements of our bodies on this planet; then it could sink, rise and move through the sky… We would return to this question again…

You can't sleep all the time!

We got down to making plans.

"At night we'll come out of the crevice, not right after the Sun sets, when the ground is heated almost to the utmost, but after a few dozen hours. We'll visit our residence too, to see what's going on there. Has the Sun gone and broken anything? Then we'll travel for a while by moonlight. We'll enjoy the view of the moon here to our hearts' content. Until now we've seen it looking like a white cloud; at night we'll see it in its full beauty, in its full glory and from all sides, since it rotates rapidly and will show its whole self in no more than twenty-four hours, which is an insignificant part of the lunar day."

Our large moon – the Earth – has phases, just like the Moon, which we had looked at previously from afar, full of dreams and curiosity.

At our present location the new moon, or rather the new Earth, appeared at midday; the first quarter as the sun set; the full moon at midnight, and the last quarter at sunrise.

We were located in a place where the nights and even the days were always moonlit. That was not so bad, but only as long as we were in the hemisphere visible from Earth. As soon as we passed into the other hemisphere, the one invisible from Earth, we would immediately lose our nighttime light. We'd be deprived of it as long as we were in that unfortunate, yet so mysterious, hemisphere. It's mysterious for the Earth, since Earth never sees it, and therefore it intrigues the scientists very much; it's unfortunate because its residents, if there are any, are deprived of both the nocturnal light source and the magnificent view.

In point of fact, are there any inhabitants on the Moon? What are they like? Do they resemble us? Until now we hadn't met any, and it would be fairly hard to meet them, since we had been sitting almost in one place and spending much more time on gymnastics then on selenography. That unknown half was especially interesting, with its black skies eternally covered at night by a mass of stars, for the most part tiny, easy to view by telescope, since their gentle gleam was neither disturbed by the multiple refractions of the atmosphere, nor violated by the crude light of the enormous moon.

Could there be a hollow there where gasses could gather, and liquids, and a lunar population? This occupied our conversations, which passed the time as we waited for night and sunset. We waited with impatience. It wasn't too tedious. We didn't forget to experiment with vegetable oil, an idea the physicist had brought up before.

In fact, we managed to collect drops of an enormous size. Drops of oil that fell from a horizontal surface would attain the size of apples, while drops from a sharp edge were significantly smaller, and oil flowed through an opening two and a half times more slowly than on Earth under identical conditions. The phenomena of transpiration took place on the Moon with sixfold strength. Thus, the meniscus of oil at the edges of a vessel rose six times higher above the level of the oil in the center.

Oil in a shot glass had the form almost of a depressed sphere…

We didn't forget about our sinful bellies either. Every six to ten hours or so we fortified ourselves with food and drink.

We had a samovar with us with a lid that screwed on firmly, and we often sipped a strong brew of the Chinese herb.

Of course, we couldn't put the samovar on in the usual way, since air was needed for the combustion of coals and kindling. We simply carried it out into the sun and surrounded it with especially hot little pebbles. It would heat up quickly, without boiling. Hot water poured strongly from the open spout, driven by the pressure of the steam, which was not counterbalanced by the weight of the atmosphere.

It wasn't especially pleasant to drink this kind of tea because of the possibility of getting badly burned, for the water went in all directions like exploding gunpowder.

Therefore, after putting tea into the samovar ahead of time, we would let it heat up a lot at first, then wait for it to cool down after we removed the hot stones, and finally we would drink the prepared tea without burning our lips. But even this relatively cool tea poured out with noticeable force and boiled weakly in our mugs and in our mouths, like seltzer water.

V

Soon the sun would set.

We watched the Sun touching the peak of one mountain. On Earth we would watch this phenomenon with our naked eyes, but here that was impossible, for there was no atmosphere, nor any water vapor, and so the Sun lost none of its bluishness, nor its power of heat and light. You could only take a quick passing glance at it without a dark glass; it was nothing like our scarlet Sun that is weak when it rises and sets!

It sank, but slowly. Half an hour had already passed since it first touched the horizon, and only half the Sun was hidden.

In St. Petersburg or Moscow the sunset lasts no more than three to five minutes. In tropical countries it's about two minutes, and only at the poles can it continue for several hours.

Finally the last particle of the Sun was extinguished behind the mountains, where it looked like a bright star.

But there was no sunset glow. Instead of a glow we saw around us a multitude of mountain peaks and other elevated parts of our surroundings lit up with bright reflected light.

This light was entirely sufficient to keep us from sinking into darkness for several hours, even if there had been no moon.

One distant peak continued to glow for thirty hours, like a streetlamp.

But then it went out too.

Only the moon and stars made light for us, and the power of illumination of the stars is negligible. Right after sunset, and even a while after, the reflected sunlight outweighed the light of the moon.

Now, when the last mountain cone had gone dark, the Moon – lord of the night – sat in state over our moon.

Let's turn our gaze toward it.

Its surface is fifteen times larger than the surface of the Moon from the Earth, compared to which, as I already said, it's like a cherry to an apple.

The power of its light is fifty or sixty times brighter than the Moon with which we are familiar.

We could read without straining; it seemed that this wasn't night, but some fantastic kind of day.

Its radiance didn't let us see either the lights of the zodiac or the smaller stars without special screens.

What a sight! Hello, Earth! Our hearts beat wearily, neither bitterly nor sweetly. Recollections burst into our souls…

How dear and mysterious now was that formerly disdained, everyday Earth! It looked to us like a picture covered with blue glass. That glass was the ocean of air around the Earth.

We saw Africa and part of Asia, the Sahara, the Gobi, Arabia! Lands of drought and cloudless skies! There were no blots on you: you are always open to the moon-dwellers' gaze. Only when the planet rotates around its axis does it bear these deserts away.

Meanwhile, those formless shreds and stripes were the clouds.

The dry land seemed dirty yellow or dirty green.

The seas and oceans were dark, but their shades were different, depending, probably, on the degree of their disturbance and calm. Over there, perhaps, the whitecaps were plying the backs of the waves so that the sea was whitish. The waters were covered here and there with clouds, but not all the clouds were snow-white, though there were few grey ones: it must have been that they were covered by fine layers above consisting of icy crystalline dust.

The two diametrical ends of the planet were especially brilliant: those were the polar snows and ices.

The northern whiteness was cleaner and had a larger surface than the southern one.

If the clouds had not moved, it would have been difficult to tell them apart from the snow. By the way, for the most part the snows lie deeper down in the ocean of air, and therefore the blue color that covers them is darker than the same tinge over the clouds.

We saw snowy spangles of smaller size scattered over the whole planet, even at the equator – those were mountain tops, sometimes so high that the cap of snow never leaves them, even in tropical countries.

There were the Alps gleaming!

There were the heights of the Caucasus!

There was the range of the Himalayas!

The snow spots were more constant than the clouds, but they too (the snows) change, disappear and appear once again with the seasons…

With a telescope we could make out all these details… We looked in admiration!

It was the first quarter: the dark half of the Earth, illuminated by the weak moon, could be made out with great difficulty and was far darker than the dark (ashen) part of the Moon when seen from the Earth.

We wanted to eat. But before we went back down into the crevice, we wanted to find out whether the ground was still hot. We came down from the stone layer we had made, already renewed several times, and found ourselves in an impossibly overheated sauna. The heat quickly penetrated through our soles… We retreated in haste: the ground wouldn't cool down at all any time soon.

We ate lunch in the crevice, whose edges no longer glowed, but a terrible multitude of stars was visible.

Every two or three hours we came out to look at the moon – Earth.

We could have examined it entirely in about twenty hours, if we hadn't been prevented by the cloudiness of your planet. A few places were stubbornly covered by clouds and made us lose patience, though we hoped to see them later, and in fact we did observe them as soon as the weather cleared there.

We hid for five days in the bowels of the Moon, and if we came out then it was only to places nearby and for a short time.

The ground was cooling, and by the end of five earth days, or towards midnight Moon time, it was cool enough that we decided to undertake our journey on the Moon, through its valleys and mountains. It seemed that we hadn't yet been in any low-lying areas.

Those darkish, enormous and low expanses of the Moon are usually called seas, although that's entirely incorrect, since there's no water there. Would we find traces of neptunic activity in those "seas" and other low areas – traces of water, air and organic life, which in the opinion of some scientists had disappeared from the Moon long ago? There is a hypothesis that all this existed on the Moon once, if it doesn't exist now, somewhere in crevices and abysses: there was water and air, but they were sucked away, they were consumed over the course of centuries by its soil, uniting with it chemically; there were organisms – some kind of plant life of a simple order, some kinds of shellfish, because where there's water and air, there you find slime, and slime is the beginning of organic life, at least of the lowest kind.

As far as my friend the physicist was concerned, he thought, and with good reason for it, that there had never been life on the Moon, nor water, nor air. If there were water, if there were air, then it would have been at such a high temperature that no kind of organic life would be possible.

Let readers forgive me for expressing here the personal opinion of my friend the physicist, which is not proven by anything.

Once we completed our voyage around the world, then we'd see who was right. And so, taking up our loads, which had grown considerably lighter due to the large quantity we had eaten and drunk, we abandoned the hospitable crevice and headed beneath the moon, which stood in one and the same place in the dark firmament, back to our residence, which we quickly found.

The wooden shutters and other parts of the house and its service buildings, made of the same material, had fallen apart and their surfaces had charred and peeled away, exposed to the Sun's prolonged action. In the yard we found shards of the water barrel blown apart by steam pressure, since we had carelessly stoppered it and left it in the hot sun. There were no traces of water, of course: it had evaporated without leaving any behind. By the porch we found slivers of glass – this from the lamp, whose frame had been made of metal with a low melting temperature: it had obviously melted, and the glass panes had fallen. We found less damage inside the house: the thick stone walls had protected it. Everything in the cellar was still in good shape.

Taking the essential things from the cellar, so as not to die of hunger and thirst, we set off on an extended trip towards the Moon's pole and into the other hemisphere, which had not yet been seen by any human being.

"Shouldn't we follow the Sun westward?" suggested the physicist, "altering our course a bit towards one of the poles? Then we can kill two birds with one stone: the first bird is to reach the pole and the dark side; the second bird is to escape the excessive cold, since if we don't lag behind the Sun we can run through places the Sun has warmed for a certain time – therefore, through places with an unchanging temperature. We can even change temperature on demand, to the extent we need to – if we catch up to the Sun, we can increase it; if we hang back, we can decrease it. This is especially good if you keep in mind that we'll be approaching the pole, whose average temperature is low."

"Oh come on, is that possible?" I remarked, in reaction to the physicist's strange theories.

"Entirely possible," he answered. "Just take into account the ease of running on the Moon and the apparently slow movement of the Sun. In actual fact, the greatest lunar circle is about ten thousand versts in length. This length has to be covered, if we don't want to fall behind the Sun, in thirty days, or seven hundred hours, to express myself in earthly language. That means, in an hour we have to cover fourteen and a half versts."

"Fourteen and a half versts per hour on the Moon!" I exclaimed. "I regard that figure with nothing but disdain."

"Well, there you go."

"We'll run twice as far without even trying!" I continued, remembering our mutual gymnastic exercises. "And then every twelve hours we can sleep for just as long…"

"Different latitudes," the physicist explained. "The closer we get to the pole, the less distance, and since we'll head precisely in that direction, then we can run more and more slowly without falling behind the Sun. However, the cold of the polar countries won't allow us to do that: as we approach the pole, in order not to freeze, we'll have to move closer to the Sun, that is, run through places that have been exposed to extended illumination by the Sun, even though they're polar. The polar Sun hangs low over the horizon, and therefore the ground is heated incomparably less, so even at sunset the ground is merely warm."

The closer we get to the pole, the nearer we must be to the sunset, to keep a constant temperature.

"Westward, westward!"

We glided like shadows, like phantoms, silently touching the pleasantly warming ground with our feet. The moon was almost full and therefore shone exceedingly brightly, presenting an enchanting picture, veiled by blue glass that seemed grow thicker towards the edges, since it gets darker the closer it is to the edge. On the edges themselves you couldn't make out either dry land, or water, or cloud formations.

Now we were seeing the hemisphere that's rich in dry land; in twelve hours it would be the opposite, the half rich in water – almost nothing but the Pacific Ocean. It reflects the sun's rays poorly, and therefore if it weren't for the ice and clouds, which gleamed brightly, the moon wouldn't have been as bright as it was now.

We easily ran up onto an elevation and even more easily down from it. From time to time we were bathed in shadow, from which more stars were visible. For now we encountered only low hills. But even the highest mountains would present no obstacles, since here the temperature of a place didn't depend on its elevation: the mountaintops were just as warm and free of snow as the low valleys… Uneven places, protuberances, abysses on the Moon were not frightening. We leapt across uneven places and abysses as wide as ten or fifteen sazhens; if they were very wide and inaccessible, then we tried to run around on one side or we stuck to the slopes and protuberances with the help of thin cords, sharp hooked sticks and shoes with cleats.

Remember our low weight, which didn't require cables for support – and it will all make sense to you.

"Why aren't we heading for the equator? After all, we haven't been there," I remarked.

"Nothing is stopping us from going there," the physicist agreed.

And we immediately changed our course.

We ran exceedingly fast, and therefore the ground got warmer and warmer; finally it became impossible to run because of the heat, for we had come to the parts that were more heated by the Sun.

"What would happen," I asked, "if we ran, regardless of the heat, at this speed and in this direction – towards the west?"

"After about seven earth days we would see first the sunlit mountaintops and then the Sun itself, rising in the west."

"But surely the Sun wouldn't rise where it usually sets!" I was dubious.

"It's true, and if we were folkloric salamanders, protected against fire, we could let our own eyes persuade us of this phenomenon."

"What happens then? The Sun just appears and then disappears, or does it rise in the usual way?"

"As long as we run along the equator, let's say, faster than fourteen and a half versts, the Sun will keep moving from west to east, where it will set. But we just have to stop, and it will immediately start moving in the usual way and, after we forced it to rise in the west, it will once again disappear behind that horizon."

"But what if we ran neither faster, nor slower than fourteen and a half versts per hour, what would happen then?" I went on asking.

"Then, as in the time of Joshua, the Sun would stop in the sky and day or night would never end."

"Can you play this sort of trick on Earth too?" I persisted to my physicist.

"Yes, but only if you're in shape to run, ride or fly over the Earth at a minimum speed of one thousand five hundred and forty versts per hour."

"What? Fifteen times faster than a blizzard or a hurricane? No, I won't try that… that is, I forgot – I wouldn't try it!"

"That's right! What's possible here, and even easy, is entirely unthinkable over there on that Earth," and the physicist pointed at the moon in the sky.

So we reasoned, sitting down on the stones, for we couldn't run any more due to the heat, which I already mentioned.

Worn out, we soon fell asleep.

We were awakened by a significant chill. Leaping up cheerfully and jumping up five arshins or so, we once again ran off towards the west, tending towards the equator.

You'll remember that we had determined the latitude of our cabin as forty degrees, and therefore there was a fair distance left to the equator. But don't think that a degree of latitude is the same on the Moon as on Earth. Don't forget that the Moon's size is proportionally smaller than the Earth, as a cherry is to an apple. Therefore, a degree of Moon latitude is no more than thirty versts, while on Earth it is a hundred and forty.

We became convinced, however, that we were approaching the equator by the fact that the temperature of the deep crevasses, which represented the average temperature, gradually increased and, after reaching fifty degrees Réaumur, stayed at that level. Then it even began to decrease, indicating that we had passed into the other hemisphere.

We determined our location more exactly by astronomical means.

But before we crossed the equator, we encountered many mountains and dry "seas."

The form of lunar mountains is perfectly familiar to inhabitants of the Earth. For the most part they are round mountains with craters in the center.

The crater was not always empty, and did not always turn out to be a recent crater: sometimes a whole other mountain rose in the center with its own indentation, which turned out to be a newer crater, but very rarely an active one – with lava inside, glowing dull red on the very bottom.

Was it not these volcanoes that in the past had tossed up most of the rocks we often found? I can't imagine they came from anywhere else.

Out of curiosity, we intentionally ran past the volcanoes, right along their very edges, and twice as we glanced into their craters we saw waves of gleaming lava.

Once we even noticed an enormous, high sheaf of light above the summit of one mountain, most likely formed of stones heated until they glowed: the tremor from their fall reached our feet, which were so light here.

Whether in consequence of the lack of oxygen on the Moon, or for other reasons, we only came across unoxidized minerals, most often aluminum.

The low, even spaces, the dry "seas" in some places, despite the physicist's assurances, were covered with clear, though small signs of neptunic activity. We liked that kind of depression, slightly dusty to the touch of our feet; but we ran so fast that the dust remained behind and dissipated at once, since it was not raised by the wind and didn't blow into our eyes and noses. We liked the "seas" because we had pounded our heels on the rocky places, and for us they stood in place of soft carpets or grass. This sedimentary layer could not hamper our pace because of its thinness, which did not exceed a few inches.

The physicist pointed something out to me in the distance, and I saw to our right something like a bonfire that sent red sparks flying in all directions. The sparks traced out red arcs.

We tacitly agreed to make a hook in our path, so we could find an explanation for this phenomenon.

When we ran up to the place we saw scattered pieces of more or less molten iron. The small pieces had already managed to cool, the large ones were still red.

"This is meteoric iron," said the physicist, picking up one of the cooled fragments of the aerolite. "The very same kind of pieces fall on the Earth," he continued. "I've seen them more than once in museums. Only the name of these heavenly stones, or rather bodies, is incorrect. The name meteorite is especially inappropriate here on the Moon, where there's no atmosphere. They aren't even visible here until they hit the granite ground and get hot as the energy of their motion is converted into heat. On Earth they're visible almost the moment they enter the atmosphere, since they're heated by the friction of the air."

After running across the equator, we decided to turn back towards the north pole.

The cliffs and mounds of stones were amazing.

Their forms and positions were quite bold. We had never seen anything like them on Earth.

If we imagined them there, I mean on your planet, they would inevitably collapse with a terrible crash. Here the capricious forms could be explained by the low gravity, which couldn't pull them down.

We ran and ran, moving closer and closer to the pole. The temperature in the crevices grew lower and lower. On the surface we didn't sense that, because we were gradually catching up to the Sun. Soon we were due to see its miraculous rise in the west.

We didn't run fast; there was no need.

We had stopped going down into the crevices to sleep, because we didn't want cold; instead we rested and ate where we stopped.

We also dozed off as we were walking, giving ourselves over to disconnected daydreams; there's no reason to be surprised at that, knowing that similar phenomena have been observed on Earth. They're all the more possible here, where standing takes little more energy than it takes to lie there (speaking in terms of weight).

VI

The moon sank lower and lower, illuminating us and the lunar landscape more weakly and then more strongly, depending on which side was turned towards us – the watery one or the land one, or on how much of its atmosphere was full of clouds.

There came a time when it touched the horizon and began to sink behind it – that meant we had reached the other hemisphere, invisible from Earth.

About four hours later it disappeared completely, and we saw only the heights that it still illuminated. But they too went dim. The darkness was remarkable. A multitude of stars! You can see that many on Earth only with a decent telescope.

Their lifelessness, however, is unpleasant; their motionlessness is far from the motionlessness of the blue sky of tropical countries.

And the black background was so oppressive!

What was that, giving off such a strong light in the distance?

Half an hour later we found that it was the mountain peaks. More and more such peaks were beginning to glow.

We had to run up the mountain. Half of it was lit up. There was the Sun! But while we ran up, the peak had already had time to grow dark, and the Sun was no longer visible from it.

Apparently, this was the line of sunset.

We set off more quickly. We flew like arrows from the bow.

We could have hurried less than that: all the same we would see the Sun rising in the west, even if we ran only 5 versts per hour, that is, if we didn't run at all – what kind of a run is that! – but walked.

But we couldn't help rushing.

And there, O miracle!

The rising star gleamed in the west. Its size quickly increased… A whole slice of the Sun was visible… The whole Sun! It rose, grew separate from the horizon… Higher and higher!

However, that was only for us, because we were running; the mountaintops left behind us were going dark one by one.

If we hadn't looked at those unmoving shadows, the illusion would have been complete.

"Enough, we're tired!" the physicist cried jokingly to the Sun. "You can go off and rest."

We sat down and waited for the moment when the Sun, setting in the ordinary way, would disappear before our eyes.

"*Finità la commedia!*"

We turned over and fell soundly asleep.

When we woke up we chased down the Sun again, just for the sake of warmth and light, without rushing, and we no longer let it out of our sight. It would rise and then sink, but it was constantly in the sky and warmed us without ceasing. We would fall asleep when the Sun was fairly high. As we woke up the laggard Sun would be crawling towards setting, but we would tame it in time and force it to rise again. We were approaching the pole!

Here the Sun was so low and the shadows so enormous that, as we ran across them, we got properly chilled. In general, the contrast in temperature was striking. Some elevated places were heated up to the point where we couldn't even approach. We couldn't run through other places, which had been lying in the shade for fifteen days or more (earth time), without the risk of getting rheumatism. Don't forget that here the Sun, even though it was lying on the horizon, heated the rock surfaces no more weakly, but rather twice as strongly, as the Sun on Earth when it stands directly overhead. Of course, this can't be so in Earth's polar countries, because in the first place the power of the Sun's rays is almost entirely absorbed by the thickness of the atmosphere. In the second place, they don't shine on you so stubbornly at the pole: every twenty four hours the Sun and its light go around any rock in a circle, though they never let it out of sight.

You'll say, "But what about heat conductivity? Shouldn't the heat pass from a rock or mountain into the cold, stony ground?" I'll reply, "Sometimes it does seep away, when the ground forms one whole with the main mass, but many granite massifs are simply cast onto the ground, regardless of their size, and only touch it or some other massif at three or four points. Through these points the heat passes extremely slowly, or better – imperceptibly. But the mass keeps heating up more and more; the rate of radiation of the rays is so slow."

We had trouble, though, not with these heated stones, but with the very chilled valleys that were lying in shadow. They interfered with our approach to the pole because the closer we came to it the more extensive and impenetrable the shadowed spaces were.

If only the seasons of the year were more noticeable here – but there were hardly any seasons: in summer the Sun doesn't rise higher than five degrees at the pole, while on Earth it rises five times higher.

And anyway, how long would we have to wait for summer, which would, most likely, allow us more or less to reach the pole?

And so, moving along in the same direction after the Sun and tracing a circle or, more accurately, a spiral on the Moon, we once again moved farther from the point that's frozen in places with hot rocks scattered over it.

We didn't want to freeze or to burn up either! We moved farther and farther… It was hotter and hotter… We were forced to move away from the Sun. We were forced to lag behind it, to keep from being roasted. We ran in the dark, decorated at first by a few shining peaks of mountain ranges. But then they were already gone. It was easier to run: we'd already eaten and drunk a lot.

Soon the moon, which we had forced to move in the sky, would appear.

There it was.

We greet you, o dear Earth!

We were glad to see it, no joke.

And how could we not be! We had been separated from it for so long!

Many more hours passed. Though we'd never seen those places and mountains, they didn't attract our curiosity and they seemed monotonous. We were tired of everything – all these wonders! Our hearts were breaking, our hearts were aching. The view that was so splendid but inaccessible from Earth only exacerbated the pain of recollections, the sores of unrecoverable losses. It would have been good at least to reach our residence as quickly as possible! We couldn't sleep! But what awaited us there, in the house? Well-known but inanimate objects, able to prick and lacerate our hearts even more.

From where did this longing arise? Before we had barely felt it. Hadn't it been overshadowed then by our interest in the surroundings, which hadn't yet had time to bore us – by the novelty?

Home as fast as possible, so at least we couldn't see those dead stars and that sky, black as mourning!

Our residence had to be close by. It was here, we'd established it with astronomical observations, but despite indubitable indices we not only couldn't find the familiar yard – we didn't recognize even a single familiar view, a single mountain, which ought to have been familiar to us.

We walked along and searched for it.

Was it here, or there!? It was nowhere.

We sat down in despair and fell asleep.

The cold woke us up.

We restored ourselves with some food; there wasn't much left.

We'd have to save ourselves from the cold by running.

As if on purpose, we didn't come across a single suitable crevice where we could shelter from the cold.

Again we ran after the Sun. Running like slaves, chained to a chariot! Running forever!

Oh, far from forever. We had only enough food left for one meal.

What then?

The meal was eaten, the last meal!

Sleep closed our eyes. The cold forced us to huddle together like brothers embracing.

And where were all those crevices that kept showing up when we didn't need them?

We didn't sleep for long: the cold, still more powerful, woke us. Unceremonious and merciless! It hadn't let us sleep for even three hours. Hadn't let us get a good rest.

Powerless, weakened by longing, hunger and the advancing cold, we couldn't run with our previous speed.

We were freezing!

Sleep started to overcome me first – and the physicist supported his friend, and then sleep started in on him – and I supported him against sleep, deadly sleep. The physicist had taught me to understand the meaning of this terrible, final drowsiness.

We held each other up and gave each other strength. As I recall now, we didn't even think of abandoning each other and thus postponing the hour of our own deaths.

The physicist was falling asleep and raving about the Earth; I hugged him, trying to warm his body with my own.

I was overcome by tempting daydreams: about a warm bed, about the fire in a hearth, food and wine… I was surrounded by my own family… They were taking care of me, feeling sorry for me… They were taking me…

Daydreams, daydreams! The blue sky, snow on the neighbors' roofs… A bird flew by… Faces, familiar faces… A doctor… What was he saying?

"Lethargy, extended sleep, a dangerous situation… Significant weight loss… He's gotten much thinner… But he'll be all right! His breathing has improved… His responsiveness is returning… The crisis is passed."

Everyone around was happy, despite their tear-stained faces…

To make this brief, I had slept a diseased sleep and now I was awake: I lay down on the Earth and woke up on the Earth; my body remained here, while my thoughts flew off to the Moon.

Nevertheless I raved for a long time: I asked about the physicist, spoke about the Moon, was surprised that my friends had come to be near me. I confused the earthly with the heavenly: first I imagined myself on Earth, then I was back on the Moon.

The doctor ordered them not to argue with me and irritate me… They were afraid I'd go crazy.

Very slowly I returned to consciousness and even more slowly regained my health.

It goes without saying that the physicist was very surprised when, after I got better, I told him this whole story. He advised me to write it down and supplement it with some explanations.

First published in Russian: 1893
Translation by Sibelan Forrester

VALERY BRYUSOV
1908

REBELLION OF THE MACHINES

FROM THE CHRONICLES OF THE THIRTIETH CENTURY

I

My dear friend,

Giving in to your repeated requests, I am embarking on a description of the monstrous events that befell me and sent my happiness to an early grave. You are right: those who witnessed the horrible catastrophe, unprecedented in recorded history, and still retained their sanity are now obliged to chronicle its details for historians of the future. Contemporary testimonies would be priceless for scholars who will study us one day, and perhaps help future generations defend themselves against the horrors that were unleashed upon us. This is why, despite how heavily the remembrance of those days that resembled delirious nightmares – days that took away everyone I loved and crippled me – weighs on my heart, I will put into writing, as dispassionately as possible, all that I observed myself and heard from other eyewitnesses.

In fact, if not for your persuasiveness and your observation that after the tragic war only a few survivors remained, I would never have taken up this responsibility. I am scarcely suited for it. I represent probably the least qualified person to undertake this enterprise, as I can only describe the events in their external form; their meanings and causes are inaccessible to me. I can only promise to represent, in as lively and clear a manner as possible, the fantastic events that have now come to be known as "the rebellion of the machines," and in the process remain as credible as possible for a person who has now crossed the boundary between waking and dreaming and is incapable of distinguishing between reality and fantasy. It is up to others, more informed and educated than I, to analyze and interpret the facts.

You know that I am an ordinary man of my time, a simple philistine who did his duty in the civil services and looked forward to spending his leisure hours on relaxation and entertainment. After spending the requisite time at work, I was happy to return to the circle of my family: to my wife, poor Maria, my two children – Andrei, your favorite, and his little sister Anna – and their grandmother, the old woman whom everyone called "dear Yelizaveta." Whatever I learned at school stayed with me in some sort of vague way, and later I never had the time or the desire to supplement my rather limited knowledge. Let those who chose the higher calling of science be concerned with it, I thought, while we ordinary citizens, having fulfilled our obligations, could happily partake of the results.

Like all our contemporaries, I took advantage of the many benefits of modern gadgets, but never thought about how their parts functioned or how they were designed. It was enough that these machines served our everyday needs, and I was completely uninterested in how this was accomplished. We pressed the required button or turned the proper dial, and received everything necessary: fire, warm or cool air, hot water, steam, light, and so on. We spoke on the telephone; over the megaphone, we heard the newspaper read out in the morning and some light opera in the evening; we would switch on the telecinema while conversing with friends and gladly see their faces come to life, or enjoy some ballet on the same apparatus; we rode up to our apartments on automatic elevators summoned by the press of a button, and went up to the rooftops the same way to catch a breath of fresh air.... Out on the streets I confidently leapt on buses, subway trains, and compartments of the imperial railways, and rode on the platform of a dirigible; in emergencies I used motorcylettes and airplanes; I used the connecting escalators between stores while shopping, and in restaurants my order arrived automatically; at work, I used electric writing machines, electric adding machines, electric multipliers and dividers. Needless to say, we used the telegraph, suspended walkways, long-distance telephones and telescopes, attended both the electro-theater and the phono-theater, took ourselves to the automatic clinic for every little ailment, and so on and so forth. Literally at every step, if not every minute, we sought the cooperation of machines, yet at no point did we ask ourselves how exactly it all worked; we only got annoyed when the administrative telephone rang to inform us about this or that machine being temporarily out of service.

As everyone knows, using machines became exceedingly simple for us. Even my little Andrei knew which buttons and knobs got heat or light, called up the newspaper or circus, stopped the elevator or hailed the passing bus, and he never made a mistake telling them apart. It seems to me that modern man has developed a special instinct for communicating with machines. As people of bygone years figured out, for example, how much force they needed to push open a door without thinking too much about it, we press a button and know that the door will swing shut noiselessly. In exactly the same way we know how to manipulate the switches so that the strains of the opera can be heard in only one room, or step off the moving walkway onto the pavement – even though a person unused to this would immediately stumble and fall. And it seems entirely natural for us to know that a slight movement of the hand, an imperceptible turn of a dial, will bring about a particular consequence. We almost believe that all this happens "all by itself," that this is in the nature of things, just as in the past, when people struck a match, they knew to expect a flame for lighting their bonfire.

Now I am compelled to become much more aware: many things needed to be sorted out, inquiries were made, and much of the information I got from the newspapers, which for two months now have been continuously broadcasting the details of the catastrophe to the whole world. Now I know (of course I knew it before, had studied it in school, but had totally forgotten about it) that the Earth is divided into eighty-four "machine zones," each with its own self-contained electric station. Each area is subdivided into districts; ours had sixteen. Each district also has a central electric station, which in turn connected with all the others. Finally, each district is split into counties, with substations in each of them that receive electricity from the central station. The district central station, serving 146 counties, was located in our Octopolis. And if the mishap affected a relatively small area, it was precisely because the majority of the communicating lines were disconnected in the nick of time. That is why the rebellion, which began at the central station, caused upheaval only in Octopolis and its neighboring thirty counties, instead of affecting all 150 of them.

I do not know if one can talk about a plan for the rebellion, about its "preparations" or "conscious deliberations." No matter how awkward it sounds, after all I have gone through, I can no longer tell the difference between the unthinkable and the possible. The machines behaved so systematically, with such diabolic logic, during the events that I am ready to acknowledge – never mind the sarcasm most people direct towards crazy "fantasists" and the way in which scientists try, through harsh criticism, to beat some reason into them – that the rebellion was definitely thought out in advance, if not consciously conceived. That would make the rebels' plan crystal clear: they began the uprising not in one of the small substations, where its impact would have been relatively insignificant, but rather at the central station, from which it would potentially spread chaos into the whole district, and then, maybe, through the communicating lines across the whole zone – a vast space approximately the size of what used to be called a country. Naturally, I have no idea whether the rebels intended to spread their revolutionary actions all over the planet.

One might add – to my embarrassment, I only learned about this recently from newspapers and lectures after suffering through my experiences – that some scientists have been predicting such a rebellion for a considerable time. It turns out that many centuries ago the similarities between organic and inorganic life had been noted. For instance, the growth of crystals is analogous to the growth of plants and animals; the fragments of a crystal are regenerated by the same "forces of nature" as those that heal a wounded living organism; pearls can suffer from disease, as can minerals; metals have breaking points of elasticity and tension; power cables "wear out" and refuse to comply if they are forced to work too hard; some elements (or substances, I am not sure exactly what they are called) magnetize spontaneously; electric currents at certain levels of condensation (I apologize again for a possible terminological error) spontaneously go live; all chauffeurs and pilots have noticed that engines "act up" without any observable cause, and so on. Incidentally, my knowledge of all this is so vague that I am the least suitable person to describe such phenomena; even in these few short lines, I must have committed many errors. I repeat: let those with more knowledge untangle the facts, and I will merely describe what I saw.

I will get to the story now and try to keep all explanations out of it. I will leave aside the "why" and "wherefore," and attempt to answer only the question of "what." Even then my responses would be limited to a small range of events: as I never left the city of Octopolis through the whole course of the catastrophe, my observations are of necessity bounded by the city limits. I am an insignificant man, a speck of dust in a gigantic tornado, yet the tornado is made up of billions of dust specks; and so my limited awareness nevertheless registered the full extent of the horror that would soon engulf the entire Earth and, as they say, the whole universe.

II

I can't say anything about how the catastrophe began. Now it has come to light that the first terrifying events – signals of the larger rebellion, so to speak – occurred at the Central Station. But what happened there, what monstrous apparition was witnessed by those working there, will remain forever unknown, since not one worker survived to tell the story. Now, following diverse speculations, they are trying to reconstruct the hellish, fantastic scenario that played out in the massive hallways of the Station: hurricanes of unexpected lightning sparks, floods of electrical discharge, noise like a million simultaneous thunderclaps, hundreds and thousands of people – engineers, assistants, ordinary workers – falling charred beyond recognition, destroyed, blasted to pieces or contorted in unbelievably tortuous dances… But all this is mere supposition, and maybe it did not happen at all this way. In any case, I cannot attest to it and certainly did not know in those minutes, or rather moments, when it all transpired.

It is remarkable that the morning alarm woke us, the entire family, as usual at 7:15. Thus, at a quarter after seven the gadgets were all working normally – assuming, of course, that they were suppressing any signs of the coming rebellion according to the conspirators' plans that we were not to be alerted ahead of time. We switched on the lights, my wife placed the automatic coffeemaker on the stove, Andrei turned on the heat in the rooms, and all our activities proceeded normally. A few minutes must have passed before the catastrophe unfolded, or else the power supply in our home may have come from a local generator rather than directly from the station; or, as I mentioned above, the rebels may have been hiding the true state of things from the city residents… The usual cacophony of motors and propellers could be heard beyond the walls.

I was in a hurry because I planned to call on my friend Stefan, who was ailing, on the way to work. Not wanting to waste time, I asked Grandma (as everyone in the family called my mother) to inform Stefan on the telephone that I was on my way. She picked up the receiver of the city telephone, brought it up to her ear, pressed the right buttons on its panel and finally the last one... And suddenly something happened that we could not immediately understand. Grandma shuddered pitifully, dropping the receiver, and then went rigid, collapsed on the couch, and fell to the floor. We rushed to her prone figure. She was dead; this was apparent from her distorted face and the absence of breathing, and the ear to which she had held the telephone was as charred as if a lightning bolt had struck it with unimaginable force.

We looked at each other with surprise as much as despair. Naturally we attempted to revive her, but I saw immediately that it was futile. "We need to call the doctor!" I exclaimed, and reached for the telephone. But my wife sprang forward, grabbed my arm, and cried, "No! No! Do not touch the telephone! Don't you see there is something wrong with it? It will kill you just like Grandma!" Grasping the truth by some instinct, Maria overcame my resistance and did not let me approach the telephone, and thus saved my life – but to no avail, alas! I would have preferred to be killed then, at the beginning of the horrors, like my poor mother.

After some argument we decided that I would go up to find the young physician who lived on the fourteenth floor of our building. I had already turned towards the door when all the lights went out. It was light enough outside, but nevertheless this event surprised us. And again Maria, with startling perspicacity, pinpointed the source. "Something is malfunctioning at the Central Station," she warned. "Be careful." Then she sternly forbade Andrei to touch any buttons or knobs; this miraculous insight, however, did not save the woman herself. I was out on the landing by then. To my astonishment, there were about twenty people gathered there, all in a state of nervous excitement. Apparently some mishap had taken place in almost every apartment: some were killed, like Grandma, while trying to talk on the telephone, others received a terrible shock switching on the telecinema, still others were boiled alive by steam bursting out of the furnace or had their hands frozen by the refrigerator, and so forth. It was clear that the machines had deviated from their normal functions and that every wire and cable concealed danger.

After exchanging a few incoherent explanations, we decided to summon the elevator. For a long time no one was willing to transmit the necessary signal. At last, an elderly man resolved to press the button. We looked on with fear, yet he remained unharmed. But the elevator car did not appear, because there was no current. After some hesitation, I ran up the stairs because I only had to climb five floors. On every landing fearful faces kept asking me what had happened. Silently I ran up to the doctor's apartment and, not daring to press the doorbell, knocked with my fist. Startled by my wild knocking, the doctor himself opened the door, as I had almost broken it down like a madman. He did not yet know anything, and listened to my rambling account with a skeptical smile; nevertheless he agreed immediately to accompany me and help Grandma, all the while assuring me that she had probably only lost consciousness.

Before my arrival the doctor had been busy with some work in his small laboratory, into which I followed him from the entrance. Now, preparing to leave with me, he seemed to want to hermetically seal something, or perhaps start something up. I am not sure what he intended, but momentarily forgetting about my concerns – or not having paid any attention to them – he carelessly extended his hand and started to manipulate some kind of switch. Obviously, the doctor's table was equipped with special wires and circuits, and suddenly, before my very eyes, a bluish spark, thick as a good-sized rope, shot out of the switch and struck a fatal blow like a small clap of thunder. And the doctor collapsed on the carpet before me, brought to his death by this domestic lightning.... I froze in [Editor's note: the text ends here].

First published in Russian: 1908
Translation by Anindita Bannerjee

NIKOLAI FYODOROV
1906

ONE EVENING IN 2217

I

It was three o'clock. Matte lenses on the streets lit up, competing with the innumerable multicolored windows overhead. Above them, the bright winter day was dying, and the sun's rays sparkled gold and red on the flowery frost covering the city's glass roof. It looked as though fiery rubies, bright emeralds, dusky, lazy amethysts, and millions of other precious stones were flashing overhead in the aluminum net's dark web.

Many of the people standing in the self-mobile looked up; the leaves of the palm and magnolia trees along Nevsky Prospect appeared dark, like bits of black velvet in a sea of fading luminescence.

The sparks from the light in the glass flickered and died. The mournful bell rang three forlorn, soft peals. The pneumatic landed noisily on the corner of Liteyny Prospect, and in two minutes motley throngs of passengers poured down its stairs and up out of street elevators, crowding into the self-mobile.

A woman who was still young, though she'd lost the first bloom of youth, stood on the self-mobile's second landing. Deep in thought, she bit her full lower lip with white, even teeth and furrowed her delicate, velvety brows. A kind of haze covered her face and clouded her blue eyes. She did not notice how she crossed Liteyny, Troitskaya Street, and the park on the Fontanka, did not notice how everyone else standing around her was looking up at the news bulletin, flaming in red letters above the crowd and announcing that the eruption in Greenland continued, despite an intense struggle to keep it in check.

"It's terrible, how weak humanity still is," said a tall, broad-shouldered lad near her.

"But this eruption is extraordinary."

"Basically, something bad's going on all over," muttered a heavyset chiliarch as he lit a long cigarette. The red light reflected from his hooked nose, pursed lips, and bulging eyes.

"You think so?" asked a woman wearing a doctor's armband.

"No need to think about it. Just listen, and you'll hear the rumble of an approaching eruption, only it won't be like the one in Greenland. It'll be a sight worse."

As if in answer to these words, something rumbled deep in the earth below their feet. It slowly moved past and went silent, like a huge sigh heaved by an enormous breast.

"That was a truck," said the woman quickly, as if hurrying to explain it.

"Not everything is that easy to explain," the chiliarch countered, and walked over to board the self-mobile.

The girl had already reached Catherine Street by the time she noticed that she'd passed her stop. She didn't feel like going back. She'd been caught, body and soul, in some kind of web, a sticky, heavy web that slowly constricted more and more tightly around her, like a viper's coils.

II

The girl got off the self-mobile and walked to the cathedral. She loved this "ancient corner." It seemed to her that shadows of the past lived here, of people who would never return. She loved these little bushes; the flower gardens laid out according to how they looked in old pictures, hundreds of years ago; the newspaper kiosk, sporting announcements printed in clumsy old-timey letters; the tiny fountain with its thin, naïve jets of water arcing, then splashing gently back into the round basin… Only the high, grey roof hanging overhead spoiled the illusion.

There were not many people here today, only a tall old man with a long black beard, and two boys. One of them particularly attracted her attention. He was thin, frail, with big blue eyes and straight blonde hair. He was probably imagining that he was a defender of the truth from bygone days, a student or a revolutionary, as he looked secretively into his small, red notebook. He looked to be no older than fifteen. The girl smiled in spite of herself as she looked at him.

Then she closed her eyes and leaned back onto the hard, uncomfortable back of the bench. She could vaguely hear the distant murmur of the self-mobile's passengers, combined with the splashing of the fountain. She felt as though she were surrounded by a huge crowd of hushed people. Timid and oppressed, with pounding hearts and anxious spirits, they'd gathered here to raise the red banner of freedom for the first time. She could hear their voices, strained and harsh with tears, she could see their naïve faces, beaming with faith and inspiration.

No one passing and looking at the girl, at her full, healthy face, at her hands folded together, at the musculature detectable even through her clothes, her pretty legs crossed one over the other, at her slender figure – no one would realize that she had travelled into the past, into the mysterious distance.

Then the girl imagined the ringing of the big bell rolling out like thick, viscous waves, settling from above onto the hard, cold earth, and it seemed to her that all she needed to do was turn around to see the red flame of wax candles, the censer's thick smoke, women in long, dark dresses with their heads bowed, and weighty male figures in leather boots, thick, rough suits, and white, starched collars. The service was ending, and crowds of people were streaming out the cathedral doors and dispersing into the streets, dimly lit with electric and gas street-lamps. And all of them were going home… to their own home… their own home… their own home…

Silently, the girl repeated these three strange words to herself, and she became sadder than she'd been all day. She caught her breath raggedly, and her breast heaved and subsided in short bursts. The soft material rustled in annoyance.

III

Only yesterday she had taken her turn with Karpov.

She was a strange girl, for sure. What attracted and amused others repelled her; what to them seemed plain, simple, and natural would produce a whirlwind in her pretty head, a whole storm of strange and incomprehensible thoughts, an oppressive aching in her soul… How the boys and girls she knew would laugh, laugh with their whole souls if she told them her thoughts. Most of them would not understand her, and she would hear, of course, the same advice from all sides: "Go to a doctor."

She wanted a family, an old-fashioned family shut off in its own circle, tightly and indivisibly bound together, the kind of loving family one could only read about in historical novels. She looked at the strong, self-satisfied guys with hard muscles and smiling eyes whom she met at work, on the streets, in the theaters, at meetings and picnics, and she insisted despondently, "No, he's not right. And he's not right… him either…" The ease with which these fellows went from woman to woman, changing their affections, was almost an insult to her, it wounded her deeply.

Like the miser in the old story, she wanted to gather up whoever she'd fall in love with and hide him, take him away from everyone else so that he was hers alone. She wanted him to love only her, for his whole entire life… And so passed the years.

Her girlfriends laughed at her: "You have a heart of stone." The boys she had turned down considered her stupid and abnormal, and little by little stopped paying attention to her.

One day, in the spring, when a fresh, scented wind was blowing in through the open roof panels and you could hear the affectionate rustling of the trees' shining leaves, she was at the university, watching Karpov's dissertation defense. Though young, the scholar had already managed to acquire a multitude of admirers.

The topic of his dissertation was "The Institution of the Family in Pre-Reform Europe." It was magnificently written, and along with brilliant scientific erudition, its author also displayed significant talent in his clear, almost tangible descriptions of the family, that ancient, closed cell that was the basis of past governments, the way a honeycomb is for a beehive.

Once he'd been granted the title of Doctor of History and left the stage, holding his head high, the hall erupted into applause. It made the metallic covering of the walls and ceiling shake, and took a long time to die down. Women and girls threw Karpov bouquets of fresh, aromatic lily-of-the-valley.

Aglaya – that was the girl's name – was already twenty-six. Twice the stern, dry chiliarch Krag had looked at Aglaya's slender figure and said, "You're avoiding your duty to society."

Not many people liked Krag, because she had such a one-track mind, an austerity, a fanatical devotion to her god, Society. Young, lazy, addle-pated women would gossip that she was aiming for District Representative. The night before Karpov's defense, Krag had found Aglaya after work, stared directly at her with glass-hard eyes, and said, "Even if you don't have anything you're especially interested in, no talents or predilections, you still have to register, at least. If you take everything you need from society, you must give what you can back to it. It's improper and immoral to shirk your duty."

"I'll think about it," said Aglaya.

"There's nothing to think about. It's crystal clear. This seems to be some new disease. When I was young, girls didn't think so much. I think the people who want that special compulsory law are right."

So now, going down the steps at the university, gripped by a cool spring wind that made her nostrils flare and her breath to come deeply and freely from her chest, Aglaya made up her mind. The very next day she went to the building where Karpov lived.

It was difficult for her to do this, and she blushed when she asked the superintendent of the house, "Does Karpov take applications?"

The superintendent smiled in spite of himself and answered, "Yes he does. Wednesdays from two to three."

Four days until the next Wednesday. Aglaya spent them in a fever, a hundred times deciding not to go and then changing her mind. Five minutes before she left her room she was not yet certain that she would go. But she went.

More than twenty women and girls were already sitting in his bright, beflowered waiting room when she arrived, and each minute brought new ones. Some were obviously embarrassed and sat with their eyes down, hands folded. Others chatted in an undertone. The room was so crowded that there did not seem to be enough places for everyone who wanted to register with this striking celebrity, and the elevators kept bringing them up in in ones, twos, and threes.

Around two-thirty Karpov came out, wearing soft house clothes and slippers. Women had already spoiled him enough, but evidently, even he was embarrassed by today's flood: he stopped short, disconcerted.

There were over fifty candidates. Karpov went to the middle of the room, offered a general bow to everyone present, and ran his eyes over faces and figures. There were no absolutely ugly ones. Everyone had her work number sewed on her shoulder, as always. Karpov pulled out a small book with gilt edges and a tiny pencil, noted down several numbers, cast a last gaze over all the candidates, and bowed again, to everyone and no one. Then he left by the same door through which he'd come.

Aglaya did not want to speak with anyone. Burning with shame, she jumped to the self-mobile's first landing. Impatient with its slowness, she got off and shoved her way through the crowd to her apartment, leaving a trail of annoyed glances in her wake.

When Krag again confronted her several days later, "You still haven't registered?" she answered furiously, with a nervous quiver in her voice, "I've registered, I've registered, leave me alone now, I beg you."

IV

Yesterday morning she'd been informed that today would be her turn with Karpov. She had expected this, yet she had also thought that it would be a very long time before she was called, which had calmed her down somewhat. The news hit her like an electric shock. Her arms and legs felt paralyzed and her head spun in a frenzy. That evening, when she washed and dressed, she was trembling.

Her knock on Karpov's door was barely audible. He was home and answered lazily, "Come in."

It was midnight, the hour she'd been assigned to visit him…

V

Now, remembering that whole evening moment by moment, she felt like burying her face in her hands and sobbing loudly, shrieking until her whole body shook.

The plaintive sound of the electric bell wafted down from the roof, and a pneumatic halted briefly, then roared onward. The humming of the crowd on the self-mobile faded as the crowd grew smaller.

It seemed to Aglaya that yesterday she had lost the dearest, the best thing in life, and that it could not be returned. She raised her eyes, as if searching the dark night sky for silent stars, but overhead all she saw was the cold, apathetic grey roof hanging over her. It seemed to Aglaya that it was pressing down on her brain, her thoughts.

Aglaya turned her gaze back to the street. The red letters of the bulletins faded and then glowed back again, bringing news from all corners of the earth:

"Pneumatic crash near Madrid. Eleven dead."

"Elections in the Tokyo region. Kamagawa won by 389 votes."

"The eruption in Greenland continues. Four divisions have been mobilized."

Aglaya read these announcements, but the meanings behind the blood red letters of the words escaped her. She looked to the right, to see the cold green letters of the evening programs:

"First auditorium. A lecture by Lyubavina on the earth's crust."

"Second auditorium. An aromatic concert."

"Third auditorium. A lecture by Karpov..."

This name hit Aglaya like a hammer and she jumped up, wanting to run away – but where could she go?

Today she wanted to be far away from people, from these self-satisfied, happy, laughing people, as monotonous as mannequins. But it would be even worse to go back to her own room, clean, light, and filled with loneliness; to be alone with herself would be the worst of all. She decided to visit Lyuba, the new friend she had become close to in the last couple months. Nevsky Prospect was empty. Only a few windows were still lit, and it was as though someone had poured an even white light over the cold, gleaming facades, and they'd frozen. Ribbons of self-mobiles flowed both ways along the buildings. There were only a few people sitting and standing in the self-mobiles, exchanging the occasional words that rang out dully in the empty street.

Aglaya boarded a self-mobile, sat down, and closed her eyes again.

VI

This time, she didn't go past her stop. She got out at building nine, walked into the entrance, and pressed the button to number twenty-seven. The answer appeared instantaneously: "I'm home. Who is it?" She answered and again the letters lit up: "Come in."

Aglaya got into the elevator and went up to the eighth floor. She took a few steps down the corridor and then knocked at number twenty-seven.

"Come in," answered Lyuba.

"Are you alone?" asked Aglaya, having difficulty trying to make out the objects in the room, which was lit only by a heater.

"Yes," Lyuba replied, getting up off the couch to greet her.

The variegated matte-glass panels of the heater threw pale shades and colors onto the walls and floor. The window curtain was up, and the weak light from the street fell in, barely delineating the window-frame.

"Can we close the curtain?" asked Aglaya, her finger already on the black button.

"Of course," Lyuba replied.

Aglaya pressed the button, and the heavy curtain lowered and covered the window, which looked cold and empty, like a dead man's eye.

"That's better. Being outside is bothering me today."

"I've just been lying here, dreaming," said Lyuba, after Aglaya had taken off her sweater and gloves.

"About what?"

"Oh, I don't even know myself. Today was the aromatic concert with my favorite numbers: Vyaznikov's "May Night," Wallace's "Storm," Poletti's "Romeo and Juliette." But I didn't want to leave my room. That "May Night" is so marvelous, you remember? It begins with the delicate scent of a fresh meadow. Then the thick, warm aroma of violets, and the smell of thick green leaves, and then the forest smells, spicy, with a hint of decay... You seem to be walking through the thick woods hand-in-hand with your beloved... and then the sharp, fresh scent of lily-of-the-valley, wafting through the air like a gossamer fabric, it's a scent that makes you breathe more broadly and freely. At that point I want to just shout for joy! And then roses, regal and in full bloom... the dawn sparkles in the dew on the roses... It's so marvelous!"

Lyuba put her hands behind her head and gazed dreamily into the heater's colored glass panels.

"Why aren't you going?" asked Aglaya, waiting the answer with such dread that it seemed as though her fate was hanging in the balance.

"I didn't want to. Can't be bothered... And lately I've had a lot of unpleasant things happening to me," Lyuba answered, then fell silent, looking intently at the heater's colored glass.

<h3 style="text-align:center">VII</h3>

"What kind of things?" asked Aglaya, to break the silence.

"Oh, the usual. Everything's falling apart again. I'm so unhappy, Aglaya, so miserable!"

"What's the matter?"

"This week I was at Eichenwald's, Kurbatov's, and Eisen's. Nothing but rejections... Although I did get in with Eisen, but not for a year and a half. And he's a musician. I don't really like musicians, I have no desire for my child to be a musician. Why am I so unattractive, so ugly? Why do I have such a long nose? I'm sure that every one of them sees my nose first and that scares them off."

"Lyuba, you're not as ugly as you think you are."

"Oh, you can't console me, I know better."

Silence again ensued. In the distance, the electric bell sounded pitiably: one, two, three...

"That bell! It's driving me mad," said Lyuba, momentarily plugging her ears with her long fingers.

"Yesterday I was at Karpov's," Aglaya murmured, almost inaudibly.

"You were!" Lyuba cried out excitedly, turning to her. "So, how was it? You're so lucky, Aglaya. Tell me everything, do you hear? Everything."

"I'm depressed... I can't talk about it. My soul feels nasty, filthy."

"But why? How I'd love to be in your place. Don't blush... Karpov is so handsome, so magnificent..."

VIII

The telephone rang abruptly, and a ray of white light pierced the room.

"Who is it?" asked Aglaya, annoyed.

"Vitinsky," Lyuba read the lighted panel.

"Let him in, please," Aglaya intervened, hurrying to prevent her friend from sending him away.

"I can't stand that reformer," Lyuba whispered, turning away from the telephone.

"Please," Aglaya repeated, folding her hands and begging.

"All right, fine…" Lyuba turned back to the telephone and said, "Come on over. Your admirer Aglaya is here too."

As soon as Lyuba turned off the telephone, Aglaya asked in annoyance, "What'd you tell him that for?"

"What? Isn't it true? But he's not my type, and I don't understand why you like him. He's troubled, somehow."

"It's his troubled nature that attracts me."

"I don't get it."

The conversation kept faltering. The friends sat in silence, each thinking her own thoughts.

"What time is it?" Aglaya eventually asked. "I haven't eaten since lunch today, but I don't feel like eating."

Lyuba raised her arm back over hear head and pressed a small button. A clock-face gleamed above the heater. "Seven thirty," Lyuba said.

"Thanks," Aglaya said, then resumed her silence.

"Did you get transferred?" Lyuba asked, after a long pause.

"Yes."

"Where?"

"The pasta factory. At least it's more fun than sorting and mailing packages."

"Well, I'm so sick of my gloves, I could… I could… Well, I can't even think of the word."

"You could just cry?"

"Exactly."

IX

They heard a knock at the door.

"Come in," said Lyuba.

A tall, well developed and muscular fellow entered.

"Is that you, Pavel?" asked Lyuba, not turning around.

"Yes, it's me. Why don't you have any lights on?" Pavel greeted the young ladies.

"Just because. I'm tense."

"I see... well, these days it's all too easy to be tense. Have you heard the latest news?"

"It's awful," whispered Lyuba.

"First, there was an explosion in the central heating station in Moscow. A cylinder of gas blew up, taking several houses with it. More than ten are confirmed dead so far, and part of the roof was destroyed. The whole city is freezing. Also, and this is the news that really excites me, seven people, members of the "Southern Society of Individualism,"[1] have been captured, interrogated, and sentenced to life imprisonment. Some of them have come and talked to us about their ideas. Yesterday in the city of Solianii they received a genuine ovation after their lecture. They weren't able to make it back to their home before the Supreme Soviet ordered them rounded up and tried at a special session..."

"It's about time someone took measures against this infection," said Lyuba.

"But where is our freedom?" asked Aglaya.

"Freedom, freedom... a hackneyed expression," answered Lyuba. "These people are undermining society, threatening calamities worse than any explosions..."

"You have to fight words with words," said Aglaya.

"And what word do you use to fight the plague?" asked Lyuba, upset. "There are words worse than plagues."

---

1. The author here makes reference to Russia's first band of revolutionaries, the Decembrists of 1825, who were organized into "Northern" and "Southern" societies.

She began to speak excitedly, getting upset and gesticulating: "Like we need these prophets! For hundreds, no, for thousands of years humanity moaned, suffered, writhed in blood and tears. Finally its troubles were solved, it solved the eternal problems: there are no more unhappy, destitute, forgotten people any more. Everyone has a place in the world, warmth, enough to eat, the opportunity to study…"

"And they're all slaves," tossed out Pavel quietly.

"That's not true," Lyuba responded heatedly, "it's not true. There are no more slaves. We're all free and equal. There aren't slaves because there aren't masters."

"There's one terrible master."

"Who?"

"The crowd. Your ghastly 'majority'."

"Stop. It's the same old story. It annoys me, I can't just listen indifferently to it," Lyuba now fell silent, wringing her hands nervously.

"But they draw me in, as if into a deep pool, into the abyss," Aglaya said softly.

"Who does?" asked Lyuba.

"Those whom you ironically call 'prophets'."

Lyuba smirked derisively, but didn't answer. Then she said, "So, should we have some tea?" She shook her head, as if shaking off unpleasant thoughts about troubled people.

"Yes," said Pavel and Aglaya in unison, then looked at each other, as if testing one another to see if they shared the same secret.

<h2 style="text-align:center">X</h2>

Lyuba took three glasses, milk, cookies, and bread and butter from the tray, then pressed the button and shut the door.

"Some light would be nice now," Pavel commented, as he took his glass. "It's a little awkward to sit in the dark."

Wordlessly, Lyuba turned a handle, and a soft light-blue light flowed from the ceiling.

Pavel took a few sips, then leaned back in his armchair and began to speak. "I'm reading old books now. Every evening I devote a couple of hours to reading."

"So what?" Lyuba asked curtly, still upset.

"I'm envious," Pavel began slowly. "I envy the free people of those times. I envy the unfortunate, hungry, and cold peasants. They lived so freely, so broadly, choosing either work or idleness according to their own free wills."

"That's the main thing, to be free to die of hunger," Lyuba tossed out.

"Yes, to be free to die of hunger."

"You can die of hunger from your own free will now, too, if you want."

"Yes, I'm free to die any moment I want, but they don't allow me to live as I'd like."

Aglaya did not take her eyes off him, catching his words hungrily. "Yes, those are my thoughts too," she finally said.

"Be quiet! You're unbearable," cried Lyuba. "Now you're going to start talking about religion." She laughed contemptuously.

"Oh, how I would like to believe!" said Pavel, caught up by her words, "to believe purely, naively, passionately, as they describe in the those books. But they stole that from me when I was still a baby. They poisoned my soul with skepticism. Now it's dead, lifeless. How I envy the old-fashioned families, with mothers and fathers instead of numbered citizens."

"You're against the communal raising of children, too?"

"Yes, I'm against it, and I'm not afraid to talk about it, I don't care how wild it sounds or how much it goes against the current postulates of Grand Science or prevailing morals."

"Be quiet, it makes me sick to listen to you. I don't believe you. It's just an act."

"Oh, no, I'm absolutely sincere. A friendly, old-fashioned family! How nice that must have been! How the children jumped for joy, meeting their father when he came home! How trusting and loving they were, pressing close to their own mother!"

"Your head is stuffed full of old nonsense. You need to stop reading and take a vacation."

"Of course, that's the best medicine!" he said mockingly. "No, that won't help. Once these feelings have awoken in your soul, you can't suppress them."

"Do you know that in Africa, near New Berlin, a society has been organized to demand from the Supreme African Soviet the legalization of the family according to the old ways?" said Aglaya.

"Yes, I heard that. I sympathize with them, very much. And if I ever get together with a woman," Pavel added meaningfully, "if I go with one it will be forever, and we will never part. If she nevertheless tries to leave me, I'll kill her and myself."

"You're completely nuts," said Lyuba. "More tea?"

"No thanks… Free people. But what about our service in the Army of Labor, as inescapable and obligatory as fate itself? What about our obligatory occupation? What are you doing now?"

Lyuba replied, "I'm at the glove factory."

"Well, there you are. How do you like it?"

"It's necessary. And besides, it only takes up four hours a day, and we do what we like the rest of the time."

"But I don't want to succumb for a minute, not a single instant, I don't want to do my cursed glass-polishing for a single minute."

"Request a transfer."

"To do what? Hammer in nails? Mix dough? I don't want to be coerced into doing anything, not even moving a single muscle."

"And why are you yakking on about this?" asked Lyuba. "You're not going to convert society. And if the majority is against you, you must submit to it."

"The majority, the majority. The damned, imbecilic majority. A rock, crushing any possible freedom of movement."

XI

Pavel jumped up and began to pace nervously. "I've been made extraneous. I've had my faith taken away. I don't know by what miracle there still are believers among us; how I'd love to have that miracle myself! I've been robbed, but nobody gave me anything in exchange, no weapon against that fearsome, monstrous enemy: death."

"What kind of weapon do you want? There never was one, except in old fairy tales."

"Faith was a weapon. Strong, fiery faith, that gives us courage in even the darkest night."

"Science gives us more than faith. It's real, not just in dreams and delusions, but actually real. It extended human life expectancy twofold. It freed man from disease. What more do you want? I think that these real blessings are more than enough to replace the illusory blessings of faith."

"What about death?"

"Didn't the faithful die, too?"

"They did, but they believed they would be resurrected." Pavel paced the room, then resumed. "Freedom," he said, "but I can't say that a single thing on this earth, a single corner of it, is mine. There's not a single corner where I can do precisely what I want, how I want."

"You so love talking about the olden days. What about the ancient Christians? I read a whole book about them recently. They shared everything."

"Yes, that's right. Everything was shared. But it was purely for love, not by coercion. I would gladly share everything with everyone, if it was for love, for fraternity."

He paused, plucking at his short beard, just long enough to curl.

"When I'm out walking along the Field of Mars,"[2] he began again, "beneath its stunning palms, magnolias, and oleanders, among its bright flowers, and I see that damned Palace of the Supreme Soviet,

---

2. The Field of Mars is a large park in the center of St. Petersburg that has existed since the eighteenth century. In the story's "2217," it is now lush with tropical vegetation, thanks to the city's "glass roof."

my hands start to shake and I believe that I could strangle those people, tranquil, cold and soulless as machines. The inflated speeches our orators give at public festivals always seem to me to be a mockery, pathetic wretchedness. I always want to answer their trite words about the prosperity of humanity with a short phrase: you're blind! Humanity is dead. It no longer exists. It was only valuable for its soul, this was what gave it the right to live… the bright impulses of the soul, the bright tears of love… and now…"

Pavel was breathing heavily. Aglaya kept her rapt gaze fixed on him and thought, "Yes. Those are my thoughts, too."

XII

"Let's walk together," Pavel said to Aglaya as she prepared to leave. "Could we?"

"Of course we can. I'd be very happy."

They went downstairs and walked out into the street. The self-mobiles had already stopped running; the lonely steps of a few pedestrians rang hollowly in the street.

"It must be a clear, moonlit night," said Aglaya, lifting her face to the sky.

"Probably so. You can see the moonlight through the roof."

"Let's go up, to the pneumatic station. I love to watch them lift off and gradually disappear in the sky. It's especially pretty on a moonlit night. They look like silvery birds."

"Let's go."

They walked side-by-side toward Liteyny, first falling into the patterned shadows of palm fronds, then showered in milky radiance. The little red lights of news bulletins flared here and there. Aglaya and Pavel climbed the stairs in silence.

"Comrade, give us some coats," said Pavel, laying his hand on the sleeping dutyman's shoulder.

"Where're you off to so late?" the man said, more bored than curious, and gave them each a set of warm clothes. "What warehouse should I write you down for?"

"We're not here for long, we just want to go for a walk on the platform," Pavel said.

"Mm-hm," the dutyman said, sitting back down in his warm, comfortable armchair.

Pavel and Aglaya went out onto the platform. A pneumatic was ready to take off and it hovered, trembling faintly. The full moon hung in the very middle of the cloudless blue sky. Its delicate, tender rays fell on the roof, stretching out to the horizon. Tall smokestacks and cornices cast blue shadows. The roof, powdered with unswept snow, sparkled. Pneumatic stations loomed into the sky like apparitions. Occasionally a pneumatic shot past with a sharp hiss, then fell toward a station, and the electric bells' pitiful peals ran across the roof.

Behind Pavel and Aglaya, two voices suddenly rang out. They both flinched.

"Ready?" asked the sender.

"Ready," replied the conductor.

"Release moorings!" shouted the sender.

The pneumatic clanged, then slipped its mooring and rose smoothly.

"Look, isn't it like a fairytale bird?" asked Aglaya. "See how it shines."

"Yes," Pavel took Aglaya's warm hand and squeezed it. Aglaya's heart stopped from a premonition of unutterable happiness.

The sender went back in, and Aglaya and Pavel remained alone on the platform, illuminated by the moon's bright rays.

"Aglaya, dear Aglaya, I love you, I love you," Pavel whispered suddenly, feverishly. "I've loved you for a long time, madly, and I want you to be my wife. I don't want you to give me a moment, or a day, a week; I'm not asking for fleeting love from you. I want you for the rest of your life, until death. If you can give that kind of love, and if you want mine, tell me 'yes'..."

Aglaya's head was spinning, her thoughts jumbled. Suddenly she turned away and pulled her hand from Pavel's hot hands.

"I'm unworthy of you," she said.

"You? You? So pretty, so pure in body and soul… unworthy of me?" whispered Pavel, tossing words out one after the other.

"Yes… yesterday I was at Karpov's… for a registered visit."

Pavel stepped away from her, staring bitterly at her pale face, as if he could not believe what he was hearing.

"Yes, yes… I'm telling the truth… Go away… Leave me alone… my darling…" she ended in a whisper.

"Please…"

"I beg you, leave me alone…"

Pavel obeyed and walked away, numb, his legs almost buckling beneath him. Soon he disappeared through the door to the stairwell.

Aglaya stood with bowed head and arms clutched around herself. Large tears burned one by one down her cheeks, then froze on her breast in little grains of ice.

A bell rang. The massive shadow of a pneumatic moved slowly in from the right, and before it could land Aglaya closed her eyes and threw herself from the platform, directly under its bright, shiny body.

Pavel wandered the empty streets for a long time. At three o'clock, crossing Morskoy Street, he looked up reflexively at the bulletins. The red letters jumped in his eyes. The news read: "At pneumatic station number three, citizen no. 4372221 threw herself beneath a pneumatic and was recovered with no signs of life. Cause unknown."

First published in Russian: 1906
Translation by James von Geldern and Anne O. Fisher

MUTINY OF THE MACHINES

A FANTASTIC TALE[1]

I

In order to understand the course of events to be recounted here, it is first necessary to clearly envision how the entirety of life is organized today.

The accelerated development of technology began in the nineteenth century. Until then, over the preceding two thousand years humanity merely resurrected the discoveries of the ancients. Structures such as Agrippa's Pantheon, the Colossus of Rhodes, and

---

1. Parables usually convey a moral lesson. Modern fiction relies on its readers, or as the last resort critics, to discern the moral of a story. Following this convention, I am not going to lay bare the allegory behind my creation. But I can allow myself to make one note. In these days of the "great war," when our opponents set all their hopes upon the technological superiority of Germany, perhaps it would not be so absurd to compose fiction that attempts to personify technology. The abyss towards which the German creed's radical convictions lead us is the dark, menacing specter that stood before the author's imagination as he conjured up the unbelievable story recounted here (Author's note).

the great Roman sanitation system, not to mention the great pyramids, compel us to acknowledge that the ancient nations commanded greater technological might than Europe in the Middle Ages, the Renaissance, the Reformation, and the "age of the philosophes." The same can be concluded from the partial information we have about the ancient Egyptians' knowledge of electrophysics or the steam engines constructed by the seers of Memphis and Thebes. The only exception was the art of war: the introduction of firearms constituted a significant step (forward or backward, it is hard to say), but nevertheless the "Greek fire" of the Byzantines pales in comparison with gunpowder. For the sake of parity, let us also take into consideration printing, which, by the way, was long known to the Chinese and evident in the Romans' practice of inscribing tablets from engravings; and Dionysus' invention of the compass, which begs some stretch of the imagination to be called "technology" despite the ancients' evident knowledge of magnetism.

All this changed suddenly in the nineteenth century. People were seized by an insane desire to instantly expand their power by a tenfold, a thousandfold, by mechanical means. Mastering the elemental forces of nature was the first goal of humankind. The second was developing specialized apparatuses to replace human labor, or, for that matter, the work done by beasts of burden and even natural forces. Finally, the third goal was the compression of space. The second objective could only be attained after the first, and the third only after the first two. But every new invention facilitated the perfection of its predecessors; they accumulated one after the other, augmenting and enhancing each another, resulting in an uninterrupted chain of technological developments with such wide-ranging influence and such a profound effect on human cognition that inventors became quite common. Every minimally intelligent person, having received some education, could invent something that would have immortalized a new Archimedes or Hieronymus two thousand years ago.

In the matter of conquering the forces of nature two things stood out: mastering steam power and commanding the forces of electricity.

The ancients were acquainted with both kinds of power, but they never dreamed of the range of their applications. Perhaps this was because the ancients, having access to another kind of elemental energy – slave labor – depended less on natural forces. The nineteenth century compelled steam to transport it and work for it. The first steamships breached the seas, iron needles of the railways tattooed all the nations from coast to coast; machines came to life, completing tasks in minutes that would have taken humans hours and even days. Electricity turned out to be even mightier. It replaced steam to a large extent, working more intensively, more comprehensively, all the while flooding cities and streets with its magical light: thoughts began to be transmitted at lightning speed across hundreds and thousands of miles, first along telegraph lines and then wirelessly, and voices traveled on the telephone; electricity preserved fleeting moments forever on the cylinder of the phonograph, the grooves of the gramophone record, and the cinematographer's film; it brought to life wonders that could only be dreamed of in previous centuries. Diverse technological facilitators developed simultaneously with them: machines for sewing, weaving, carding, and spinning. Machines replaced humans in the fields, plowing, seeding, harvesting, hulling, and milling in their stead; machines replaced humans in the factory, and the men who formerly wielded the chisels, hammers, choppers, and anvils began to merely supervise the steel monsters; machines replaced humans at home, writing and cooking, washing and keeping accounts for them. Finally the machines called "internal combustion engines" were invented, which drove automobiles and ships with turbines, burrowed submarines under water, and unleashed dirigibles and airplanes in the sky...

Such was the state of affairs at the cusp of the nineteenth and twentieth centuries. Steam, electricity, and "internal combustion engines" enabled humankind to conquer space. Not even taking into account the conquest of both poles, the penetration of desolate deserts, and flights to rival the birds, distances between points on the globe shrunk a hundred times. What used to be a journey of many weeks was now a matter of a day; places which, until recently, only fearless pioneers could breach became resorts for bored tourists; news of the day could be broadcast to readers in a few minutes; thoughts, perilously transmitted by slaves carrying letters along dangerous high roads in the distant past, could now be instantly transmitted via telegraph and telephone.

Finally, humans have tapped into a new mighty form of energy: radium. This force was unknown in any previous era, although as far back as two thousand years ago people were treated with radioactive mud and witches exorcised the ailing with amulets containing a tiny piece of radium. But the twentieth century has put radium to a thousand uses. Humanity has forced radium not just to cure but also illuminate the body, and to serve its needs like steam and electricity. Machines powered by radioactivity have emerged, terrifying in their all-consuming power as well as in their ability to kill anyone who is not careful around them. These secret inventions contain the potentials of great benefit to humankind together with great harm to the uninitiated.

The final frontier of the same era was the discovery of methods that came to be called "mutation," that is the capacity of transforming one form of energy into another without complex mechanisms. Previously, for example, electricity was produced out of steam power. The mutation method enabled any form of energy to be converted into the most convenient one. The most salient example of this method consists of unleashing energy latent in radioactive materials, which were previously inaccessible for practical uses. In this way humanity gained virtually unlimited supplies of electrical energy, obtained, moreover, with such speed and force that its production exceeded the worldwide demand. The potential of using electric power became real in all walks of life, for all scientific, social, and personal applications in all human societies across the planet. Electricity was ready to be used everywhere and by everyone. It became as ubiquitous as air and perhaps even more so; every day, every minute, so much electric energy was produced that anyone could consume it at their discretion, at will, just for entertainment, and still count on unlimited amounts being held in endless reserve for hundreds of years thanks to the same mutation method – with the insignificant rate of loss at 0.0001% per year.

This was the situation at the beginning of the age that saw notable initiatives of "technological cooperation" of all humankind and "technological organization of the entire globe."

II

At that time, the population of the earth was – let's round up the numbers – five billion people. A quarter of this population – perhaps even more than a quarter – lived in metropolitan cities, or the so-called capitals of the world, of which there were 122 with each city housing 10 million people. The same percentage, that is about a quarter more, lived in smaller cities and towns, of which there were several thousands with a population of a half million each. The other half of humanity, two and a half billion, were by the old definition agrarian people, although the term had lost its traditional meaning. Villages or hamlets did not exist in their old sense anymore. There were either small townships with specialized functions – factory-town, university-town, library-town, hospital-town – or isolated settlements of people working the land. They could be raising crops or digging for construction, or conversely engaged in forestry and animal husbandry; still others would just settle outside of town by personal preference. Superior communications made distances between these habitations immaterial: personal airplanes took people to the nearest underground station in a few minutes, from there to the nearest capital in half an hour by "automatic cigars," and in a few more hours to any place in the world. If those who lived in these "miniature" specialized towns could be added to the "urban" population, it is obvious that almost the whole planet's population had run to the urban centers. Outside the cities – that is between the polar caps, high mountains, and deep forest – lived a maximum of 400 to 450 million people, less that 10% of the earth's population.

City life, which is the only kind of life worth discussing in this day and age, was completely homogenous, thanks to the availability of electricity and other forms of energy discussed above. Physical labor, or indeed physical effort of any sort, almost completely disappeared from human life except in sports, athletics, and games. People still amused themselves by flying airplanes, riding electric trains, and sailing on motor submarines, and they still played ball and ran, swam, or jumped for exercise; there were still misfits who walked or rode bicycles, supported the old institution of boxing, and sparred at fencing matches, but all this belonged to the same sphere of entertainment as card games, billiards, or chess. People were so physically inactive that doctors had to issue warnings about muscular atrophy, decreased mobility, or impairments in arm movement.

From the moment he awoke, man fell under the regime of the machines. An automatic alarm sounded at the time of awakening; dressing and washing took minimum effort with the help of automatic gadgets. Leaving an apartment in a multistoried building, he would press a button to call the elevator and descend directly to the depths of the "metropolitan" or "imperial," depending on the destination. Automatic subterranean walkways would transport him without any physical effort to the final destination, whereupon another elevator would take him up to his place of work. Since every aspect of work was also automated, human effort was required only for accounting. All production was carried out by machines; all trade was automated; goods were transported from country to country and across oceans... [Editor's note: the text ends here].

First published in Russian: 1915
Translation by Anindita Bannerjee

RED STAR
IN RETROGRADE

PROFESSOR DOWELL'S HEAD

I. The First Encounter

"Please, take a seat."

Miss Adams sank into a deep leather chair. While Professor Kern opened and read her letter, she glanced swiftly around his office.

What a gloomy room! But a good place to work: there were no distractions. A lamp with an opaque shade cast just enough light to illuminate the writing desk, which was heaped with books, manuscripts and proof sheets. The solid black oak beneath was barely visible. The wallpaper and the curtains were dark-colored. Only the gold-seamed bindings in the heavy bookcases gleamed in the semi-darkness. An ancient wall-clock slowly and portentously measured out time with its long pendulum.

Transferring her gaze to Kern, Miss Adams smiled at the thought that someone had very successfully styled him to match his office.

His heavily built, rigid, solid frame looked like part of the furniture; it might have been carved out of the same black oak. His large glasses in their tortoiseshell frames resembled clock dials. His steel-grey pupils swung like pendulums, crossing from one line of her letter to the next. His right-angled nose, straight slash of a mouth and square, forward-thrusting chin gave his face the look of a stylized decorative mask, carved by a Cubist sculptor.

You should see a mask like that above a mantelpiece and not a writing table, Miss Adams thought.

"My colleague Smith has already spoken about you. Yes, I need an assistant. You're a medic? Excellent. Seven dollars a day. You'll be paid every week. The work isn't difficult. But I impose one non-negotiable condition."

Drumming his dry fingers on the desk, Professor Kern asked an unexpected question.

"Can you be silent?... Women are all so talkative! You're a woman – that's unfortunate. You're an attractive woman – that's even worse."

"But what has that got to do with—"

"Everything! It has everything to do with it. An attractive woman is a woman twice over. That means she has twice as many feminine failings. If you haven't got one yet, you'll soon have a husband, or a fiancé, or a gentleman friend. And then all secrets will go to the devil!"

"But—"

"No 'buts'! You must be as dumb as a fish. You must keep silent about everything you hear here. Can you accept this condition? I must warn you: failure to observe this condition will entail extremely unpleasant consequences for yourself. Extremely unpleasant!"

Miss Adams was puzzled and intrigued.

"I'm willing, provided there isn't anything not entirely—"

"Anything criminal, you wanted to say? You may put yourself completely at ease. Nor are you in danger of being saddled with any responsibility. Are your nerves in good condition?"

"I'm healthy…"

Professor Kern nodded. His dry, sharp finger pressed the button of an electric bell.

The door opened silently. In the half-darkness of the room, as if on a half-exposed photographic plate, Miss Adams could just see the shining whites of a pair of eyes; then the glint of a Negro's gleaming face gradually appeared. His black hair and suit melted into the dark curtain behind the doorway.

"John, show this young lady the laboratory."

The Negro nodded, inviting her to follow, and opened a second door.

Miss Adams entered a completely dark room.

A switch clicked, and the brilliant light from a hemispherical ceiling lamp filled the room. Miss Adams involuntarily covered her eyes. After the gloom of the office, the pure whiteness of the walls was blinding. The glass panels of the cupboards shone with glittering surgical instruments. The steel and aluminium of various apparatuses shone with a cold light. Polished copper components reflected a heavy, yellow gleam. Pipes, retorts, machines. Glass and metal.

In the middle of the room stood a large dissecting table. The headless corpse of a man lay on the table with the rib-cage exposed. By the table was a glass case, holding a pulsating human heart. Narrow tubes led from the heart to various containers.

Miss Adams turned her head away; suddenly she saw something that made her shudder as if from an electric shock.

A human head was watching her – only the head, without a torso.

It had been fixed to a square glass panel, which was supported by four tall, shiny metallic legs. From the severed neck and the arteries, two tubes led away to the containers through an opening in the glass. A third, thicker tube connected the head to a large cylinder. The cylinder and the containers were supplied with taps, manometers, thermometers, and other devices Miss Adams didn't recognize.

The head looked at her attentively and sorrowfully, blinking its eyelids. There could be no doubt that the head was alive. Separated from its body, it led an independent and fully conscious existence.

In spite of the shocking sight before her, Miss Adams could not fail to notice that this head looked astonishingly similar to a famous scientist who had died not long before, the surgeon Professor Dowell, celebrated for his experiments with the revival of organs extracted from fresh corpses. Miss Adams had attended his brilliant public lectures more than once, and she clearly remembered that high forehead, the distinctive profile, the wavy light-brown hair and beard silvered with grey, the sky-blue eyes… Yes, this was Professor Dowell's head! Only his lips and nose had become sharper, drier, his temples and cheeks drawn in, his eyes had sunk into their sockets, and his white skin had acquired the dark-yellow tinge of a mummy's. But living, human awareness sparkled in his eyes.

Miss Adams felt her the roots of her hair tingling. But, as if she'd been bewitched, she couldn't look away from those pale blue eyes. The head soundlessly moved its lips.

That was too much for Miss Adams' nerves. She sensed that she was close to fainting. The Negro supported her and led her out of the laboratory.

"This is horrible… it's horrible," Miss Adams said over and over, sinking into the armchair.

Professor Kern drummed his fingers on the table without speaking.

"Tell me, was that really the head of…"

"Of Professor Dowell? Yes, it's his head. The head of Dowell, my late respected colleague, whom I restored to life. Unfortunately, I was only able to resurrect his head. We can't have it all at once! Even so, we scientists are invading the 'inalterable laws' of nature, challenging death itself and snatching their daily bread from miracle-workers and from God himself. But we can't have it all at once, as I say! Poor Dowell was suffering from a disease for which there is still no cure. As he was dying, he willed his body to be used for the scientific experiments that he and I had carried out together. 'My entire life has been dedicated to science. I hope my death may serve science too. I would prefer for my body to be excavated by a fellow scholar, not a graveyard worm,' he said.

That was Professor Dowell's legacy. And so I took his body. I managed not only to resurrect his heart, but his consciousness – his 'soul,' to use the terminology of the masses. What's horrible about that? Until now, people have always thought death was horrible. Hasn't humanity been dreaming of resurrection from the dead for a thousand years?"

"I would prefer death to such a resurrection."

Professor Kern gestured vaguely with one hand.

"Well, yes, it has its inconveniences for the person resurrected. It would be unpleasant for poor Dowell to be shown to the public in this… incomplete condition. That's why we're keeping this experiment a secret, by Dowell's own wish. Moreover, we still haven't completed the experiment."

"And how did Professor Dowell – that is, his head – express this wish? Can the head speak?"

For just a moment, Professor Kern looked embarrassed.

"No… Professor Dowell's head doesn't speak. But it listens, understands and manages to reply with facial expressions…"

And clearly wishing to change the subject, he asked, "And so, will you accept my offer? Excellent! I shall expect you tomorrow by nine in the morning. But remember: silence, silence, and silence!"

II. The Secret of the Forbidden Tap

Miss Adams's life had not been easy. Her father died when she was seventeen, and she had to shoulder all the responsibility for caring for her sick mother and younger sister. The small resources remaining after their father's death did not even suffice for her to finish college. She had to study and support her family. For several years she worked as a proofreader for a newspaper. Once she qualified as a doctor, she tried in vain to find a position. She had offers to travel to South America, to those Godforsaken places where yellow fever raged. Miss Adams was reluctant to bring her family there, but she didn't want to leave them either. Professor Kern's proposal offered a way out of her situation. In spite of all the strangeness of the job, she accepted without hesitation.

Miss Adams was unaware that before Professor Kern had offered her the job, he had exhaustive enquiries made about her.

She had now been working for Kern for two weeks. Her duties were not difficult. During the course of the day, she had to monitor all the machines that kept the head alive. At night, John took her place.

Professor Kern had shown her how to handle the taps for the containers. Indicating the big cylinder from which a thick tube ran to the head's throat, Kern forbade her in the sternest terms from opening its tap.

"If you were to turn that tap, the head would instantly perish! At some point I will explain to you my system of nourishing the head and the function of this cylinder. For now, all you need to know is how to handle the machines."

However, Professor Kern was in no hurry to provide the promised explanation.

A small thermometer was inserted deeply into one of the nostrils of the head. This had to be extracted at fixed times in order to record its temperature. Even the containers were provided with thermometers and manometers. The temperature and pressure of the fluids had to be monitored. But the well-regulated apparatus never caused any trouble, operating with the accuracy of clockwork. Last of all, a particularly sensitive piece of equipment attached to the head's temple registered its pulse, automatically plotting it on a chart. The typewriting ribbon had to be changed at fixed intervals. The contents of the tanks were refilled before Miss Adams' arrival.

Miss Adams was now somewhat accustomed to the head, and had even become friendly with it.

When she entered the laboratory in the mornings, with cheeks rosy from walking in the fresh air, the head smiled weakly at her, and its lids trembled in a sign of welcome.

The head was unable to speak. But a form of sign language was soon established between them, although it was limited strictly to words that could be expressed as gestures. The head blinked once to say "yes" and raised its lids high for "no." The silent movement of its lips helped a little.

With the help of the head's language of gestures and Miss Adams' ordinary speech, they even managed to have conversations based on questions and answers: Miss Adams would ask questions, and the head would signal "yes" or "no."

"Well, how are you feeling today?" Miss Adams asked.

The head smiled and lowered its lids to say, "Quite well, thank you."

"How did you pass the night?"

The same gesture.

Miss Adams would fire questions at the head while efficiently performing her morning duties. She checked the apparatus, the temperature, the pulse. She made notes in a journal. Then, with the greatest care, she washed the face of the head with water and alcohol using a soft sponge, then wiped it down with super-absorbent cotton wool. She washed the eyes, ears, nose, and mouth. Special tubes were inserted into the nose and mouth for this. She tidied the hair.

Her hands touched the head swiftly and skilfully. Its face wore a contented expression.

"Today is a wonderful day," Miss Adams was saying excitedly. "The breeze is light and chilly; the sort that makes you want to fill your chest with air. Look how brightly the sun is shining. It's just like spring!"

The corners of Professor Dowell's mouth curved down sorrowfully. His eyes turned regretfully to the window and then paused upon Miss Adams.

She blushed, mildly annoyed at herself. With a woman's instinctive sensitivity, she had tried to avoid mentioning anything unattainable for the head, which could unnecessarily remind it of its pitiful physical state.

She felt a certain maternal pity for the head, as she might for a helpless, malformed infant.

"Well, let's do some work!" Miss Adams said hurriedly to rectify her mistake.

In the mornings, before Professor Kern arrived, the head was occupied with reading. Miss Adams would carry over a heap of the latest medical journals and books and show them to the head. It looked through them; when it came to an article it needed, it wriggled its brows. Miss Adams would place the journal on a stand, and the head would plunge into reading. Miss Adams learned to tell, by following the movements of its eyes, which line the head was reading in order to turn the pages at the right moment.

When it wanted to make a note in the margins, the head made a sign, and Miss Adams would run her finger down the lines, following the head's eyes, and make a pencil mark in the margin.

Miss Adams did not understand why the head made these marginal notes; but she did not expect to get an explanation with their simple language of gestures, so she did not ask.

Once, however, when she was passing through Professor Kern's office during his absence, she saw a pile of journals on his writing table with the marks she had made at the head's indication. And on a sheet of paper, in Professor Kern's hand, several of these marked passages had been copied out. This gave her food for thought.

Suddenly remembering this, Miss Adams could not restrain herself from asking:

"Tell me, why do we mark these sections in scientific articles?"

Professor Dowell's head displayed annoyance and impatience. The head stared meaningfully at Miss Adams, then at the tap from which the tube ran to its throat; it raised its brows twice. This indicated a request. Miss Adams understood that the head wanted her to open the forbidden tap. This was not the first time that the head had made this request to her. But Miss Adams explained the head's desire in her own terms: clearly, it wanted to end its joyless existence. Miss Adams could not make up her mind to open the forbidden tap. She feared the responsibility; she feared losing her job.

"No, no!" Miss Adams answered the head's request with terror. "If I open that tap, you'll die! I don't want to kill you, I can't do it, I'm not brave enough!" A spasm ran across the head's face from impatience and consciousness of its own helplessness. The head ground its teeth.

Three times the head energetically looked upwards, opening its eyes wide…

"No, no, no… I won't die," Miss Adams understood the head to say. She hesitated.

The head began to move its lips soundlessly, and it seemed to Miss Adams that the lips were trying to say:

"Open it, open it, I beg of you…"

Miss Adams' curiosity was piqued to the highest degree.

She could sense that there was some mystery here. Even before this, she had not quite believed Professor Kern's words about the fatal nature of the forbidden tap.

Meanwhile, an immeasurable sorrow shone in the eyes of the head. The eyes asked, begged, demanded; it was as though all its human power of thought, all its stored-up willpower was concentrated in that gaze.

And Miss Adams made up her mind.

With her heart beating fast and a trembling hand, she carefully opened the tap part of the way.

Immediately a hiss sounded in the head's throat. Miss Adams heard the head's voice: weak, uninflected, crackly, like a broken gramophone.

"I… th..thank…k…. you!"

The forbidden tap released air compressed in the cylinder. Passing through the head's throat, the air stimulated the vocal cords to move, allowing the head to speak. The muscles of the throat and vocal cords could no longer function normally, and therefore air passed through the throat with a hissing sound even when the head was not speaking. And the damaged vocal cords lent its voice that uninflected, rattly timbre.

The face of the head expressed satisfaction.

But at that very moment they heard footsteps in the office and the noise of a lock opening – the laboratory door was always locked with a key from the office side.

Miss Adams narrowly succeeded in turning the tap off. The hissing in the head's throat stopped.

Professor Kern entered.

III. The Head Spoke

About a week had gone by since Miss Adams discovered the secret of the forbidden tap.

During this time, relations between Miss Adams and the head had grown even friendlier. In the hours Professor Kern spent at university, Miss Adams opened the tap, sending a moderate stream of air into the head's throat, so that the head could speak in an audible whisper. Miss Adams spoke softly too. They were afraid that the Negro might overhear their conversation.

Their chats worked a visible improvement on Professor Dowell's head. His eyes became livelier, and even the sorrowful wrinkle between his brows smoothed out.

The head spoke eagerly and at length, as if rewarding itself for the period of enforced silence.

The night before Miss Adams had dreamed about Professor Dowell's head, and she had wondered afterwards: did the head dream?

"Dreams…" the head whispered softly. "Yes, I dream. And I cannot tell whether this brings me greater sorrow or joy. I dream that I'm healthy, full of strength, and I wake up doubly bereft. I am reduced both physically and morally… After all, I am deprived of everything that living people enjoy! Only consciousness, like a curse, is left to me…"

"What do you dream about?"

"I have not yet dreamed about myself in my current situation. I see myself as I was once… I see my family, my friends… Not long ago, I dreamed about my late wife and lived the springtime of our romance over again. Long ago she came to see me as a patient; she had hurt her leg getting out of a motor-car. We first met in my reception room. We somehow felt a bond straightaway. After her fourth visit, I invited her to look at a portrait of my fiancée which was lying on my writing desk.

"'I will marry her if she accepts my proposal,' I said.

"She walked over to my desk and saw the little mirror lying there: she glanced into it, laughed and said:

"'I don't think she'll say no!'

"Within a week, she was my wife. I dreamed that scene not long ago…" The head's expression lit up with the memory, but grew sombre again at once. It was as if a ray of autumn sunlight had momentarily pierced a shroud of grey autumn clouds, before being quenched.

"How infinitely long ago that time was!"

The head grew thoughtful. Air hissed quietly through its throat.

"Last night I dreamed about my son… How I would love to see him once again!… But I wouldn't dare to put him through this ordeal… He thinks I am dead…"

"Is he grown up? Where is he now?"

"Yes, he's grown up… He's almost the same age as you or a little older. He has finished university…At the moment he should be in Italy, with his mother's sister… No, it would be better not to dream! Now I lead the life of an almost bodiless spirit. How laughable and foolish the dream of non-corporeal existence seems to me! We are sons of the earth, creatures of flesh and blood. And we can only be happy with and on our native clay. Do you know what it means to live without a body, to exist as consciousness alone? I am tormented not only by my teasingly real dreams. When I am wide awake, my sensations torture me. Strange as it might seem, sometimes I imagine that I can feel my body. I suddenly want to breathe in with my whole chest, or spread my arms wide, as one does after sitting too long. And sometimes I experience a paralysing pain in my left leg. Laughable, isn't it? As a doctor, however, you should understand. The pain is so real that I involuntarily look down and, of course, I see through the glass below me only empty space and the flagstones of the floor… From time to time I imagine that I am about to suffer an attack of breathlessness, which makes me almost glad of my 'post-mortem' state, which at least frees me from asthma. It is all simply the reflex action of brain cells, somehow linked to the life of the body…"

"How dreadful all this is!" Miss Adams burst out.

"Yes, dreadful… Strange, when I was alive I imagined that I lived a life purely of the mind. Truly, I somehow managed not to notice my body, utterly buried in my academic studies as I was. And only when I lost my body did I realize what I was missing… The world of bodily sensations! How many pleasures it offers! Now, like never before in my whole life, I think about the scents of flowers or fragrant hay at the edge of a wood, of long walks, of the noise of surf… In losing my body, I lost a world – the whole beautiful, ungraspable world of objects which I had never noticed, objects which can be touched and handled, feeling at the same time one's own body – oneself! Oh, how eagerly I would give up all of this chimerical existence just for the joy of weighing in my hand a single cobblestone! I envy the porter laboring under the weight of the load on his back… I have only now understood that even physical pain carries a dose of pleasure. Pain is the cry of a living body!… yes… I suffer most of all from lack of tangible sensations. If only you knew how much pleasure I derive from the touch of the sponge, when you wash my face in the mornings! And the touch of your hands… If you want to make me happy, stroke my face with your hand."

Miss Adams touched the head's dry and chilly forehead with her hand.

"My thanks!… And here is yet another request… which may strike you as peculiar. The touch of your hair! Could you somehow bend over and touch your hair to my cheek? If only you knew what a pleasure that is!"

The head looked at her pleadingly.

Miss Adams felt embarrassed. She was embarrassed not only by the request, but by the particular expression in the head's eyes. This was not the first time she had noticed that expression…

"Well, not too much at once! Let's leave this for another time!" she said, and a faint blush spread over her cheeks.

She felt that more than the simple act of touching was involved. She would have done it out of pity, but something close to disgust stopped her, and she sat without moving….

An expression of deep disappointment and sorrow appeared on the head's face.

"The poor thing!" thought Miss Adams and, by an effort of will, she quickly stood up, laughed casually and brushed the head's cheek with her hair.

"Now, there you go!" she said in the same tone she would use with a spoiled child, after fulfilling its whim.

That evening, assessing her impressions, Miss Adams could not sleep for a long time. And when she slept she dreamed of the head once again… of Professor Dowell's sorrowful eyes… Miss Adams was running through corridors, pursued by the head. Her path was blocked by closed doors, they opened with an effort, the head began overtaking her… She could already hear the hissing whistle of air behind her…

Miss Adams woke up with a rapidly beating heart.

"It seems my nerves are not what they should be…"

IV. Death or Murder?

One day, looking through medical journals before going to sleep, Miss Adams read an article by Professor Kern about his scientific work. What caught her attention in this article were Kern's references to certain studies by other scholars. These were all the extracts from scientific books and journals which Miss Adams had noted, instructed by the head, during their morning sessions.

The next day, as soon as she had an opportunity to speak with the head, Miss Adams asked:

"What does Professor Kern work on in the laboratory when I'm not here?"

The head replied after a hesitation:

"We continue our scientific work."

"That includes all the notes you take for him? But do you know he is publishing your work under his own name?"

"I imagined as much."

"But that's scandalous!"

"Perhaps so… But what can I do about it?"

"If you can't, I certainly can!" Miss Adams exclaimed furiously.

"Hush… It would do no good. It would be laughable for someone in my situation to claim copyright. Money? What can I do with it? Fame? What could fame do for me? And then… If all this were exposed, the experiment would not be finished. And I myself have a vested interest in it. I confess that I would like to see the results of my research."

Miss Adams thought about it.

"Yes, a man like Kern is capable of anything," she continued quietly. "Professor Kern told me, when I applied to him for work, that you died from an incurable illness and that you yourself willed your body for scientific research. Is that true?"

"It's a difficult subject for me… I could be mistaken… It is the truth, but possibly… not the whole truth. Kern and I were working together on the revivification of human organs, extracted from a fresh corpse. Kern was my assistant. The crowning moment of my research was to be the solution of the question of whether a human head could be restored to life. I had finished all the preparatory work; we had already revivified the heads of animals, but we were not going to publish our successes until we succeeded in demonstrating the revivification of a human head. Before this final experiment, the success of which I never doubted, I gave Kern a manuscript about my scientific work to be prepared for publication. At the same time, we were working on another scientific project, which was also close to its solution. At this time I suffered one of my terrible attacks of asthma – the very same disease I was trying to overcome. I had long struggled with asthma: who would win? And it is certainly true that I had willed my body for anatomical research – although I never expected, that my own head would be revivified. Thus it was… during this final attack of asthma, Kern was beside me and gave me medical assistance. He injected me with morphine. Perhaps the dose was too great, or perhaps my asthma won the fight…"

"What happened then?"

"Then I woke here, on this glass panel, after a deep sleep... My body was lying on the dissection table, and Kern was opening the ribcage. Here, as you see, my heart is beating in this glass vessel..."

Miss Adams looked at the head in horror.

"And after that... after that you continue working with him? If it hadn't been for him, you would have conquered the asthma and been a healthy man by now... he is a thief and a murderer, and you are supporting his rise to fame? You are working for him! Like a parasite, he feeds on your mental functions; he has turned your head into a sort of accumulator of creative thought, which he exploits to earn fame and money. And what about you? What does he give you? What sort of life do you have? You are deprived of everything! You are a miserable amputee, with your desires still alive inside you! Kern stole the whole world from you! Forgive me, but I don't understand you! And yet you can really work for him meekly and calmly?"

The head smiled sorrowfully.

"The revolt of the head? Would that achieve anything? What could I do? Why, I'm deprived even of a man's ultimate option: to do away with myself."

"But you could refuse to work with him."

"And I did refuse. In a manner of speaking, I rebelled, like the angels. But my rebellion was not provoked by Kern using me as a thinking machine. In the end, how important is the name of the author? The important thing is that my idea went out into the world and had its effects. I rebelled solely because it was difficult for me to get used to my new existence. I preferred death to life. I'll tell you about one incident that occurred at that time. For some reason, I was in the laboratory, alone. Suddenly a large black beetle with nippers on its head flew in at the window. Where could it have come from in the center of an enormous city? I do not know. Perhaps it was brought in by a car returning from a trip into the country. The beetle started circling around me and settled on the glass panel of my table, beside me. Squinting, I followed the progress of this repulsive insect, unable to flick it away. The insect's tiny feet slid over the glass and, buzzing, he moved slowly towards my head. I don't know if you can understand me… I have always felt an exceptional degree of disgust, a sense of revulsion for such insects. I could never bring myself to touch them with a finger. And here I was, helpless before this insignificant enemy. As far as he was concerned, my head was just a convenient place for take-off. And he continued slowly approaching, rustling his little feet over the glass. After several efforts, he managed to cling on to the hairs of my beard. For a long time he scrabbled around, getting lost in my hair, but he stubbornly climbed ever higher. Then he crawled over my tightly squeezed lips, up the left side of my nose, over my clamped-shut left eye, until finally, after reaching my forehead, he fell to the glass, and then on the floor. What a pointless incident! Yet in my then emotional state, it shook me severely.

"And when Professor Kern came in, I categorically refused to continue our scientific work. I knew that he would not exhibit my head publicly. He would not keep a head which might act as evidence against him unless it was useful for his research. Therefore he would kill me. That was what I was counting on. War broke out between us. He swiftly resorted to rather cruel measures. Attaching electrical conductors to my temples, he released a current, constantly increasing it. It felt as if someone were drilling into my brain with a white-hot drill.

"He looked at me, but my lips whispered: 'No!'

"Then he started to put chemicals in my feeding tubes which caused new kinds of tormenting pain in my head.

"I could not be swayed.

"He left, beside himself with rage, showering me with thousands of curses. I celebrated my victory.

"For several days, Kern failed to appear in the laboratory, and every day I expected to be liberated by death.

"On the fourth or fifth day he arrived as if nothing had happened, merrily whistling a tune.

"Without glancing at me, he started continuing our work. For two or three days I observed him without taking part. But the work could not fail to interest me. And when he made a series of mistakes in carrying out his research, mistakes which could have destroyed the results of all our efforts, I could not restrain myself and made a sign to him.

"'About time too!' he said with a satisfied smile, releasing air to pass through my throat. I explained his mistake to him and since that day I have continued to supervise the work… He outwitted me!"

V. Victims of the Big City

It was twilight. The laboratory was quiet. Only the air hissed softly, passing out of the head's throat. Miss Adams was sitting with her head in her hands. Suddenly she heard the voice of Professor Dowell's head.

"I am tormented by a single desire… A crazy desire… for you to kiss me!"

A pained smile appeared on the face of the head.

"Are you shocked? You didn't expect an… admirer, in my condition? Calm down! It isn't what… what you think. I know that I can arouse only revulsion. The revived head of a corpse!… My body has long been in the grave… But try to understand me: one cannot live by thought or consciousness alone… Try to understand what you mean to me! You are young, beautiful! Men will fall in love with you and you will give them the gift of your kisses. But to no-one in the world will your kiss give as much as it would to me! For me, you are not merely a woman. For me, you are life, all of life in all its variety. By kissing you, I would be touching life, touching everything you touch, all that I can only long for hopelessly. If you spurn me, I will be hopelessly unhappy… This is not a passionate kiss! What sort of passion can a head feel, without a body? Take a look: my heart is beating peacefully in its glass vessel. It is not capable of love. This is a symbolic kiss. A kiss of life, glittering, triumphant life, taking pity even on that tiny, dwindling spark which still glows inside me… Don't leave me to feel like a corpse until the end! Take pity on me… Kiss me!"

During this speech Miss Adams sat silent and pale, gazing at the head with wide-open eyes. Only her fingers, rubbing together, gave away her disturbance. A sorrowful crease extended between her brows. Within her, a profound feeling of pity battled with involuntary physical revulsion.

After a long pause she slowly stood up, walked over to the head… kissed it… and suddenly gave a brief shriek and sprang away.

The head had bitten her lip.

Miss Adams was so shocked, frightened and embarrassed that she sank almost senseless onto her chair. But the eyes of the head watched her seriously and calmly.

"I thank you… I am grateful! Don't imagine that I've gone out of my mind… That wasn't a fit of insanity. Alas! I thought about this for a long time before I acted. You see, don't you, that there is nothing, nothing I can do in this world of living people and real objects. And I wanted to leave in this world a tiny trace… a trace of my will… and this was the only way I could do it. I will think how you will walk home with this mark, along noisy streets, among other people. Perhaps someone will notice this trace in that world, so far from me – this trace that I have made – and he will think, that someone—"

The head suddenly paused and whispered:

"Forgive me! That was selfish, but I didn't have the strength to resist... It may be that my reason is really starting to betray me…"

By the strange logic of emotions, her unpleasant experience with the head's kiss inspired in Miss Adams a storm of indignation against Professor Kern. Ever since Miss Adams had learned the head's secret, she had detested Kern with all the force of her spirit. And this feeling grew with every passing day. She fell asleep with this feeling; she woke up with it. She dreamed terrible nightmares about him. She was practically ill with hatred. Recently, when she met Kern, she could barely restrain herself from flinging the word "Murderer!" in his face.

Her manner with him was strained and cold.

Quite possibly, this state of mind worsened her ever more unstable nerves. The days she spent in company with the revived head of a corpse, and everything that she had learned from it: none of these shocks could pass without leaving some trace. Little wonder that she blamed Kern for everything.

"I forgive you," Miss Adams said heatedly, "although you don't deserve it! You frightened me and caused me pain… But I won't forgive Professor Kern! I'll report him! I will shout from the rooftops about his crime! I won't rest until I have deprived him of his stolen fame and revealed all his crimes! I won't spare myself…"

"Softer… calm yourself… I already told you that I have no desire for revenge. But if your moral feeling is outraged and requires vengeance, I will not try to dissuade you… but please do not hurry… I beg you to wait until our experiments are concluded. Kern and I need each other now, after all. He cannot finish his work without me, but neither can I, without him. And that is all I have left… I cannot create anything else. But the work I have begun must be finished…"

They heard steps in the office.

Miss Adams swiftly closed the tap and sat down with a book in her hand; she was still very agitated. Dowell's head lowered its eyelids, like a man plunged in reflection.

Professor Kern entered.

He looked suspiciously at Miss Adams.

"What's the matter? Are you upset by something? Is everything in order?"

"No… nothing… everything is in order… I have some family problems…"

"Let me take your pulse."

Miss Adams unwillingly extended her arm.

"It's beating more rapidly… Are your nerves affected? I admit this is a difficult job for the nerves. But I am happy with your work. I am doubling your wages."

"I have no need of it. I thank you."

"'I have no need of it!' Who doesn't need money? You have a family, after all!"

Miss Adams made no reply.

"Well then. We must make some preparations. We will transfer Professor Dowell's head into the room behind the laboratory. Temporarily, my dear colleague, temporarily! You're not asleep?" he addressed the head. "Tomorrow two fresh corpses will be brought here, and we will turn them into a couple of well-spoken heads and exhibit them to the academy. It's time we made our discovery public."

And Kern once again looked at Miss Adams with some mistrust.

So as not to reveal her dislike too clearly or too prematurely, Miss Adams forced herself to ask a question, the first that came into her head: "Whose corpses are being brought?"

"I don't know; no-one knows. Because right now these are not yet corpses; they are living, healthy individuals. Healthier than we are – that I can say with confidence. I need heads from absolutely healthy people. But tomorrow death is lying in wait for them, inevitably. And within an hour of dying, no longer, they will be here – on the dissecting table. I've already made all the arrangements."

Miss Adams, who considered Professor Kern capable of anything, gazed at him so uncomprehendingly and challengingly that he was momentarily abashed; but then he roared with laughter.

"Nothing could be simpler! I have ordered a pair of fresh corpses from the morgue. The fact is, you see, that the city – this modern-day Moloch – demands daily human sacrifices. Every day, by the inevitability of natural laws, several people perish in traffic accidents; not counting accidents in factories and building sites. And now these doomed, perfectly happy, strong and healthy people will peacefully fall asleep today, not realizing what tomorrow has in store. Tomorrow morning they will rise, cheerfully singing a song, dress to go – as they think – to work, but in reality, to meet their inevitable death. At the same time, in another part of town, singing just as carelessly, their accidental executioner, some chauffeur or goods driver, is also dressing. Then the victim will leave his apartment, while the executioner will, at the opposite end of the city, drive out of his garage or tram park. Overcoming the flood of traffic in the streets, they will steadfastly travel towards each other – without knowing it – to the fateful intersection of their paths. Then, for one brief instant, one of them will be distracted – and it's done! Statistical charts, recording the number of victims of traffic accidents, rise by one point – precisely by that point the chart required to fulfil its own prediction.

"Thousands of accidents must occur to bring them to that fatal point of intersection. Yet, nonetheless, everything is inflexibly completed with clockwork precision, placing both hands at the same point on the face of the clock for a single instant, although they move at different speeds."

Professor Kern had never been so talkative with Miss Adams before. And as for this unexpected generosity!

"He wants to trick me, to buy me," thought Miss Adams. "He seems to suspect that I have guessed or that I even know a great deal. But he'll never manage to buy me!"

VI. The Laboratory's New Inmates

That complicated mechanism, known as probability theory, directed thousands of chance happenings towards a single point in time and space, and the next morning two fresh corpses were indeed lying on the dissecting table in Professor Kern's laboratory.

The two new heads, intended for public exhibition, were not to know about the existence of Professor Dowell's head. And this was why Professor Kern had had the forethought to move the latter into an adjacent room.

The first corpse belonged to a workman aged about thirty, who had died in a traffic accident. His powerful body had been cut in half. An expression of fear was frozen in his glassy, half-open eyes.

Professor Kern, Miss Adams and John, all in white gowns, were working on the corpses.

"There were some other bodies," Professor Kern was saying. "There was a worker who had fallen from scaffolding. But he might have suffered brain contusions from the impact. I also rejected several suicides who had poisoned themselves. This chap here seemed as if he might do. And then there's this… lady of the night as well. I won't swear that her blood is good quality, but there wasn't any other choice."

With a jerk of his head he indicated the corpse of a woman with a beautiful, but faded, face. It still showed traces of rouge and mascara. The face was peaceful; only the raised brows and half-open mouth expressed a kind of childish surprise.

"A singer from a quayside bar. She was killed instantly by a stray bullet during a quarrel between some drunken sailors. Right in the heart, can you see? You couldn't aim so well if you tried!"

Professor Kern worked swiftly and confidently. The heads were separated from the bodies and the corpses removed.

A few minutes later, the heads had been transferred onto elevated tables. Tubes were run into the throat, the main vein and artery.

Professor Kern was in a pleasantly excited state of mind. His moment of glory was at hand; he had no doubt of success.

The stars of the scientific world had been invited to Professor Kern's forthcoming speech and demonstration to an academic society. The press, skilfully manipulated, had published advance articles praising Professor Kern's scientific genius. His portrait appeared in journals. Kern's exhibition, with his astonishing experience in the revival of dead human heads, was regarded as grounds for national celebration. All the glory of the discovery was credited to Kern. Only one medical journal mentioned, in passing, the name of the late Professor Dowell, "who carried out several experiments in this direction."

Miss Adams read these articles greedily. They gave her a kind of bitter pleasure, feeding her hatred for Professor Kern.

Whistling cheerfully, Professor Kern washed his hands, smoked a cigar and gazed with self-satisfaction at the heads arranged before him.

"Ha, ha! Not only John's head is on the plate, but Salome's as well! What an encounter this will be. All that's left to do is open the taps, and… the dead will come to life! We really are setting up as rivals to the Lord God! Well, miss? Look lively! Open all three taps. That large cylinder contains compressed air, and not poison, ha, ha…"

For Miss Adams this was anything but news. But with almost unconscious cunning, she gave no sign. He frowned, becoming suddenly serious. He walked right up to Miss Adams and, snapping out every word, said: "But in Professor Dowell's case, I must ask you not to open the tap. He has… damaged vocal cords and…"

Meeting Miss Adams' mistrustful look, he added with irritation:

"In any case – I forbid you to open it, unless you wish to bring very serious unpleasantness on yourself…"

And, brightening up once again, he sang out, "Well, let's get started!"

Miss Adams opened the taps.

The laborer's head was the first to give signs of life.

Hardly noticeably, the eyelids quivered. The pupils grew more transparent. The skin color changed almost imperceptibly.

"Circulation is established. All is going well…"

Suddenly the eyes moved, turning towards the light from the window. Consciousness was slowly returning.

"He's alive!" Kern exclaimed cheerfully. "Turn the air flow up higher!"

Miss Adams opened the tap more widely.

Air whistled through the throat.

"What's this?… Where am I?" were the head's first, barely audible words.

"In the hospital, my friend!"

"In hos-pit-tal?" The head moved its eyes, looked downwards and saw the empty space beneath it.

"But where are my legs? Where are my arms? Where's my body?"

"It's not there, my good fellow! It was smashed into bits. Only your head is in one piece; we had to cut off your body!"

"What do you mean, cut off? Well, no, I won't allow it! What kind of operation is that? What am I good for now? A head on its own can't earn a crust of bread! I need hands! Nobody's going to hire me without hands or feet… I'll walk out of hospital… hell! Nothing to walk on! What do I do now? I have to live, I have to eat! I know your kind of hospital – you keep people for a couple of days, then you sign them out: cured! Well, look how you've cured me! No, I won't allow it!" he repeated firmly.

His incorrect pronunciation, his wide, sunburned, freckled countenance, the naïve expression of his blue eyes – all these marked him out as a country dweller, possibly from a far-off land. Privation had forced him away from his native fields, the city had chewed up his young, healthy body…

"Maybe I can get some compensation for this? And where is he?" the head suddenly recalled. Its eyes widened.

"Who's 'he'?"

"Why, that fellow – who ran me over? There was a tram, and another one, and then a car, headed straight for me…"

"Don't worry! He'll get what's coming to him. The number of the goods van was written down: 4.711, in case that interests you. What is your name?" asked Professor Kern.

"My name? They called me Tom. Tom Beggins, that's me."

"Well, then, Tom… You won't need anything and you won't suffer from hunger, thirst, or cold. We won't throw you out on the street, have no fear!"

"What do you mean, are you going to feed me for nothing, or show me at street fairs for money?"

"We'll certainly show you off, but not at street fairs. We'll show you to scientists! And now, it's time for you to rest!" And, after glancing at the woman's head, Kern said, "It seems Salome is making us wait a long time!"

"What's this? Another head without a body?" asked Tom's head, indicating the head of the woman.

"As you see! So that you wouldn't feel too dull here, we took the trouble to find you a young lady companion! Please shut off his air supply, Miss Adams, so that his chatter won't disturb us for a while!"

Kern removed a thermometer from the nostril of the woman's head.

"The temperature is higher than that of a corpse, but still low. For some reason the revivification is proceeding slowly…"

Time passed. The woman's head did not revive. Professor Kern began fretting. He walked anxiously around the laboratory, looking at the clock; every step he took on the stone floor rang out loudly around the whole room.

Tom's head watched them with puzzlement and silently moved its lips.

Finally, Kern approached the woman's head and attentively examined the glass tube, encased in rubber, running into an artery.

"There's the problem! The tube is too loose, and the circulation is going slowly. Give me a wider tube!"

Kern changed the tube, and within a few minutes the head came to life.

The head of Watson – that was the woman's name – reacted more strongly to her revivification. When she had completely regained her senses and started speaking, she began screaming weakly and begging them to kill her rather than leave her looking like such a monster.

"Ah, ah, ah… my body… my poor body… What have you done to me? Save me or kill me! I don't want to live without a body! Let me at least look at it! No, no, there's no need… It doesn't have a head… how awful… how awful!…"

When she had calmed down a little, she said:

"You say you revived me. I may have little education, but I know that a head can't live without a body. What is this: a miracle or a magic spell?"

"Neither the one nor the other. This is a triumph of science."

"If your science can work miracles like these, then it should be able to do more. Give me another body! That ass Teddy shot a bullet through mine… But there must be lots of girls who shoot themselves in the head. Cut off one of their bodies and stick it on to my head. Only show it to me first. You have to choose a beautiful body. Otherwise I just can't… A woman without a body! That's even worse than a man without a head!"

And, turning to Miss Adams, she asked:

"Kindly give me a mirror!"

Looking in the mirror, Miss Watson studied herself long and seriously.

"Awful… Could I ask you to tidy my hair? I can hardly do my own…"

"Well then, everything's turned out well," said Professor Kern, turning to Miss Adams. "Your work has increased. Your wages will be increased proportionately. I must be off."

Kern glanced at the clock and, stepping close to Miss Adams, whispered to her:

"In their presence," he indicated the heads with his eyes, "not a word about Professor Dowell's head!"

And, the raised heels of his boots clattering loudly, he left the laboratory.

Miss Adams went off to inform Professor Dowell's head.

Dowell's eyes gazed at her sadly. A sorrowful smile made his moustache tremble.

"My poor, poor dear!" whispered Miss Adams. "But soon you will be avenged!"

VII. The Heads Entertain Themselves

The heads of Tom and Miss Watson found it almost harder to adapt to their new existence than had Professor Dowell's. His intellectual resources were greater than theirs. His head was occupied with the same scientific tasks which had absorbed him in life. He had "felt" his body only when he lost it. Tom and Miss Watson were simple people, with primitive requirements and feelings. Lacking their bodies, their existence lost almost all meaning. No wonder that they very quickly grew listless, like birds accustomed to freedom, suddenly trapped in a cramped cage. Tom found captivity particularly difficult.

"Can this really be life?" he said. "Sticking up like a stump; I must have stared holes in all the walls."

Kern was very troubled by the mood of his "prisoners of science," as he jokingly called them. The heads could pine away from gloom, putting an end to their temporary existence even sooner than the day they were due to be exhibited.

Thus Professor Kern did everything in his power to cheer them up.

He obtained a projector, and Miss Adams and John screened a program of cinema films for them in the evenings. The white wall of the laboratory served as their screen.

At first, this entertained them. But soon the sight of people moving around started making them even gloomier. Even the "king of the screen," Charlie Chaplin, had no effect.

"Look at him, carrying on like a scalded cat," grumbled Tom's head. "If he were shut up like this, he'd soon stop leaping around!"

Miss Watson was irritated by watching beautiful women at their toilette.

"Turn it off… I don't want to watch the way others live!" she said.

They took the projector away.

The radio entertained them for slightly longer. But music, especially dance tunes, agitated both of them.

"God, how I used to dance to that number!" cried Miss Watson.

They were forced to resort to other forms of entertainment. Miss Watson was troublesome, constantly demanding a mirror, contriving new hairdos, asking to have her eyes made up with eyeliner, or her face powdered and rouged. She was annoyed by Miss Adams' incompetence; the latter had never managed to grasp the mysteries of make-up.

"Can you really not see," said Miss Watson's head crossly, "that the right eye has been underlined a touch more thickly? Raise the mirror higher!"

She asked to be brought style magazines and fashionable fabrics, and made them drape the table to which her head was fixed.

"So that I'm spared the sight of my mutilated self…"

She even indulged herself in whimsies. In a fit of belated modesty, she suddenly announced that she could not sleep in the same room as a man; she asked to be shielded at night by a screen.

"Protect me, at the very least, with a book!"

And Miss Adams made a "screen" from a large open book, placing it on the glass surface beside Miss Watson's head.

Tom was no less troublesome.

He announced that he could not live without food, even though he was unable to feel hunger.

"How can anyone feel full with your little pipes and tubes? Give me Irish stew – with pepper, and plenty of it!"

With extreme caution, they drew the tube out of his throat and began to "feed" him. His pleasure in chewing was all the greater since it proved that he had not lost his sense of taste. One piece of food at a time was placed in his mouth, as if he were a raven fledgling. The chewed food fell from the opening in his throat onto the floor.

Once he demanded whisky. The whisky flowed straight through him, without making him tipsy. As soon as he was able to speak again, he swore roundly.

"This is all trickery. I'm not a gutter-pipe! I want to get drunk!"

And Professor Kern was obliged to make him happy by intoxicating him mildly with ether.

Tom's mood became playful.

"Miss Watson! Allow me to offer you my hand and my heart, or at least my head, if you'll have me. Let's get married and have lots of little heads. Ho, ho!"

Miss Watson made no reply, but Tom was already trying to sing.

Sometimes they sang a duet. Their weakened vocal chords were unreliable; the duets were dreadful.

"My poor voice… If only you could have heard how I used to sing, before!" Miss Watson would say, pitifully raising her eyes to heaven.

In the evenings they grew thoughtful. The strangeness of their situation forced even these simple souls to consider the great questions of life and death.

Miss Watson believed in immortality; Tom was a materialist.

"Of course, we're immortal," Miss Watson's head would say. "If my soul had died with my body, it wouldn't have returned to my head."

"And where did your soul reside, in your head or in your body?" Tom would ask acerbically.

"In my body, of course – it was everywhere," Miss Watson's head would answer uncertainly, suspecting a trap behind the question.

"So in that case, your body's soul is now wandering in the other world, without a head?"

"You're headless yourself!" Miss Watson would say indignantly.

"Actually, I do have a head. But I have nothing else. What if your body's soul came back from the other world?" Tom did not relent. "What if it returned through that rubber tube? To say hello, how are you? Tell me, what did you see in the other world? What news have you heard? No," he said, growing serious, "we are like machines. Release the steam – we start working again. But if we're smashed in pieces, no amount of steam can help."

And each of them sank into thought.

VIII. Tom Dies a Second Time

Exhibition day for the heads was approaching.

Professor Kern was anxious and ever more often sent mistrustful, testing glances Miss Adams' way. But outwardly he was twice as kind to her.

The night before Kern's formal presentation to the scientific society, the head of Tom unexpectedly fell sick.

In the morning, when Miss Adams came to relieve the Negro, Tom's head was already unconscious.

Professor Kern ranted at John for not waking him in the night, as soon as Tom's head took ill.

"I thought Tom was asleep, and when I looked at him in the morning – he was dead…"

"You were asleep yourself, you ass!'

Kern went to work on the head.

"Oh, how horrible," hissed the head of Miss Watson, "he's died! I'm just terrified of corpses! And I'm also afraid of dying… what did he die of?"

"Shut off the tap with her air supply!" ordered Kern angrily.

Miss Watson fell silent halfway through a word, but she continued to stare fearfully and pleadingly into Miss Adams' eyes, helplessly moving her lips.

"If I can't bring this head back to life within twenty minutes, we'll just have to throw it out!" said Kern.

Fifteen minutes later the head gave some signs of life. The eyelids and lips trembled, but the eyes stared blankly, without any thought. After another two minutes the head uttered several disconnected words. Kern was already celebrating his victory. But suddenly the head felt silent again. Not a single nerve moved on its face.

Kern looked at the thermometer.

"The temperature of a corpse. It's over!"

And forgetting that Miss Watson was there, he angrily seized the head by its thick hair, wrenched it off the table and hurled it into a large metal bucket.

"Put it in the freezer! We'll have to open it up and find out why it died."

The Negro swiftly picked up the bucket and went out.

Miss Watson's head watched him, eyes wide with horror.

Kern took giant paces around the laboratory, agitatedly twirling between his fingers a cigar he had forgotten to light.

The death of Tom's head reduced the effect of his exhibition by half.

Finally, he turned towards the head of Miss Watson, who had continued to follow him with her wide-open eyes.

"Well then. Today at eight in the evening you will be taken into a crowded meeting. There you will have to speak. Answer the questions that they ask you briefly. Don't chatter about anything unnecessary… Do you understand?"

Kern opened the tap for air, and Miss Watson whispered:

"I understand… but I'd like… please…"

Kern walked out without listening to her.

Miss Watson began preparing herself for her excursion into society.

Forgetting about the death of Tom's head, she was engulfed by worries about her appearance. She tormented Miss Adams with her hairstyle and her "tattoo," as Miss Adams mentally called the cosmetic decoration of the head.

Miss Watson's head unexpectedly announced that she could not venture out "looking like this," and she demanded that a body be made for her from a corpse and swathed in fashionable fabric. Kern was forced to intervene.

"The hall," he said to her, "will be full of heads with bodies. You, however, possessing only a head, will be the most original woman in the gathering."

Miss Watson was convinced by this argument, and she abandoned her whim.

Kern grew more and more worried. The task facing him was not easy; he had to transfer the head to the meeting hall of the scientific society. The slightest jolt could prove fatal for the head's survival.

Had Tom's head still been alive, the chances of success would have been double.

A specially equipped motor-car was prepared. The table on which the head was placed, with all its equipment, was set on a special tray with wheels for pushing across the floor and with handles for carrying on stairs.

Finally, everything was ready. At seven o'clock in the evening they set off. Miss Watson's head, curled, combed, painted and wrapped in veils, was glowing with anticipation of her outing in society.

IX. Triumph Spoiled

The huge white hall was flooded with bright light. The auditorium was filled with the grey hair and shining pates of men of science, swathed in black waistcoats and tails. The glass of thousands of spectacles sparkled. The boxes and stalls were allotted to élite members of the public, claiming some connection to the scientific world.

The ladies' splendid costumes, glittering with diamonds, suggested the atmosphere of a concert hall or a speech by a celebrity.

A restrained hum filled the overcrowded hall.

Below the stage, at their little tables, press correspondents fussed around like excited ants, sharpening their pencils for their stenographic reports.

To the right of the stage a row of movie cameras had been arranged, in order to record on film every moment of Kern's fascinating exposition and of the revivified head's appearance.

An honorary committee was assembled on the stage, chosen from the most important representatives of the scientific world. A podium was erected in the middle of the stage, with a microphone for broadcasting the speeches by radio to the entire world. A second microphone was placed in front of the head of Miss Watson. She was looking down from the right side of the stage, glowing all over from pleasure. The lessons in "tattooing" had not been wasted on Miss Adams; her skilful and moderate application of make-up lent Miss Watson's head a fresh and attractive appearance, softening the troubling impression that the head was bound to make on an unprepared observer. Miss Adams and John stood near her table.

At precisely eight o'clock Professor Kern walked up to the podium.

The gathering greeted him with lengthy applause.

He was paler than usual, but full of dignity.

A movie-camera creaked into action. The anthill of pressmen fell silent and gave their full attention. Professor Kern began his speech.

This was a brilliantly delivered and cunningly structured talk. Kern did not forget to mention the "preparatory, but very worthy work of the prematurely deceased Professor Dowell." But, after paying his dues to the work of the dead man, he did not neglect to mention his own "modest service" also. The listener could not be left with any doubt that all the honor of the discovery belonged entirely to him, Professor Kern.

His speech was repeatedly interrupted by applause. Hundreds of opera-glasses were trained on him. The men's opera-glasses, with no less interest, were directed towards the head of Miss Watson, whose enchanting smile never faltered. She considered herself the star of this brilliant gathering, and grew drunk on her own success.

But Miss Adams' face was furious and deathly pale.

At a sign from Professor Kern, she opened the air tap, and Miss Watson's head had the pleasure of uttering a few phrases.

"How do you feel?" an elderly scientist asked her.

"Oh, wonderful, thank you!"

This response brought smiles to the lips of the audience. Several successive naïve responses made the whole hall laugh. This spectacle had proved more interesting than the public in the lodges and the stalls had expected.

Although Miss Watson's voice was flat and toneless, with a whistle caused by the flow of air under high pressure, and although the sound lacked any modulation, her speech produced an unusual impression. Many world-famous actors never heard such a storm of applause.

The simple-minded Miss Watson, accustomed to applause in small bars, took all this enthusiasm as personal praise. Unable to curtsey – a shortcoming she bitterly regretted – she lowered her eyelids languidly and delighted the hall with her bewitching smile.

Miss Adams' agitation was rising constantly. She started shaking with nervous fever, and she pressed her teeth together tightly to stop them chattering. "Now!" she told herself several times, but every time her resolve failed her. The atmosphere oppressed her. After every missed opportunity she tried to calm herself with the thought that the higher Professor Kern's reputation rose, the lower he would fall.

The speeches began.

A little old grey man approached the podium – one of the greatest scientists in America.

In a weak, cracked voice he spoke about Professor Kern's ingenious discovery, about the omnipotence of science, about victory over death, and about America, which had given birth to such great minds and given the world the greatest scientific achievements…

At the moment when she least expected it, a sort of whirlwind of long-restrained fury and hatred overwhelmed Miss Adams and bore her onwards. She was no longer in control of herself.

She flung herself onto the podium, almost knocking the astonished old man off his feet, practically pushed him away, took his place and with a deathly pale face and feverishly burning eyes like one of the Furies on the trail of a murderer, she breathlessly began her fiery, confused speech.

The entire hall was rocked by her appearance.

At first Professor Kern looked troubled and made an involuntary movement in Miss Adams' direction, as if to restrain her. Then he turned swiftly to John and whispered a few words in his ear. John slipped out the door.

In the general confusion, no-one paid any attention to this.

"Don't believe him!" shouted Miss Adams, pointing at Kern. "He is a thief and a murderer. He stole Professor Dowell's research! He killed Dowell! Even now he continues to work with him… He tortures Dowell. He forced Dowell by torture to continue his scientific work and claimed it as his own… Dowell told me himself that Kern poisoned him…"

Confusion turned to panic amongst the public. Many rose from their seats. Even some of the correspondents dropped their pencils and froze in postures of astonishment. Only the camera operator, who had seen it all before, was energetically turning the handle of his machine and enjoying this unexpected caper, which guaranteed that his film would be a *succès de scandale*.

Professor Kern was entirely in control of himself. He stood by calmly, wearing a pleased smile.

After waiting for the moment when a nervous paroxysm prevented Miss Adams from speaking, he used the pause that followed to turn to the guards stationed at the door of the auditorium. He spoke to them calmly and authoritatively:

"Take her away! Can't you see that she's suffering a fit of insanity?"

For some time the guards stood without moving; perhaps they too were affected by the scene. But Miss Adams made their task easier. A hysterical fit shook her body, and with a crazy laugh she collapsed near the podium.

They carried her away…

When the general agitation had calmed a little, Professor Kern mounted the podium and apologized to the gathering for the unfortunate incident.

"Miss Adams is a nervous, hysterical girl; she could not cope with those powerful anxieties which she was forced to bear, spending day after day in the company of the head of the *corpse* (Kern emphasized the word) of Miss Watson, after I artificially brought it to life. Miss Adams' psyche has given way. She has gone out of her mind… Naturally, we will take good care of this victim of scientific duty!"

It was as if the scythe of Death the Reaper had passed over the hall. And thousands of eyes stared at the head of Miss Watson with horror and pity, as if at a corpse that had crawled out of the tomb. The mood of the hall was irretrievably spoiled. Many of the public left, without waiting for the end. The speakers hastily read their prepared speeches and congratulatory telegrams, awarding Kern honorary membership of and honorary doctorates from various institutions and scientific academies; then the meeting was closed.

Just before the very end the Negro appeared behind Professor Kern and, nodding imperceptibly to Kern, started to remove Miss Watson's head for the return journey. The head had immediately wilted, looking tired and frightened.

Only once he was alone in the sealed car did Professor Kern give way to the rage boiling up inside him.

He squeezed his hands into fists, ground his teeth and swore so loudly, that his driver stopped the motor-car several times and said, "Hello?" into the communication tube.

X. The Madwoman

It was a medium-sized room with a window onto the garden. The walls were white. The white bed linen was covered with a light grey blanket. There was a white table and two chairs of the same shade.

Miss Adams sat at the window and stared vaguely into the garden. The sun's rays gilded her red hair. She had grown much paler and thinner.

From the window, she could see the paths where small groups of patients were wandering. Around them fluttered the white robes of the Sisters.

"They are mad!" she spoke softly, gazing at the strolling patients. "And I am mad too! What nonsense! And this is all I managed to achieve!"

She wrung her slender hands until her finger bones clicked.

It was a month since she had found herself in a suburban hospital for the mentally ill, thanks to Professor Kern's efforts to take care of the "victim of scientific duty."

The fact that her nerves genuinely were in lamentable condition after the infamous evening had made it all the easier for Professor Kern to place her in a psychiatric institution. She had lost her job, and she was tormented by worry about her family. Worst of all, she was aware of the utter hopelessness of her situation. She was too dangerous to Kern. And her stay in the psychiatric ward could be prolonged indefinitely… It was possible that even the authorities would not be very concerned about her. They had treated Kern's speech as a kind of national triumph. America boasted about him to the whole world. It would now be unfortunate to show the world the other side of the coin: the rivalry, greed, and dishonesty among those who were considered the scientific élite…

Professor Kern had fulfilled his threat about "the gravest consequences" that would ensue if she failed to protect his secret. They might have been worse. She would expect anything from Kern. He had had his revenge, but he had escaped vengeance for what he had done to the head of Professor Dowell. Miss Adams had sacrificed herself in vain. This knowledge unbalanced her mental state even more.

She was close to despair and ready to commit suicide.

Even in here she felt Professor Kern's influence. Other patients were allowed meetings with family and friends. She was kept in the strictest isolation.

In spite of this, she had succeeded in making friends with one of the custodians. This woman, with the greatest secrecy, sometimes brought her newspapers. In one of these papers she read about herself:

"Miss Adams, formerly employed by Professor Kern, was placed in a psychiatric institution after the fit of insanity which afflicted her during Professor Kern's presentation to a scientific society. Doctors consider her condition to be serious, offering little hope of a cure."

"There's my sentence!" whispered Miss Adams, dropping the newspaper on her lap.

In the next issue she managed to find out that Professor Kern's premises had been searched immediately after his presentation.

"As might have been expected," the short article recorded, "Professor Dowell's head was not found. It was later established that his death followed an asthma attack, such as the patient had suffered for a long time. Thus the last remaining doubts – if anyone had indeed been in doubt – about Professor Kern's innocence were dissipated. The entire story was no more than the delirium of Miss Adams' sick imagination."

"Could the head really have perished? Poor Professor Dowell!" thought the girl.

Miss Adams found no more articles about the matter. It had been supplanted by other sensational stories.

In the mornings, the doctors visited Miss Adams.

"Well, how are we doing?" They always asked the same question.

She hated them: either they were all ignorant, unable to tell a healthy person from an invalid, or they were in Kern's pay.

She did not answer them, or else she replied with uncharacteristic rudeness.

And they would leave, shaking their heads disapprovingly, possibly sincerely convinced that they were dealing with a mentally ill woman…

Someone knocked on the door.

Miss Adams, thinking that the custodian had brought tea, said indifferently, without turning her head from the window, "Come in!"

Someone entered. A young, male voice spoke just behind her:

"May I see Miss Adams?"

This was so unexpected that the girl turned sharply. Before her stood a young man dressed with elegant simplicity. There was something familiar about his face. But Miss Adams could not remember where she might have seen him.

"That's me…"

"Allow me to introduce myself: I'm Arthur Dowell. Professor Dowell's son."

"So that's where the resemblance comes from! The very same eyes, open forehead and oval face," thought Miss Adams.

"How did you… reach me?" she asked in amazement.

Arthur Dowell smiled.

"Well, that wasn't easy! You are well guarded. I'll admit that I was forced to use a minor subterfuge. And even now I only have a few minutes. Let me come straight to the point. I was living in England with my aunt, when I learned from the newspapers about the events surrounding Professor Kern's presentation and your… noble speech in my father's defense. I could not remain uninvolved in this matter. It concerns my father's name…"

He wanted to say "my *late* father's," but he couldn't.

"…as well as the fate of his scientific work and the secret of his death. Moreover, you have suffered from this affair. I see you here in captivity. Now is not the moment to speak of my gratitude for your self-sacrificing act. I know Kern slightly and, I admit, I considered him capable of everything that you spoke about on that night. I didn't believe the story of your insanity. And now, seeing you, I am convinced I was right. Mad people don't look like you. But I want to be convinced from your own lips of the truth of everything that you said. Was it all true?"

"Yes, it was true!"

"I believe you… What a shameless act! What's more, I want to ask your opinion: would Kern have kept my father's head? How unfortunate, that I was detained by illness! I am afraid I have come too late!"

"Unfortunately I know no more than you about the fate of Professor Dowell's head. I can only say that the head was needed to finish a certain major project."

"In that case… it must be found! But first of all you must be freed! I shall take care of that. And remember, please; my name is not Dowell, but Bean; I'm your cousin. Do you understand me? This way we shall reach our goal sooner!"

Someone knocked at the door.

"Sadly, our meeting is over. But I hope that we will soon meet again in different circumstances. I wish you all the best!"

And he left as unexpectedly as he had appeared.

Miss Adams continued to stand, her eyes fixed unwaveringly on the door.

Then she whispered, "Could I really be freed?"

XI. Free

"Are you certain that the car aimed for you on purpose?" Arthur Dowell asked Miss Adams.

"I am perfectly certain," she replied. "I was walking along a side street with little traffic. I had already noticed a black Ford which seemed to be slowly following me. When I was crossing the street, the driver suddenly accelerated, sending the car straight towards me. I darted out of the way. The driver swerved after me. I was only saved by a carriage which accidentally blocked the path of the car."

"Yes… you must be more careful! Kern can have no peace while you are at large!"

This conversation was taking place in Miss Adams' small living room, on the fourth day since her newly minted cousin Bean had succeeded in freeing her from the psychiatric institution. This had proved no easy task. The management of the asylum initially refused point-blank, claiming that the nature of Miss Adams' illness presented great danger for anyone around her, and that it was impossible to take her out of the asylum.

But Dowell-Bean was insistent. He took responsibility for Miss Adams, persuaded, insisted, finally demanded an expert opinion given in the presence of a legal representative. Further resistance could have had unpleasant consequences for the asylum, and the management were forced to concede.

Miss Adams was welcomed at home as if she had risen from the dead.

Her elderly mother looked at Arthur with delight, as on the savior of a daughter whom she had lost hope of ever seeing again.

Arthur spent all his time with the family, discussing plans for finding the head.

On the fourth day her mother's joy was overshadowed by the incident with the car which almost crushed Miss Adams.

"The same motor car had already tried to cut me down at an intersection," Miss Adams continued. "I observed the driver plainly."

"You would do better to stay at home for a few days!" said her mother anxiously.

"Yes, you must be extremely careful," said Arthur. "The struggle is seriously heating up. It's possible that Kern has guessed that I am here. Your escape put him on his guard. We must take swift and decisive measures. When I was on my way here, I considered getting in to see Kern under a false name, perhaps as a doctor wishing to work with him, to earn his trust, in order to be admitted to the secret laboratory…"

"But what about the family resemblance?" asked Miss Adams.

"Yes, the resemblance… although I have changed significantly since the days when Kern knew me. After all, I have spent the last several years in England. But this plan is already out, because it would take time to fulfil. And Kern will be more suspicious now than ever."

"What if we tried to reach him through John, the Negro who works for Kern? Kern treated him roughly, and I don't think John was especially devoted to him," Miss Adams suggested.

"Perfect! We have to try."

And then and there they worked out a plan of action.

They found a reliable individual, whom they invited to attempt the task.

Bill – that was the individual's name – quickly struck up an acquaintance with John in one of the cheap restaurants where John usually spent his free time.

John eagerly swallowed the whisky and soda his new friend offered him, but his tongue did not wag.

To all Bill's searching, apparently accidental questions, John either remained silent, or assured him that he knew nothing.

After two or three unsuccessful evenings, Bill was forced to show his hand. He offered John two hundred dollars if he could just tell him whether the head of Professor Dowell was alive and where it could be found.

But John, looking innocent, continued to insist that he knew nothing.

Bill doubled and then tripled the reward, without success. Finally, he offered two thousand dollars.

John's eyes blazed with greed. For a moment, he hesitated. Then finally he announced, looking innocent:

"Well, if only I knew!"

Plainly Professor Kern was paying John very well indeed, since even a sum such as that failed to tempt him.

The only result was to convince Bill that John knew about the head's fate; but for one reason or another, he was staying loyal to Kern.

When Bill communicated this to Arthur Dowell, Dowell decided that any further bribery would be useless.

"If John is loyal to Kern, then Kern has already been informed about everything. That means your escape, Miss Adams, and our attempt to bribe John; all of this will have warned Kern sufficiently of the threat assembling against him. For Kern to continue to keep my father's head under these circumstances – no matter how necessary it is to him – would be either extreme courage, or irrational carelessness. If it is not already too late, we must not delay another day. We can still declare open war. I am Professor Dowell's son, and I have every right to demand a renewal of the legal investigation and the carrying out of a second search. Either my cards, or Professor Kern's, will fold. I consider your presence during the search, Miss Adams, to be absolutely essential."

"And what if that scoundrel kills her!" old Mrs. Adams squeaked in terror.

"I will go no matter what!" Miss Adams announced determinedly.

"I hope that no danger will threaten your daughter. We will be present there with a court detective and plenty of policemen!"

That very same day Arthur managed to arrange matters with the investigative authorities. The search was arranged for the following day, at eight in the morning, before Professor Kern left his house.

XII. The Final Meeting

John the Negro opened the heavy oak door.

"Professor Kern is not at home."

The policeman who had appeared on the scene obliged John to admit the unexpected guests.

Professor Kern, seeing Miss Adams enter the office, threw her an annihilating glance, then immediately assumed an expression of wounded virtue.

"If you please," he said icily, holding the laboratory door open wide.

The detective, Miss Adams, Arthur and Kern went inside.

Miss Adams' heart beat fiercely as she saw the familiar surroundings where she had experienced so much heartrending emotion.

They found the head of Miss Watson in the laboratory. It was still living, although very much withered. The cheeks had lost their blush and taken on a dark-yellow hue, like a mummy. When she saw Miss Adams, she smiled and blinked.

In the hope of finding out any information at all, Miss Adams opened the air tap.

But Miss Watson's head knew nothing about the head of Professor Dowell. As usual, she babbled all sorts of nonsense. She complained that her hair had been cut; she complained that she was bored and that she was never taken out of the laboratory any more; she recalled Tom.

"What do you think of me? Tell me, does the short haircut spoil my looks? Oh, how I wept when they cut my hair… My hair… that was the last bit of my womanhood!"

They entered the room adjoining the laboratory.

There they found two heads.

The first was the head of a boy, as curly-haired as a Raphael cherub. But the spinal cord extended from the base of his small head downwards into a liquid-filled vessel, lending him the appearance of some monstrous tadpole. Clearly, Kern was continuing his scientific experiments. The boy's dark blue eyes stared at the newcomers with childish curiosity.

The second head was that of an elderly man with close-shaven hair and an enormous meaty nose. Over its eyes the head had a pair of perfectly dark glasses.

"Its eyes hurt," Kern explained.

"That's all I have to show you," he added with an ironical smile.

Disappointed, Arthur Dowell headed for the door. The detective and Kern followed him towards the exit.

"Wait!" exclaimed Miss Adams. And stepping towards the head with the fat nose, she opened the air tap.

"Who are you?" asked Miss Adams.

The head moved its lips, but its voice made no sound. Miss Adams released a strong current of air.

Then they heard the whistling mutter:

"Who are you? Is that you, Kern? Uncover my ears! I can't hear you."

Miss Adams looked in the ears and extracted thick wads of cotton wool.

"Who are you?" she repeated the question.

"I was Professor Dowell."

"But what about your face?"

The head spoke with difficulty.

"My face? Yes... even my face was taken from me... A minor operation... paraffin injected under the skin... Alas... only my brain is still my own, in this strange container... But even that is refusing to obey... I am dying... Our experiments... My experiments are unfinished. Although my head has survived longer than I had considered theoretically possible..."

"Why are you wearing glasses?"

"My colleague has recently come to mistrust me," the head even attempted to smile, "he has deprived me of the chance to hear and see... the glasses are not transparent, so that I couldn't reveal myself before guests he mightn't want... but I seem to recognize your voice... take off the glasses."

Miss Adams removed the glasses.

"Miss Adams... Greetings, my dear! And Kern said that you had left! I don't feel well... I cannot work any longer... These are the last experiments... the boy... with the spinal cord... But I will not finish them... My colleague Kern kindly declared an amnesty for me yesterday. If I don't die by myself today, he will liberate me tomorrow."

And suddenly, seeing Arthur, who, astonished by the sight of his father's head, stood transfixed, the head cried out gladly:

"Arthur! My son!"

For an instant life seemed to return to the head. The dull eyes grew bright.

Arthur approached his father's head.

"My dear father! What have they done to you?"

"Well… it's all fine… I have seen you one more time… after my death…"

The vocal cords were barely working any more; Dowell's head spoke in short bursts. In the pauses, air whistled out of its throat.

"Arthur… kiss my brow… if it is not too unpleasant for you…"

Arthur bent over and kissed him.

"There… now it is good."

The detective walked over to the head.

"Professor Dowell, can you give us information about the circumstances of your death? I am a detective…"

The head looked dully at the detective, not understanding. Then, evidently having grasped the situation, the head glanced towards Miss Adams and whispered:

"I… told… her… She knows everything."

"Good…." the head whispered one more time, with just its lips, after a pause, and its eyes grew cloudy.

"It's the end!" said Miss Adams.

For some time they all stood in silent grief.

"Well, anyhow, the case is clear!" the detective interrupted the painful silence. And, turning to Kern, he pronounced firmly:

"Please follow me into the office. I need to take a statement from you."

Kern silently obeyed. They went out.

Arthur sank heavily onto a chair beside his father's head and laid his own head on his hands.

"My poor, poor father…"

Then he rose. Silently and firmly, he squeezed Miss Adams' hand.

From Kern's office, a shot rang out.

First published in Russian: 1926
Translation by Muireann Maguire

ANDREI PLATONOV
1926

THE LUNAR BOMB

1. KREUZKOPF'S PROJECT

Peter Kreuzkopf, an engineer and the son of a miner, was in his country's capital city for the first time. He was in ecstasy at the maelstrom of automobiles and the rumble of surface railways. There must have been practically no one living in the city other than mechanics! But no factories could be seen. Kreuzkopf was sitting on a bench in the downtown park, but the factories were built on swamps in the outskirts, in the fields where wastewater was dumped, out beyond the airstrips of worldwide aviation lines.

Kreuzkopf was young and penniless. He had quarreled with the mine administrators, who wanted to extract money from nothing but compressed air, raised a fuss at his mine, was taken to court and fired, and then came to the capital.

The train arrived early, but this strange city was already full of vigor: it never awoke because it never went to sleep. Its life consisted of steadily accelerated motion. The city had no connection to nature. It was a self-enclosed concrete and metal oasis, completely isolated and alone in an abyss of the world.

Kreuzkopf's gaze was attracted by a sumptuous theater made of dusky dull stone. The theater was large enough that it could have been an airship station.

Peter Kreuzkopf's heart was pierced with grief. His young wife Erna, who had once loved him, had stayed in Carbomort, the coal town from which Peter had come. Peter admonished her: "There's no sense breaking up, Erna. We've lived together seven years. Things will get easier. I'll go into the city and start working on the Lunar Bomb, and they'll pay me for it, surely."

But Erna was tired of promises, tired of the coal haze of the mine, the narrow life of Carbomort, and the monotonous, ugly faces of the unchanging workers, particularly two persons from among Peter's friends, narrow specialists who consciously believed themselves to be the atoms of human knowledge. The most frequent conversation Erna heard was the words of Mertz, Peter's coworker: "We live to know things!"

"But what you don't know," Erna replied, "is that people don't live to know things…"

Peter could understand both Erna and his friends, but they didn't particularly understand him. Erna was an aristocrat, the daughter of a coal baron and educated at the Sorbonne. She detested Peter's friends, the craftsmen, electricians, and inventors that sat around in her living room getting into needless arguments with Peter till midnight.

Kreuzkopf knew he had little in common with Erna. He was half self-taught, an engineer by trade, while she had mastered all the latest "flowers of culture" that were out of his reach.

And Erna had left him to be with her own kind. Kreuzkopf grieved and did not know what to do all alone amid this multitude of people.

☆

The general feeling of preoccupation, the electric advertisements, the smell of exhaust, and the roar of rumbling machines magnified Kreuzkopf's sadness tenfold. He remembered the bygone years of his life, full of labor, trust in people, technical inventiveness, and devotion to his beloved wife. And now it had all been destroyed by inscrutable elemental forces: people had deceived and betrayed him, and they did not need his labor; his wife found another love and grew to despise him; and his creation led him to loneliness and poverty.

"Is there really no salvation? Death? No, let me crushed by the unconquerable. Or else I will conquer all that is visible and invisible!"

Kreuzkopf stood up, wiped his face with a dirty handkerchief, and set out for the Science and Technology Commission of the Republic. He did not think their green desks to be of much use; he knew the irony hidden in those boxes in those offices, and the dull ignorance of the professors. But he had nowhere else to turn. He was received by the chairman of the Commission, a railway engineer. Kreuzkopf laid out his proposal, complete with illustrative graphics.

The proposal concerned a "Lunar Bomb," a kind of transportation tool capable of moving in any gaseous environment, within the atmosphere or outside it. A metal sphere filled with the payload would be attached to a disk installed in a fixed position on the earth. The sphere was attached at the edge of the disk, and the disk itself was positioned either horizontal to the earth's surface, at an incline, or vertical, depending on where the missile was to be sent: to a station on Earth or to another planet.

The disk was rotated sufficiently for the missile to arrive back from its destination station. When the disk, in the proper position for the direction of the launch, reached the required number of revolutions, an automatic device separated the sphere from the disk and the sphere took off at a tangent. All this was done based on a formula for centrifugal force adjusted by a coefficient for environmental resistance.

A safe landing on earth (or another planet) was provided for by automatic devices on the missile itself. When approaching a solid surface, a circuit in the device was closed and a certain quantity of an explosive was detonated in the same direction as the flight. The recoil acted as a brake on the flight, and the fall became a smooth and safe descent. The missile's ascent was also safe and smooth because the speed of the launching disk started at zero.

Kreuzkopf proposed launching the first missile in a curved path that would take it around the Moon, close to its surface, then return it to Earth. The "Lunar Bomb" would have all the equipment required to automatically record the temperature, gravitational force, general environmental conditions, and structure of the electromagnetic sphere in the interplanetary space near the Moon. And finally, movie cameras with special microscopes would capture everything passing by the missile. Of course the design of all this equipment must take the hurtling state of the "lunar bomb" into account.

Kreuzkopf was guided by a secret thought: there were a lot of humans on earth, passing the days of their unrepeatable lives in stifling crowds that gathered around the shriveling veins sustaining the earth. Kreuzkopf hoped to open up new virgin sources of sustenance for life on earth, run hoses from these sources to the earth, and use them to swallow up the meanness and the burdened, cramped feeling of human life. And then, when the endless depths of the alien celestial gift were opened, people would feel more of a need for other people…

"We're expecting a good harvest," the Commission chairman said contemplatively after hearing him out. "Industry is up and running, new construction is underway… Yes, we can ask for the money. How much do you estimate you need? Six hundred thousand? Okay. But we need to put the entire matter before the Commission Plenum and get their approval, and only then can we take the proposal to the government… The Plenum is meeting on – today is Tuesday – they're meeting on Friday. Personally I'm in favor of your proposal. As far as I can see there are no mistakes in your calculations. So, are you free on Friday?"

"I am at your disposal," Kreuzkopf replied.

"Okay then, see you Friday. All the best."

"Goodbye." Kreuzkopf left. He hadn't expected to be paid such attention. But now what could he do until Friday, three days from now, and where could he get something to eat?

The city ceaselessly rioted with life and work. It was noon in torrid summer. Kreuzkopf bought a cheap newspaper. He began with the classifieds: "Engineer wanted… travel required… travel required…" Nothing useful. Here's one: "Design engineer wanted… for generators." Kreuzkopf didn't have detailed knowledge in that field. Another one: "Temporary driver wanted for testing dynamics of new types of automobile engines…" This would work. Kreuzkopf had had two cars (gifts from his wife during the first year of their life together). He knew how to drive quite well and he liked doing it.

Kreuzkopf was hired and, to his amazement, would be paid more than what he'd earned at the mine. They offered to take him on at the garage on Wednesday morning. Kreuzkopf spent the rest of the day and the whole night sitting on a park bench. Thoughts of the past tormented him.

2. A TRAGEDY ON THE HIGHWAY

In the morning Kreuzkopf set off for the outskirts of the city, to the garage and his new job. The garage was open but the manager wasn't around. Morning was ablaze. Kreuzkopf smoked and fought against sleep.

At last the manager arrived and Kreuzkopf was given a car. At first glance it looked like a 90-horsepower Hispano-Suiza, but there was something different about it: the wheel diameter was greater and the radiator was a semicircle. The engine was sealed. A separate compartment, also sealed, held all the necessary recording instruments.

Kreuzkopf pulled out. The car handled smoothly and had furious pull despite the cold engine. Dead weight was placed in the passenger seats. Kreuzkopf was told to put 300 kilometers on the odometer before lunchtime and then return.

The highway lay empty. Kreuzkopf shifted to fourth, floored the gas, and flew like a brick. The odometer read 104 kilometers. But the motor warmed up and the thrust increased. 118 kilometers… The wind rushed past on that quiet morning. Nature spread out all around. Smoke streamed from the pipes of a crematorium in the distance.

Calmer, forgetting his heart's sadness, Kreuzkopf gained speed. 143 kilometers… The road is deserted, our past is dead, and ahead is the wind, the road, and the rising needle of the speedometer.

And suddenly a cow appeared. Kreuzkopf steered past without braking. A slight turn followed, and the speed caused the car to skid a bit. Kreuzkopf disengaged the clutch and saw the curly-haired head of a child a meter away from the car…

Kreuzkopf yanked the wheel to the left and pulled the hand brake all the way. The car shook and the gashed roadway threw up dust, but the right headlight struck the child and his head split open at the cranial sutures. Thick blood poured over his shirt. His long eyelashes drooped down to half cover his undamaged eyes, and his plump crimson lips formed a bow that would never again be untied.

Kreuzkopf grew numb at the suffering that tore his body. In distress and fighting the dark despair surrounding him, he cried out, jumped from the car, and fell to the child's corpse. It was quiet all around. The engine was silent and the city in the distance gave off an even hum.

Kreuzkopf stood up, lifted the child in his arms, and laid the body in the car. It was a boy. His cap had the word "Ocean" written on it. The blood clotted and the bleeding stopped. The boy was about five years old.

Kreuzkopf started the car and slowly pulled away, looking for the mother with his eyes while driving around potholes so as not to shake the little body. But there was no one around. Kreuzkopf threw off his cap and sped away, giving the speedometer needle a sharp jolt. And tears mixed with dust rolled down his face in dirty streams. He wept with his chest pressed against the wheel. The child's small body flopped from the seat to the floor and shuddered from the shaking, as if having convulsions.

Kreuzkopf turned onto a side road and quickly stopped the car. There was a pit next to a boundary marker. He got out of the car with the corpse and laid it in the ready-made grave. The child's face had now begun to wrinkle, and the slightly open eyes had grown white and rolled back. Kreuzkopf took some water out of the radiator and washed him clean, then quietly kissed him on his clean lips, as bitter tears again washed the boy's face again.

"I will never forget you, my dear, warm boy...," Kreuzkopf whispered, sore with sorrow like a burning fire. He cut off a lock of light hair and took it for himself along with the "Ocean" cap, then filled in the grave using tools from the car's kit. After filling in the pit he felt such longing for the boy that he wanted to dig him out.

"I will atone for you, dear boy," he whispered, then went to the car. "Forget Erna! From now on my eternal tenderness will rest here!"

Kreuzkopf noted the location of the grave and set off. He drove slowly, pressing the Ocean hat and the tress of fine blond hair to the wheel with his hand.

Back at the garage Kreuzkopf got his salary advance and left for the city. He bought an evening newspaper, hoping to find the name of the boy, and in it he found: "His parents are pleading... he left the house at six in the morning... his name is Goga... four and a half years old, blond, very friendly, wearing a cap that said "Ocean"... the Rompa beet farm... Mr. Femm, director..."

"Goga Femm," Kreuzkopf whispered. "But what can I do? His mother will die if I tell her he's been crushed by a car!"

Friday arrived. Kreuzkopf went to the Central Science and Technology Commission to defend his project and was successful. He argued and fought desperately, and held the dead boy in his memory.

The Commission passed the project and it went to the government. It would be at least a month before he knew the result.

Kreuzkopf continued breaking in cars, and killed time in the evenings at the movies or in aimless wanderings along the seething streets.

At one point a letter came from Erna, who had somehow discovered his address: "Peter, I've married an engineer named Nimt. Before the New Year we will be leaving for Brussels. It would be nice to see you as a friend sometime. One cannot erase the past all at once. We will be in the capital from 20 to 25 August, staying at the Hotel Mayon. They tell me you are quite unhappy and that you're working as a driver. If you will permit me, I can ask my husband to remove any obstacles in the way of your career. I certainly know you to be a very talented man. Write back to me in Carbomort. Erna." Kreuzkopf wrote nothing in response, naturally.

Weeks passed. Kreuzkopf was highly valued in his new job, and once he even took part in an official race, winning second prize. At last he was summoned by the Commission. The government had given an answer: the funds requested in the estimate would be disbursed in equal payments over two years. The work could begin, and all results from study of the interplanetary route and the Moon would be the property of the government.

3. A CONSTRUCTION ACCIDENT

Kreuzkopf was jubilant. He drove out to the boy's grave and saw that it was now covered with saltbush, that the field was deserted… and that his heart was becoming overgrown with the fat of forgetting. On the road he cried and tore dried heads of grain off their stalks. But having no one close to him, knowing no friends, he instead sent a telegram to Brussels: "Erna, the bomb will be launched in two years. I'm building it." Erna's response was: "I'm glad. A hearty handshake."

Kreuzkopf had never in his entire life known such success. He could not restrain himself: in his room he sang confused songs in a strange voice, and he went drinking with the other drivers.

Construction began. At the launch pad, open to the entire sky, a foundation was poured for the 120,000 horsepower electric motor, the transmission mechanism, and the support bearing – the base for the launching disk. At the same time a branch was brought in from the main high-voltage line to power the electrical engine, and a transformer was installed.

Kreuzkopf was beside himself, with energy seething inside him like steam in an engine. He would have taken just half a year to build the whole system of structures to develop the flying force of life in the Lunar Bomb, but the funding was to be drawn out over two years. The missile itself was being built by the Monte-Monde Machine Building Trust, and it was to be completed within five months.

But a black cloud followed Kreuzkopf: while they were blasting the foundation pit for the support bearing, forty workers were electrocuted, including five of the best specialists in the country. Such were the findings of the specially-appointed commission. But a technical review clearly established that there was no current at a life-threatening voltage at the work site. Nevertheless, forty bodies were wrapped in rough canvas and shipped to their families in five trucks.

The work was stopped. Kreuzkopf kept silent and undertook no steps to get the construction back on track. It was physically apparent that his heart was breaking apart inside him. He had unwittingly killed the workers. True, Kreuzkopf had previously tested his method in the mine, with no people present, and the mine rocks were turned to fine dust.

The method involved sending electromagnetic waves into the material to be turned from mineral to dust at just the right frequency and length to coincide with the natural oscillation of the electrons in the material's atoms. These artificial waves agitated and magnified the electron pulse in the atoms, and each atom would then burst, part of it converted to an unknown and undetectable gas, and part to a light powder.

Knowing (with theoretical certainty) that electromagnetic waves with such a structure were harmless to people, Kreuzkopf aimed his machine at the foundation pit and put it into operation, saying not a word. And he sowed death among the people.

It was strange that the investigator did not see Kreuzkopf as a criminal: his tormented heart was plainly to be seen on his face and in his eyes.

The work was resumed, but it went slowly and Kreuzkopf did not hurry the workers. But soon another snag was encountered, having nothing to do with Kreuzkopf: large amounts had been embezzled from the project's funding, and the treasurer and division manager had vanished. Kreuzkopf was accused of administrative negligence and even, in a particularly foul denunciation, of complicity.

Kreuzkopf made no effort to defend himself. The work was suspended. The government appointed a Special Technical Commission to review the entire project, and Kreuzkopf was convicted and sentenced to solitary confinement for a year.

4. THE INVENTOR IN PRISON

Once in his cell, Kreuzkopf began to collect himself. For long weeks he lay on his bunk and thought. Summer burned out, the leaves fell, Erna was in Brussels, Goga Femm was in his grave, and those forty workers had also turned to dust. All he had ahead of him was a dead dream – the lunar mission.

Kreuzkopf fell ill with some sort of intestinal disease. He was transferred to the prison hospital. Inaudibly, wearing shoes, autumn trod through nature along the fallen leaves.

As he convalesced, Kreuzkopf took walks along the hallway on the third floor of the hospital. The hall ended at an open window looking out on a quiet park where belated birds were singing.

Kreuzkopf went up to the open window and looked for a long time at the dwindling twilight air and the agony of the plant life. Then all at once, without a running start, he threw himself out the window. His prison cap flew from his head, and his dressing gown covered both him and the guard on whom Kreuzkopf had fallen. After plunging unexpectedly into a soft body, Kreuzkopf choked on his own blood as it gushed from his broken lungs. But he knew that he was alive. The guard lay dead beneath him, with his feet resting on his own head, broken in half at his pelvis.

Kreuzkopf was convicted again for his escape attempt and for murdering the guard, and was sentenced to eight years including the time served for his previous crime. Kreuzkopf could not prove that he had been seeking a tight grave, not a free life.

Time became hazy and inexhaustible: days passed like years, and weeks passed, slowly, like generations. Kreuzkopf was doomed. He developed the art of not thinking, not feeling, not counting time, not hoping, and hardly living: this made it easier by a thread.

The engineers' association in his country petitioned the government to consider reducing Kreuzkopf's sentence in order to finish building the Lunar Bomb. The government was still waiting for the findings of the Special Technical Committee's review of the project as a whole.

Snow was on the ground. Kreuzkopf was corroding his brain and growing deadened and savage. The Special Committee completed its work: the design was valid, and as long as the bomb did not encounter any stray meteors on its way to the Moon, the missile would be able to reach the lunar periphery and return, though it would be impossible to foresee all that might occur on the interplanetary route. The Special Committee took the liberty of stating its opinion that Kreuzkopf, as an engineer, had exceptional creative talent and was extremely knowledgeable.

The government agreed to release Kreuzkopf on bail to the Engineers' Association. The whole country was pleased with the government's decision. All believed Kreuzkopf to be a rare genius combined with a fearsome antisocial creature, a murderer and mysterious vagabond, but that regardless he should be given the chance to complete the Lunar Bomb. Public opinion was driven not by compassion but by curiosity.

Kreuzkopf was freed. He took a long time to adjust and had difficulty recalling that which had once been habitual.

The work began anew. Kreuzkopf was now in charge of the purely technical and design work. The chief engineer was another person: the electrical engineer Nimt, Erna's second husband. Nimt had gained the trust of the government and the Engineers' Association and was now making a career out of Kreuzkopf's fashionable project.

Kreuzkopf was incapable of relating to the things around him properly and tactfully. He was indifferent to all the change, interested only in the matter of lunar research, and he performed his work steadily, diligently, and automatically. He had developed a somnolent nature, and he spent all his non-working hours sleeping alone at home. After prison, solitude had become his passion. He found it burdensome to interact with people at work, and he did not go into town. Nimt behaved cordially with him, but remained vague and distant.

Erna did not visit the construction site once. She lived with Nimt in the city.

5. IN THE CAPITAL OF METALWORK

At last the missile was ready. It had taken a long time to get the launching disk installed with exact precision: the disk was to be installed at a particular angle to the geometrical surface of the earth, and this angle needed to be adhered to with absolute stringency, since the disk's angle of inclination would determine the Lunar Bomb's flight path.

In spring the work was halted for five months to await the new fiscal year and the second half of the funding, as the money for the current year had been used up.

Nimt went abroad with Erna to Kissingen. Kreuzkopf was given paid leave until the work could be restarted. He went to the famous electrometallurgy plants in Stuasept. He was interested in the plants' experiments with extraction of deep iron ore in the Aldagan foothills.

The plant directors gave Kreuzkopf a letter of introduction to the chief engineer in Aldagan, and he set off. It was 4000 kilometers away. Kreuzkopf went by train. The train was pulled not by a steam engine but by a gas engine, which had replaced the short-lived locomotive.

The gas locomotive consisted of a gas engine on wheels. The whole undercarriage was the same as that of a steam locomotive, but the cylinders used compressed air instead of steam: the energy from the engine's gas generator was transferred pneumatically to the driving wheels. The gas locomotive was the least expensive engine for transportation: it operated using gas produced by coal, wood, peat, straw, oil shale, brown coal and other poorly burning coals, and any sort of smoldering waste from which combustible gas could be wrung.

The gas locomotive pulled with it two storage cars containing the strongly compressed gas which the engine used for power. Small gas plants were placed every 300 to 400 kilometers, producing gas from whatever cheap fuel was underfoot nearby. The gas locomotives collected gas from these plants as steam engines used to collect water from water tanks at water stations.

Compared to a steam engine, the gas locomotive hauled four times cheaper. Kreuzkopf was interested in these machines, entered so quickly into use for transportation, and he happily watched through the window as the gas locomotives took steep slopes without losing any speed at all.

A year had now passed since Kreuzkopf had first arrived in the capital. It was summer again. Heat hummed in the expanses of fields, and the farmer's hard work fought fiercely with the heat for the moisture of the plants, for the satiety of the big cities, and for the lunar flight.

Kreuzkopf had noticeably gone gray, aged, and lost his childlike interest in unnecessary things. He felt as if he were waning, as if he had few years left, and life, the rarest of events, was stealing away from him.

Kreuzkopf would have liked to have a friend, a quiet heart-to-heart conversation, and that simple warmth that speaks indistinctly of kinship and compassion among people. But he lived in a dusky dream. People respected him and kept him at a distance. He was considered unusual, both for his genius and for his crime, but Kreuzkopf was a normal, simple person. Abstractions and lofty coldness were alien and hateful to him. He liked ardent action, not celestial contemplation.

On the second day the train entered a country composed of fearful slopes and valleys: the foothills of the great Aldagan range, which arose out of the tropical sea and vanished into the icy abyss of the Arctic Ocean.

Stuasept Station, and a kilometer away was the capital of metalwork: the directorate of the iron ore industry, the mining academy, the board of the electrometallurgy plants, and a million-kilowatt hydroelectric power facility.

Kreuzkopf went right to the worksite for extraction of deep ore. The administrators greeted him simply and sincerely. The mining engineers had before them a leading expert from a different field, and nothing more.

Everyone knows that mining iron ore 300 meters deep is not economically justifiable, but here they were conducting trials to prove otherwise. The hydroelectric station generated a current of hundreds of thousands of horsepower for the electromagnets, whose poles were aimed at underground iron ore deposits.

Giant chunks of ore, howling and roaring like the thundering of an earthquake, tore through the earth's shell and flew out to the daylight surface, trying to reach the pole of the electromagnet. When the ore broke through the last layer of soil cover, a special device cut the current in the electromagnet and the electromagnet was moved aside. Then the boulders of ore tore out from the depths with a scorching wind heated by friction against other rocks, flew a hundred meters, and fell to their mother earth, burrowing in slightly.

A self-propelled hoist lifted the pieces of ore in a pincer-type bucket, dipped them in a pond for cooling, and lifted them onto a conveyor belt. The conveyor belt then delivered the ore to a blast furnace.

Despite the enormous amount of force needed to extract the ore from below the earth using the electromagnet, this force was only in use for a few moments, and then the electromagnets were charged by current from the energy of water falling through the dam. Thus the deep ore came out costing no more than the shallow ore mined using conventional methods. And there was something monstrous and unnatural in metal that flew out from under the earth, grinding and anguished on the way.

In the evening Kreuzkopf ate dinner with the supervising engineer for magnetic mining, whose name was Skorb. A calm, middle-aged man and one of the designers of the powerful mining electromagnets, Skorb had a quiet temperament and a fierce capacity for work. Skorb was alone. His family, a wife and two daughters, had drowned in the mountain river's spring floods twenty years ago. Skorb then took his vengeance on the river: he built regulating structures on it that made any flooding impossible. And since then Skorb had lived alone, not counting the thousand electricians, metalworkers, mechanics, and miners, all good friends of Skorb's.

After spending the night with Skorb, Kreuzkopf left for the capital. The gas locomotive once again sputtered into action, and the wheels began to murmur. The lush summer floated in the eternal shining of the sun.

6. FLIGHT OF THE "LUNAR BOMB"

After arriving home at the dead construction site, Kreuzkopf did not know what to do: it would still be at least four months until the work could begin again. And so he unwittingly took to reading. Once he bought a book at a tent by an ancient wall, went home, turned on the light, opened the book, and there saw:

I am kin to grass and beast,
And to the burning star;
I believe in your breath
And the evening heights…

After that there were some rather dull words, but then once more:

I am not wise, but am in love,
I do not hope, but pray.
I am forgiven for everything,
I do not know things, but I love.

Kreuzkopf was entirely gripped by enchantment with this indistinct thought, a thought mixed with ardent and mournful feeling. He read and read, as the room grew yellow from dawn and electricity. That day he bought another dozen and a half books, judging them to be interesting simply by their titles, which included: *A Journey in Reeking Gas* by Burbar; *Blue Roads* by Vogulov; Schott's *Time of Zenith*; *The Anthropomorphic Revolution* by Zag-Zagger, *Moon Fire* by Ferrent, Berkman's *Antisexus*; *Has History Always Existed, and Will It Continue, and What Is It in the End Anyway?*, the philosophy of Gorgond, as well as a few others.

Kreuzkopf was struck by the world of books. He had never had time for reading. He washed and scoured his brain, which had been oppressed by suffering, monotonous work, and mute anguish. He saw entirely new people, gloomy, burning, moving, roaring with passion and ecstasy, perishing in the expanse of thought, triumphing in a square meter in a stone niche in a wall, seeking a righteous land and finding a desert, wandering the sand and stumbling onto water, leaving for countries of fanatics, trading the warmth of home for the wind of a nighttime road…

People passed before Kreuzkopf not as a mass, but as wanderers, beggars, vagabonds rambling blindfolded. Kreuzkopf unexpectedly discovered that literature knows no happiness, while happiness itself, wherever it be found, only foretells coming trouble, an earthquake of the soul.

The harvest was already underway in Kreuzkopf's country. Straw burned in the furnaces of field engines and threshed the grain. The leaves fell from the trees for the goats to chew on. Snakes swallowed berries and made the birds flutter in the trees. A multitude of children was born from the harvest, and good writers appeared. Broadcloth mills were built, and fruits and vegetables were prepared in advance for the winter.

The new fiscal year began. The board of directors for construction of the Lunar Bomb disbursed the second half of the estimated cost of the work. Kreuzkopf, Nimt, and five hundred laborers got to work.

Week after week passed in exhausting labor, labor that required extraordinary precision, in which the conquest of the Moon depended on every thread of every nut.

The launching disk was completed. The "Lunar Bomb" had long been ready. The electric motor, the transmission, and all the gauges and breakers were installed. All that remained was to place all the research equipment and the securing hardware on the missile itself.

This was done quickly. The Construction Board was disbanded and replaced by a Science Office for Lunar Research. It was directed by a famous astrophysicist, Academician Lesuren, with Nimt staying on as his deputy director for technology. Kreuzkopf, as before, was named the design engineer.

The Science Office set the launch date for 19-20 March precisely at astronomical midnight. This was the time at which the Moon was in the most favorable position for aiming the launch. At midnight on 20 March the missile would be automatically released from the rotating disk and the Lunar Bomb would fly in the direction of our satellite. Then, eighty-one hours later, it would return to Earth and land near the city of Koro-Korotanga.

In pursuit of a sensation, the newspapers wrote about the mission in such detail that both Lesuren and Nimt were careful at first to send corrections of printed items, but then they gave it up, reasoning that newspapers are not made for news and accurate information, they are a habit, like a smoke for the tired brain.

"The whole world" came to the launch site of the Lunar Bomb. The government was in no mood for superfluous expenses, so it limited itself to construction of a huge circus arena around the structure.

Kreuzkopf pondered. It was the tenth of March and the launch date was coming soon. If equipment were added to the Bomb to produce oxygen and absorb carbon dioxide, a person could go up with it. After all, the flight was only to last eighty-one hours.

Kreuzkopf appealed to the Science Office for Lunar Research, stating his desire to fly to the Moon on the Bomb, and argued in detail for the utility of adding a living person to the Bomb.

The Science Office sent Kreuzkopf's appeal to the Government, which rejected it. Kreuzkopf wrote a second appeal: "The Government did not purchase the patent for the Lunar Bomb from me, and I, Kreuzkopf, remain the only person who knows the details of the design. I do not give my permission for my invention to be placed into operation, and, in practical terms, no one will know how to activate it properly without me. I, Kreuzkopf, also refuse to accept any monetary compensation. I exchange my compensation for the chance to fly in the Bomb."

According to the patent laws in effect in the country, Kreuzkopf was perfectly right. He had left the government no way out, and it gave consent for him to board the Lunar Bomb.

The news of Kreuzkopf's flight on the Lunar Bomb caused a stir in society. But soon everyone decided that this was a dramatic suicidal gesture. On 19 March, at eight o'clock in the evening, Kreuzkopf boarded the Bomb. Kreuzkopf boarded and the missile was sealed at the workshop, after which the missile was taken at once to the disk. Kreuzkopf thereby deflected public attention away from himself. By ten o'clock the entire arena, out to the very last tiers, was full.

There was abundant lighting and music, vendors sold water, kvass and ice cream, and taxi cabs waited on duty – the usual accompaniment to a rare event.

Three minutes before astronomical midnight they started rotating the disk. The electric engine roared. Five giant fans sent whole clouds of cold air through the motor as it hummed and heated up, and the air flew out the other side dry, harsh, and scorching, like a desert cyclone. The oil in the machines was cooled with icy sprays from turbine pumps, and still an acrid smoke hovered around the disk and the whole structure. The bearings were heated to excess, and oil burned in ice.

Despite its precise placement and flawless installation, the disk rumbled like artillery and a volcanic eruption, so great was the number of revolutions. Smoke came from the edge of the disk, which was starting to burn from air friction.

Nimt was numb with fear: the slightest failure of the tiny detaching device at this moment would cause an untold catastrophe: the disk was operating in the vicinity of hundreds of thousands of living spectators...

The meter was now showing the number of rotations required for launch: 946,000 per minute. A half-second remained before the missile would detach from the disk. At 24:00 the astronomical clock would connect the current controlling the detacher. This device would release the Bomb from the disk, and the Bomb would take flight due to the kinetic force it had accumulated during its time on the disk.

Nimt set the rotation controller to maintain speed: the calculated rate had been reached.

The beacons on the launch pad started shining at once: the signal that the Bomb had taken flight. No one noticed the moment of the launch itself. The missile's initial speed was incomprehensibly high, and human sensation is powerless when the technological spirit of humanity breaks nature.

The disk continued to turn from inertia after Nimt disconnected it from the driving clutch plate. Only four hours later was it possible to stop the rotation using the full force of the magnetic brakes' death grip.

Around fifteen thousand spectators lost their hearing, and another ten thousand sustained some sort of nerve contusions. No one had expected to see such a wild, impassioned elemental force, roaring like judgment day, in the form of a technological device.

7. MESSAGES FROM INTERPLANETARY SPACE

The Lunar Bomb was equipped with a specially designed radio. This radio was to be used for receiving messages from Kreuzkopf roughly every hour (Kreuzkopf could not have a watch), and the waves from the radio could be used to determine the interplanetary position of the Bomb from Earth.

All information from Kreuzkopf was received by the Office of Lunar Research in the person of Lesuren himself, and it was Lesuren who personally performed all the calculations of the Bomb's position and carried out the tracking of it.

The journalists had been paid for the special editions and were now turning their money into beer. However, the first day after the launch one newspaper did present an article on Kreuzkopf entitled "In Search of a Grave," which foretold the destruction of both Kreuzkopf and the Lunar Bomb.

Here are Kreuzkopf's reports from interplanetary space, in sequential order:

1. Nothing to report. The instruments show a coal black sky. The stars are unbelievably bright. There was weak friction between the missile and something else. The instruments could not find the cause. I feel free. I am reading a book called *Manor House* by Andrei Novikov, which I happen to have brought. It's an interesting work.

2. A lot of blue flame passed by the Lunar Bomb. I can't say the reason. There was no increase in temperature.

3. The flight continues. I feel no movement, of course. The instruments and equipment are working. Send my greetings to Skorb in Aldagan.

4. The Moon is falling on my Bomb. A small fireball sped by parallel to the missile in the same direction. The Lunar Bomb passed it.

5. The Bomb is moving in sharp bursts. Strange forces are contorting its path, tossing it up and down, and making it very hot, though there should be only ether all around.

6. The bursts are getting stronger. I can feel the movement. The instruments are ringing from the vibration. The landscape of the universe looks like a painting by the long dead iurlionis: the stars are crying out in the cosmic ocean.

7. The oscillation continues. The stars are physically rattling as they tear along their paths. Their movement is, of course, agitating the electromagnetic environment, and my universal radio receiver is turning the waves into songs. Report that I am at the source of earthly poetry: someone on Earth conjectured about celestial symphonies and excitedly wrote verse. Tell people that the song of stars has a physical existence. And tell them that there is a symphony here, not a cacophony. Send as many people as possible up on interplanetary bombs to the heavens: it's frightful, exciting, and everything makes sense. Invent receivers for this celestial sound.

8. The flight is calm now, no shaking. Half of space is filled with purple rays that flow like moisture. What this is I do not know.

9. I have discovered an electromagnetic ocean all around.

10. There is no hope of returning to Earth. I am flying in a blue dawn. The instruments measure the electricity in the environment at 80,000 volts.

11. The Moon is approaching. Voltage is 2 million. Darkness.

12. An abyss of electricity. The instruments are in chaos. Fantastic things happening. The sun is roaring and small comets screech as they run by: you can't see or hear anything through the mica of the atmosphere.

13. Clouds of meteors. Judging by the shining, and by the electromagnetic effects, they are metal. Fires or lights are shining on the larger meteors, shining with a flickering light. I've seen nothing shaking here.

14. The environment of the electromagnetic waves where I am has the property of evoking within me powerful, irresistible, and uncontrolled thoughts. I cannot cope with this whispering. I'm no longer in control of my own brain, though I'm fighting it so much I'm sweating heavily. But I can't think what I want to or about what I want to, I keep thinking of what I do not know, I remember events, breaks in clouds, the sun bursting through – I remember everything as if it occurred and is true, but none

of this happened to me. I am thinking of two distinct subjects awaiting me on a rugged hill where there are two decayed pillars with frozen milk on them. I continually want to drink and save my canned food. I nibble at a fish, but want to eat a whole shark. I am trying to conquer these thoughts born from electricity that penetrate into my brain like lice into a sleeping body.

15. I just returned from steep mountains where I saw a world of mummies lying in ragged grass... [Signals unintelligible – Lesuren]. Everything is clear: the Moon is 100 kilometers away. Its effect on my brain is terrifying. My thoughts are not my own. They are induced by the Moon. Do not consider what I said before sane. I am lying here a pale body: the Moon is continually feeding me incandescent mental power. It seems as if the missile is thinking as well, and the radio is murmuring comprehensibly of its own accord.

16. The Moon is passing by at forty kilometers: desert, dead mineral, and platinum haze. I am passing by slowly, no more than fifty kilometers per hour, judging by eye.

17. The Moon has hundreds of cracks. A sparse green or blue gas is coming out of these cracks... I have regained control of myself and have acclimated.

18. The gas is coming out of some of the cracks like a maelstrom. Is this a natural element or the mind of a living being? Probably a mind. The moon is one enormous, monstrous brain.

19. I cannot figure out the reasons for the eruptions of gas. It seems I will have to open the hatch of my Bomb and jump out. It will be easier for me. I'm going blind in the darkness inside the missile, and I am tired of seeing the wide open expanse of the universe only through the peepholes of instruments.

20. I am going inside the clouds of lunar eruptions. Millennia have passed since I separated from the Earth. Are the people to whom I am signaling these words still alive? Can you hear me? [19 hours have passed since Kreuzkopf took off – Lesuren.]

21. The Moon is beneath me. My Bomb is descending. The cracks in the Moon are emitting gas. I cannot hear the passage of the stars anymore.

22. Tell everyone, tell them that people have been horribly mistaken. The world is not what they know it to be. Can you not see the disaster in the Milky Way: there is a roaring blue cross-stream. It is not a nebula or a star cluster…

23. The Bomb is descending. I am opening the hatch to find a way out. Farewell.

First published in Russian: 1926
Translation by Keith Blasing

RAYS OF LIFE

(EXCERPT)

Chapter 17: "The Curve Shoots Upwards"

Among the various instruments that were helping to bring Anna back to life, there was one whose function did not become clear to Nikolai until later. It seemed to be an ordinary electrocardiogram, an instrument for measuring the heartbeat. It consisted of a small box with a round eye that glowed green, and inside the green was a dark shadow in the shape of a butterfly. By observing the pulsations of the butterfly's wings, one could follow the heart's "action current," as Ridan called it.

In and of itself, this apparatus did not present any particular mystery: its construction, which was based on the principle of cathode oscillations, was clear. The beats of the heart were transmitted to the machine by two wires, which were in turn attached to electrodes glued to either side of the chest cavity.

The device had been turned on as soon as they took Anna out of the cylinder and laid her on the operating table. By that time, over three days had passed since the moment of her death. Yet immediately the cardiograph's "butterfly" had started to furl and unfurl her trembling wings. In this dead, immobile heart a charged electrical life was still pulsing. Therefore, the heart wasn't completely dead! Some kind of life was still there after all!

Now Nikolai started to understand Ridan's musings about "real" and "false" death. What we are used to calling death is not really death. It's just a pause. The remarkable scientist Bakhmetyev, working with anabiosis, was right: an organism that has been struck down by death is actually like a clock, whose pendulum has been stopped by a hand.[1] All you need to do is push the pendulum, and the clock starts to tick again. Ridan took this concept even further.

"Real, irrevocable death arrives only at the moment when the proteins that make up living tissue fall apart," he reiterated. "If that hasn't happened yet, then life can be resurrected. If the cause of death is the destruction of one of the organs – whether a lung, a heart, or a stomach, then that organ can be removed and replaced with a new, healthy one, often taken from an animal – and the whole organism will live again. That's the theory. And we have already advanced to the practical application of theory. We were able to do so thanks to the 'conserving apparatus' that you, Nikolai, have invented. Soon we will arrive at a time when death 'by accident,' that is, by the failing of this or that organ, will no longer exist. We will create reserves of live organs that are ready to function, and we will use them as necessary, just as today we use the preserved blood of those who have died for transfusions to those who are still living. Futhermore, Nikolai Arsentievich, I am certain that this very condition, which up

---

1. The Russian biologist Porfirii Bakhmetyev (1860-1913) experimented extensively with methods to induce anabiosis, a state of suspended animation at extremely low temperatures, in insects, fish, and bats. Research on anabiosis continued, although with less public fanfare, well into the Soviet period. Nikolai Krementsov discusses Bakhmetyev's notable career in *Revolutionary Dreams: The Quest for Immortality in Russian Science and Fiction* (Oxford, 2011). Matthias Schwartz provides the fullest account of Dolgushin's novel and its contemporary contexts in *Expeditionen in Andere Welten* (Berlin 2014).

until now we called death – and rushed to bury or burn the body – we will come to understand as the opposite: one of the most powerful healing methods at our disposal."

"What?" said Nikolai, who was completely taken aback by this progression in Ridan's prognosis. "We are going to heal by death?"

"Yes, heal by death. The dead can't be sick. All illnesses depend on the functioning of living organisms. Temporary death, with very few exceptions, closes down all bodily functions and cuts off everything that feeds the pathological process. It stops the disease."

"And when the person is resurrected, and bodily functions resume, the illness will pick up where it left off?"

"No. Once the pathological process has been cut off, an external force or infection is required to restart the process. A functioning organism is only capable of supporting illness, it can't initiate it."

In these conversations, Nikolai was always deeply struck by the novelty of Ridan's ideas. Ridan's fanatical faith in the power of human reason was contagious. Nikolai needed this inspiring faith now more than ever, because when he was left alone with his own thoughts, he was ready to fall back into doubt and despair, to lose hope again.

Another night and another day had passed since the last little golden sparks of happiness had danced in Nikolai's heart, which was darkened by doubts. He had hoped that it would be just a few more moments – and Anna would look up at him, smile, and recognize his love, which he had for so long kept hidden both from her and from himself....

None of that had happened. For days Anna lay on the operating table with a beating heart and quietly breathing chest – yet still as immobile as ever, still completely lifeless. As before, her eyelids were slightly opened, but they only fluttered in response to a touch. There were no signs of consciousness.

"What is happening?" asked Nikolai, with a despairing glance at Ridan.

"Nothing," he said, and Nikolai sensed the same sense of anxiety in his voice. "We'll have to wait..." Ridan looked for any opportunity to distract himself from the doubts that threatened to overcome him, so he talked, and talked… "In the animals that I brought back to life after a ten-minute death, the brain resumed its functions within seven or eight minutes. Simka the ape was also dead for about ten minutes, but it took twenty hours for him to come back to consciousness. I think that the more complex the brain of the organism, the more deeply its cells are damaged by carbon-dioxide poisoning at death. After all, death is accompanied by the cessation of oxygen to the brain, oxygen that the blood conveys from the lungs to the brain. It's quite possible that the brain of a person takes much longer to restore. We'll have to wait…"

At nine in the evening, Natasha telephoned to the operating room to say that Vikling had arrived.

"Ah, Vikling!" answered Ridan. "Take him to the cafeteria, I'll be there shortly."

Nikolai had expected this call and followed Professor Ridan.

"Are you really thinking of meeting with Vikling?" he asked.

"Of course."

"No, Konstantin Alexandrovich, you will not go. I'm sorry, but this part of the set-up has been vouchsafed to me. Everything is prepared, and your appearance is not part of the program. It would be insane to subject you to this danger. Vikling is perfectly aware that Anna's life is in your hands, and, at the last minute, if he sees that he can't save himself, he may do something unexpected."

"Sure, maybe," Ridan shrugged, "meeting with him does not exactly flatter me."

Meanwhile, in the cafeteria, the silent drama was already starting to unfold.

Natasha had been initiated into our secret a few days earlier. Since then, she had mostly stopped crying, but her mood had grown darker. A feeling of insult had compounded her pain: why had Ridan hidden from her what he was doing with Anna until now?

When Nikolai explained everything to her and told her that Anna was still breathing, Natasha looked mistrustfully at him with her dark, searching eyes; then, with sudden comprehension, she laughed, threw herself at Nikolai and sobbed on his chest. This was happiness, and from that moment on, her grief disappeared. Without any hesitations or doubts, she was immediately convinced that Anna would return to life, and everything would be as it was before.

When Nikolai told her about Vikling's arrival, her emotions boiled to the surface just as violently.

"I sensed this would happen! I hated him from the very beginning! How could you all have believed him, when in his every movement and every word, something rings false!

She triumphantly swore to Nikolai that she would not give herself away in even the slightest gesture as she welcomed Vikling. And now she was leading him into the cafeteria.

"Please, have a seat, Alfred."

He sat down, still crumpled with sadness, warily glancing into Natasha's eyes.

"How is Anya, Natasha? You, probably, already know something…"

Oh, how hard it was to resist temptation! The desire to torture this despicable person, to toy with him like a cat with a mouse, was so strong; she wanted to start a conversation full of innocent hints that would alarm him terribly. It would be so easy now to make him sense his own impending doom, to get revenge for his betrayal, his crime, for everything… No, she did not have the right, she had promised.

"I don't know a thing," she answered unexpectedly loudly.

That was a signal. Vikling saw the door directly in front of him open suddenly, and a man in an army camouflage shirt quickly stepped out of the room and stood by the wall. Vikling recognized the man and broke out into a cold sweat. Then he noticed the revolver in the man's hand…

Vikling glanced around rapidly. There were three doors in the room. Next to each one stood a person with a weapon. Yet another person emerged out of Nikolai's room and walked directly towards Vikling, calmly and confidently.

"Alfred Vikling, if I am not mistaken?" he asked politely.

"Yes, that's me! What kind of ridiculous mystification is this?" Vikling cried, growing pale.

"I am from the Operations Division of the People's Commissariat for State Security. I have orders to arrest you. Kindly raise your hands… Search him," he ordered.

"Wait a minute!" Vikling objected. "There must be some kind of mistake. On what grounds do you arrest me?"

"I can tell you on what grounds. You are accused of the attempted murder of Anna Ridan."

"What nonsense! Natasha, you know how things happened. Call the professor…"

"The Professor is busy," said Nikolai as he entered the cafeteria, "and he asked me to convey to you that he cannot help you in any way. He himself agrees with the charges brought against you, based on information obtained directly from Anna Konstantinova."

The last words Nikolai uttered struck Vikling like a bolt of lightening. His eyes grew wide, his knees buckled, and one could see how much effort it cost him to take the first step towards the door…

Three more days passed in anxious anticipation. Anna lay in the same condition – at least, so it seemed to Nikolai – and once again his hopes changed to despair.

Ridan, on the other hand, continued with his observations, analyses, and experiments, and each day he detected new signs of awakening life in the organism of his daughter. Her somatic system had already reestablished itself. Her digestive organs had started to work, supplying her blood with the products of miraculously transformed proteins, carbohydrates, and fats, all of which Ridan delivered to her stomach in complex solutions. Anna's half-open eyelids, which frightened Nikolai more than anything else, finally closed. Her whole body was ready for movement. A few peripheral muscles started to twitch on their own, as if preparing their strength for much more significant contractions.

Yet still no "orders" came from her higher organs. The complicated departments of her brain, containing the secrets of thought and the enigma of consciousness, were silent. She was in a deep, unconscious sleep.

"Don't worry, Nikolai Aresentievich, we will wait, hope, and keep at it," Ridan said repeatedly, which did not do much to boost poor Nikolai's fading hopes.

On the other hand, released from the sharpest pangs of bitter grief, Nikolai finally recalled his interaction with the German, with the last radiogram that he sent to Ufa. At the time, Nikolai did not know that this communist sympathizer and underground antifascist activist was named Hans Rickert.[2] As Nikolai deciphered the text of the radiogram, he became convinced that the fascists had tried to set up an airwaves defense system to intercept the German underground's communications. True, they had not been able to pinpoint Hans' exact location; it's not that simple; an experienced operative who knows he is being hunted can always throw off his pursuers. Still, they managed to once again block Hans' messages. All he could do was repeat with alarmed insistence that the Germans fascists intended to attack the Soviet Union, and then add a few more words to the explanation of Gross's method that he had begun previously. In short, there was still no clarity. He had not said a word about whether the fascists had gotten Gross's machine to work again, and Nikolai was more and more convinced that they hadn't: Gross's colleague had blown up the blueprints and the model along with himself in that Munich explosion.

---

2. We know from previous chapters that an apolitical, Jules Verne-like German inventor named Gross has invented a machine quite similar to Ridan and Nikolai's machine, a "generator of miracles" that uses electromagnetic waves to stimulate processes in the brain and body. Whereas the Soviets want to use this machine to create "rays of life" (e.g., healing cancers, bringing moribund bodies back from the threshold of death), the Germans want to create "rays of death." Vikling's job as a spy was to track Soviet progress on perfecting this technology. The "Munich explosion" was a sabotage act perpetrated by communist workers in Munich to halt the death rays' production.

Vikling knew nothing about all of this beyond what had been reported in the papers. All he was supposed to do was get the encryption key so that they could decode the messages coming out of Munich. Instead, as it emerged in the conversation Nikolai had with the prosecutor, Vikling, apparently devastated by the thought that Anna might come back to life, lost hope in getting off scot-free. He fled. Of course, Vikling would hardly have believed in Anna's miraculous resurrection if not for the prosecutor's carefully planted mention of the information Ridan had obtained through the "generator of miracles." Nobody had access to those facts except Vikling himself and Anna!

The prosecutor got the impression that Vikling was genuinely remorseful for his espionage and sabotage activities – he was so eager to expose himself and everyone who had been involved, from Moscow to the factory in the Urals.

Vikling turned out to be the son of a powerful Moscow financier who had emigrated during the first days of the Revolution. Masquerading as a German named "Alfred Vikling" enabled him to easily "escape" back to the Soviet Union from Germany in 1936. This was the Gestapo's trick: the real Alfred Vikling, who was a fairly well-known member of the German anti-fascist intelligentsia, had been secretly captured and, in all likelihood, executed. It would have been nearly impossible to unmask the switch, since both the real and the false Vikling had the same profession, and they were remarkably similar in their physical appearance. In fact, when the Gestapo handed over the real Vikling's documents to the spy Vikling, they didn't even bother to change the identifying photographs. Furthermore, the "new" Vikling was assigned to go undercover as an embedded spy, so for many years he did not engage in any espionage functions at all. His only task was to find a foothold in Soviet society, acquire people's trust and an appropriate position – a task at which he excelled.

Yes, he was determined to "win over" Anna Ridan as well. Not only for professional reasons…

His first explicit assignments were to participate in the sabotage operation in the Ural factory, and to intercept Nikolai's radio communications. These missions did not fall on fertile soil. "Vikling" was no longer the person he had been, and he acted unwillingly; his earlier anti-Soviet convictions had dimmed considerably during the time spent living in his original homeland. Only the fear of death was stronger. Anna's murder, which he committed in a fit of insane fear, along with his subsequent exposure and arrest, was simply too great a burden for him to bear. He "gave up" and revealed everything that could possibly be useful to those who protected the safety of the Soviet Union.

Nikolai did not tell any of this to the professor, so as not to divert him from his stressful work. He didn't tell Natasha, either. Why cloud Natasha's mood by revealing these terrible memories, when all her grief had immediately turned to boundless joy when she saw her one and only sister coming back to life? A lucky person! Natasha was capable of simply loving, simply suffering, and just as simply rejoicing, without allowing unnecessary doubts to color her pure feelings. Now she simply believed that Anna would live again, and she threw herself into helping Ridan.

Whereas Nikolai… poor Nikolai! It was not at all easy for such a reticent person, finally touched by love just as it was tragically snatched from him. Fate had pulled him into this terrible maelstrom, buffeted him from side to side, first by tempting him with imminent happiness, then by meting out a terrible blow…

He was completely derailed. Days went by – endless, dark, hopeless days. Never before had he felt so empty, and so useless. He couldn't work. He couldn't help Ridan, other than taking turns with Natasha watching over Anna. He tried to read, conscientiously leafing through the pages, only to realize that he hadn't retained a thing…

Sometimes he started to think about his own behavior, and then he couldn't understand what was happening to him. Why was he not able to do anything that didn't relate to Anna? How could Natasha, sitting in the same place by Anna's bedside, carry on with reading her textbooks, solving problems, or sewing something? How did Aunt Pasha take on all the tasks of caring for the family, without missing a thing, and only allowing herself to occasionally interrupt her cleaning to stare intently at Anna's completely immobile face?

"Apparently the professor is right, something is wrong with my nerves," Nikolai concluded. "Or else I just have an unfortunate personality…"

On the morning of the tenth day a band of murky clouds stretched along the eastern horizon. The grey dawn broke slowly. The barometer fell.

Ridan sent Natasha off to sleep and stayed alone with Anna. Last night her body had been wracked by some kind of tumultuous process of awakening. Isolated tremors and the twitching of individual muscles suddenly become much more intense and convulsed her whole body. It was as if her muscles were quivering from the desire to move freely. The process continued for an hour and a half. Then, suddenly, all movement ceased. Anna once again lay in a deep, motionless sleep, seemingly even deeper than her previous slumber…

Ridan sat next to her and tried to figure out what had happened. Was it a step on the path to reanimating the functions of the brain, or, on the contrary, a burst of activity like death throes – after which everything goes backwards, towards death…

By ten in the morning, the clouds had spread over Moscow, the first streaks of lightening rent the sky; in the garden the dusty trees began to sway, welcoming the desired storm. The rain poured down in sheets, full of lightening, thunder, and wind.

Morose and unshaven, Ridan abruptly tore himself away from his thoughts, went to the window and flung it open. The sharp scent of storm tore into the operating room. A clap of thunder resounded with a dry crack, and the rain slanted down like a golden curtain.

Ridan approached Anna again.

He saw… Maybe it just seemed that he saw it? Of late, his exhausted eyes often betrayed him… No, he saw, and he heard, a deep exhale, the first to disturb the far too even rhythm of her calm breathing. Next her lips moved, and lightly parted…

Nikolai awoke to the ring of the telephone and grabbed the receiver before he was even fully awake.

"Come here! Natie too!" the voice was exultant. Nikolai understood. Pulling on his clothes as he went, he ran into the operating room.

Natasha caught up with him at the doorway, barefoot and in her robe. Ridan, without saying a word, moved to the side, as if ceding to them a place near the table. They bent over Anna, anxiously looking into her face, her lips, her wet eyelashes that had just closed….

"Anya," Natasha said softly but surely.

Suddenly her eyelids opened, and her brows raised slightly. Anna looked up, transferred her gaze to Nikolai, and then wearily closed her eyes again.

"Kolya…" – a barely audible whisper.

Beside himself with happiness, forgetting everything in the world, Nikolai planted a hot kiss on her cheek.

Natasha was frightened by this movement – maybe it was too much? – and taking his head gently in her hands, she moved it away. When they both turned around, Ridan was no longer in the room. Nikolai ran to the adjoining laboratory and found Ridan at the far side of the room, elbows propped up against the window sill, holding a handkerchief to his face. His shoulders were shaking.

People always strive for happiness.

Everyone understands happiness in their own way, everyone strives for it, chases it, waits for it, in their own way. But then it arrives, and within a few days, even within a few hours, we get used to it, so that, like the beating of our heart, we cease to feel it happening, it's just there. This is personal, local happiness. It is fleeting. You would think that nothing could be more dear than grasping back life, which gives us the ability to create joy, multiply it, instill happiness in others – how many times has it happened to nearly every one of us, that somehow we were able to swerve away from a crushing, fatal blow of fate, to remain alive? Did the happiness of life that we snatched and saved last long? No, just for a moment!

The Ridans' happiness, on the other hand, was boundless and wide, like an ocean; it buoyed them up with a seemingly endless power. Each of them felt it as their own personal happiness: Anna lives, Anna will live, there will be no more of the terrible grief that had gripped them before. The Ridans were transformed, as if they themselves had returned to life, their faces beamed. They no longer avoided each other's glances, as people stricken with grief will do; on the contrary, whenever they ran into each other they eagerly caught the other's eyes, in order to again burst with joy, embrace each other and squeeze each other's hands. They started to love each other more sincerely and more openly.

But they also recognized something else – that a miracle had occurred. After all, this *was* a miracle! What had previously been impossible had been made possible. Reason had achieved new power over nature. Ridan's miracle would be a gift to all of humanity. That is why their happiness flowed out like an ocean....

Anna did not get up immediately.

The first illumination of consciousness still lacked the full complexity, the organized memory of a normal mind. At first, there was only simple apprehension. There was also an unfathomable weakness, of the muscles and of the nervous system. After her first word, which Nikolai did not so much hear as intuit, Anna fell back into a deep sleep. Six hours later, she opened her eyes again. This time her eyes reflected fear, and her breathing betrayed agitation.

"Where… is he…," was all that her father managed to catch as he bent over her.

He understood. In just a few phrases, he relayed to Anna the most important information about Vikling. Anna calmed down.

Ridan did not let down his guard for a moment; he could not permit the tiniest mistake or allow for any complications. Anna was watched constantly – on his orders, somebody had to be by her side at all times, day and night. As before, he conducted daily analyses of her condition. Every morning, Ridan and his irreplaceable colleagues – Vikenty Sergeyevich and Ivan Lukich – checked over everything in Anna's system, squeezing, bending, knocking, and poking her weak body until they had an exquisite understanding of its internal process, and were able to take measures to correct any detected deviations.

One week after her first awakening, Anna began to learn how to walk again. After two weeks she was able to go into the garden for the first time. The analyses and check-ups ceased. Rehabilitation was proceeding at full force, and quite rapidly.

As soon as Anna had gained back enough strength, Ridan called in the criminal investigator, who had long waited for the opportunity to get needed testimony from the victim. For the first time, the Ridans heard from Anna the whole story of the horrible events in Ufa.

Nikolai could hardly wait to be alone with Anna after her meeting with the investigator. He was in agony and could barely contain himself. After all, they had still not breathed a single word to each other about the most important thing! Up until now, he had even concealed his glances in her direction, which burned with uncontrolled ardor. He was not sure if this was necessary, but he didn't want to risk upsetting her. After all, Ridan had strictly forbidden any mention of Vikling and the catastrophe in Ufa.

But now it was out!

The evening went by slowly. Nikolai sat alone in the dining room, holding up the newspaper, but all the while thinking about what Anna would say…

At about ten o'clock, Natasha emerged from Anna's room in a robe, with a towel in her hand. She looked at Nikolai in surprise.

"What are you waiting for? We don't have to watch her around the clock anymore, haven't you been told?"

"No, nobody said anything," Nikolai answered, and Natasha caught the agony in his voice. She smiled at him encouragingly.

"Go on. You have half an hour. I'm going to take a shower."

Nikolai walked over to her bedside silently, looking intently into Anna's eyes. It seemed to him that she read his thoughts and that her eyes were calling to him. Anna was also silent. Then she reached her hand out to him, exactly the gesture he had longed for. He took the weak, thin little hand with the long, slender fingers and pressed it to his cheek, to his whole face, and kissed it. Anna's eyes, huge and dark, followed him openly and seriously, as if barely able to take in all of what cannot be fully encompassed. She sat up and drew her knees to her chest.

"Today I told the investigator everything," she said. "Except I didn't mention the most important thing, because for him it's not relevant… It's not relevant for anyone except us… When I fell asleep there, behind the bushes, before Vikling showed up, I had a dream. I dreamt that I was standing in water, and the light was so blinding that I couldn't open my eyes and did not know where to go. I was scared, and I called out to you…. and you came, and lifted me up in your arms and carried me to the shore. And you said, 'This is how we will be together… forever together…' As soon as I woke up, I remembered this dream."

"Anyutka, my darling, that's exactly what I wanted to say to you today!"

He jumped up and without thinking grabbed her up in his arms along with the blanket, pressing her to him and kissing her. He carried her around the room. She seemed weightless.

"Is this what it was like, Anya?"

"Yes, exactly, Kolya! Does this mean – it will be forever?"

"Forever, Anyutka!"

"Me, too… forever! And now put me back down on the shore. And leave. There's nothing more we need to say today, isn't that true? Kolya, I'm so happy…"

"I am also happy, Anya. Sleep well… if that's possible."

He ran out of the room, feeling that at this moment, he absolutely needed to be alone.

First published in Russian: 1939/1958

Translation by Yvonne Howell

THE NUR-I-DESHT OBSERVATORY

Air hissed loudly through the brakes, and the even clanking of the wheels faded into a steady hum. Outside the train car window, a snow cloud of dust was swirling.

The conversation stopped abruptly, and a lieutenant colonel glanced out the window, now pink in the rays of the setting sun. But the train built up speed and barreled relentlessly forward, taking its passengers toward the new wartime fates that the new year, 1943, held in store for them.

A naval officer who had taken part in the conversation went out into the corridor and sat down on a folding bench, pondering the indelible cruelty of war, which leaves nothing unmarked. Ramshackle villages flashed by outside the window of the battered train car.

One of his compartment mates, a tall, young artillery major, stopped nearby. From their very first meeting, the naval officer had been struck by the controlled energy emanating from the major's entire dexterous and trim figure. His eyes, which seemed exceptionally bright against his darkly tanned face, were amazingly calm, but some force radiated from inside them that the naval officer had determined from the start to be a sign of unyielding joy in life that was well masked through a habit of self-restraint.

The major extended his hand.

"Lebedev," he introduced himself. "I overheard the conversation you were having with our neighbors and the hard time they were giving you. I liked your claim that people have a right to joy. I think the people who took the other side are right. But you, of course, are also right. Such is the dialectic of life. These days, people experience a sense of joy less frequently than other feelings… And then there's the fact that human joy can stem from causes that appear to be utterly inexplicable at first glance."

After a moment's hesitation he added:

"I'll tell you about a curious episode in which I myself wound up playing a role quite recently."

It grew dark. They entered the compartment and settled into their places on the top bunks. The tightly drawn window shade made the compartment, lit by a single small lamp, especially intimate. The naval officer lay on the top bunk across from the major and listened to his story. It had so little in common with the scene around them that at times a part of his consciousness seemed to fly off to a distant sun-drenched and vast land…

I was called up three months into the war. I went through the relentless battle of retreat. For seven months the enemy's bullets and shrapnel spared me. There's no point telling you everything I experienced… Before the war I was a geologist, a worshipper of our indomitable nature, and a dreamer. The drudgery of war and the devastation and atrocities inflicted on my native land by the invading hordes, hard on a peace-loving soul like mine, almost broke me. But I got through it and soon was hardened, like the hundreds of comrades who fought beside me. My dreams vanished without a trace. I grew thick-skinned and morose. All that was left of my soul was an excruciating void – a void that was filled only when I fought the enemy, only when my batteries hit the mark.

In March, I was seriously wounded and taken out of commission for several months. After treatment in the hospital I was granted leave and sent to recuperate at a resort in Central Asia. I tried to argue and gave them all the reasons why I should be sent to the front immediately; I said that I was completely alone in the world – nothing did any good.

In short, in late July 1942 I found myself on a train speeding me across the vast Kazakh steppe toward the hot sun.

At night, I often stood by an open window. The wind, which smelled of wormwood, dry and fresh, wafted around me welcomingly. The weightless dark of the steppe accentuated the plain's primeval lack of habitation. But my mind was somewhere else – far to the west.

In the end, nature's pristine serenity worked its magic, and after a week of travel I somehow softened a bit inside. Most importantly, I became more attentive to the world around me.

After Arysa, the sweltering daytime heat in the scorching train became agonizing, and I was happy to get off at a small station late one night. The bus from the sanatorium wasn't coming until morning. I had no desire to trade the soft cool of the southern night for a place to lay my head inside the station. I sat down on my suitcase near a lamppost and, breathing in the nocturnal freshness, examined my surroundings. The train was still standing there. Its passengers were strolling along the crunching gravel by the glow of lamplight. After lighting a *papirosa*, I began to look them over.

A young woman who was walking back and forth along the platform caught my eye with the attractive combination of a green dress, reddish bronze suntan, and ash blond hair.

Something set her apart from the crowd. Even now I remember my first impression; I suppose it was the joyful freshness that emanated from her entire being.

Clearly looking for someone, she now stopped, shook her short hair, and, after raising her round face to the light, protruded her lips in a funny pout. Sensing my stare, the young woman looked me straight in the eye, turned her back on me, and walked away.

The train pulled out of the station. The red light of the last car was lost amid dark hillocks; all but two of the lamps went dark. For a while, I continued to sit on my suitcase in the dusk of the now quiet station. For the first time in a long while my soul was at peace, perhaps because of the cool darkness around me, perhaps because I could sense the vastness of the nighttime steppe.

I began to feel cold and reluctantly made my way toward the station. The tiny waiting room had little lighting. Behind a low wooden partition was a section for wounded soldiers with nobody in it. The wind was rushing in unhindered through an open window. I lay down on a bench, although I had no desire to sleep. Light footsteps sounded in the dimly lit room. I turned and recognized the young woman I had encountered on the platform. She looked at the benches occupied by sleeping Uzbeks and hesitantly approached the partition separating my section. I rose to greet her and invited her to settle on a free bench. She thanked me and sat down on the bench, throwing back her head and squeezing her knees tightly together. As soon as she appeared, this station, adrift in the steppe, suddenly seemed less desolate. Apparently, the young woman had no intention of sleeping. I decided to ask her a few of the sorts of questions travelers ordinarily ask one another, and she responded curtly and without enthusiasm. Nevertheless, we gradually struck up a conversation. Tatyana Nikolayevna, or simply Tanya, was a graduate student at the Institute of Asian Languages in Tashkent and was accompanying a famous archeology professor on an expedition. The professor was studying the ruins of an ancient astronomical observatory built approximately a thousand years ago in the foothills of a mountain range two hundred kilometers from the station. Tanya's duties included restoring and translating Arabic inscriptions found on the ruin's walls and stones.

"Doesn't it seem silly to you, after the front, after this," she lightly touched my arm, which was in a sling, "that people are working on this sort of thing?" She glanced at me, looking somewhat embarrassed.

"No, Tanya," I responded. "I'm a former geologist and believe in the importance of science. Also, it means that my comrades and I are defending our country well if you're able to do your job far from the war…"

"So that's how you see it!" Tanya smiled and grew silent, sinking into thoughtfulness.

"You said that the observatory is in the remote steppe. How did you get here?" I asked, to get the conversation going again.

Tanya gave me a rather detailed account of the expedition to the ancient observatory. Its members were few: the professor, Tanya, and her fifteen-year-old brother, who was helping to map the site. Laborers were hard to come by, of course. Although it wanted to assist the expedition, the nearest collective farm could only spare two old men, who left after working just two weeks. Nobody else would come, so the job of clearing the ruins ground to a halt. The professor sent a letter to his institute requesting that a graduate student who had stayed behind in Tashkent to work on his dissertation be sent to do some simple clearing and help complete the job. Tanya was there to meet this new comrade, but he was not on either of the two trains that had come and gone. She had sent a telegram to Tashkent asking what was going on and was expecting a reply in the morning.

"That's the whole story," she said, suppressing an annoyed sigh. "It's a shame! You can't imagine how interesting the work is and what an amazing place Nur-i-Desht is! Nur-i-Desht – that's the name of the observatory ruins. It means 'Light of the Desert.'"

"If the place is as wonderful as you say it is, why did your old men take off?"

"There are underground tremors, quite strong and frequent. Everything shakes, a loud rumbling comes from deep underground, and stones and earth spill down from the ruins' walls. Our laborers thought the tremors were a sign that a major earthquake was coming that would kill us all…"

I thought about everything Tanya had told me, and when I was ready to ask her a question I saw that she was sleeping peacefully with her head lolled to one side.

After carefully positioning my rolled up greatcoat to give her a little support, I moved to the neighboring bench, lay down, and fell asleep.

When I awoke, the young woman was gone. There were more people in the waiting area, filling the small space with their colorful robes and the sounds of an unfamiliar language.

After washing up, I went to find out about the bus. The news was not reassuring: the bus was late and could be expected only after lunch. I walked around the station, hoping to find Tanya. After circling the entire building, I went out into the steppe, but the sun, which was already scorching, drove me into the shade of the station garden. In the distance I caught sight of Tanya's green dress by the entrance to the telegraph office. She was sitting, lost in thought, on the stone stoop under an acacia.

"Good morning. Did you get your telegram?" I asked.

"I got it… Semyonov joined the army, so nobody's going to be coming. What will I tell Matvei Andreyevich? He'll be so disappointed!"

"Who is Matvei Andreyevich?"

"My boss, the professor. I told you about him yesterday," she said with a hint of annoyance.

At this point I had an idea that immediately cheered me up.

"Listen, Tanya. Take me along to help!" I said. "I certainly won't be any worse than your old men."

Tanya looked at me with surprise.

"You? But you're supposed to be undergoing treatment. And besides…" She stopped short, glancing at the sling holding my arm.

I noticed this glance, took my arm out of the sling, and made a few rapid movements with it.

"Don't worry, Tanya. My arm works, and the only reason it's in a sling is to prevent swelling. I can't keep it lowered for long," I explained. "And after all, I'm going there to recuperate, not to undergo treatment. What difference does it make where I do that? You yourself were singing the praises of this Nur-i-Desht of yours."

The young woman wavered. Her gray eyes grew cheerful.

"Everything will be fine," I continued facetiously, "so long as that professor of yours doesn't keep me on soldier's rations…"

"Of course not! We have plenty of food! But what about your sanatorium? And it's a difficult trip to our place…"

"Difficult how? You're getting ready to make it for the fourth time."

"I may not be tall, but I'm strong," Tanya replied. "You know how we get there? There are trucks that go from here to a state farm – that's 120 kilometers. From the state farm they usually give us a horse to the village of Tuz-Kul, a small collective farm, and the road to it is awful: sand and stone. From Tuz-Kul we have to get a camel and make it through about thirty kilometers of arid sand. I can't stand riding camels: you sit there as if you're on a huge barrel, rocking back and forth, like a pendulum. And the camel, you know, goes exactly four kilometers an hour, no more, no less."

I soon had Tanya convinced, and long before sunrise an empty three-tonner was bouncing along the potholes like a rubber ball, carrying us southeastward, away from the bluish line of snowy peaks and in the opposite direction from the sanatorium. We sat on the floor of the driver's compartment exchanging cheerful glances. Conversation was impossible – you'd bite your tongue off. A dense, rust-colored dust cloud whirled behind the truck and gradually widened, obscuring the hills beyond which stood the train station we had left behind. After about three hours on the road, a dark line of poplars that had been looming on the horizon parted before us, revealing two rows of little white houses separated by a straight street as wide as a city square. The regular rows of pyramidal poplars extended their green towers skyward, and to the left and right, gentle slopes bristling with light yellow clusters of needlegrass ran down to the village.

The truck stopped by a babbling irrigation ditch not far from the state farm's office. I still have fond memories of the simple, heartfelt hospitality shown us by this remote state farm. We decided to set out as late as possible: the cool of night is the best time for traveling. Catching sight of a spacious tarantass, Tanya chuckled softly.

"You're a handy fellow to have around, Ivan Timofeyevich: they're taking us in a tarantass in your honor."

An agronomist who was also traveling to the collective farm took on the duty of coachman; Tanya and I settled down in the basket and we began moving into a weak breeze. The dark steppe enveloped us under low, warm stars.

Soon I could feel that Tanya's shoulder was often touching mine. And then her curly head came to rest peacefully on my shoulder. Time passed. The velvet breeze brought out its cold claws. The predawn chill kept us in a state of semi-wakefulness.

Tuz-Kul did not strike me as a pleasant place. A bare hillock with a few recently planted poplars was dotted with low huts plastered with reddish-brown clay. At six in the evening we set out into the sands accompanied by a guide and a camel loaded with provisions. I decided to follow Tanya's example and proceeded on foot, walking by her side. Low sandy mounds were overgrown with bluish brambles. Walking was not at all easy, and I was surprised by my companion's endurance. Our legs became mired in the shifting sands, which emanated a suffocating heat – it was easy to imagine what it must be like to walk here during the hot daytime hours. After a brief halt under the glow of sunset, we entered a saxaul thicket. The luminous face of my watch showed quarter past twelve when the sand came to an end and we were relieved to feel the firm ground of the rocky wormwood steppe beneath our feet.

Off in the distance and rather high up there was a red glow surrounded by a cloud of golden haze.

"That's our campfire," Tanya explained. "They're up late – must be waiting for me."

The resonant voice of a boy rang out in the darkness:

"Matvei Andreyevich, Tanya's here!"

My first encounter with the professor took place by firelight. He was a small, round man with a square face. His intelligent eyes were covered by large, thick glasses. I had been lagging behind a bit, trying to coax the stubborn camel closer to the fire. After greeting Tanya, the professor called out toward me:

"Show yourself, Semyonov! Where are you hiding there? Tell us what's going on in Tashkent."

I stepped into the circle of light around the campfire. The professor started, adjusted his glasses, and looked at Tanya.

"Who is this? And where's Semyonov?"

"Semyonov didn't come, Matvei Andreyevich," Tanya replied guiltily, in a barely audible voice.

"I don't understand anything! What kind of a joke is this?" The professor grew angry.

I walked up to him, reached out my hand, introduced myself, and then briefly explained why I was there.

"What are you saying! How can that be? You're a wounded major, a decorated warrior. It's not right, my friend, it's not right!" the professor grumbled, casting angry glances at Tanya.

She kept silent.

"And, on top of that, your arm… My, my!…Will you really be able to work?… I didn't expect this sort of silliness from you, Tanya."

I burst out laughing. With my good arm I grabbed a heavy bundle that had been unloaded from the camel and easily raised it over my head. Tanya applauded. The professor seemed somewhat appeased.

"Well, well… What am I to do with you?"

"Try me out on the job. If I'm not a fit, you can kick me out," I said humbly.

Tanya snickered. The professor's glasses flashed as he glared at her.

"Oh, those girls! They're forever… They do just fine, but show them a man in uniform and it's all over. So be it. Have some tea, settle in, and we'll see."

In the end, everything worked out. When the professor learned that I'm a geologist and therefore familiar with archeology, he completely got over the shock of my showing up.

The next morning, the Nur-i-Desht observatory really did strike me as an exceptionally agreeable place. Atop a high, rocky hill stood a semicircular wall, on the far side of which was a squat tower. Both ends of the wall were straddled by massive arches resting on thick, cube-shaped bases. Between the cubes, a beautiful Arabian-style portico had survived that retained the traces of gold lettering against a turquoise background. Between the tower and the arches, a deep, funnel-shaped hole had been dug and lined with tufa. Most of the hole was taken up by the precisely sculpted concave marble arc of an astronomical quadrant that descended and then rose in two pieces with a space between them. Some sorts of symbols and markings had been carved into the sides of the arc. Shallow steps, carved with perfect regularity, descended in parallel with the arc.

The professor did not linger at the observatory.

"We've already examined everything here," he told me. "Now we'll be working over there." And he gestured toward the end of the wall's right-hand wing, near which stood the remains of crumbling arches and a narrow, spired tower. "As you see, the astronomical observatory is well preserved. Of course the bronze parts of the quadrant's arc and other instruments were plundered long ago, back before the Mongol invasion. But this spot, where we'll be continuing our investigation, must have been where the instruments were stored, the star maps and books, and the astronomers may have lived here. Part of the building was carved out of the cliff. We still need to figure out what some of the entrances, wells, and caverns were used for. Whatever was built on top has collapsed, piles of crushed stone and sand are blocking the entrances to the spaces below, and I still don't have a clear understanding of this building. It looks more like a little fort than an observatory… Well, let's get to work…" And with that, the professor plunged under an archway crusted with dust and covered in dry grass.

All three of us followed him.

It was pleasantly cool in the semidarkness of the square room under the arch. Arming myself with a hoe-like instrument – a *ketmen* – and, following the professor's instructions, I got down to work raking away the pile of earth and stone that had accumulated as the neighboring arch settled. I was going full steam and dripping with sweat. The piles of earth I was excavating kept growing on either side of the room. The professor, very pleased, ordered me to rest and took charge of the *ketmen* himself. Then Tanya did some digging, and I took another turn. We were immersed in sweat and dust for a long time before we finally broke through to a low, spacious cavern that was barely illuminated through slits in the rocks supporting the arches above. The professor and Tanya were immediately drawn to some smooth stone tablets piled in a corner. Nothing in this dark and featureless cavern interested me, so I began to examine the adjoining rooms. Doorless passages as narrow as slits connected another three caverns which, unlike the first ones, had high ceilings. They were all completely empty, but at the end of the second room stood a broad, sturdy cylindrical structure of gray stone. Around the outside of the cylinder wound a narrow, crumbling staircase, the top of which disappeared into a chaos of debris obstructing a square hatch. Lower down the cylinder, some black openings, so small even a rat couldn't fit through, caught my eye. I looked into one, and spent a long time studying the darkness until I thought I could detect a faint glow. I took another look, and again I saw a barely discernible light. I called the professor. He reluctantly tore himself away from his examination of the tablets and followed me. I pointed out the cylindrical structure, but the professor did not express the slightest interest.

"Look, Tanya," he said to the young woman walking behind him, "that's the base of the outside tower, the one that looks like a minaret.

That's the only thing that survived: it was built of the strongest diabase."

To my comment that there seemed to be a glimmer of light inside, the professor replied:

"But what could possibly be there? Some sort of decorative tile fell in. They accessed the tower using the outer staircase, and the only reason they kept it hollow was to economize on materials. There's no way to get inside."

He started to head back, but stopped short:

"Now here's something that really is important!"

And the professor pointed beyond the protruding frame of a narrow doorway to a crumbling cavern wall. Under the rubble was a barely visible step – apparently the beginning of a staircase leading someplace below.

"You see, Tanya, I told you that there had to be another level, a third story, the lowest. This is the first way down that we've managed to discover. Here's where we'll dig. What time is it, Ivan Timofeyevich?" the professor asked, apparently struck by a sudden thought.

"Almost five."

"Well! That explains why I'm so hungry. Let's head up right away."

Above ground, we were met with dry heat and blinding light that dazzled the eyes after the darkness under the arches. I made way for Tanya and the professor to pass me and stayed behind to get a better look around from atop the observatory mound. On the level ground to the left of the mound stood our two tents. Both the mound and this flat area sat on the summit of a broad, dome-shaped hill, part of a group of eight similar hills covered in sparse, wiry grass that was nothing like the cheerful green grass of our north. The angular tips of black stones sprinkled with coarse sand poked through its bristles. The stones protruding out from under a thin cover of earth on the observatory's hill were of a different, lighter shade. So in terms of hue, the observatory mound stood out rather sharply among its black brethren.

The nine hills clustered together at the edge of a boundless plain that gradually sloped downward toward the south, while to the west, my right, almost at the very horizon, rose a jagged strip of distant, snow-topped mountains. On that same side, the plain was intersected by a narrow, winding ribbon of molten steel; the river ran down from the mountains, skirted the observatory hill and, turning eastward, was lost amid the sands. Below the observatory, the yellow steppe spread in every direction, dotted with bushes of silver wormwood and thorny blue acanthus plants. Farther in the distance, to the north, the steppe was outlined at the edge of the sands by a dark ribbon of saxaul trees.

Calm, expanse, pure mountain air, and the blue of a heavy sultriness overhead…

What a lucky twist of fate had brought me here! What more could my soul require? I was seized by a joyous feeling of conciliation with myself and with nature.

"Ivan Timofeyevich," I heard Vyachik, Tanya's brother, calling me. "Suppertime!"

"Where did you disappear to?" Tanya asked by way of greeting. "I had a marvelous swim, and I wanted to ask you along. We're going to eat now, so swimming will have to wait till evening."

After supper and a brief rest, we again went to dig out the stairway the professor had discovered. It led into a broad cavity carved out of the sandstone and was filled from top to bottom with all sorts of debris. Given the pace of progress, it was clear that several days of our combined effort would be needed to excavate the stairway.

After we finished our day's work, I reminded Tanya of her promise. She led me down a narrow path along the riverbank to the foot of the second hill. I followed her in silence, listening to the steady sound of the rapids, whose fast trickles fractured the sunlight. At a turn in the stream, Tanya stopped.

"Sit here and wait for me. Vyachik and I built a dam so the water would be waist deep."

She disappeared behind a bluff in the riverbank, and I lay down on the prickly grass and pointed my face to catch the weak breeze. The babbling of the stream lulled me to sleep.

"You fell asleep? Hurry up. It's marvelous!"

Fresh and cheerful, Tanya stood before me – the unblemished beauty of youth in harmony with the water and sun. I jumped up and descended the steep bank. Before me I discovered a small weir across from a miniscule sandy beach. Two twisted saplings, like sentries, guarded this pristine bath from the low right bank. I quickly figured out how to lie down without being swept away by the cold current. The swim was amazingly refreshing. Back at the tents, the professor and Vyachik awaited us with tea.

"How did you like your swim?" the professor inquired. "Ah, let's put the geologist to the test! You didn't notice anything in the river? No? My dear major, you've forgotten everything on the battlefield! We know from the chronicles that the ancient name of the river is 'Ekik,' which means carnelian. And you can find red stones among the pebbles in the riverbed. Take a look when you have a chance."

Excavating the lowest level proved to be more difficult than anticipated. The downward sloping cavity kept filling up with showers of earth and stone. I had already been working four days from morning to late at night. My muscles were infused with new strength. It was as if fresh new feelings were emerging from some unknown corner of my soul, like the green shoots of spring – feelings just as infinitely calm and bright as the nature around me. I was possessed by a confident joy in life: fatigue and unhappiness almost vanished from memory. As it should be for any completely healthy person, my body ceased to exist; all I was conscious of was the pleasure of abundant energy. Now I can break these feelings down into separate elements, but back then it was different and they were expressed, actually, in a sense of heightened delight in the land where the Nur-i-Desht ruins were located. I racked my brain, trying to understand the secret behind the enchantment of these desolate rocky hills and forlorn ruins amid a baking ring of steppe and sand. I shared my impressions with Tanya and the professor. They agreed with me.

"I have to admit, I don't understand it at all," Matvei Andreyevich said. "I only know that I've never felt as well as I do here."

"'Well' is putting it mildly," Tanya chimed in. "For my part, I'm filled with radiant joy. It seems to me that this ancient observatory is a temple… I can't really express it clearly… the earth, the sky, the sun, and something mysterious and beautiful that imperceptibly permeates this ungoverned space. I've seen plenty of much more beautiful places, but I've never been as captivated as I am by these seemingly unimpressive ruins."

Another workday ended after dark, but I had no desire to sleep.

Night came. We lay down by the campfire. At the zenith of the black cupola above us shone blue Vega; from the west, golden Arcturus twinkled like an owl's eye. The stardust of the Milky Way radiated a silvery heat.

Just above the horizon, red Antares was gleaming; and to the right were the faint contours of Sagittarius, the Archer. There lies the center of the monstrous sidereal wheel of the Galaxy – the central "sun" of our Universe. We will never see it – the Galaxy's axis is hidden behind a gigantic curtain of black. These countless worlds must also contain life – alien and diverse. Off in the inaccessible distance, they are inhabited by beings like us, possessed of the power of thought… And there I was, beguiled, looking up at these worlds with a sense of yearning, unsettled by a vague premonition of the impending greatness of humankind's destiny. But great only once we manage to overcome the dark brutish forces that still dominate the earth, obstinately, bestially eroding – destroying – the precious advances of human thought and imagination.

"Are you sleeping, Ivan Timofeyevich?" the professor's voice broke the silence.

"No, I'm looking at the stars… They are especially clear and close here."

"Yes, they knew what they were doing when they built the observatory; the air here is exceptionally translucent. Then again, the sky is translucent and vibrant almost everywhere in Central Asia. That's why the people here are expert stargazers. You know, the Kyrgyz call the North Star the sky's silver stake. Three horses are tied to that stake. Four wolves are eternally chasing the horses, but they are never able to catch them. When they do, it will be the end of the world. Isn't that a poetic way to look at Ursa Major's rotation?"

"Very nice, Matvei Andreyevich! I recall reading somewhere about the sky in the Southern Hemisphere. High up, where the Southern Cross glimmers, there is a bright star cloud in the Milky Way, and next to it is an absolutely black spot – a huge, pear-shaped cluster of dark matter. The first seafarers called it the Coalsack. An ancient Australian legend sees this spot as a gaping hole, a chasm in the sky, and another legend sees it as the incarnation of evil in the form of an Australian ostrich, the emu. The emu is at the foot of a tree formed by the stars of the Southern Cross where it lies in wait for an opossum who has taken refuge in the tree's branches. When the emu catches the opossum, the world will come to an end."

"Similar story, different animals," the professor replied lazily.

"Tell me please, Matvei Andreyevich: who 'knew what they were doing' when they created Nur-i-Desht? When was it built, and why is it in such a deserted spot?"

"Uyghur astronomers were working here, pupils of Arab wise men. And the place became uninhabited after the Mongol invasion. There are ruins all around here, signs of habitation. There's no doubt that seven hundred years ago this was a thriving, populous place. You need a lot of knowledge and skill to build an observatory like this."

The professor stopped short. Something had happened. At first I couldn't figure out just what it was. By the second jolt it became clear that the earth had started to shake beneath us, as if a wave of stone was rippling across the surface. At almost the same moment we heard a distant roar that seemed to come from deep below us. The dishware clattered in its crate and the tower of wood in our campfire collapsed. The jolts came one after another.

It all ended just as unexpectedly as it began. In the sudden silence we could hear dislodged rocks tumbling down the slopes and the sound of something spilling into the observatory ruins.

In the morning, when we showed up at the spot where we had been working every day, we were met by startling changes caused by the nighttime earthquake. The left side of our dirt pile had collapsed, revealing a shallow niche in the wall to the right in the shape of a pointed arch. Inside the niche, covered with dust and clumps of earth, we could see a stone tablet with a string of symbols written in Arabic Kufic lettering, utterly unintelligible to the uninitiated.[1] Excited about the discovery but, at the same time, upset that the staircase had been buried again, we quickly brushed off the inscription that for so many centuries had been hidden under the dry, dusty earth. The letters on the smooth, bluish tablet were deeply engraved and covered with some sort of beautiful orange glaze with a shimmer of green. Tanya and the professor took on the task of deciphering the inscription while Vyachik and I got to work clearing the stairway.

Matvei Andreyevich straightened up and issued a loud sigh:

"Too bad! Nothing important! Although it does confirm information already preserved in the historical record. The inscription says that by order of such-and-such, in such-and-such year, in the month of Qaus – that's Sagittarius in Arabic, Tanya?"

"Yes."

"So, in November, construction was completed in the area of Nur-i-Desht, by the river Ekik, on the hill… what is that, Tanya?"

"I don't quite understand the name – something like shining chalice."

"How poetic! On Shining Chalice Hill, on the site where royal paints had previously been mined… Aha, this is up your alley, major.

---

1. Kufic writing is an Arabic script distinguished by wide geometric letters linked together.

Where are the remnants of these mines and what might they have been mining?"

"I don't know; I haven't noticed any mines."

"You were a geologist, weren't you?" the professor asked in feigned indignation.

"Wait, Matvei Andreyevich. I'll finish digging out your stairway, then let me go wander around for a few hours. A geologist just might come in handy. So far, I've been walking the same route every day: the river to the cavern, the river to the tent."

"Aha!" the professor burst out laughing. "You've been walking in an archeologist's shoes for a while, your nose to the ground. But you're right: we should proclaim a day off. There will be no digging tomorrow – take a walk around, do some investigating. Tanya, of course, will deal with the laundry... No? What's going on? You also want to walk around, learn some geology? Well, well..."

"What else does the inscription say, Matvei Andreyevich?" I interrupted the professor.

"Next it says: to commemorate a great deed, this inscription has been made and an ancient vase with a description of the construction has been interred inside a wall."

"But professor, finding the vase would be extremely important in studying the observatory, wouldn't it?"

"Of course. But it doesn't say where it was interred. Obviously, it must be in the foundation. How will we find it? We can't even get the staircase dug out."

In the morning, hoping to shoot some wildfowl, I asked Vyachik for the Berdan shotgun. The professor saw Tanya and me off with a derisive farewell speech, and we embarked on our journey around the Nur-i-Desht hills. Apparently, none of the members of the little expedition had strayed far from the ruins, since all their time had been spent working. The day was exceptionally sultry and quiet, and there was not the slightest hint of a breeze to chase away the dry heat rising out of the rocky soil. After a long time walking across the hills and clambering up and down slopes, we were overcome by thirst. We walked down to the stream, drank our fill, and started to wade barefoot through the riverbed. Large pebbles slid around underfoot. Through the clear water, among black and gray pebbles, multicolored pieces of opal and chalcedony, smoothed by the current, occasionally caught our eye. We were both absorbed in hunting for beautiful stones, and only once our feet had turned numb with cold did we climb up onto the bank and start to warm ourselves on the stony shore as we sorted through our loot.

"Put the red ones here, Tanya. That's carnelian – a gem very highly valued in antiquity that supposedly has some sort of curative power."

"Most of them are red. Look at this one, what a beauty!" Tanya exclaimed. "Did you find that one? It's translucent and gleams like a pearl."

"That's a hyalite, the most valuable kind of opal. You can make yourself a brooch out of it."

"I don't like brooches, rings, earrings – nothing but bracelets. But if you just give it to me as a present then I'll be grateful… But why did you pick up those three stones? They're dull, not any good."

"What are you talking about, Tanya! How can you find fault with my very best find? Look." And I lowered a plain white pebble into the water. The stone became translucent and glimmered with flecks of blue.

"How beautiful!" the young woman exclaimed in amazement.

"That's right, this homely stone turns out to be magical. And in ancient times it was considered magical. It's a hydrophane, also called 'the eye of the world.' It's very porous and so it isn't see-through when it's dry. As soon as its pores fill with water it becomes translucent and very beautiful. That's true of all varieties of quartz; there are many more sorts that differ in terms of tint, value, and beauty."

"What did you learn from our excursion today?" Tanya asked.

"I now have an understanding of the makeup of this entire area. It actually turns out to be nothing interesting: ancient granites and strata of black quartzite with veins of quartz running through them. The hill that the observatory sits on is a little different from the others: it's composed of very dense, glassy quartzites. The pretty stones in the riverbed were deposited there as the quartzite eroded – there must be quite a bit of chalcedony and opal in the veins, in the interstices and incrustations, and throughout the fissures."

"And where is the mine mentioned in the inscription?"

"I still don't know. You saw for yourself – there wasn't the slightest trace. Maybe it's hidden beneath the observatory ruins."

"That's bad! Matvei Andreyevich is going to poke fun at us again," Tanya concluded. "It's time to head back. Look, the sun is already setting. We'll get back after dark as it is."

The red fire of sunset gave the hills' sloped shoulders a sharp silhouette. The total stillness accentuated the desolate silence of the surrounding sands. When we reached the observatory hill, the last glow of sunset had been extinguished in the west.

The ruins, barely discernible by starlight, greeted us in silence. A lone scops owl gave a melodious hoot off in the distance.[2] The place was rather menacing at night; a vague foreboding gripped us, and we crept stealthily along, whispering, as if we were afraid of waking something slumbering amid the gloomy walls.

Suddenly, I felt as if my daytime fatigue had vanished, replaced by a rush of energy. The dry, still air coming off the sun baked walls, despite its warmth, seemed exceptionally fresh. Every now and then, a pleasant, barely perceptible tingling ran over my skin.

"I don't feel tired at all," Tanya whispered to me, moving so close that our shoulders were almost touching. "There's something in the air here."

---

2. The scops is a small owl found in southern Europe, Russia and Central Asia.

"Yes, I would say that the air is as if we were next to an electrical generator. Touch your hair, Tanya: it's sticking out all over the place all of a sudden."

Tanya ran her hand over her hair, trying to smooth it out, and a multitude of tiny blue sparks flickered under her fingers.

"Like before a storm," Tanya commented, "except the sky is clear and there isn't a hint of humidity, quite the opposite."

"Strange. In general, a lot of things in this place are inexplicable…" I began, but stopped short when a faint greenish glow coming from a gap in the wall caught my eye.

We were approaching the main structure, the one with the quadrant's arc. I took a closer look and noticed the faintly visible glow of several letters of an inscription on the inner wall of the portico.

"Look, Tanya!" I led my companion to a collapsed part of the wall.

In the pitch blackness under the arches, the curlicues of lettering outlined by a greenish-yellow glow stood out clearly.

"What is that?" Tanya whispered excitedly. "There are inscriptions all over the place here, but they don't glow."

"All of those inscriptions were done in gold. That's right, isn't it?"

"Yes, that's right," Tanya confirmed.

"But this one… Wait a minute…"

I carefully slipped into the portico and lit a match. The mysterious glow instantly vanished. Before me there was nothing but a dark, broken down wall. But I did manage to notice a surviving tile fragment covered with a smooth glaze and orange-greenish lettering.

"This was done in the same sort of enamel as near the stairway in the cavern, not gold."

"Let's go take a look right away!" Tanya urged.

"Let's go," I agreed, and asked: "Have you ever been to the observatory at night, you or the professor?"

"No, not once."

"In that case, let's go to the camp first – but don't tell the professor anything. We'll have dinner, and we'll continue our investigation after everyone goes to sleep, if you want. And if you're tired, I'll go on my own."

"You've got to be kidding! How could I be tired? It's all so mysterious and interesting!"

"Excellent. But one condition, Tanya: not a word to the professor. I myself don't understand what's going on yet, but if you and I come up with some sort of explanation, we'll have quite a surprise for Matvei Andreyevich in the morning!"

Tanya gave me a warm, firm handshake. We quickly walked down the hill to the campsite where, as usual, a small fire was blazing. After grumbling at us for being late for supper, the professor started to interrogate me about the results of our excursion. As Tanya had predicted, Matvei Andreyevich lavished my poor self with good-natured mockery as soon as he learned that I hadn't found any traces of the paint mine.

"Fine, better not to ask what you found there in the darkness with Tanya… Come on now, don't be angry! Show us your stones… What a lot of carnelians! We could get a whole sack of them in just a few days. Carnelians aren't highly valued anymore, another example of the wisdom of human experience that's been forgotten with the passage of time. It used to be that all of Near Asia valued this stone as much as the most precious gems. They made bracelets out of it, necklaces, buckles. And they believed that carnelians protect people against many diseases. Most curious of all, it turns out that this belief was not simple superstition. I recently learned…" the professor fell silent as he held the red stone up to the firelight.

"What did you learn, Matvei Andreyevich, tell us?" Tanya asked.

"It's very simple: doctors are starting to test treatments using carnelian. It turns out that they almost always have some radioactivity – weak, you could even say negligible, equal to the total radioactivity in the human body. But it is specifically because there are only tiny traces of radium in carnelians that they have a beneficial effect on the nervous system, restoring some sort of equilibrium in it, or something like that – I'm no expert."

"Radium?" I was suddenly transfixed by a vague hunch, and thoughts of electrical discharges, glowing inscriptions, and orange-greenish paints began to swirl through my mind. I leapt to my feet impatiently, but immediately got a hold of myself and hurriedly took out a pack of cigarettes.

"What's come over you, Ivan Timofeyevich? It's as if something just stung you," the professor asked in surprise. "But perhaps it's time to sleep. Let's get an early start tomorrow – we'll probably finish digging out the entrance. You two do as you please, but Vyachik and I are turning in."

Tanya and I were left alone. I nervously smoked my *papirosa*, waiting for the professor to fall asleep so we could take candles for our nocturnal investigation into the secrets of the Nur-i-Desht observatory.

Finally, Tanya got two candles and I grabbed a heavy crowbar from under the pile of tools.

"What's that for?" Tanya looked perplexed.

"It'll come in handy. We might have to get a rock out of the way or dislodge a slab."

Below, in the stony caverns, total darkness reigned. We felt our way down the familiar path without lighting any candles. Turning to the right, into the slit-like doorway, we reached the niche in the stairway. Tanya let out a cry: a large panel weakly but distinctly shone with a string of Kufic letters. The same sort of golden yellow string of glowing letters extended up and down the arch over the stairway.

"I see," I thought out loud. "There isn't much light here during the day…"

"Meaning?" Tanya asked impatiently.

"Wait and ask me after I solve the whole puzzle. Let's go up, to the quadrant. We'll probably find more traces of glowing inscriptions… Wait! Give me a candle. Let's have a look in here."

I recalled the mysterious glow inside the base of the astronomical tower that I had seen on the first day and decided to try getting inside. Using the crowbar, I started to carefully pry away a stone that was firmly fused into the masonry above a narrow ventilation slot. After some persistent effort, the stone began to yield. I pressed harder and, after maneuvering the stone toward me, I freed it from the masonry. The second gave way more easily. There was now an opening large enough for my head and an arm to hold a candle.

The candle's flame illuminated the tower's rounded, narrow interior, which extended far upward into the darkness. To the left of the hole I had broken through was a broad, rough-hewn stone supporting a large, wide-necked vessel covered in a thick layer of dust, its glaze faintly glimmering through the grime. Based on the vase's shape, even I could tell it was old.

"The vase, Tanya, the vase!" I cried, and stood aside so she could look into the hole.

"It's too tight to squeeze through. How will we get it?" she asked, suppressing an excited gasp.

"Just a moment."

Inspired by the discovery, I quickly managed to remove another two stones. Once inside the tower I hurriedly drew back: to the right of the stone that supported the vase and behind it gaped the darkness of a well. Narrow steps spiraled down to a ledge inside the tower. I handed the vase to Tanya through the hole and said:

"Wait for me, Tanya. I'm going down."

"No, no, I'll go with you: who knows what's there…" She became flustered and fell silent.

Our eyes met, and I… In short, I climbed down, keeping my hands against the wall for support. I then helped Tanya, who was right behind me.

The well was not deep. In fact, it turned out not to be a well at all, but an uneven, slightly sloped passage cut into the rock face. A chill penetrated our light clothing. But rather than the cold, stagnant air of a dungeon, this air was pure and fresh, like the ozone-rich air at the top of a mountain. At a depth of several meters, the passage widened into a large, rugged cave with pitted walls grooved with narrow furrows trailing off in all directions. I already knew what to look for: here and there in the cracks of siliceous shale and quartzite and at the bottom of the furrows, there were small ochreous lemon-yellow and orange blotches.

"And here's where they mined the paints, Tanya! But they were no ordinary paints."

We climbed back up. Over Tanya's objections, I committed sacrilege: I carried away the vase without waiting for morning. Pressing the heavy vase to my chest, I stepped cautiously, afraid of tripping. Near the portico we put down our precious find and slowly circled the building. It turned out I was right: we discovered the glow of lettering in several other places as well. The quadrant's arc was also embellished with glowing strokes.

After climbing down to the stream, we carefully removed the vessel's lid. There was nothing but dust inside. We then washed the vase on the outside, silently carried it to the tent, and placed it by the head of the professor's cot, gleefully anticipating how surprised and stunned he'd be in the morning.

"Well, now tell me!" Tanya whispered into my ear. "I'm not going to be able to sleep anyway until I find out."

Moving away from the tent, we settled down at the edge of the stream, which was running into the dark steppe with a melodious babble.

"As it turns out, it's all very simple, Tanya. There's a deposit of uranium ore here, which means there's radium. These yellow spots are uranium ochers. They're used in ceramics for a long-lasting glaze with vibrant and pure colors: orange, greenish yellow, olive. Uranium ores are found in incrustations and in the cracks of quartzites and were used even back in antiquity, but radium – radium! – there were probably traces of it, along with the uranium, in the siliceous beds of light-colored quartzites. And I believe that the entire observatory hill, which is composed of these quartzites, emanates radium. Quartzites should be weakly radioactive. Radium salts, when mixed with other minerals, can make unusually durable luminous paints. Today, these luminous compounds have many uses, especially in warfare. It turns out that the ancient astronomers also knew this secret and, perhaps, the very name "Nur-i-Desht" – "Light of the Desert" – also comes from the strange phenomena at the observatory. There hasn't been a lot of research into radium yet. We know that it ionizes air, builds up electricity and ozone, kills microbes, and can neutralize toxins. Now I understand the mystery behind the exceptionally joyous effect this place has: a huge bed of radioactive quartzites, not encased under other rocks, has created a large field of weak radiation, apparently at a level optimally beneficial to the human body. Think back on what the professor was saying about carnelians. And today, with no wind, there was more than the usual buildup of radium. You and I immediately noticed that tonight. Quite an unexpected and interesting discovery, isn't it?" And I placed my hand on top of hers.

"Yes it is," Tanya said coldly and quickly stood up. "Well, we should get to sleep. It's already late."

A bit puzzled by Tanya's sudden standoffishness, I stayed at the riverbank. All my thoughts whirled around my unexpected discovery. I continued to find more and more evidence confirming my theory and spent a long time sitting in the darkness. Finally, I began to lose my way in the labyrinths of chemistry and wandered off to bed.

I awoke to the sound of the professor's loud cries as he called out to us. The vase was taken out into the light. Bright orange, brown, and olive-colored stripes ran up and down it, with a pattern of velvety greenish-black glowing enamel in between. The glaze's exquisite tones could only have been achieved using uranium compounds – yet another confirmation of my night-time discovery in the blinding light of day!

When I shared all my ideas with the archeologist, his joyous excitement was a sight to behold! I added that the radium emanation could explain the greater clarity of the air immediately above the observatory.

"Now you're going a bit far," the professor objected. "But as for our state, I completely agree. This is not just a place of light, but a place of joy. But why is our Tanya sad today? What happened?"

"Nothing, Matvei Andreyevich, I'm just fine."

After taking a second look at the mine, we got back to work on the stairway. By the end of the day we had managed to clear a small opening, and we took turns crawling into it. There was a cavern there with several rooms. I'm not sure what the archeologist saw there, but it seemed to me that the cavern was just as empty as all the ones I had seen before.

A sunset wind raced across the steppe; clouds of pink dust rose above the silver-gray carpet of wormwood. The professor and Vyachik walked ahead, while Tanya, lost in thought, slowed her pace, lagging behind. I caught up to her and took her by the hand.

"What's wrong, Tanya? You're always so cheerful, lively, and suddenly... It seems to me you've changed since our discovery yesterday."

The young woman looked me squarely in the face.

"I don't know whether or not you'll understand, but I'll say it anyway... Nur-i-Desht truly is a place of joy. And I thought that joy was inside me, from me, that I was strong, free, and happy. And then you came along..." she hesitated, "stern, withdrawn, scorched by the flames of war. And you also became serene and joyous... And then it turns out that the only reason for all this is radium... So if it hadn't been for radium," her voice dropped almost to a whisper, "we wouldn't have had the amazing enchantment of these days at the ancient observatory."

Tanya turned away, tore her hand from mine, and ran down the hill. I followed her slowly, pausing to survey the ruins of Nur-i-Desht.

"Light of the desert – yes, without doubt, light both for my soul and for the desert. It won't be fleeting; the joy of my days at the Nur-i-Desht observatory will always be there!"

Once again, as we had many times before, Tanya and I were sitting outside the tents by the campfire as it was burning out. The golden glow of the ancient vase radiated beside us, a shining chalice of bygone but undying human hopes.

"Dear Tanya," I said. "Here, my heart has come back to life, and it has opened… to you. Who knows? Maybe the scientific advances of the future will offer a deeper understanding of the effect radioactive substances have on us. And who's to say that we aren't under the influence of many more radiations – cosmic rays at the very least. Up there," I stood and reached toward the starry sky, "all sorts of energy could be streaming, emanating from the dark depths of space… the particles of distant stellar worlds."

Tanya rose and made an impulsive movement toward me. Her clear eyes reflected the ashen starlight.

In the heights above us, piercing the glistening clouds of the Milky Way, shone Cygnus the Swan, stretching out its long neck in eternal flight toward the future.

First published in Russian: 1944
Translation by Nora Seligman Favorov

ALEXANDER KAZANTSEV
1946

EXPLOSION

THE STORY OF A HYPOTHESIS

An image from distant childhood is engraved in my memory. High ground ends abruptly at the water, as if sliced by a gigantic knife. The broad river makes a sharp turn. Its banks are wild, rocky, forbidding. Immediately beyond them is the ageless taiga.

Our boat is traveling along the Upper Tunguska, as the Angara is called here. Only the helmsman and I stay on board through the shallows. All the others, including my father, are pulling the tow-rope. Now the shallows are behind us and everyone is rowing. I've taken my place at the stern and feel every bit the captain. Our ship is a galley. We are dauntless corsairs, off to discover new lands beyond the ocean. Hey, who's up in the crow's nest? What's that island on the horizon? A floating island? Sound the whistle! All hands on deck! Rafts, one after another, come out from behind dark cliffs that obscure half the sky. We hear bleating.

The captain knows exactly what's going on. The cursed slave traders have robbed the natives, herded their livestock onto the floating island, and stowed the shackled slaves deep down in the hold. I can see that now's the time for a noble seafaring feat. Have at them, corsairs, forward!

It is a quiet, quiet morning. Not a cloud in the sky. Off in the distance is the faint rumble of yesterday's shallows.

I curse the splashing of our oars. The despicable slavers mustn't notice a thing. The galley is fast approaching the floating island. The sheep and the hut on the lead raft are clearly visible. But I know it's really the deckhouse of the slavers' captain. There he is, the one with the beard, in a blue shirt, stepping outside to look at the sky. He stretches, scratches his back, and then yawns and makes the sign of the cross over his mouth. Quiet, oarsmen! We must approach the enemy unnoticed and then immediately take him by storm. Off to the left, a squirrel rustles the foliage. If he looks… Quiet, so quiet. You can barely hear the splashing of the oars.

And suddenly, a horrific blow. I hunch down. I'm crying. I've forgotten all about the corsairs. The raftsman falls to his knees in surprise. His mouth is open. The sheep are bleating and rushing straight for the water. And then a second blow, more horrific than the first. The door to the hut bursts violently open, but nobody comes out. To the left, beyond the taiga, something flashes, rivaling the sun.

"Hang on!" my father's voice barely reaches me. The air – thick, heavy – slams down on me with a jolt. I grab the boat's side, I scream. I'm echoed by the terrified, frenzied bleating of the sheep. I can see the sheep being toppled into the water, one after another, as if a giant hand was sweeping them off the raft. A giant wave is coming down the river. I see how the now empty raft breaks into pieces. Its logs are suddenly upright. Our boat is tossed as if we're going down rapids. I swallow water and try to catch air with my mouth. My fingers open, and, drenched, I tumble down to the bottom.

There, the water smells of fish. And all of a sudden it's totally quiet.

A distant memory, a page from my childhood diary. There it is, a dog-eared brown notebook labeled 1908. Back then, thirty-eight years ago, two hundred and fifty kilometers from the spot where the sheep were swept from the raft into the water, a terrible meteorite fell into the taiga. In Siberia, this event has been much written and talked about.

Why did I need my old notebook? Why is my desk piled high with articles and books about the Tunguska meteorite?

Full of polemical ardor and argumentative fury, I pick up a piece of paper. Yes, I'm ready to argue!

Perhaps it is best to start the story from the moment when, on the morning of April 3, 1945, two men came to see me at the journal's editorial office. Each of them placed a bulky envelope on my desk.

One of them, a man of gigantic height, put a large suitcase on the floor. He was extremely stoop-shouldered; it appeared as if he was studying something on the floor. He had large, chiseled features. Pensive light blue eyes peered out from under shaggy eyebrows that had grown together. His companion sat upright in his chair without touching its back. He was slender and a bit narrow in the shoulders. His horn-rimmed glasses gave his face, which featured rather prominent cheekbones, an expression of erudition.

"Yu-yu-your journal," the giant began, stumbling over the letter y, "would no doubt be interested in a scientific debate that will be settled during an Academy of Sciences ethnographic expedition to the Podkamennaya Tunguska region."

"If you can call the assertion and refutation of nonsense a scientific debate," the man in glasses commented caustically.

"I would ask that yu-yu-you not interrupt me," the first visitor turned to him ferociously. "I offer yu-yu-you two envelopes." He was now speaking with me as if he did not notice his adversary. "They spell out two hypotheses in regard to a strange ethnographic puzzle."

"Would you be so kind as to acquaint me with the essence of the debate?" I requested.

"Are yu-yu-you aware that in northern Siberia, east of the Ye-ye-Yenisei, there lives a people, the Evenks? People our age – of course

I'm not talking about experts – sometimes incorrectly call them the Tungus. Evenks belong to the ye-ye-yellow race and are related to the Manchurians. They were once warlike invaders who encroached into Central Asia. However they were squeezed out by the Ya-Ya-Yakuts, and, after retreating to the north, they took refuge in the impenetrable forests of Siberia. True, the Ya-Ya-Yakuts also had to relinquish the flourishing land that they had conquered to stronger invaders – the Mongols – and also depart for the Siberian forests and tundra, where they became the Evenks' neighbors…"

"Sergei Antonovich is so fond of ethnography that he never passes up an opportunity to promote that science," my second visitor interrupted. "I'll take the liberty of formulating his thought: neither the Evenks nor the Yakuts are indigenous to Siberia."

He spoke with demonstrative seriousness, but the slightly lowered corners of his lips lent his mouth an expression of faintly discernible mockery.

"And I'll prove it! Here! Would yu-yu-you care to have a look?"

With a groan, Sergei Antonovich bent down and opened his huge suitcase and, to my utter astonishment, removed a gigantic yellow bone. He triumphantly placed it on the table before me, on top of the manuscripts.

"What's that?" I drew away involuntarily.

"A tibia of the indigenous inhabitants of Siberia," Sergei Antonovich announced dramatically, looking at me with happy, luminous eyes.

"Indigenous inhabitants?" I cringed as I tried to imagine what someone with such a bone would look like.

"It is the tibia of an elephant," Sergei Antonovich dispelled my assumptions.

"In Siberia? Elephants? Mammoths perhaps?" I asked doubtfully.

"Elephants! It was I who found this bone. Last ye-ye-year I crisscrossed the taiga's swamps and crests, crawled up and down inaccessible hills in search of fossils, any fossils, and just imagine – at the sixty-fifth degree north latitude and one hundred fourth degree east longitude I stumbled upon an elephant graveya-ya-yard. Mountain ridges, like a gigantic fence, had blocked access to a plateau from all sides. The hot Siberian sun had melted a layer of permafrost and… Here, have a smoke," he extended his cigarette case.

"Thanks, I don't smoke."

"I myself sawed off the material for this cigarette case from an actual elephant tusk – straight, not curved like a mammoth's. For three weeks I ate nothing but cow parsnip. That's a plant from the umbrelliferae family much better suited for making flutes than edible dishes. I left all my provisions at the elephant graveya-ya-yard so that I would be able to carry this bone and part of the tusk back with me."

"It should be noted that Sergei Antonovich selflessly loaded himself up with these curious bones in addition to samples of valuable ores he had found. An amateur ethnographer, an amateur paleontologist, and on top of all that, a professional geologist."

The giant glanced at his companion.

"Study of the exposed geological strata led me to conclude that Siberia had a hot, African climate before the last glacial period. It was roamed by elephants, tigers…"

"And, naturally, black Africans lived there, as our distinguished scholar is prepared to assert."

"Yes, I'm certain that a tribe of indigenous, pre-glacial Siberians existed and, perhaps, even had descendants who have survived to the present. In the wilds of the Siberian taiga there are legends of a mysterious black-skinned woman…"

"There is a colorful description of an encounter with her from Kuleshov, an Angara hunter," Sergei Antonovich's companion said, removing his glasses so as to wipe them with his handkerchief. Squinting, he was looking over my head, off into the distance. "Thanks to Sergei Antonovich's kind persistence, I have learned it by heart. Imagine: a roar, a rumble, and wet, black stones amid white foam. Almost scraping the cliffs overhanging the riverbank, a small boat is bouncing over the rocks. The boat's high nose is plunging into the foam. In it stands a black-skinned woman wearing nothing but a loincloth. Long, red hair flutters and blows in the wind. Kuleshov was ready to swear that she was of gigantic height. He didn't manage to see her face. The hunter said that she is shaman to some old folks. She was probably going through the rapids without clothing because she was afraid they would weigh her down if she fell overboard."

"I maintain that this is the last descendant of pre-glacial Siberians," Sergei Antonovich placed his huge fist on the desk. "Her distant heredity has left its mark on that woman!"

"That's a curious little conclusion, unsupported by the slightest rationale. No reasonable person would be likely to arrive at such a conclusion."

"I'd like to see yu-yu-you reject it when we get there," Sergei Antonovich bristled. "I have made up my mind to take yu-yu-you with me, even though yu-yu-you're an armchair physicist, and the expedition party is already complete. I'll take yu-yu-you along as my opponent and won't let yu-yu-you spend a minute on your electrons and neutrons until yu-yu-you give in and recognize my hypothesis."

The physicist smiled.

"We are asking you to unseal the envelopes," he turned to me, " and publish the hypothesis that we will be sending you via telegraph from Vanovara, where the interdisciplinary Academy of Sciences expedition led by Sergei Antonovich is heading."

"And please telegraph me in Vanovara to let me know what abstruse gibberish this distinguished, thoroughly negative scholar has sealed in his envelope," Sergei Antonovich muttered.

My feuding visitors bade me farewell and left. I started to wonder, looking at the envelopes left behind on my desk, what could possibly have provoked such discord between experts from two entirely different fields?

"Excuse me," I was addressed by a quiet voice. Looking up, I saw the physicist before me. This time his eyes were serious, his lips tightly pursed. "I came back to warn you that my envelope really does contain a hypothesis, but it has nothing to do with the black-skinned woman, which would undoubtedly come as quite a shock to dear

Sergei Antonovich, who has forbidden members of his expedition to be distracted by extraneous questions."

"What is your hypothesis about?" I asked, intrigued. This business was becoming increasingly tangled.

"About the Tunguska meteorite."

"The one that fell close to the Vanovara trading post in 1908?"

"The one that never fell to earth."

Never fell to earth?! Shattered rafts, swimming sheep, and a glow above the taiga all passed before my mind's eye.

"Were you there when it fell?" I could barely contain myself.

"There are no special expeditions there, and I took the opportunity of my dispute with Sergei Antonovich over the matter of the black-skinned woman to visit the region. I want to establish certain details and then I will send you a telegram asking you to unseal the envelope. You will understand what needs to be done."

His manner was perfectly matter-of-fact as he explained all this with a disarming tone of certainty.

"I have my reasons for not telling anyone about my hypothesis just yet. I will acquaint Sergei Antonovich with it when we arrive there. Otherwise he just might refuse to take me with him. And now, good-bye!"

My extraordinary confidant extended his hand and told me his name. The day had delivered yet another shock: before me stood a famous theoretical physicist. I gazed at the door that shut behind him, trying to make sense of what had just taken place. The story of the black-skinned woman somehow faded into the background. It was now an entirely new thought that bothered me.

There was no meteorite?!

No, I would not give in so quickly! I was ready to fight. I saw the disaster's glow with my own eyes and felt the gigantic explosion's air wave. My mind was made up. I would refute the famous physicist's hypothesis, whatever it might be.

I dug into my files and took out everything relating to the Tunguska meteorite, which I had at one point taken a special interest in. There was the entry from my childhood diary. There was also a quote from the speech that L.A. Kulik gave to the Academy of Sciences in 1939: "The fact that the Tunguska meteorite fell at approximately seven o'clock on the morning of June 30, 1908, has been noted by numerous observers…under clear skies and in calm weather… After the fireball fell on the taiga, a 'pillar of fire' rose above it toward the sky, and then three or four powerful blows rang out that could be heard a thousand kilometers away. The blast of air drove giant waves down rivers and knocked people and animals off their feet. Fences were flattened, construction sites were damaged, houses shook, and objects hanging in them swung."

How can you say there was no meteorite, my esteemed friend? Or do you trust your incisive intuition over the testimony of many thousands?

Yet here we have the objective recordings of insensate instruments. The air wave was twice registered in London, meaning that it circled the globe twice. Seismograph stations in Irkutsk, Tbilisi, Tashkent, and Jena registered surface waves with an epicenter in the area of the Podkamennaya Tunguska.

What do you have to counter that, my dear learned physicist? Conceit incarnate?

I leafed through a multitude of eyewitness accounts:

"A fireball brighter than the sun…a pillar of fire seen for hundreds of kilometers…black clouds of smoke that turned into a storm cloud in the clear sky…glass cracked 400 kilometers away…"

This testimony came from the Irkutsk Seismograph Station's correspondence network. It cannot be ignored. To continue: "it swept away tents," "it finished the reindeer," "it stirred the forest" – that was from the Evenks.

"A burst of heat like your shirt was on fire…" – that was from a worker in Vanovara. Even near Kansk, 800 kilometers from where it fell, a locomotive driver, alarmed by the crashing noise, brought his train to a halt.

No, my distinguished but foolish adversary, the time when L.A. Kulik was compelled to prove that a meteorite fell on Tunguska has passed. Since then, Kulik has led several expeditions to the area. Traces of staggering destruction were discovered there: the taiga was blown down to the ground over an area of eight thousand square kilometers. You will see for yourself a gigantic span where trees fell, where the trunks of giant larches lie, their roots, unscrewed from the ground, pointing to one spot – the center of the phenomenal catastrophe. You will be convinced that over a radius of thirty kilometers not a single tree was left standing, and at a radius of sixty kilometers, trees were uprooted at all elevations. An explosion of that force would require hundreds of thousands of tons of the most powerful explosives.

Where could all that energy come from? I will give you the same answer, my dear scientist, that you would give a schoolchild. A meteorite, maintaining its orbital velocity, hit the earth, and all its kinetic energy was instantly converted to heat, which is tantamount to an explosion.

I will direct your attention, my learned adversary, who has never been to the area of the Tunguska disaster, that for local inhabitants, the meteorite's fall is not in dispute. The natives claim that not a single local has gone near the spot where dazzling Ogdy, the god of fire and lightning, came down from the sky. It has been cursed by the shamans. Only during the first days after the disaster did the Evenks walk through the wind-flattened forest, looking for the charred carcasses of their reindeer and the ruined huts where their belongings had been stored, and saw fountains of water that gushed out of the earth for three days. It would perhaps be better, my adversary who no doubt deserves a better fate, if instead of a hypothesis that disavows an obvious phenomenon you came up with an explanation for the local inhabitants' enduring fear.

And finally, the last unexplained phenomenon that attests to a cosmic connection.

A photograph lies before me on my desk that was taken by a local schoolteacher in Narovchat in Penza Province. The photograph was taken at night, one day after the meteorite fell in Siberia. And here is a reference to Academician Fesenkov – still alive and kicking – who was at the Tashkent Observatory that night waiting in vain for darkness to fall so he could commence his observations.

After the meteorite fell, across the entire region, from the Yenisei Basin to the Atlantic Ocean, and even in Central Asia and along the Black Sea, there were white nights such that you could read at midnight. At an altitude of 83 kilometers, shining silver clouds of unknown origin were observed.

There's a problem for you to solve, my dear adversary, vainly yearning for laurels. Explain the connection between this phenomenon and the meteorite that fell, but don't compromise yourself by disputing the established fact of a fallen fireball.

In short, I was infected with polemical fervor, and a biting, brilliant article that would smash to bits the anti-meteorite hypothesis, whatever it might be, was already in my inkwell. I could barely wait to learn the contents of the envelope I'd been given.

But my impatience, along with my polemical fervor, was put to the test.

Between April 3 and August 14, 1945, I received no news from the men who had entrusted me with their manuscripts.

A report about the notorious atom bomb dropped on Japan distracted me from any thought of the physicist, the geologist-ethnographer, and their hypotheses. But a telegram I received instantly cast everything in a new, unexpected light:

"Compare 30 June 1908 seismic data from impact and second American present. Searching for black woman."

There was no doubt. My physicist was referring to the atom bomb I had heard about on the radio.

I admit that I felt as if I had been hit in the head by a heavy sack.

In a state of excitement, I dug into the details of the test bomb's explosion in New Mexico, where from the site of a vaporized steel tower, a pillar of fire could be seen for many dozens of kilometers. With intent focus, I read descriptions of the explosions in Hiroshima and Nagasaki, where a blinding fireball of gases reaching temperatures of twenty million degrees traveled upward, leaving behind a column of flame that burned through clouds and billowed across the sky into a gigantic mushroom of black smoke.

My hands trembled as I compared these details with descriptions of the Tunguska taiga explosion that I had painstakingly prepared for a debate.

To verify my findings, I spent time at the Academy of Sciences, in the Meteorite Committee, and obtained additional material about the "Tunguska Fall." While there I also learned of the death of the scientific secretary for meteorites, L.A. Kulik. This renowned Russian scholar voluntarily stepped forward to defend the Motherland during the very first days of the Great Patriotic War with the same faith in victory that amazed the world during his investigations into the Tunguska meteorite.

How sad that this outstanding scientist was not able to complete his research by comparing the seismic recordings from the meteorite and an atomic explosion!

With help from the Academy of Sciences institute, I managed to perform this comparison.

One feature of the seismograph readings from the Tunguska impact was a record of two jolts, separated by a time interval correlating to the distance between the seismograph station and the site of the explosion. The second jolt that reached the monitoring stations was from the airwave, which traveled from the site of the explosion more slowly than the wave that passed through the earth's crust.

Analysis of readings from the seismographs monitoring the atomic explosion in Nagasaki fit the picture painted by the recordings from June 30, 1908, with amazing precision. Could it really have been that back in 1908 we were already dealing with the first atomic explosion on earth?

Before me lay the envelope concealing the thoughts of the Russian theoretical physicist who had ingeniously divined an atomic reaction in the Tunguska disaster. I could barely control my irritation at the scientist who was off searching for some red-haired black woman in the taiga instead of publishing his ideas. I decided that my wavering was excessive. I unsealed the envelope.

My conjectures were proven right. My theoretician had foreseen everything.

Yes, the Tunguska disaster, in which explosions were heard a thousand kilometers away, a disaster that caused unprecedented destruction and an actual earthquake, that generated a blinding ball of gas that reached temperatures in the tens of millions of degrees and was then transformed into a pillar of fire shooting upward that was seen at a distance of 400 kilometers – this disaster could only have been an atomic explosion.

The physicist assumed that the meteorite that entered the earth's atmosphere, whose weight he determined to be one hundred kilograms at most – not thousands or hundreds of thousands of tons as previously believed – was, unlike most metal meteorites, not made of iron-nickel, but of uranium, or of even heavier transuranium elements, unknown on earth.

The enormous temperature that the meteorite built up as it flew through the earth's atmosphere was one of the conditions making a nuclear explosion possible. The meteorite exploded, discharging its atomic energy without ever touching the ground. Most of its mass instantaneously vaporized and the rest was converted into energy equal to the energy produced by two hundred thousand tons of explosives.

This explains why L.A. Kulik was unable to find any trace of the meteorite or its crater. There was nothing at the center of the windfall but a swamp that formed over the permafrost layer.

Finally, my physicist's hypothesis explained the last two remaining puzzling aspects of the Tunguska disaster. The mysterious silvery clouds that illuminated the earth at night were remnants of the meteorite's radioactive substance blasted up to the Heaviside layer by the force of the explosion. Their atoms' radioactive decay caused the surrounding air to glow.

The superstitious fear of the Evenks who wandered the windfall during the first days after the disaster was directed toward the "wrath" of dazzling Ogdy, god of fire and thunder. Everyone who spent time in this cursed place died of a horrible and baffling illness that covered internal organs with ulcers. The poor Evenks wound up victims of the nuclear decay of minute remnants of the meteorite that scattered over the area of the disaster.

How brilliant and astute my physicist's ideas now seemed! After all, this was the very phenomenon with which the Japanese were confronted in Nagasaki after the atom bomb exploded. The decay of the remaining atoms could continue for one-and-a-half to two months.

The upcoming issue of our journal with the physicist's article had already been laid out and sent to the printers when I received a telegram from him in Vanovara: "Hypothesis wrong. Destroy manuscript. Saw black woman. Heading back."

I was beside myself with indignation. Once again I refused to believe the physicist.

It would be hard for anyone else to imagine how reluctant I was to part with the hypothesis that the meteorite caused a nuclear explosion! I could not, simply could not force myself to telephone the printer.

But what was I to do? What proof that he was wrong could the physicist have found at the site of the disaster?

Another telegram, again from Vanovara, was delivered. I unfolded it with trembling hands: "Last descendant pre-glacial black Siberians found. Publish."

I stared at Sergei Antonovich's telegram in bewilderment. What bearing could the pre-glacial black woman have had on the hypothesis about the nuclear explosion? Finally I realized that there was no getting to the bottom of this. At the very least, that would require the imagination of a crazy person. Giving up on any and all conjecture, I unsealed Sergei Antonovich's envelope and tried to figure out whether his article would be the right length to replace the other, which had already been incorporated into our upcoming issue.

I became so engrossed in my professional duties I failed to notice that my door had opened and a bearded man had entered my office in muddy boots that were tracking dirt on my parquet floor. After unfastening his fur jacket and removing his *ushanka*, he reached out his hand like an old friend.

Looking inquisitively at this stranger, I muttered a polite greeting and…suddenly I recognized him.

The beard! The missing glasses! But how did he get to Moscow so quickly? The telegram had only just arrived!

I grabbed it and looked at the dispatch date: well, of course…there was a delay.

"The manuscript…" the physicist blurted, breathing heavily. He had apparently been walking fast. "I rushed here from the airport…"

"The journal is still at the printers," I replied. "But where are your glasses?"

The physicist gave a dismissive wave.

"They broke."

He silently sat down, took a tobacco pouch out of his pocket, rolled a cigarette with his brown, calloused hands, and fumbled as he tried to retrieve his flint. I offered him an electric lighter. The visitor smiled awkwardly.

"Gone a bit wild," he remarked laconically as he lit up.

We sat facing one another in silence. I examined my transformed scholar. He now seemed broader in the shoulders. A healthy tan and thick, curly beard gave him the appearance of a strapping young buck. Inhaling the smoke from his strong, cheap tobacco, he stared pensively into the corner. His thoughts were somewhere far away.

"Curious?" he asked concisely.

"Of course!"

"You know," he looked at me, and suddenly, squinting myopically, was transformed into the theoretical physicist I had known, "until now, I had never slept in the forest, and I had only seen a swamp from a train car window. I couldn't stand mosquitoes, so I never went to the dacha. I bathed twice a week," he flicked ash on the floor and then grinned and gave me a guilty glance. "In short, I've gone a bit wild," he added, not quite coherently.

We again fell silent.

"You'd probably like to know just why it was I traveled to the site of the Tunguska disaster, what I was looking for there? I'll start with the taiga landscape where the trees were blown down. Just imagine: at the disaster's center, around the swamp that used to be considered the main crater where, supposedly, the explosion had the strongest impact, the forest was left standing. The trees, which were knocked down everywhere else within a radius of thirty kilometers, are standing rather than lying there. Huge sticks are sticking up out of the ground, and new growth is already sprouting among them… That's what's left of the trees; their roots are long since dead, they have no bark – it was scorched and fell away. All the branches were sheared by monstrous winds, and the knots where the branches once were are charcoal. Telegraph poles – that's what these trees look like. Only a vertical hurricane could have left them standing, a hurricane that blew down from above."

My visitor took a deep drag of his cigarette and, with evident pleasure, blew a thick cloud of smoke up to the ceiling. I did not interrupt his silence.

"This was the image I needed," he continued, apparently finding it difficult to tear himself away from his thoughts. "Why was this dead forest left standing? Only because the trees in that spot were perpendicular to the blast wave. And that could only have been the case if the explosion took place above the earth! Gases rising to a temperature in the hundreds of thousands of degrees, after traveling at a tremendous velocity, sliced off branches, scorched trees, and left behind a vacuum. The cold air that rushed into it put out the fire."

"So there was an explosion after all?" I was almost glad.

"Yes, at an altitude of five kilometers above ground. I calculated this altitude based on the area of the dead forest left standing. A simple geometry problem."

"If the meteorite didn't make contact with the ground, it could only have been a nuclear explosion. Now I'm prepared to defend your hypothesis even against you!" I exclaimed earnestly.

"That's interesting," the physicist remarked. "A scholarly duel? Go ahead and make your case!"

And so we entered into a rather strange debate. The physicist did, in the end, wind up being my adversary, but we had exchanged roles.

"What could have caused the meteorite to instantaneously explode?" the physicist asked, puffing on his cigarette.

"We've got to assume that it was made of a uranium isotope with an atomic weight of 235 capable of a so-called 'chain reaction.'"

"Correct. Either a uranium or a plutonium isotope. Now, describe what this chain reaction looked like, and you'll immediately see the weakness of the hypothesis you're defending."

"I'll be glad to. If the atoms of a uranium isotope are bombarded with neutrons, which have no electric charge from elementary particles of substance, when a neutron hits, the nucleus will split into two parts, releasing tremendous energy and emitting, on top of that, three neutrons that break up neighboring atoms, which in turn emit three neutrons each. There's your description of a continuous chain reaction that doesn't stop until all the uranium atoms decay."

"That's all correct. But tell me, what is needed to trigger an atomic reaction?"

"The first atom has to break apart; the first nucleus has to be hit with a neutron."

"Exactly. But there's a trap hidden here. Do you know how far apart atoms are from one another? The distance between them is like the distance between planets, if we put atomic nuclei on a planetary scale. Just try to hit a planet – a nucleus – when you're flying along like a comet, as we can imagine neutrons to be. Physicists have calculated how thick a layer of uranium the neutron would have to pass through in order, based on probability theory, to hit an atomic nucleus. Some calculate that to trigger a chain reaction, the so-called critical mass of uranium needed would be at least eighty tons."

"That's not true! You're resorting to dirty tricks. That's what they used to think. Just one kilogram is enough to start a nuclear reaction."

"I agree," the physicist smiled. "You're beating me at my own game, but you don't realize I have another trick up my sleeve. Yes, it's true that a neutron stream can't start a chain reaction in a half-kilogram of uranium, but in a kilogram it definitely can. What does that mean? We seem to have already established that the meteorite that fell had to have at least a kilogram of uranium-235 isotope."

"Absolutely right."

"But we also need flying neutrons. Tell me, what started the reaction? Where did the neutron stream come from?"

"Cosmic rays? After all, they do have flying neutrons, don't they?"

"You've done your homework, you've definitely done your homework," the physicist grinned. "But that same sort of neutron stream was also present outside the atmosphere. Why didn't the meteorite explode there?"

"The speed of the neutrons should play a decisive role here. At a high velocity, neutrons might not do much damage to a nucleus, like a bullet that goes through a board but doesn't knock it over."

"Remarkably true," the physicist banged his fist on the desk. "To start a chain reaction, flying neutrons have to slow down."

"If the high temperature, the heating up of the meteorite as it moved through the atmosphere, affected neutron velocity…"

"You've fallen into the trap!" the physicist cried, jumping to his feet. "You've been crushed, dear opponent! It's time to start making assumptions. 'If'! There's no 'if'! I don't know how the Americans made their atomic bomb, but, without meaning to, you and I have figured out its entire 'mechanism.' Yes, the hardest thing the Americans had to do was slow down the neutrons. And it's doubtful they could have done that without heavy water."

"That's true, the Americans really did use heavy water. How well informed you were, off in the taiga!"

"I was well informed before the taiga, not in the taiga. I'm a theoretician after all. Theoreticians are supposed to see solutions to problems far in advance, many years before they're solved by practitioners, empiricists. So in the case of our meteorite, it's hard to imagine that there could have been any inhibitory elements in place that would have been activated at just the right moment. After all, these elements were put in place in the American atomic bomb artificially."

"So what were you searching for in the Tunguska taiga if before going you knew that no nuclear explosion could have occurred?" I jumped up, ready to pounce on the physicist, who had just refuted his own theory with devastating dispassion.

"I was looking for something that might have been there before the disaster. For that, I lugged a mine detector over many a kilometer, while being sucked dry by those damned mosquitoes."

"A mine detector?" I stared at the physicist and was silent for a few moments as I thought something through.

"And did what you found there change your views?" I almost shouted. "Do you really think that the explosion might have been manmade, that we were dealing with an atomic bomb?"

"No," the physicist replied calmly. "The nuclear explosion was not caused by a bomb."

"I give up. I can't do this anymore. So, none of it's true… You didn't find anything?"

"Yes, over the course of a month and a half in the area of the windfall I did not find the meteorite crater, any fragments or traces of the meteorite, or any metal objects that might have been there before the explosion. That's not surprising. Even trees were pushed four meters deep into the peat. But…"

"But what? Don't torment me… Tell me, what did you find there?"

"Don't interrupt. I'll tell you everything in the proper order."

"I give up. I'm not your adversary anymore; I'm just going to listen. But please allow me to write it down."

"As I already told you, my search with the mine detector yielded nothing. Since the expedition was only beginning its work, under the terms of my agreement with Sergei Antonovich, after my search in the area of the windfall I had to join him in the search for his idiotic black-skinned woman of the taiga. Of course, at that point, I didn't think that she could disprove my initial hypothesis. We got ourselves some Evenk guides, and, riding their reindeer, set out on our journey."

"The nuclear explosion and the black woman! What's the connection?" I groaned.

"You promised not to interrupt."

"But a scientist like you has to have some logic. Well, fine. I'll keep quiet."

"For about two months we tirelessly hunted for the last of the tribe of black-skinned Siberians. We learned that she was alive and was practicing something akin to shamanism somewhere. We finally caught up with her at a nomad's camp near a village with the amazingly melodious name of 'Taimba,' which doesn't sound anything like either Russian or Evenk. An Evenk brought us there, Ilya Potapovich Lyuchetkan, who once upon a time served as guide for Kulik himself, despite the fact that the shamans forbade this. Lyuchetkan was ancient, with a wrinkled, brown face and such narrow eyes that they almost always seemed to be closed.

"'The shamaness is a strange woman,' he said, stroking his smooth chin. 'Forty years ago, maybe less, she came to the Khurkhangyr clan. Ruined, she was.'

"We knew that Evenks use the word 'ruined' for both people suffering from a concussion and the insane.

"'She couldn't speak,' Ilya Potapovich continued, 'she screamed. She screamed a lot. She couldn't remember anything. Healing, she knew. Could heal with just her eyes. She became a shamaness. Many years she spoke to no one. A strange person. A black person. Not one of us, but a shaman… a shaman… Here, there are still many old Evenks. The Russian tsar is long gone. The merchant who took furs from the Evenks is long gone, but they still have a shaman. Other Evenks drove their shaman away long ago. They got a teacher. We'll write a forest newspaper. But here there is still a shamaness. Why do you want to look at her? It would be better if I showed you a hunting cooperative. I'm telling you, *bae*.'

"Sergei Antonovich kept trying to find out what clan the shamaness came from, hoping to determine her ancestry. But all we managed to establish was that before she showed up in the Khurkhangyr clan, nobody knew anything about her. Perhaps she lost her memory and the ability to speak during the meteorite disaster, and it looked as if to this day she still hadn't recovered.

"Lyuchetkan told us:

"'Under the tsar, the Evenks were forced to get baptized, but they kept their shamans; they didn't want to obey the tsar. They kept on worshipping the black loon, the taimen fish, and the bear. But now they've driven away the shamans.'

"He also told us about the black shamaness' strange rituals.

"She performed her rituals in the early morning, with the rising of the morning star.

"Lyuchetkan woke Sergei Antonovich and me up. We got up quietly and went out of the tent. The stars scattered across the sky looked to me like the debris of a universal nuclear disaster.

"In the taiga, the forest never ends; there are no clearings. In the taiga there is only swamp.

"The shamaness' cone-shaped tent stood right at the bog's edge. The solid wall of larches parted and lower stars were visible.

"Lyuchetkan stopped us.

"'You have to stand here, *bae*.'

"We watched as a tall, stately figure came out of the tent, followed by three old Evenk women who looked tiny in comparison with the shamaness. The procession made its way through the marshy swamp in single file.'"

"'Take poles, *bae*. You'll fall – it will hold you up. We'll go around the long way if you want to watch, if you want to have a laugh.'

"Like tightrope walkers, holding our poles for balance, we walked through the swamp, which was living and breathing beneath our feet, with the tussocks to our right and left undulating as if they were ready to shoot into the air. Even the bushes and young trees were swinging, grabbing hold of the poles and, it seemed, trying to block our path.

"We turned at a stand of young saplings and stopped. Over a black, jagged line of forest and circled by a small aureole, shone the morning star.

"The shamaness and her companions were standing in the middle of a marsh with arms raised. I then heard a low, prolonged tone. And as if in response to it, a distant forest echo sounded, repeating the tone but at some sort of multi-octave pitch. Then the echo, reverberating even louder, faded into a strange, indistinct melody. I realized that this was her, the shamaness, singing.

"So began this indescribable duet for voice and forest echo, both of which were often singing at the same time, blending into an unintelligible but entrancing harmony.

"The song ended. I did not want to move – I couldn't.

"'That's a prehistoric song. Yu-yu-you see, my hypothesis about pre-glacial people was correct,' Sergei Antonovich whispered excitedly.

"That day, we sat in the shamaness' tent, brought there by Ilya Ivanovich Khurkhangyr, a wrinkled old man without a single hair on his face. This forest dweller, who has never known dust, didn't even have eyelashes or brows.

"The shamaness was wearing a rather beat-up looking Evenk parka decorated with colorful strips of cloth and ribbon. Her eyes were hidden behind a fur hat pushed forward onto her forehead, and her mouth and nose were wrapped in a tattered shawl, as if to protect against cold.

"We were sitting on the floor of the dark tent on some foul smelling hides.

"'Why have you come? Are you sick?' the shamaness asked in a low, velvety voice. I immediately recalled the song at the swamp that morning.

"Giving in to a sudden impulse, I moved closer to the black-skinned shamaness and said to her:

"'Listen, *bae* shamaness. Have you heard of Moscow? There are many stone tents there. We have built a large ship there. This ship can fly. Better than birds – to the very stars,' and I pointed upward. 'I'll return to Moscow and then I will fly into the sky in that ship. I'll fly to the morning star, the one you sing songs to.'

"The shamaness leaned toward me. She seemed to have understood.

"'I'll fly into the sky on this ship,' I went on excitedly. 'Would you like me to take you with me to the morning star?'

"The shamaness looked at me with terrified eyes that were absolutely blue.

"Total silence reigned in the tent. Someone's intently focused face was looking at me from the darkness. Suddenly I saw the shamaness begin to slump slowly down, and then writhe, and then grab at the hide. Biting it with her teeth, she began to roll on the ground. Gurgling sounds came from her throat – I couldn't tell if she was sobbing or uttering some incomprehensible words.

"'Ay, *bae, bae*,' the aged Khurkhangyr cried in a feeble voice. 'What have you done, *bae*!... What you did was bad, *bae*. Very bad… Go, get out of here, *bae*, right away. The star is holy, and you were talking… it's bad.'

"'How could yu-yu-you offend their faith? What have yu-yu-you done?' Sergei Antonovich whispered angrily.

"We hurried out of the tent. Lyuchetkan ran to get the reindeer with uncharacteristic speed.

"I have never seen such peaceable, gentle people as the Evenk hunters who live in the forest, but now they were unrecognizable. They glared at us in sullen hostility as we departed the nomad camp.

"'Yu-yu-you have ruined an Academy of Sciences ethnographic expedition,' Sergei Antonovich, who held back his reindeer to draw even with me, was so overcome he could barely speak.

"'Your hypothesis is wrong,' I growled, and dug my heels into my antlered steed.

"Sergei Antonovich and I had a falling out and did not speak once during the three days spent waiting for the hydroplane from Krasnoyarsk.

"Only Lyuchetkan was happy.

"'Good going, *bae*,' he smiled, reducing his eyes to two horizontal wrinkles across his brown face. 'You sure showed that the shamaness is nothing but a ruined person. I'll write about it in the Evenk forest newspaper. Let all the forest people know!'

"Strange thoughts were racing through my mind. The hydroplane had already arrived, the strong current tugging at its mooring ropes. A boat had delivered me to the plane, but I still couldn't tear my eyes away from the opposite bank of the Podkamennaya Tunguska.

"Beyond the cliff, so steep it looked as if it had been chopped by an ax, the river seemed to reluctantly turn to the right and head toward the site of the nuclear disaster. But on the opposite bank you couldn't see anything but the swaying tops of already yellowing larches, covered by an early snowfall.

"Suddenly, I noticed a figure jumping up and down on the cliff top. Shots rang out. It was a man, and, next to him, a creature with antlers!

"It was an Evenk with an elk!

"Not hesitating for a moment, I got back into the boat to return to the other side. I was startled by a loud thud when the massive Sergei Antonovich also jumped into the boat. Our native guide rowed as fast as he could. The Evenk stopped shooting and began to make his way down to the river.

"Our boat was going so fast it jumped half way up the rocky shore.

"'*Bae, bae*,' the Evenk cried. 'Hurry, *bae*! *Birda khok* time. None at all. The Shamaness is dying. She asked us to bring you back. She wants to tell you something.'

"For the first time since our quarrel, Sergei Antonovich and I looked at one another.

"A minute later, the elk was racing through the year's first snowfall, between the steep river bank and the golden-gray wall of taiga.

"I once heard that elk can run eighty kilometers an hour. But to experience that first hand, clinging to the sled for dear life… To see the yellowed larches flash by so fast they blur into a solid wall…To squint as the snow flies into your eyes… No, I can't convey the feeling of this extraordinary race across the taiga! The Evenk seemed to be in a delirium. He drove the elk with wild cries and whistles. Clumps of snow kept hitting us in the face as if we were in a blizzard. One cheek or the other was always burning with cold from the hurricane-force winds.

"We arrived at the camp. I wiped the powder from my eyes. It was during that wild ride that my glasses broke.

"A crowd of Evenks was waiting for us. In front stood the aged Khurkhangyr.

"'Hurry, hurry *bae*! There's not much time left!' Tears were streaming down his cheeks, one after another.

"We ran to the tent. The women stepped aside to let us through.

"The tent was well lit. There was the crackle of resinous torches. In the middle of the tent, a body was stretched out on something like a table or high bed.

"I involuntarily shuddered and grabbed Sergei Antonovich by the arm. Frozen in deathbed majesty before us, with barely any covering, lay a beautiful statue that looked as if it had been cast in iron. The unusual proportions of the tar-black face were startling and hard to compare with anything. And would one really compare the beauty of a cliff of wild, black stone with the Hellenic beauty of a Greek temple?

"Intrepid energy and suppressed sorrow had caused these feminine lips, compressed in pain, to contort. Stern brows arched up from the delicate bridge of her nose as if in intense effort. Her brow protruded strangely, making her motionless face alien, unfamiliar, unlike anything I'd seen before.

"Her hair, which spilled down her shoulders, simultaneously shimmered bronze and silver.

"Has she really died?' Sergei Antonovich bent down to listen to her heart.

"'It's not beating,' he said in alarm.

"The lashes of the black goddess quivered. Sergei Antonovich recoiled.

"'Her heart is on the right side!' he whispered.

"The old women were standing in a circle around the table, leaning intently forward. One of them approached us.

"'*Bae*, she will speak no more. She will die. She asked to tell you. When you fly to the morning star, be sure to take her with you…'

"The old woman started crying. The black statue lay motionless, as if she really was cast in iron.

"We quietly left the tent. It was time to go. There was a danger that the river could freeze and the hydroplane wouldn't be able to take off. And so… here I am."

The physicist fell silent. He stood up and paced the room, clearly upset.

"She died?" I asked hesitantly.

"I'll go back, I'll definitely go back to the taiga again," my visitor stated. "And maybe I'll see her."

We had already added a few sentences to his hypothesis about the nuclear explosion when Sergei Antonovich entered the room, also with an unruly beard.

"Have you published my hypothesis about the black-skinned woman?" he demanded, so agitated he dispensed with any greeting.

Instead of responding, I handed him the page that contained what the physicist had dictated to me. Dumbfounded, Sergei Antonovich sat quietly for several minutes with the paper still in his hands. He then rose, asked me for his article back, and methodically tore it into neat little shreds.

I reread what we had added to the physicist's hypothesis: "There is also the possibility that the explosion took place not in a uranium meteorite, but in an interplanetary spaceship that ran on atomic energy.

After landing at the upper reaches of the Podkamennaya Tunguska, the travelers may have spread out to study the surrounding taiga when their ship was destroyed in some sort of accident.

"Propelled upward to a height of five kilometers, it exploded, the gradual release of atomic energy having turned into a runaway chain reaction in the uranium, or some other radioactive substance present on the spaceship in the quantity needed to fuel its return to an unknown planet."

First published in Russian: 1946
Translation by Nora Seligman Favorov

RED STAR REFORMING

THE SPONTANEOUS REFLEX

Urm had gotten bored.

Strictly speaking, boredom, as a reaction to uniformity and monotonous surroundings or an internal dissatisfaction – a loss of interest in life – is intrinsic only to humans and certain animals. In order to be bored, one needs, so to speak, a means of being bored: a finely and perfectly organized nervous system. One needs to be able to think, or at least to suffer. Urm did not have a nervous system in the usual sense of the word, and he was not able to think, let alone suffer. He only perceived, remembered, and acted. But just the same, he had gotten bored.

The thing was that, after the Master had left, there was nothing new around for Urm to remember. Add to this the fact that the accumulation of new impressions was the basic stimulus that directed Urm's actions and motivated him to said actions. He was driven by an inexhaustible curiosity, an inexhaustible thirst to perceive and remember as much as possible. If there were no unknown facts and phenomena, then some had to be found.

But Urm's surroundings were familiar to him to the last visual detail, to the last undertone. He remembered the vast square room with rough cement walls, low ceiling, and iron door from the first moment of his existence. It always smelled here of heated metal and transformer oil. An indistinct low hum could be heard from somewhere above. People could not hear it without special instruments, but Urm heard it perfectly well. The fluorescent lights on the ceiling were extinguished, but just the same Urm saw the room perfectly well in infrared and in the pulse signals of his locators.

And so, Urm had gotten bored, and he resolved to set out in search of new impressions. A half-hour had passed since the Master had gone. Experience suggested to Urm that he would not return anytime soon. This was very important, because Urm had once embarked on a little stroll around the room without having been ordered to do so, and the Master, who caught him in this activity, made it so that Urm could not even move his locator horn. Now, it seemed he did not have to worry about this.

Urm teetered and heavily stepped forward. The cement floor rang out under his thick rubber soles, and Urm stopped for a moment to listen, and even bent over. But in the range of sounds emitted by the vibrating cement there was not a single new one, and Urm again made for the opposite wall. He walked right up to it and took a sniff. The wall smelled of wet concrete and rusted metal. Nothing new. Then Urm turned around, gouging the wall with his sharp steel elbow, cut diagonally across the room and stopped in front of the door. Opening the door was not a simple matter, and Urm did not grasp right away how it should be done. Then, extending his toothed claw of a left hand, he nimbly grabbed the lock lever and turned it. The door opened with a weak, drawn-out groan. This was diverting, and Urm spent several minutes opening and closing the door, now quickly, now slowly, listening closely and committing the sounds to memory. Then he stepped across the high threshold and found himself facing a staircase. The staircase was narrow, with stone steps to the first landing, and fairly long. Urm in an instant counted eighteen steps to the first landing, where a light was burning. Then, taking his time, he went up. From the landing another staircase led upward, wooden, with ten steps, and a wide corridor opened to the right. Hesitating for a moment, Urm turned right. He did not know why. The corridor was no less interesting than the stairs. But it is probable that Urm did not like the look of the wooden steps.

Warmth emanated from the corridor, and it was brightly illuminated in infrared. The infrared light was being emitted by some ribbed cylinders, mounted not far above the floor. Urm had never before seen steam radiators, and the ribbed cylinders interested him. He bent over and hooked one of them with both claws. A brief crack rang out along with the groaning of metal, and a thick cloud of hot steam swelled up to the ceiling. A stream of boiling water gushed under Urm's feet. Urm raised the cylinder up to his head, attentively looked it over, and examined the torn edge of the pipe. Then the cylinder was cast aside, and Urm's soles squelched through the puddles. Urm went to the end of the corridor. There above the low door blazed a red sign. "Caution! No Entry Without Protective Suit!" Urm read. He knew the word "caution," but also knew that this word always applied to people. To him, to Urm, this word could not apply. He extended his arm and gave the door a shove.

Yes, here there was a great deal that was interesting and new. He stood in the entrance to a vast room, filled with objects of metal, stone, and plastic. In the middle of the room, a meter above the floor, rose a round concrete structure resembling a low pillar, covered with a shield of iron or lead. Numerous cables ran from it in all directions toward the walls, along which stretched marble panels with gleaming instruments and switch handles. An enclosure made of copper wire surrounded the concrete pillar, and gleaming articulated rods hung from the ceiling. The rods ended in pincers and claws, just like the ones on Urm's arms.

Urm, treading inaudibly across the ceramic tiles of the floor, walked up to the copper meshwork and made a circuit around it. Then he stood for a moment and walked around it a second time. There was no opening in the meshwork. Then Urm lifted his foot and effortlessly strode through the meshwork. Torn shreds of copper cobweb hung from his shoulders. But, before he took the two steps to the concrete pillar, he stopped stock-still. His head, round as a schoolroom globe, warily turned right and left: the ebonite shells of his acoustic receptors extended and stirred, his locator horns shuddered. The leaden lid on the pillar emitted infrared light, apparent even in the heated building. But, in addition to this, it was emitting some sort of ultra-radiant emanation. Urm saw well in x- and gamma rays, and it seemed to him that the lid was transparent, with a narrow concrete well opening under it, filled with glowing dust. In the depths of Urm's memory a command surfaced: *leave this place at once*. Urm did not know when and by whom this command had been issued. Probably, Urm came into the world already knowing it, as he knew many other things. But Urm did not obey the command. Curiosity turned out to be stronger. He bent over the pillar, extended his claws and with some effort lifted the lid.

The flood of gamma rays blinded him. Red lights on the marble panels blinked on, and a siren began howling. He saw for a moment, through the transparent silhouettes of his arms, the interior of the concrete pit, then threw the lid down, proclaiming in a low, hoarse voice:

"Opasnost! Gefahr! Danger! Weixian! Abunai!"

A booming echo bounded around the room and faded away. Urm turned the upper portion of his body one hundred and eighty degrees and hastily made for the exit. The shock in his status meters brought about by the flood of radioactive particles drove him away from the concrete pillar. Of course, neither the hardest radiation nor a mighty flood of particles could do Urm the slightest harm; even spending some time in the active zone of a reactor would not threaten Urm with serious consequences. But, in creating Urm, his masters had embedded in him a tendency to stay as far away as possible from sources of intense radiation. Urm went out into the corridor, painstakingly closed the door behind him, and, stepping over the ribbed cylinder of the radiator, once again found himself on the staircase landing. Right away he saw a Human hurriedly coming down the wooden staircase.

The Human was considerably shorter than the Master. It had on loose-fitting, light-colored clothing, and its hair was strangely long, and golden in color. Urm had never seen such people before. He drew in some air and sensed the familiar smell of white lilac. At times the Master gave off the same scent, though much more faintly.

Half-darkness reigned on the landing, and the staircase behind the woman was brightly illuminated, so she could not immediately discern the outline of Urm's enormous body. Rather, hearing his footsteps, she stopped and called out angrily:

"Who's that? It is you, Ivashev?"

"Hello, how do you do?" said Urm huskily.

The woman screamed. From the half-darkness a gleaming head with bulging glass eyes, excessively wide armor-plated shoulders, and thick articulated arms advanced on her. Urm set foot on the lowest step of the wooden staircase, and the woman began shrieking again.

Never before had a Human failed to answer Urm's greeting. But this strange, high sound, shrill, penetrating and certainly inarticulate, did not resemble any of the standard answer templates that Urm knew. Intrigued, Urm purposefully moved forward after the retreating woman. The wooden steps groaned and cracked under his feet.

"Back!" screamed the woman.

Urm stopped and tilted his head, listening closely.

"Back, you monster!"

The command "back" was familiar to Urm. According to this command, he was to turn the upper portion of his body around and take several steps in the opposite direction until he heard the command "stop." But commands usually originated from the Master, and, besides that, Urm wanted to investigate. He once again began to ascend the steps, until he found himself in front of the entrance of a small, brightly lit room.

"Back! Back! Back!" screamed the woman.

By now Urm did not stop anymore, though he was going slower than he might. The room interested him: two desks, chairs, a drafting board, a bookcase, and thick folders. While he opened drawers, untied the strings on the folders and read aloud the notes that had been made in black ink in the margins of technical diagrams, the woman slipped into the room next door, hid behind the couch and grabbed the telephone handset. Urm saw this, as he had an optical receptor on the back of his head, but the small longhaired human no longer interested him. Walking across the papers spread all over the floor, he set off on his way. Behind his back the woman shouted into the telephone:

"Nikolai Petrovich! Nikolai Petrovich, it's me, Galya! Nikolai Petrovich, Urm broke into our office. Your Urm! Urm! Uniform, Romeo, Mike… Didn't you hear the siren? Yes! I don't know… When I ran into him he was coming out of the big reactor room… Yes, yes, he was in the reactor room… What? Apparently not. They already know about it at the central station."

Urm did not bother to listen. He went into the foyer and there stopped stock-still, redoubling the movements of his black locator horns. Something large, gleaming, and cold hung on the opposite wall. It seemed in infrared to be a grey, impenetrable square, and it flashed and shone silver in ordinary light, but this was not what confused Urm. In the strange square stood a black monstrosity with wiggling horns on its head, which was round like a schoolroom globe, and Urm could not understand just where it was located. His visual diastimeter instantly informed him that it was twelve meters, eight centimeters to the unfamiliar object, but his locator negated this report. *There is no object there. There is a smooth, nearly vertical surface at a distance of… six meters, four centimeters.* Urm had never before seen the like, and his locator and his visual receptors had never before given him such contradictory readings. At the beginning of his existence a desire had been inlaid in his very physical being to make everything he happened to come into contact with clear and understood. So he resolutely walked forward, noting and recording on the way the relation that had emerged: "The distance according to the visual diastimeter is equal to the distance according to the locator, divided by two"… He walked into the mirror. The glass flew apart in a clangorous rain of shards, and Urm, leaning against the wall, stopped. Clearly, there was nothing left to do here. Urm scraped at the wall, sniffed, turned; paying no attention to the police officer on duty who, white as a sheet, was hanging from the lever of the air-raid siren, and, crunching through broken glass, he strode towards the exit. The driving snow surrounded him.

As Nikolai Petrovich was throwing down the handset, Piskunov was already in the entryway, hurriedly buttoning his fur coat.

"Where are you going?"

"There, of course…"

"Wait, we have to decide what to do. If that hunk of metal starts horsing around in the electrical station…"

"It'll be fine if it's just the electrical station, " Ryabkin interrupted him. "What about the lab? Or the warehouse? Or what if he drops by over here, in the village?"

Nikolai Petrovich was thinking intensely. Piskunov shifted impatiently from one foot to the other, holding onto the doorknob.

"We have to run over there all together," gingerly suggested Kostenko, "Find him and… well, grab him!"

Piskunov just winced, while Ryabkin, rooting around the rack in search of his fur coat, shouted angrily, "That's a great idea: grab him! What do you think we should grab him by? His pants? He weighs half a ton, one of his fists can punch with a force of three thousand kilos. It's ridiculous. You're new here, Kostenko, so you should just keep quiet…"

"Everybody listen," said Korolev. "Here's what we'll do. I'll call the dorm and raise the student trainees. You, Ryabkin, run to the motor pool… Dammit, everyone is probably at the club… Run over there anyway, find at least three drivers. We have to get the tracked bulldozers… Is that right, Piskunov?"

"Yes, yes, and as soon as possible. But…"

"Piskunov, you get over to the Institute. Figure out where Urm is and call the motor pool right away. Kostenko, you go with him. Clear? I just hope that devil doesn't get through the gate!"

Jostling and stepping on each other's feet, they tumbled out onto the porch. Ryabkin slipped and butted his head into Kostenko's back, and Kostenko fell on all fours with a crash.

"Dammit, just dammit!"

"What, your glasses?"

"No, everything's fine."

A fierce wind drove clouds of dry snow over the ground, mournfully howled in the power lines, and hummed deeply in the iron lacework of the high-voltage towers. Dim rectangles of light fell from the windows of the cottage, and all else was plunged into impenetrable darkness.

"Well, I'm off," said Ryabkin. "Be careful over there, friends, don't stick your necks out if you don't have to."

He stumbled again and for a minute floundered in the snowdrift, muttering obscene obscenities at the damned snowstorm, that pig of an Urm and generally all those accessory to the incident. Then his light-colored fur coat was glimpsed by the wicket gate before it disappeared in the eddies of swirling snow.

Piskunov and Kostenko were left alone.

Kostenko huddled up against the bitter cold.

"I don't understand," he said. "What on earth are the tractors for?"

"And what would you recommend?" inquired Piskunov.

"No, I just don't understand… Do you want to destroy Urm?"

Piskunov exhaled sharply.

"Urm is a unique machine, the creative result of the last several years of work by the Institute of Experimental Cybernetics. Do you understand? Why would I want him destroyed?"

He lifted up the tails of his fur coat and made his way through the snowdrift. A confused and timid Kostenko followed after him. The snow-covered field lay before them, the highway behind them. Right across the highway was the electrical station.

So as to shorten their path, Piskunov turned off of the highway and went through the vacant lot where a foundation pit had been excavated in the fall for a new building. Kostenko could hear Piskunov muttering something as he stumbled over an ice-covered pile of bricks and rods of rebar. It was difficult going. Beyond the shroud of the snowstorm they could just make out the Institute's sparse chain of lights.

"Wait a second," Kostenko said finally. "By God, it's hard going! Let's rest for a minute."

Piskunov squatted down next to him. What had happened, after all? He knew Urm like no one else at the Institute. Every little screw, every electrode, every lens of that marvelous mechanism had passed through his hands. He had thought he could calculate and predict each of his movements under any circumstances. And now this. Urm had "willfully" come out of his basement and was now strolling around the electrical station. Why?

Urm's behavior was governed by his "brain," an extraordinarily complex and delicate apparatus composed of germanium-platinum foam and ferrite. While an ordinary digital machine has tens of thousands of circuits (the elementary parts that receive, store, and deliver information), Urm's brain employed nearly eighteen million logic cells. They held the programmed reactions for a multitude of situations, for different variations of changes in circumstances, and they anticipated the execution of an enormous number of different operations. What could have influenced the "brain," the program? Emissions from his atomic engine? No, his engine is surrounded by thick shielding made of zirconium, gadolinium, and boron steel. In practical terms, not a single neutron, not a single gamma ray could pierce the shielding. Then his receptors? No, the receptors had been in ideal working order just this evening. Then the whole of the matter is in the "brain" itself. The program. The complex new program. Piskunov himself had overseen the programming and... The programming... That was it!

Piskunov stood up slowly.

"A spontaneous reflex!" he said. "Of course, it's a spontaneous reflex! I'm an idiot!"

Kostenko looked at him fearfully.

"I don't understand…"

"But I do. It's obvious… But who would have thought? Everything was going so well."

"Look!" Kostenko suddenly yelled.

He gasped and jumped to his feet. The greyish-black sky over the Institute was lit up by a tremulous blue explosion, and against this blaze, surprisingly well defined and at the same time unreal, the silhouettes of black buildings sprang up out of the whirling of the snowstorm. The sparsely lit chain of lights that defined the walls of the Institute blinked and went out.

"It's the transformer!" said Piskunov hoarsely. "The substation's right across from the reactor tower. That's were Urm is… and the guards…"

"Let's run!" Kostenko proposed.

They set off running. This was no simple matter. The oncoming wind swept them off of their legs, and they tripped in holes filled with dry snow, fell, got up, and fell again.

"Faster, faster!" Piskunov urged.

Tears, either from the wind or from the excitement, covered his face, froze on his eyelashes as blurry little drops of ice, made it hard for him to see. He grabbed Kostenko's arm and dragged him, still muttering hoarsely:

"Faster, faster!"

Apparently, the explosion over the Institute had been noticed in the village. On the outskirts, a siren began howling anxiously, the windows of the cottages where the guards were stationed lit up, and the blinding ray of a searchlight skimmed over the field. It plucked snowy barchans and the latticed pillars of the of the high-voltage towers out of the darkness, slid along the stone wall that surrounded the Institute, and, finally, came to a stop at the gate. Next to the gate small black figures moved around rapidly.

"Who's that… over there?" asked Kostenko, catching his breath.

"The guards. The police, probably…" Piskunov stopped, wiped his eyes, his voice was failing him. "They've locked… the gate. Good thinking! That means… Urm's still over there."

Apparently, the alarm had been raised. Now not one, but three searchlights were feeling along the walls of the Institute. One could see snowy whirlwinds dancing in the blue light. Through the noise and the wind's howling the sound of shouts reached them; someone was cursing angrily. Finally, motors roared to life, the clank of treads could be heard. The gigantic bulldozers were coming out of the vehicle fleet.

"Look, Kostenko," said Piskunov. "Look closely. We are present at the most unusual round-up in the history of humanity. Look closely, Kostenko!"

Kostenko looked skeptically at Piskunov. It seemed to him that tears were running down the engineer's face. Of course, they could have been from the wind.

Meanwhile, they could now hear the clank of treads not only from behind, but also to the right. The bulldozers were on the highway. They could already see the shaky sparks of headlights. There were five such sparks.

"Five against one," whispered Piskunov. "He doesn't have a chance. His spontaneous reflex arc won't help him here."

And then something suddenly changed all around them. Kostenko could not even tell right away just what had happened. As before, the snowstorm howled; as before, clouds of dry snow tore around over the ground; as before, the motors of the bulldozers roared, threatening and confident. But the searchlights were no longer gliding along the field. They had come to a dead stop at the gate. But the gate was wide open, and no one was next to it.

"What the devil?" said Kostenko.

"Surely he didn't…"

Piskunov did not finish, and, not bothering to consult one another, they set off running to the Institute. They were not two hundred meters from the gate when Piskunov, running in front, flew into a man with a rifle. The man cried out in terror and was about to flee in another direction, but Piskunov grabbed him by the shoulders and stopped him.

"What's happening?"

The man crazily turned his head, clad in its police cap, swore, and finally came to his senses.

"He broke out," he said. "He broke out. He pushed the gate over and left. Almost stomped on Makeyev. I'm heading into the village for back-up..."

"Where did he go?"

The police office waved to the left without conviction.

"That way, I think... To the highway..."

"That means he'll run into the tractors any minute. Let's go."

They would remember what happened next for the rest of their lives. Out of the whirling snowy darkness something huge and formless came towards them, red and green blinking lights stung their eyes, and a sharp voice with no intonation pronounced,

"Hello, how do you do?"

"Urm, stop!" screamed Piskunov desperately.

Kostenko saw the policeman run, saw Piskunov raise his arms and shake his fists. Then a monstrous figure, wreathed in steam, a baleful scarecrow, went past him, raising high its legs, thick as logs, and melted into the snowstorm.

After carefully closing the door behind him, as he always did if the door was not broken, Urm took a step and stopped. Everything around him was full of sounds, movements, and emanations. He saw the night as a multicolored faery kaleidoscope of radio waves. Thirteen and a half meters in front of him was a squat building with wide windows, covered with iron grating. Its walls emitted bright infrared light. From the building he heard a low, powerful hum. A million snowflakes swirled around in the air. As they settled down on Urm's faceted sides, hot from the fire of his atomic engine, they instantly melted and vaporized.

Urm swiveled his head and decided that the nearest and most interesting object of study could only be the squat building across the way. He found the entrance immediately, noting a path on the downwind side. Low fir trees were planted all around the building, and pausing for a moment, he broke off one of them and examined it. Then he opened the door and went in.

Two humans were sitting next to a table in the close, narrow little room. As he appeared they leapt up and stared at him in horror. He closed the door behind him (and even threw the bolt) and stopped before them.

"How do you do?" he said.

"Comrade Piskunov?" one of the humans asked in confusion.

"Comrade Piskunov has stepped out. Would you like to leave a message?" Urm informed him coolly.

The humans did not interest him. His attention was drawn by a small, hairy creature that was cowering against the wall. *Warm, alive, smells strongly, not a Human*, determined Urm and said, "Hello, how do you do?"

"Grrr..," answered the creature with a bravery born of despair, baring its sharp, white teeth and pressing still more firmly into the corner.

Urm was absorbed by the dog and completely indifferent to the fact that the policemen had deftly barricaded themselves behind the table and filing cabinet and had begun to hurriedly undo their holsters.

Whining piteously, with its tail between its legs, the little dog dashed past Urm. But Urm was far more nimble than a dog. He was more nimble than the most nimble animal in the world. His torso turned a half circle in a lightning-quick and silent motion, and a long extending arm, like a telescope, snatched the dog up by its side. At that moment a shot rang out: one policemen's nerve had failed him. The bullet rang off the armor that covered Urm's back, and ricocheted deep into the wall. Plaster rained down.

"Sidorenko, stop shooting!" yelled the other policeman.

Urm released the quivering little dog and set his sights on the humans, pale but very resolute, holding their weapons at the ready. He sniffed the air with curiosity. The unfamiliar smell of smokeless gunpowder was diffusing in the air. The little dog cowered under the policemen's legs, but Urm had already lost interest in it. He turned and went to the next door, which was adorned with the image of a skull and crossbones pierced by a red lightning bolt. The policemen, struck dumb in wonderment, watched his clawlike fingers fumbling with the ribbed barrel of the lock. The door opened. Then they got a grip on themselves and both raced after him:

"Stop! Get back! You can't!"

They clung to his armored sides, grabbing his pillar-like legs, hot as a stove, forgetting everything in the world in terror at the single thought of what chaos this iron monster could wreak in the substation. But Urm simply did not notice them. Their efforts made no impression whatever on him; they may as well have been trying to stop a moving tractor. Then one of them, pushing his comrade aside, emptied his entire magazine into Urm's head, point-blank, from below. The substation chamber, flooded with light, rang with the din of gunshots.

Urm reeled. The ebonite shell of his right acoustic receptor flew apart in splinters. His crooked locator horn broke loose and hung there, dangling on a wire. The sound of broken glass rang from the ceiling.

Urm had never before been subjected to an attack. He lacked an instinct for self-preservation and had no experience fighting with humans. But Urm could put facts together, could make logical conclusions and choose a behavior path that maximally ensured his safety. All these mental operations took him a fraction of a second. In the next moment he turned around and started towards the humans, threateningly displaying his terrible claws.

The policemen split up. One ran behind the panelboard, and the other leapt behind the massive steel housing of the closest transformer, hurriedly reloading his pistol.

"Sidorenko! Run to the watchman's booth, call them, raise the alarm!" he shouted.

But Sidorenko had no success in running to the door. Urm moved far faster than a human, and the moment the policeman came out from behind the panelboard, Urm took two steps and stood before him. Then the humans resolved to run out simultaneously. This, too, was unsuccessful: Urm zipped from the panelboard to the transformer with the speed of an express train.

The panelboard broke in half from Urm's ungainly lunging, the wind whistled through the bullet holes in the windows and the glass ceiling.

Finally, Urm got tired of that game, and he resolved to leave the humans in peace. He stopped suddenly in front of the transformer and decisively thrust his hands under the housing. The policemen took this opportunity to go hurtling headlong to the watchman's booth. At the same instant, a deafening crack rang out, everything around was lit up by a blinding blue flash, and the lights when out. The acrid smell of burnt metal, smoke, and hot varnish poured out of the room. The deafened, dispirited policemen did not comprehend right away what had happened. And then the watchman's booth shivered from heavy footsteps, and a reedy voice pronounced in the darkness:

"Hello, how do you do?"

The door bolt clicked, and the door opened with a creak. For a moment the outline of the iron monster could be seen in the dim rectangle, and the door closed once again.

Urm walked around the grounds of the Institute, sinking into the snow and lifting his legs high. The Institute was plunged in darkness, and darkness offered little to help even Urm's infrared vision. He could make out only the weak radiance around his stomach and legs, on which snowflakes melted and vaporized. A few weakly phosphorescent human silhouettes could be glimpsed between the buildings. Urm paid no attention to them and went along, orienting himself by locator readings – though one locator horn had been smashed by the bullet, making it impossible for him to determine distances correctly.

The faraway lights of the village, barely visible gleams through the snowstorm, drew Urm's attention. Then the bright blue rays of the searchlights blazed on. He went up to the wall, hesitated for a moment and turned left. He was well aware that walls always have doors. And before long he ended up at the gate. It was a large gate, made of iron. The main thing, though, was that it was locked. On the other side of the gate he could hear the alarmed voices of the humans; a bright blue light pierced through the chink.

"Hello," said Urm, and heaved at the gate. The gate did not give way: it was firmly locked. From somewhere far away he could hear the clank of metal. There, beyond the gate, something very interesting was taking place. Urm pressed harder, then stepped away, threw back his head and struck the gate at a run with his armored chest. The voices beyond the gate fell silent, and then someone yelled uncertainly:

"Back! Hey, careful you don't shoot that devil!"

"Hello, how do you do?" said Urm, ran back and struck again. The gate collapsed. The bolt turned out to be stronger than the hinges built into the concrete wall, and the gate fell flat as a plank onto the snow. Urm walked over it past the scattered policemen and plunged into the snowstorm that was raging in the open field.

He marched onward, continuously struggling to recover his balance on the dug-up earth covered by a swelling sea of dry snow. Suddenly, an emptiness opened up beneath him, and he fell. The snow sizzled underneath him. He had never fallen before, but an instant later he had already dug his hands into the earth, extended them to their full length, and drew his legs up under him.

He regained his footing and stood for a moment, looking about. The lights of the cottages gleamed before him. To the left, very close by, loomed three human figures; further away vehicles growled, moving towards the gates in a line. Urm turned to the left. Going past the humans, he recognized one of them as the Master. The Master could deprive him of his ability to move. Urm remembered this very well and began to walk faster. The Master dropped out of sight behind him in the whirls of the shifting snow.

He emerged on a flat place where the snow was plowed smooth. A bright light illuminated him from head to foot. Unwieldy metal monsters, carrying heavy shields before them, moved towards him and came to a stop, snorting angrily.

Urm stood five steps from the lead bulldozer, slowly turning his round head to the right and to the left and repeating:

"Hello, how do you do?"

Nikolai Petrovich Korolev jumped down from the tractor. The driver yelled in a panic:

"Comrade engineer, where are you going?"

At that moment, Piskunov appeared on the highway. Disheveled, his hair standing on end (his fur hat was left behind somewhere in the vacant lot), his hands thrust deep into the pockets of his wide-open fur coat, he went around the bulldozer and stopped before Urm. There were not more than five steps between them. Urm loomed like a giant over the engineer, like a tower, his faceted sides gleamed in the headlights, his stomach, wreathed in steam, shone with moisture; his round head with its large glass eyes, splayed-out receptor ears, and locator horn resembled the frightful and ridiculous pumpkin masks that village boys use to scare girls. His head danced smoothly as his eyes followed Piskunov's every move.

"Urm," said Piskunov loudly.

Urm's head froze in place; his articulated arms were glued to his sides.

"Urm, listen to my command!"

Urm answered:

"I am ready."

Someone laughed nervously.

Piskunov stepped forward and placed his gloved hand on Urm's chest. His fingers quickly slid along the armor, feeling for what would settle the matter: the switch that linked the computational-analytic portion of Urm's brain to his power and movement system. And then something unexpected happened, unexpected for everyone except Piskunov, who feared it more than anything. Apparently, Urm's memory had saved an association linking this movement by the Master to an instant inability to move. Piskunov's fingers had barely touched the key when Urm turned sharply. His armored hand cut through the air above the head of Piskunov, who just managed to duck, and Urm, in no rush, started back along the highway. Nikolai Petrovich was the first to come to his senses.

"Hey, guys!" he yelled. "Bring the bulldozers around from the right and the left. Cut off his path to the gate… Piskunov, hey, Piskunov!"

But Piskunov did not hear him. While the bulldozers crawled in both directions away from the highway, diving into the clouds of snow, he set off running after Urm.

"Urm, stop!" he yelled in a high, breaking voice. "Stop, you brute! Come back! Back!"

He ran out of breath. Urm was going ever faster, and the distance between them gradually widened. Finally, Piskunov stopped, shoved his hands into his pockets, and, drawing his head into his shoulders, watched him go. Nikolai Petrovich and Ryabkin ran up to him. Kostenko came up last.

"What's gotten into you?" asked Korolev angrily.

Piskunkov did not answer.

"He's not obeying," he said. "You understand, Kolya? He's not obeying. It's clearly a spontaneous reflex."

Nikolai Petrovich nodded.

"I was thinking the same thing."

"Obviously!" exclaimed Piskunov. "You'd have the same degree of success letting a train pick its own time and itinerary…"

"What's a spontaneous reflex?" asked Kostenko timidly.

No one answered him.

"And just the same, in spite of everything, this is really something." Nikolai Petrovich blew his nose and shoved his handkerchief into his inner pocket. "He's not obeying! Of all things…"

"Let's go!" said Piskunov decisively.

Meanwhile, the bulldozers had spread out in a half-circle and began to converge around Urm, who was unhurriedly shuffling along the highway. One of the bulldozers crawled out onto the highway ahead of him, with its back end to the gate, another came up at him from behind, the remaining three approached from the sides: two from the left, one from the right. Of course, Urm had long since noticed that he was being surrounded, but he probably thought nothing of it. He continued moving along the highway until his chest ran up against the bulldozer. He pressed, the tractor teetered just a bit; the driver grabbed at the levers with a tense face. Urm took a step back and hit it at a run. Iron clanged against iron, and bright sparks could be seen cutting the snowy darkness under the straight beams of the headlights. At that moment the blade of the rear bulldozer hit Urm's back. Urm froze stock-still, only his head slowly turned on its axis, just like a school globe. From the right and left approached two more bulldozers and securely closed the remaining avenues of retreat. Urm found himself in captivity.

"Comrade engineers! Comrade Piskunov! What should we do now?" yelled the driver of the first machine.

"Comrade Piskunov has stepped out. Would you like to leave a message?" said Urm.

He took a swing and struck the blade. Then he did so again and again. He hit steadily, like a boxer in a training session, knocked back slightly with every blow, and splashes of sparks hailed from under the clanging of his club-like hands.

Piskunov, accompanied by Nikolai Petrovich, Ryabkin, and Kostenko, approached him.

"We have to do something quickly, or he'll disable himself," said Ryabkin anxiously.

Piskunov climbed without speaking onto the tread of the tractor, but Ryabkin grabbed him and pulled him back down.

"What's the matter?" asked Piskunov with annoyance.

"You're the only person who knows Urm intimately. If he lays you out… this whole thing could last for months. Someone else should do it."

"He's right," said Nikolai Petrovich hastily. "I'll go."

One of the workers who were standing around the engineers broke in:

"Maybe you could choose one of us? We're younger, quicker…"

"I'll do it," said Kostenko somberly.

"That won't work," said Nikolai Petrovich. "Don't let Piskunov go."

He threw off his fur coat and climbed onto the tractor. Then Piskunov tore loose from Ryabkin's embrace.

"Let me go, Ryabkin."

Ryabkin did not answer. Kostenko approached from the other side and firmly gripped Piskunov by the shoulders.

And Urm was raging. The lower half of his body was securely clamped by the bulldozers, but the upper part moved freely, and he turned from side to side with lightening speed, pounding the iron blades with backhanded blows of his steel fists. Shreds of steam circled above him in the snowy darkness. "The force of one blow of his fist is three thousand kilos," recalled Kostenko.

Nikolai Petrovich, setting his teeth, squatted down between the bulldozers at Urm's feet and waited for the right moment. His ears hurt from the clanging and crashing. He knew that Urm had noticed him: the glass eyes, now and then glimmering warily, would turn to him.

"Easy, easy," whispered Nikolai Petrovich soundlessly. "Easy, my dear Urm. Take it easy, you scoundrel!"

Some sort of new sound arose amid the blows, something cracked, either Urm's steel hand or the blade of the bulldozer. There was no more time to delay. Nikolai Petrovich dove under Urm's fist and pressed up to his side. And then Urm surprised everyone. His arms fell to his sides. The crashing ceased, and once again they could hear the snowstorm howling over the field and the tractors snorting. Nikolai

Petrovich, pale and sweating, straightened up and reached his hand to Urm's chest. A dry click rang out. The green and red lights on Urm's shoulders went out.

"It's over," Piskunov croaked out and closed his eyes.

People began talking right away in exaggeratedly loud voices; laughter and jokes could be heard. The drivers helped Nikolai Petrovich get out from under Urm and lowered him to the ground. Piskunov embraced and kissed him.

"And now," he said abruptly, "to the Institute. We will work. It will take a week, a month… We'll have to beat this nonsense out of him and finally make him an Urm: a Universal Roving Machine.

"But what was it that happened with Urm?" asked Kostenko. And what is a spontaneous reflex?"

Nikolai Petrovich, tired and drawn after the sleepless night, said, "You see, Urm was constructed by order of the Department for Interplanetary Communications. He differs from other highly complex cybernetic machines in that he is intended for work in conditions that cannot be predicted by even the most ingenious programmer. On Venus, for instance. Who knows what the conditions are there? Maybe it is covered by oceans. But maybe by deserts. Or jungles. For the time being people cannot be sent there: it's too dangerous. Urms will be sent, dozens of Urms. But how should they be programmed? The trouble is that, at the current level of cybernetics, it is still impossible to teach a machine to 'think' abstractly…"

"What do you mean?"

"For a machine there is no general dog. There is only this one, that one, a third dog. If it meets a fourth dog that doesn't resemble the first three, the machine won't know what to do. Roughly speaking, if Urm is programmed for a definite reaction only in relation to a mutt, he will be unable to react the same way in relation to a pug. It's a simplistic example, of course, but I presume that you understand me. And *this* is one of the basic differences between the smartest machine and the dumbest person: an inability to operate in abstract categories. Anyway,

Piskunov attempted to compensate for this shortcoming by creating a self-programming machine. He gave Urm's 'brain' a reflex chain, the essence of which boils down to filling vacant memory cells in a self-governing fashion. Piskunov calculated that, once he "fills up on impressions," Urm will be capable of picking the most beneficial line of behavior for every new event. This is the most advanced model of consciousness in the world. But we got an unexpected result. Well, Piskunov had theoretically allowed for such a phenomenon, but in practice… To put it succinctly, the new reflex arc generated dozens of secondary reflexes not anticipated by the programmers. Piskunov has christened them spontaneous reflexes. With their appearance, Urm ceased to function according to his basic programming and began to 'direct himself.'"

"What do we need to do now?"

"We'll try a different approach." Nikolai Petrovich stretched and yawned. "We will perfect the analytic capabilities of the 'brain,' the receptor system…"

"But what about the spontaneous reflex? No one is interested in it?"

"Oh, Piskunov has already thought something up… In a word, the first ones on unexplored planets and in unexplored oceans will still be Urms. We will not have to risk people… Listen, Kostenko, let's get some sleep, OK? You'll be working here and will learn everything, I give you my word."

First published in Russian: 1958
Translation by Kevin Reese

SODA-SUN

The author of a hypothesis implicitly acknowledges the possibility of a mistake, so that in the course of rigorous experimentation the hypothesis can be overturned, verified, or transformed into something different.

— Academician N. Semenov

The richest ideas are the most specific and subjective ones. That which is truly individual represents infinity in embryonic form.

— V. I. Lenin

1. For What, Actually?

They said that he wasn't serious, just chasing after sensations. As I left, I looked at him and thought that it was the other way around: he's very serious, because he seriously loves what is sensational. This was his position:

"Think about it: what is a sensation? *Sensus* is feeling, a sensation shakes your entire core with feeling. What is so bad about that, if a person loves being shaken up? Life moves along soberly, people are occupied with mundane things. Then one day a person looks up and sees that life is moving along soberly and people are occupied with mundane things. So now what? What is the point of our efforts? Food? New clothes? A chance to travel? Travel to where? You can't out-distance old age, and everything that is given to you to see in this life, you'll eventually see from the window of a train or maybe from the window of a spaceship. For God's sake, we won't even have spaceships unless we start building them. When will that be? In the meantime we wait, while life slowly dribbles out, like wine from a leaking leather pouch."

When they told him to leave, he asked me:

"Are you sure that archeology is only important for the history of material culture? Why study this material culture to begin with?"

"This is why you are being fired," I said. "If you would dig deeper…"

"No, my dear teacher, that's not why they are firing me. They are firing me precisely because I want to dig deeper. To me, digging deeper is the task of archeology."

"Bad pun."

"No," he said, "it's not a pun. You are all just pretending. Insofar as archeology needs funds, you pretend that you are studying cultures of the past in order to help those of the present. But how does it help? Maybe you'll find a few decorative pieces, and yet another skull, at which the smart ninth graders on a museum field trip will gawk, although the really smart ones will spend their time gawking at the girls in the excursion next to theirs."

"They're right to fire you."

"Of course they're right. They're trying to remove the witness to the crime."

"What crime? Think about what you are saying!"

"Exactly – I am saying what I think. People don't like it. Listen to me! Why did you get into archeology? You wanted to dig deeper and find something sensational. Am I not right? You were still a child then, a treasure-hunter, a romantic. Of course the adults around you, the unhappy ones who in an entire lifetime never came close to digging up Tutankhamun's faded little coffin, were quick to explain to you that archeology is very difficult work, not just chasing after something sensational. But is that really so obvious? What if archeology *is* hunting for the sensational, and this is its very essence? The greatest finds of archeology have helped humankind understand itself. Isn't that true? Is there anything more sensational than self-understanding? Gradually you grew up, and our monkey's instinct for imitation forced you to disavow your own thoughts. Yes, archeology is very difficult work! Yet what is this work for, if it does not lead to sensational finds, the kind that make our entire being tremble and shake with the feeling that humankind has opened its eyes and stared at its own face?

"I still think you talk too much," I warned.

"Fine, sign my dismissal," he said. "You're chasing the only poet out of your guild of antique junk dealers."

They fired him. He was always a master of creating sensations. Perhaps most absurd is the fact that we let him go, and now we are preparing for an expedition based on his materials.

I hope that was the last sensation. We've had enough. Archeology is simply a science that is necessary for... for what, actually?

2. Such Was His Logic

He was a strange guy. There was always a vague smile flickering across his face. Nobody could understand what exactly he wanted out of archeology – or, for that matter, out of life.

One night, as the expedition sat around a campfire, he came out and said, "*Salut alaikum*."[1] At the time, nobody guessed that this was not just an attempt at being fashionably witty, it was the formula of his personality. He greeted the world around him through a strange mixture of modern and ancient salutations.

---

1. *Salut* is a very informal greeting that conveys a breezy familiarity with French slang, whereas *alaikum* conveys respect for the traditional Arabic greeting "peace be upon you" (*salaam alaikum*).

Every person is in some ways two people. We all know this. For the most part, our double self lives peacefully and presents only one side to the outside world. The world judges us by this side. The other side lies in wait, to appear only when the time is right, in extraordinary circumstances. Then it is said that so-and-so turned out to be a hero, or, on the contrary, a real villain. What does this mean? Nothing more than the fact that the hidden side was able to adapt better, or, on the contrary, could not adapt, to a given set of unusual conditions. Under ordinary circumstances, we would see the other side, the person we see under conditions that we like to call "normal." But are our conditions ever really normal?

Let's say I go to work every day to a job that I am thoroughly sick of, but I know how I behave at that job. If you gave me a job that I love, would I behave differently? We don't know. It's always assumed – give a person something he or she likes to do, and everything will be fine. In fact, this is just where it starts to get the most complicated. One person will joyfully immerse himself in a beloved occupation and not ask for anything more in life. Another will experience his favorite occupation solely as a means for getting ahead and gaining the advantage over others. A third will be frightened by the freedom and spiritual space that opens up when one does what one loves, and this person will never crawl out of his boring but comfortable shell. Instead, he will secretly envy the bold ones, rejoice when they fail, and spend his whole life obstructing their way.

Perhaps the most complicated case is when a person searches long and hard for what inspires him the most – and suddenly he stumbles upon it and is blinded by the brightness. If you let a nightingale out of its cage, it flies straight up and then falls down dead, having swallowed too much of the sky. If you let it fly around a room first, this can be avoided. Perhaps.

I was probably the only one among all of us who guessed what was going on with him. I understood that he belonged precisely to the fourth case. Therefore his two sides did not coexist in harmony, but were constantly at war with each other. You could see it in everything he did. He would be telling us crazy, hilarious stories, everyone would be rolling with laughter, and his eyes would crinkle merrily, but the rest of his face looked long and sad. One lovely morning, when you could just barely hear the knocking of a generator motor in the distance along with the lowing of oxen behind the mud walls of the village, I saw him coming toward me and smiling with the rest of world. But when he came closer, I saw that there were tears in his eyes.

He was interested in the problem of the devil. Are you surprised? Naturally, he did not mean the devil invoked by mystics and religion, but the real devil. He was convinced that there actually was such a thing – that there was something *real* that provided the motive for all legends, folk tales, stories, and countless works of art. Like all modern people, he understood that the devil is just a personification of the force of evil; that is, of all those forces, both natural and manmade, that we can't figure out and that we find easier to ascribe to an imaginary demon. In that case, however, why do we depict the devil as something non-human, whereas God looks human? Evidently, because God is an ideal person, that is, a person who brings the world only good, whereas the devil is something harmful, and therefore must be depicted as some kind of monstrous, inhumane creature. But if that is so, and "God" is conceptualized as an ideal human – that is, as the ideal of a real creature – then we should be able to conceptualize a monstrous real creature, onto which we have projected all our unhappiness. This was his logic.

3. He Was Working As a Research Assistant

He was dumped from our expedition for good reason, when after working for free for a month, eating only out of our community rations, he announced his crazy idea. Basically, he was fired because this idea of his, once he had voiced it, acquired a strange attractive power. Something devilish started to happen. Here we were, devoutly modern young people, for whom even Hemingway was starting to seem old-fashioned, suddenly obsessed not only with ancient grave mounds, but with ancient texts in which we tried to find the real, actually existing prototype for the image of ungodly horror. Names like Swedenborg and Jakob Boehme[2] came up in conversations over boiled green tea and cans of beef stew. At first, I tolerated the half-joking talk of visionaries, basilisks, newts, and dragons. Who doesn't like fairy tales? Archeology needs whimsicality just as much as math. Fantasy cleanses the mind, among other things. Let them have fun, I thought, take a break from logic. But when things began to get out of hand – when Valya Medvedeva, a nice, calm girl, announced that we should look for prototypes of the devil in fossils of prehistoric animals, and Pasha Bidenko countered that our concept of the devil derives from a deep knowledge of human nature – I decided to put an end to it.

"Look, my friend," I told him. "Why don't you leave us in peace and go your own way."

He went his own way just as he had arrived. Smiling vaguely, he left the campfire, leaving a whiff of insanity and incomprehensible longing in his wake.

The dig continued successfully. We found traces of an advanced material culture. We came across a market square, ancient trading stalls, weapons. We loaded boxes of artifacts, numbered and wrapped in tissue paper, to be transported back by all-terrain vehicles. When the cold season arrived, our expedition wrapped up its work in the field and returned to Moscow to systematically sort through and describe what had been found.

We ran into him in the Academy of Science's Institute of Archeology. He was working as a research associate.

4. It's Demagogy!

How he managed to wheedle his way in remained a mystery, but the fact remained: this man, who had no academic degrees, no published articles, not even any serious training, was already working as a scientific research associate at the Institute by the time we returned. It was not at all clear how he'd managed to get this position. In fact,

---

2. Emmanuel Swedenborg (1688-1772) was a Swedish scientist who became an influential mystic, theologian, and interpreter of spiritual destiny, in books such as *Heaven and Hell* (1758), his account of the afterlife. Jakob Boehme (1575-1624) was an influential German mystic and theologian.

it seemed suspicious. Rumors circulated. Opinions were divided. The rumors became more incredible. Some decided that he was a member of a secret sect, while others assumed he was an auditor sent from the Department Against the Misappropriation of Socialist Property. Only I knew the improbable truth.

The personnel manager, whom no one had ever seen laugh (although he occasionally smiled politely), accosted me while doubled over with silent laughter, wiping away tears:

"He's hilarious!"

"Who?"

"That carpet clown. Before he worked here, he must have been in the circus!"

"You're kidding," I said.

"How can you not laugh? Look at the photo he brought over to human resources."

It was the usual 4.5x6 photo, except his face was covered in paint. I nearly choked.

"Don't worry, Vladimir Andreyevich," said the manager, "later he brought a real photo. I just kept this one for fun."

"Photos are not the issue! I'm going straight to the director. You're turning science into some kind of circus."

"That's exactly what it is, a circus, Vladimir Andreyevich. And nothing will come of going to the director, because he has already approved the hire." He said something else, but I didn't listen.

My conversation with the director went like this:

"I know, Vladimir Andreyevich, I know. Have a sip of water…"

"Thanks."

"Tell me, Vladimir Andreyevich, in your opinion, is it possible for, say, a Soviet deputy to be a clown?

"I don't know. In my view, that seems ridiculous.

"Bravo. We have the same opinion."

"Why?"

"I answered his question exactly as you just did. Literally in the same words. And he said, 'A clown is an artist, and it is quite possible for an artist to become a people's representative. It begs the question, why can't a clown become a scientist?' Do you object, Vladimir Andreyevich?"

"Yes. It's demagoguery."

"Then read this. Sit down. It's sixteen pages long."

5. Secrets

It was an article that conveyed the following in everyday, non-scientific language:

Among the Italian masters who took part in the construction of the Moscow Kremlin, the most well-known was Aristotele Fioravanti. As a result, the common assumption is that he was the main architect. However, it turns out that the person who designed the most important parts of the Kremlin – the towers and the walls – has been nearly forgotten. There are only two structures like this in all of Europe, in Moscow and in Milan. At the time, they looked like twins. The unique peaked turrets on the Moscow towers were constructed much later. The name of the unknown architect is inscribed on the inside wall of the Spassky Tower: "Pietro Antonio Solari of Milan."

None of this was entirely new. Perhaps it's true that until now, nobody had specifically enumerated the parts designed by Pietro Antonio, so his fundamental contributions to the construction of the Kremlin had not been fully acknowledged. One could use this information and accentuate it more in various brochures. The interesting part was still to come... The article went on to show that Pietro Antonio Solari was a scion of the Milanese Solari family, whose members were all artists, engineers, and so forth. Since all of Milan's artists would sooner or later meet while working at the court of Lodovico il Moro, uncle of the sickly duke Gian Galeazzo Sforza, and since for some reason the entire Solari family left Milan in 1490 – that is, the year Pietro Antonio arrived in Moscow – and since Christoforo Solari was a student of Leonardo da Vinci's (this is now officially acknowledged), and since at that time Leonardo da Vinci himself was building the Milan castle, it becomes clear why the Moscow emissaries invited the unknown Pietro

Antonio to build their most important structure and did not hand the construction of the Kremlin over to the internationally famous Fioravanti. Our official histories have conveniently forgotten Pietro Antonio, because who wants to admit that Moscow's great Kremlin, "the fourth Rome," was built by some second-rate engineer? Instead, let's celebrate Aristotele Fioravanti! But in fact it turned out that by inviting Solari, they were actually inviting Leonardo himself, one of the most enigmatic figures in history. For instance, did you know that the first map of America that actually depicts "America" as a separate continent surrounded by ocean was found in the papers of Leonardo da Vinci? So what, you ask? So, it means that Leonardo's map was made before Magellan's, who was the first to confirm with his own eyes that America was a separate continent, and not the other side of India, as Columbus and Amerigo Vespucci had thought.

I hardly noticed the degree to which I got sucked in by this clown's arguments.

According to him, the builder of the Moscow Kremlin was one of Leonardo da Vinci's apprentices. Great, that's excellent – it changes our entire view of Europe, and of Russia's relationship to Italy. But why conclude that Pietro learned from Leonardo? Weren't there a lot of masters around at the same time that Leonardo was working on the Milan castle? And besides, Leonardo didn't build the Milan castle by himself, there were many others. There would have to be some direct proof of the relationship. And guess what? There was.

If you follow the wall that overlooks the Moscow River, you will find strange openings along the top of its battlement. These crenels are strange because they are not openings between the merlons, as is usually the case, but holes inside the merlon, just above the base of each "tooth."[3] As we know, battlement merlons were not decorative: warriors stood behind the merlons while pouring boiling tar through the openings between them. But in this case the openings are in the

---

3. A *merlon* is the solid upright section of a battlement or parapet in medieval architecture or fortifications, sometimes pierced by a narrow slit through to which to observe the enemy. A *crenel* is the space between two merlons. These features together give the Kremlin walls their "toothed" appearance.

merlons, and so low to the base that it would be impossible to even crouch behind them. However, an opening with no purpose cannot exist in a fortification wall.

It turns out that one of Leonardo's drawings contains a sketch of a certain apparatus with openings in the solid parts of a crenellated wall. Poles are inserted through the openings to the outside, and logs are lashed to the poles in a long line. Within the walls, the whole thing is connected to a system of levers. When an enemy army attempted to breach the walls by running up ladders, the defendants would push down the levers, causing the horizontal line of logs outside to pop up and topple over all the ladders. That is the purpose of those unusually placed openings. In order to use Leonardo's secret in the Moscow Kremlin, Pietro must have known about them directly.

6. Soda-Sun

What do we know about the past, when we know so desperately little about the present? To think that we want to predict the future as well! We accumulate facts, wrap them up in tissue paper, place them on shelves, and completely fail to capture the hidden connection between things. It's some kind of obsession with us. Wherever *he* shows up, nothing seems stable anymore – instead there's chaos or bedevilment of some sort. Although, is he really that far off the mark? Indeed, what is the point of our perennially fading, perennially resurrected profession?

They called him Soda-Sun.

The American pilots who flew shuttle flights over Berlin and then came to our base for a drink greeted him with incoherent howls of joy. He shielded them from German airstrikes while they ran from their base to ours. He single-handedly shot two Messerschmitts down into the sea, while a third one lay smoking on the horizon.

"A whiskey-and-soda, for you!" they cried.

"*Soda-solntse!*" he answered, parting his lips to catch drops of a fleeting rain shower that blew through the open window while the sun still shone outside.

Someone translated for the Americans: soda-sun. The Americans laughed again and got happily drunk. From then on they called him Soda-Sun. Whenever he appeared at the base, the mood lightened. He was tall and thin, with chestnut brown eyes, lucky in his undertakings and sweet with the girls. The girls from ABW – the Air Base Wing – groaned when they heard his whistle. He always whistled the same tune:

The golden days flew by
A thief's reckless love,
O you, my raven horses
You black steeds of mine.

He didn't engage in any romances, and no one knew who this "reckless love" might be. He didn't drink, other than snatching drops of rain after a flying a mission without a single mishap. He always flew away from the Messerschmitts in the direction of the sun. His bright wings dissolved in the blinding disk.

I'll line my sled with wraps
Braid ribbons into their manes,
Flying with ringing bells,
I'll snatch you up along the way.

Then he disappeared for the last time into that solar disk. His wings sparkled and dissolved into the blinding brightness. After that, nobody saw him again. He disappeared.

The American shuttle-pilots finished another flight and showed up at our base, unbuttoning their Canadian jackets.

"Soda-Sun!" they shouted, looking for him.

"Soda-whiskey," corrected the new girl tending the bar.

They got drunk again, but this time morosely. One of the airmen kept crying and shouting "Soda-Sun," as if he'd find him somewhere in the room.

We escaped their crazy chase.
Stop crying, my dear, please stop.
The black steeds have not betrayed us,
And nobody will ever catch us.

The night he appeared at our expedition's campfire, I recognized him immediately by his whistle. He whistled the same song of thief's love and raven-black horses. I recognized him immediately, even though he had filled out and his face danced with constantly shifting expressions. A total circus. Now he had been accepted into the Institute of Archeology on the basis of his da Vinci article, and he turned out to be a clown. He was going through a trial period.

I never let on that I knew him. And he didn't recognize me as the humble technician who helped lift the tail of his silver plane, but now had a doctorate and served as his boss. I'm old now, I don't want to see chaos anymore. When I look at him, I remember how he was called Soda-Sun and how he caught drops of rain with his bright lips. Those poor little drops – there are thousands of them. Now it is nighttime, and it's raining. The drops fall flat and disappear. But every drop is someone's sea. Somebody with bright eyes is rowing across to the other shore. We are all oceans inside, oceans surrounding a continent. And I decided to let him be, let him do his thing. In the name of Soda-Sun, I'll help him, help him get whatever he wants. Nothing has changed. I'm the technician, and he's Soda-Sun, except he's injured, and I have to help him fix his silver wings.

"What kind of help do you need?"

He thought about it.

"Tenderness…" he said.

"What?"

"I work well," he said, "when I am loved."

"Soda-Sun…" I let it out, unable to resist.

His close-set eyes widened.

"I recognized you right away," he said quietly, "which is why I went up to the campfire, back there, in Kherson… I had an old piece about Leonardo," he said. "When I saw you at the campfire, I thought, why not become an archeologist?"

"That's absurd."

He swallowed and put out his cigarette.

"Don't be upset," he said as he left.

The sun came through the window of the room. I took some cool water from the carafe. Soda-Sun…

7. An Elderly Man Was a Boy

I signed the necessary papers, and he left the Institute, this time forever.

I went to see the director.

"Don't even think about asking me, Vladimir Andreyevich," said the director. "I've had enough of this craziness."

"But we're going ahead with his expedition anyway."

"Yeah, but without him," said the director.

"Didn't he do a lot for us?"

"He did plenty," said the director. "Plenty. Our institute has become the center of a hellish uproar. Sensationalism. Priests swarming around. As if it's not bad enough that our findings ended up supporting religious ideas instead of debunking them.

"Quite the contrary. If we can prove the existence of an actually existing prototype for the devil, then that puts an end to about half of any religious system. What kind of devil can there be if it has an anatomy, real flesh, and a metabolism? And what kind of religion can make do without the devil?"

"Alright, let's take another example. Why did he have to bring up that 'slave poet' Mitus, who supposedly might be the actual author of the epic *The Lay of Prince Igor*?[4] All he did was bring the wrath of

---

4. "The Lay of Prince Igor" is an epic poem that was probably composed in the late twelfth century, and fixed in written form as early as the thirteenth century. As such, it is by far the most important and renowned example of medieval Slavonic language, and it occupies a place comparable to the "Song of Roland" or "Song of the Niederlungen" in Slavic national mythology. Therefore it

the entire Slavic professoriat upon us. They don't even want to hear about Mitus! He did it simply to be obstreperous. It's not as though he proved that the court jester Mitus was actually a great poet!"

"It's true that he could not prove authorship, but he made some interesting findings. First of all, the medieval chronicles refer to a *slav* poet, not a slave poet. In those times, all names ending in 'slav' designated princes and kings: Yaroslav, Bryachislav, Mstislav, and so on are specifically noble names. All other names – your Dobrynyas, your Putyatas – are for non-nobles. Now, how could a person designated as 'Mitus,' a word which has been interpreted as slang for 'one who mutters' or 'one who mixes words' – in short, a jester – also be a noble? Well, he combed through all the sources and did not find any other examples of this slang usage. Instead, in the documents of the Carpathian Slavs who emigrated to Canada, he found that among the Lemko ethnic group the *name* Mitus occurs to this day. Finally, he even found genealogical records of the Mitusov family, which traces its noble lineage all the way back to the Slavic singer of tales, Mitus."

"Sensationalism. Troublemaking." The director was adamant. "This is not serious work, this is provocation in the name of scholarship. He is going too far. Like all dilettantes, he's searching for sensational ideas. I give him credit for tenacity, though. He could become a real scholar."

"He could become anything. He is a real human being. As a human being, he was offended on behalf of a great poet, who the specialists decided was a simple jester. As a human being, he wanted to show that anybody can become anything. He is a human being, Sergei Aleksandrovich, whereas you and I are just specialists."

I shouldn't have said that. Sergei Aleksandrovich did not appreciate my little witticism. For him, "specialist" is a sacred category.

"In any case," I said, "these things were just small digressions from his main work. The main task is to find the locus of the evil spirit, or whatever you call it."

---

has also been the object of endless controversies over authorship. Here, Soda-Sun seems to reconcile both the scholarly supposition of the author's Carpathian identity and the patriotic theory that this great work of art was composed by someone of noble lineage.

"What are you talking about?! I can't believe it! This is the twentieth century! I am a dues-paying member of our professional organization. I study ancient Greek folklore. I'm learning old-fashioned Lipsi dances from T.V.[5] We don't need to be ridiculed. Can you imagine the following announcement: the Institute of Archeology of the Academy of Sciences initiates a new study on the origins of the devil. *Please!*"

"As you like," I sighed. "If you look at it that way, it does indeed seem ridiculous."

Thank God he hasn't remembered the incident involving that woman, I thought to myself. Then I realized: he couldn't remember it. Because during those 24 hours our director – a scholar, a specialist, an elderly man – was a boy.

8. We Are Going Because of Him

We're launching the expedition without him. I go along with mixed emotions. Everything is strange on this strange journey: the fact that I am going without him and in all likelihood will never see him again; the fact that we are going to verify the hypothesis of the person that we fired; and the fact that we are going to Turgai.

I never thought the Kazakh village of Turgai would reappear in my life after it played such a large role in it once before. It's as if I am once again twenty years old, my parents and loved ones are still alive, and I'm just starting my scientific career, as if half a century had not passed since that time.

It was the summer of 1912. A few brigades from the Department of Land Improvement were working on the Turgai steppe. The brigades had been given the task of elucidating hydrological conditions, in order to provide a water supply for future resettlement plots. Along the Kara-Turgai River, a brigade under the supervision of the mining engineer Mokeyev found several very large teeth, a long spine, and a foot bone. During the same summer, a Mining Institute student by the name of Gorbunov, on a different brigade, found rich fossil layers a

---

5. *Lipsi* is a German style of improvisational ballroom dance that was developed in the late 1950s in the GDR to counter the more sexual rock n' roll.

bit to the west, on the river Dzhilanchik. He was able to gather a large number of elk and tiger bones. These fossils were all delivered to the geological museum of the Academy of Sciences, which in the following summer of 1913 directed that same Gorbunov to proceed with further exploration of both sites. Gorbunov, student of the Mining Institute, was me. My secret ambition was to find the bones of a mammoth. That expedition was a turning point in my life and brought me unexpected success.

The Turgai region was carved out of a part of the Central Asian steppe populated by the nomadic Kyrgiz people. It was gently hilly country, dotted with reed-rimmed saltwater and freshwater lakes. I put in supplies for the caravan, hired some local Kyrgiz to help with the dig, and set out on the expedition. Along the way, my Kyrgiz told me that, in a different place, on the shores of one of the salty lakes, there are much larger fossil deposits than the ones by Lake Dzhilanchik. They called the place Battle of the Giants.

You can imagine what I felt when I heard about a "battle of the giants." I was overcome by a mixture of smoldering excitement and almost superstitious dread that the local stories might not pan out. These conflicting emotions forced me to examine my true motivations and face my real calling; in other words, it was a revelatory moment. I forgot all about the Mining Institute, the instructions of my bosses, and about the fact that I even had a boss. I immediately turned the expedition toward the Salt Lake, although I had always been considered a person who valued steady judgment and discipline above all else. Without a doubt, my decision was a breach of conduct, but I could not resist the temptation of finding those mammoth bones.

I found them. We returned with the bones. At this point, I was met with a bitter disappointment.

I had been sent to collect the fossils of some heretofore unknown elk and tiger specimens, and instead I had come back with the bones of a mammoth that had been discovered long ago and was well-known to experts in the field. Nevertheless, the boxes arrived. Even though no one was particularly interested in the mammoth, we opened one of the biggest boxes and looked inside. At the very first glance, it became clear that these bones exhibited features that could not be a mammoth's. What was it? It seemed to be a completely new, unknown and gigantic animal. Disappointment abruptly turned to keen interest, and the technicians unpacked the rest with a great deal more care and attention.

The colossal skeleton of the five-meter tall *Indricotherium*[6] that hangs in the Historical Museum will always be the monument to my first success. Yet now we are setting out on an expedition without *him*, even though we are going because of him.

9. Without Pills

He was driven out because everyone got tired of him.

It started when I asked him why, exactly, he had begun to investigate Mitus and Leonardo.

That was my first mistake.

"I was interested in the Mitus question because I don't know any foreign languages," he said.

"What do foreign languages have to do with it?"

"The dawn of our millennium was a time of remarkable poetry. In Germany they had the "Song of the Nibelungen," in Spain they had "El Cid Campeador," in England, "The Ballad of Robin Hood," in France, "Song of Roland," and in Russia, "The Lay of Prince Igor." It was easier for me to read in a Slavic language than any of the others."

"So what?"

"One gets the impression that all creative forces at the turn of the first millennium went into poetry – anonymous poetry, at that."

"Let's say that's true. And your point is…?"

"My point is that the epoch of the Renaissance, which occurred in the middle of the millennium, was supposed to exhibit its creative force in more rationalistic forms. And that was indeed the case – literature

---

6. *Indricotherium*: a prehistoric herbivore that lived in the forests of Central Asia roughly 20 to 30 million years ago. A predecessor to the elephant and the rhinoceros, it is the largest land mammal ever discovered.

became a form of philosophy, drama a form of public intellectualism, and the fine arts overlapped with the natural sciences."

"All points that have been made before. It follows that…?"

"It follows that if you look at humanity as a whole, not as an aggregate of many individuals, but as an organism, then the first two stages look a lot like the first two stages in the Theory of Reflection, i.e. direct experience, followed by abstract reasoning. It follows that the final stage, coming at the end of our millennium, should be marked by action in the form of creativity. And what does this mean?"

"Well, what *does* it mean?" I said. "You twist things around. Creativity is a form of action, so how can there be 'action in the form of creativity'? People were creative a thousand years ago, five hundred years ago, and today they create as well."

"But what do they create?" he asked. "Where are the unique creations of culture, the great works, the synthesis of poetry and reason? Today all of our analyses, investigations, discoveries and theories are just a heap of fragments, a demolition job, a search for the truth. They take apart the universe like a watch and then try to put the parts back together, but a bunch of little pieces don't fit. Is this really what we mean by creativity?"

"People have always sought the truth, both moral and scientific."

"Yes, but what for? Why so much seeking, but so little actual inventing?"

"People are inventing enough! We hear about new inventions every day…"

"We hear about them! That's the point – there should be so many that we don't even hear about them. You don't hear about it when they release another pair of shoes or an automobile, because those aren't things that are talked about, they are things that are made. No, our age does not like new inventions. It likes research. What is the most difficult job to have? Being an inventor. But a researcher… well, all of our institutes are in fact scientific *research* institutions. Why is that? Because research means researching what nature has already designed for us. Invention, on the other hand, is an act of human consciousness, a creative action, a synthesis."

"There wouldn't be any invention without research."

"Sure, but without inventions there wouldn't be anything. There wouldn't be life. Man differs from the monkey not in his research of the cudgel, but in inventing the cudgel. Nowadays we are simply afraid of inventors, afraid that they will disorganize production. Yet we're long overdue in producing inventions, not just objects. Production should produce inventions. Then there can't be any disorganization, because it will already be written into the plan – to produce something new."

"How are you going to accumulate all these inventions? An invention is not the same as shoes or a car," I said.

"Exactly. This is different, because nobody knows what creativity really is, where it comes from, or how you should serve it." Then he added, somewhat reluctantly, "although Leonardo knew."

"How do you know that he knew?"

"By his results. The list of his inventions alone is dozens of pages long. It's exhausting just to read it," he added sadly.

"Leonardo was a genius!" I pronounced grandly.

"Genius!" he was practically yelling. "Doesn't it occur to you that his whole way of thinking must have been different from ours? Doesn't it look as though a genius is actually a person who has figured out a different way to think? And the rest of us… we try to use logic."

"Well what else…"

"Whaddya mean 'what else?' What is logic? It's an instrument. Instruments get old. It doesn't bother you that Euclidean geometry doesn't work anymore?"

"Some people still use it."

"Of course, for certain tasks. For flat surfaces. But any flat surface is a segment of a sphere. On this sphere the sum of the angles of the triangle will never be equal to 180 degrees. You can also still use a hammer, but there are better implements out there."

"With what do you propose to replace logic?"

"If our brain is capable of sudden discovery occasionally, then it is capable of this all of the time. If Mendeleyev discovered the periodic table in his sleep, it means that at that moment his brain was thinking the right way."

"That's ridiculous!" I exploded angrily. "He slaved over that table for years, trying to figure it out, before it 'came to him in his sleep.'"

"That's correct. He 'slaved over it.' What's so great about that? It only means that for years he was thinking the wrong way, logically picking apart each variant, thinking linearly. When there were enough lines, they finally converged into single bundle, and it worked."

"There is no other way to do it."

"Oh yeah? And what if suddenly there is?"

"And you have it."

"Chopin once said: 'When I sit down at the piano, I just start to improvise, until I come upon the blue note…'[7] What that means is that his whole being resonated with the right harmony at the right time. He followed that note, and produced a masterpiece."

"Uh-huh…. And how do you suggest we plan these bursts of creativity?"

"You don't need to plan the creativity, you need to plan the people who are capable of being creative. Even now we don't plan production, we plan the output of our production. The production process itself is the result of the output."

"Then how are you going to plan these creators, how do you know who will be a good inventor?"

"Everybody will be."

"Even you?"

"Even me."

"Is this why you decided to become such a loose cannon?"

"Partly," he said modestly. "When I first tried to call Professor Glagolev and tell him that I have interesting new data about the authorship of "The Lay of Prince Igor," he hung up on me. I called

---

7. George Sand used this term to describe an evening with Chopin and Delacroix, when Chopin tried to find the color "blue" in music.

again and asked: 'If I found a manuscript with Mitus's signature on it, would you still not believe me?' He laughed and said 'What a joke,' and hung up on me again. I thought, 'You want a joke? Well, why not? Why not laugh at all you conceited people?' After all, the real joke is not when the people laugh at the clown, but when the clown laughs at the people."

He cast a sidelong glance at me.

I felt a flush of embarrassment, but asked "Well, did you find this all-powerful mode of thinking?"

That was my second mistake.

"Yes, I found it."

It was time to teach him a lesson.

"Great," I said. "Let's have a demonstration."

"Why demonstrate?" he said. "I'll bring the pills tomorrow, that's all."

"What pills?"

"Take them, and you yourself will start to think creatively."

He wasn't even laughing, the jerk.

"Fine," I said. "I'll try your pills."

He nodded and left. In the meantime I had a shot of vodka. Without pills.

10. Flour and Sugar

What happened next was ridiculous.

He showed up the next day with some kind of homemade pills. Six tablets.

"There aren't any more," he said. "I need the rest for myself." The little punks who knew what was going on all jostled forward with their eager little hands outstretched. Six of them grabbed the bait.

"You're going to get poisoned!" the others yelled at them.

"You won't be poisoned," he assured them.

They took the pills, chasing them down with water from our carafe.

"Alright guys, don't get too pumped up," he said.

"The work day has already started," I growled.

Our group moved down the hallway, giggling obnoxiously. The six poisoned ones were in front. I was disgusted with myself, both because I had wanted to take one of the tablets myself, and because I wasn't bold enough to do so.

I couldn't sleep that night. I sucked on one of my own creativity pills – Valium.

At first, nothing in particular happened at work the next morning. He just ignored the smirking and kept making the rounds of all six pill-takers, asking them how their work was going, and in so doing, he distracted them from their work, because after all each of them was supposed to be concentrating on a problem. Still, I let him be. I felt sorry for him. Once again I recalled who he had been and who he had become, and how hard it was to find your place in life without your silver wings. Poor Soda-Sun.

That morning, five out of six problems were solved. Brilliantly. The only one of the six who hadn't solved his problem was our most talented and productive researcher, Pasha Bidenko. The hallways grew quiet. The five of them looked completely startled and flushed. Valya Medvedeva sat in the corner of my office crying.

"From happiness," she explained. "And from despair. I think I'm in love with him…."

He was surrounded by a vacuum of fear.

We barely made it through the day.

That night I dreamt that I was flying, swooping down through the burial grounds of the Minusinsk cultures, grabbing clay jugs from their graves. The jugs contain creativity pills, and I flew off with them in the direction of the sun.

The next day I planned to go to the director and report what had happened.

Pasha Bidenko stopped me in the hallway. He could barely keep his eyes open.

"This is torture," he groaned with exhaustion.

"What?"

Flour and sugar," he said. "There's nothing else in them. In those pills. Zilch. I spent all night analyzing them."

11. That Was Just the Beginning

After the whole fiasco, after we vigorously interrogated him and took measures to ensure that the scandal would not expand beyond the walls of our institute and make us a laughingstock in scientific circles, after I managed to push through my suggestion that the best solution was not to fire him, but to send him off on an expedition… I asked him quietly, just as he was climbing into the expedition vehicle with his sleeping bag:

"Why did you do it to begin with?"

He leaned over the side of the truck to answer.

"So our scholarly friends would stop strutting around as if they know everything."

"Ok, fine. But still, why did five out of six achieve such spectacular results?"

"Two reasons. The first you will have already guessed – their imaginations lost all inhibition and they started to think more freely and independently. The second reason is that I myself prompted them toward the answers to the problems they were working on."

The truck moved out of the institute parking lot in a noxious cloud of exhaust. That was it.

Actually, that was not it at all. That was just the beginning. On the expedition, things continued.

No sooner had he left than I immediately remembered his name was Soda-Sun. I always remembered this at the times when I didn't see him. Now both my annoyance with him and our senseless condemnation of his former profession seemed petty. Why shouldn't he have had another profession? Does the profession really determine the person? A person is determined by what he brings to a given profession. Humankind has thousands of needs, and each need spawns a profession. The important thing is what each person brings to humanity through his profession. When a talented person came to us with his ideas, we just gaped at him and called him a clown. Maybe a clown is exactly what we needed. We are always afraid of appearing silly, which allows any jerk to shower us with flattery and praise until we end up adopting his ethical code. While we wallow in our pride, we are completely conned. A clown is a surgeon who operates on our ethics. A clown is a poet of laughter. With one little word he pokes a hole in our conceit. I didn't get it at the time, but now I do.

Now I get it, but as he headed out with the expedition, I was thoroughly irritated. He was exceptionally good at irritating people, that clown. Stupid clown! After all, I was his friend, and he knew it. Why did he have to taunt me as well? Never mind, I thought, don't be petty, help him. So I helped him. I made sure he got on the expedition. I thought about it a lot, sending him on an expedition I would have gone on myself, if I had the strength. I sent him to the place where my career had started. He'd put in enough time comparing historical documents. Let him get back to the basics. Let him go to Turgai. So he went. And it turned into a mess.

At first we didn't hear a word from the expedition, even though communication these days is hardly as difficult as it was in 1913. Then, a crazy letter arrived.

The worst part wasn't the fact that the letter was filled with all kinds of ideas on all kinds of topics, none of which had any direct relationship to the archeological task at hand – the highest mark of a dilettante. That much I expected – I knew who we were dealing with. What was most absurd was the soppy beseeching at the end, which sounded almost like mockery. He begged me to use radioactive dating to establish the age of the *Indricatherium* I had dug out of the ground in 1913, and send him the results immediately.

12. Whaaat? I Exclaimed

Let me explain the radiometric method to those who are not familiar with it.

We take a bone from an ancient burial place and incinerate it in a special oven. We catch the carbon dioxide that is released and then measure the radioactivity of the carbon in the sample. Radioactive carbon dating works on organic material because all living organisms absorb carbon-14 – a radioactive isotope of ordinary carbon. After the plant or animal dies, the carbon-14 it contains slowly decays. If we compare the amount of radioactive carbon left in the bones to the amount of regular carbon in the atmosphere, which varies only slightly, we can determine the age of an object with a high degree of accuracy. This is all true, but it only works for organisms that died less than 40,000 years ago. *Indricotheria* went extinct millions of years ago. Therefore, my entire department laughed at the request in the letter.

"I hate him," declared Valya Medvedeva.

"Pasha," I said to Bidenko, "He's asking for a stint in remedial ed. Do you want to take him on this time?"

"Sure," said Pasha. "If you get me a little piece of bone from your *Indricotherium*."

"Good," I said. "We'll send him back an official answer on Institute letterhead. With an official seal."

It wasn't hard to call the museum and pay a visit to my beloved colossus. My five-meter-tall beauty was still in one piece, and the sign underneath it included my name. I sighed.

While I immersed myself in reminiscences, the museum technicians brought me a small sliver of bone. I forgot to mention that at the time, I had brought back an entire skeleton as well as a few other bones – all of the bones had been caught in the same landslide; therefore, they were all of the same age. I thanked my museum colleagues and handed the piece of bone to Pasha Bidenko. As for myself, I sat down to write that clown a devastating letter, in which I poured out my accumulated anger, laid out what we all thought of him, and lectured him about how a responsible scientist should approach the field. As I was writing, I could see his long face with that smile of his, and I realized that a big letter would only mean more scoffing on his part. I tore up the letter and wrote a brief note on the letterhead: "For some reason no radioactivity can be detected in the bones of the *Indricotherium*." I underlined the words *for some reason*, got the office to put an official stamp on the letter, and signed it "Dr. V. A. Gorbunov, PhD."

When I got home that evening, Pasha Bidenko called to tell me that, according to radiometric analysis, the bones were only 5 thousand years old.

"Whaaat?" I exclaimed.

13. It Was All Very Sad

Why does everything in life pale after a while? Probably because everything we encounter only looks close to what it should be, but falls short of being the best version, and you keep thinking there must be something better out there. Fashions change. Yesterday's clothes are no longer attractive, yesterday's beauty seems to fade, yesterday's thoughts are ignored, yesterday's happiness makes you feel awkward (what were you so happy about anyway, you idiot?), yesterday's joy turns out to be yesterday's naïveté. Now I wised up and my teeth were set on edge.[8] We look for salvation in endless quests, but endless questing is endless hunger. Of course, it's pleasant to imagine that a delightful dish of perfection lies just ahead of us, but doesn't that dish remind you of the clump of hay tied just beyond the donkey's nose? The poor donkey keeps walking on and on, his hunger never filled, as the clump of hay moves further into the distance at the exact same rate as the donkey moves toward it.[9] Why should we wait for the future to solve today's problems? The future will have its own problems, but we will not be in that future.

Try to recall. Let your body recall. When was the last time something did not pale with repetition, did not grow boring after a while? Flip through everything you can think of, and suddenly you remember the touch of someone else's hand, that feeling – the feeling of tenderness.

---

8. From Ezekiel 18: 1-2. The proverb "The parents ate sour grapes, and now the childrens' teeth are set on edge" has been interpreted to mean that one must take personal responsibility for one's own sins. The childrens' teeth ache not because their parents ate those sour grapes, but because of their own unwise actions.

9. Official Soviet political rhetoric insisted that the "radiant future" of full communism was just ahead, on the horizon. By the 1970s, the endlessly receding "radiant future" had become the butt of sardonic jokes, whereas this passage makes the same point in a more elegiac mode.

Every shade of that feeling: from the fierce tenderness of the soldier who drops his sword to pick up a slain enemy's child, feels her pressed to his stony cheek, and commands the rest of the world "don't touch her," all the way to the melting tenderness of a lover's embrace.

Only tenderness is unambiguous and cannot abide falsehood, masks, or deceit – it's either there, or it's not. We experience this tenderness too rarely, we almost don't notice the role it plays in our lives. But perhaps it plays the most important role of all. When reptiles still lumbered over the earth, it's not as though any lizard-philosopher noticed the little creature slipping out of its hole, the one who carried his own warmth in his blood and did not depend on changes in the weather. The big lizards left, and warm-blooded creatures filled up the world.

Plus, I still want to talk about hematomas.

"Whaaat?" I asked.

Although I didn't need to ask, because I was sure of the answer. I'd just forgotten it, over the past half century. That is, I didn't exactly forget, but I'd chased it deep down into the depths of my mind, where we keep the memories of things that never came to be, but still live within us. We stay sane by habitually avoiding this dark spot like a bruise, like a hematoma in our psyche. A hematoma is nothing more than a localized pooling of blood that the surrounding tissue won't absorb. If you don't touch it, it will just stay there like a harmless foreign body, but if you disturb it, it can cause trouble. "Harmless" in a hematoma is a relative term; after all, something dead in a live body cannot be neutral. In a live body, everything must be alive and participate. There are two ways to get rid of a hematoma: remove it surgically, or, theoretically at least, reanimate it. There's a third way – give up. Obviously there is nothing worse than giving up, which is a bad end. And nothing better than reanimation, which is a good start.

Therefore, when I exclaimed "whaaat?," the question, the yelp of surprise, was not in response to Bidenko's statement, even though he had just announced in a bored voice that the animal we thought had disappeared millions of years ago had perished as recently as the age of the Egyptian pharaohs. It turns out my gigantic beast was on this earth at the same time as humans, which makes it a real question for archeology. Unless it's a mistake. Bidenko was mistaken, the instruments were mistaken, who knows who was mistaken, maybe the museum director mistakenly delivered the wrong bone sample. The most important thing for an old fart like me (who once upon a time was young and not afraid of sensations and thirsted for the kind of thrills that shake up your whole world and make you feel like anything is possible – youth thinks this is the way life should be, and chases after thrills constantly, incoherently, charging behind every rock in hopes of finding something – naturally, old age, with the wisdom of its scars, proceeds methodically and correctly, but less passionately, in the name of self-preservation, in the name of preserving what's left of his strength he tells himself that if the grapes are still green you shouldn't eat them, but he feels the astringency on his soul anyway; the guy who never risked anything and diddled away his youth ended up with nothing in old age except his comfort and his fear of the unexpected…), the most important thing for me, an old fart, was that when I lucked upon a big find in my youth, it seemed like the fulfillment of a presentiment; but when I was stunned by the reanimation of my long-dead fossil in old age, it seemed like the reanimation of a long-dead hematoma.

In other words, all these reflections on tenderness and reanimation of dead matter were necessary for me to understand myself, and were the reason why, when I yelled "whaaat?," it suddenly came back to me that a month ago, when I had walked out of my office and for the first time and called him Soda-Sun, he said "don't!" and slapped my hand.

It also came back to me that fifty years ago I had guessed that my colossal beast was only a few thousand years old, and not millions of years old, as the scientists had subsequently affirmed.

As I walked along the street, I felt like a boy whose loved ones were still alive and nearby, and whose life was all ahead of him. I felt immortal. The wind was blowing and tearing at the flaps of my coat, but I didn't care. It was raining as well, but I didn't notice the rain and my eyes were dry.

"Haha, just you wait, all you old farts," I muttered, my heart pounding. "I'll still show you, this is just the beginning… "

I didn't know at the time exactly what was just beginning, but I felt ready for anything. Let it be a circus or some kind of hellfire, I didn't care. At least something had started! However, in the end, it was all very sad.

14. The Human Skull

I'll never forget those days, full of happiness and secret striving.

At first nobody believed the results of Pasha Bidenko's analysis, least of all Pasha himself.

"Ridiculous," said the director.

They retested. The results were the same. Did it cause a sensation? No, of course not. They could have mixed up the bone samples in the museum. A meeting was called. It was decided to take a piece of bone from the skeleton itself, in a place where it could be easily repaired and restored. They tested again… the *Indricotherium* I had found in 1913 was five thousand years old.

A sensation? Try a complete scandal!

Nevertheless, the fact is that at age 23, I had voiced my supposition that the bones I had found were relatively recent. However inexperienced I may have been in those years, even I could tell that the animals whose bones I was digging up had perished in some kind of unnatural circumstances. It didn't look like a natural death. The bones of all sorts of animals were mixed up and tossed all over the place, all of them in one layer, which means they were not a result of successive changes in the earth's crust. That was the crux of the matter, which made me think of Pushkin's lines: "oh field, field, who strew you with dead bones?" It resembled either a battleground of various animals, or a cemetery, or, more likely, a dump. The whole mishmash was located quite close to the surface, in layers that could not be more than a few thousand years old, as even I, a student at the Mining Academy, could figure out. At the time, I suggested that these animals, including the *Indricotherium*, existed not so long ago. I was laughed at. Now my suggestion was confirmed, a full half-century later. At least, according to the analyses. They have decided to launch a comprehensive expedition to conduct "high-level" excavations. I am supposed to go, but I don't feel like it. The original plan, to be simple and honest, has already accrued too much baggage. It's all his fault again, that Soda-Sun.

He was summoned back to Moscow immediately. He hung out somewhere for a few days, then appeared at the institute. It was hard to tell whether he was the victor or the accused. They demanded a report, and he wrote a very reasonable one, in which he explained why he had requested the dating analysis: because among the bones he found close to my old dig, he'd discovered a human skull.

15. After That They Fired Him

He brought us the skull.

The skull was new and smooth. It wasn't some kind of *Pithecanthropus* either; it was a contemporary skull, the same, for example, as mine, except even more contemporary, since this skull still had all its teeth, which is more than I can say for myself. The skull looked so new that we immediately ran an analysis to date it, in order to rule out the obvious possibility of a counterfeit or fraud. The analysis came back: five thousand years old. Well then!

This all looks good, does it not? No, it looks bad. At the end of his report he had written: "In addition to the bones of extinct animals there was found a sculpture of a woman of extraordinary beauty."

"What woman?" We were stunned. "Where is she?"

"I took her home," he said. "I'll bring her tomorrow."

"We'll see you tomorrow, then," said the director.

I did not intend to wait until tomorrow. I could feel it in the pit of my stomach. What the hell kind of woman was this, for god's sake! I was tied up on the phone all evening, trying to reach someone on the expedition. I finally got through in the middle of the night.

"Hey, it's me." I say. "Yes! Hello! How are things?"

The distant squeak of a girl's voice: "Fine… Going well…"

Another voice cuts in: "Are you connected?"

"Yes, we're connected."

"Go ahead then, talk…" the voice says encouragingly.

"I *am* talking!" I yell.

"Did something happen?" asked someone at the other end. "How was the report?"

"The report was not bad," I answer. "Tell me, what do you know about this woman? Where did he find her?"

"Oh, she's a beauty!" they squeak. "Have you seen her? What do you think?"

"I don't know yet. We'll see her tomorrow."

"Are you still talking?" interrupts the voice.

"You're the one who is talking! Let us talk!" I scream into the receiver.

"Your time is up," says the voice.

"Hello! Hello!"

That was it.

The next day we gathered in my department. So many people showed up that we had to push all the tables to the walls and stack them on top of each other. Pasha Bidenko stretched out regally on top of the highest table, close to the ceiling, smoking a cigarette. He didn't believe anything, and he looked down upon the proceedings both literally and figuratively. A chess table we had dragged in from the lounge stood in the middle of the room, hemmed in on all sides by senior scholars. The table supported a plywood shipping box. Cotton padding protruded from its half-open top. Silence reigned. The only sound was the unpleasant scrunch of nails being pulled out of wood with the pliers wielded by Soda-Sun.

He removed the top and plunged two hands into the dusty cotton.

"Hold onto the box," he said.

Hands reached forward and grabbed the box.

He pulled out a dark pillar of padding and set it down on the instantly cleared table. The box was already floating over peoples' heads and toward the door, through which it crashed to the floor in the empty hallway. Layer by layer, swaths of cotton dropped to the table, each layer lighter and whiter than the last, until it looked like a pile of sea foam. Everyone held their breath. If it weren't for the buzzing in one's own ears, it would have been possible to hear the steady beat of a single collective heart when all that remained was the last swath of cotton, finer than mist, just a shadow of fabric, through which the features of a beautiful face with half-closed eyes became visible.

All hearts stopped. Hands moved the last veil aside. A sharply defined upper lip. A thick, lush lower lip. The dusky golden color of old wood. The mouth was just barely smiling. She looked a little bit like Nefertiti, but in a different mode. More like Aelita, the Martian princess. She glanced out knowingly thorough lowered eyelids.

Something crashed. Everyone jolted, as if from an electric shock. It was nothing. Pasha Bidenko had tumbled down from the ceiling.

Everyone looked stunned. The director swallowed with difficulty. Something moved through the solid mass of people. It was Pasha Bidenko.

"… an analysis," he wheezed. "I don't believe…"

"I forbid it," said the director and licked his dry lips.

"Why not?" said Soda-Sun.

He grabbed the pliers and quickly broke off a chip of wood near the base of that beautiful neck. He handed it to Bidenko.

"You are a barbarian, a vandal," the director said to the poor clown. "Get out of here!"

"Thank you, everyone," said Soda-Sun. "Honestly, thanks."

He sighed deeply, smiled his smile, and began to squeeze his way toward the exit.

The director pushed everyone back from the table. With trembling hands he gathered up the cotton and began to re-wrap the beautiful face. He clucked something to himself and his elbows flailed out, so that he resembled a large hen. Everyone understood that this was his expression of winged exaltation. We had never seen our director like this before.

"Vladimir Andreyevich," clucked the director. "Call security… get the key for the safe… we'll lock the safe."

If he could have, he would have called in the tanks. I hesitated. He looked at me with fury.

"You, too?" said the director. "Really, even you? Bidenko can be forgiven… although you don't need to be a specialist to see what we have here."

"True, you don't need to be a specialist," I said.

I left to carry out the director's orders.

The next morning Bidenko confirmed, smiling guiltily: "Yeah… the same five thousand years."

I called the clown.

"Why did you do that…" I asked wearily.

"I was joking," he said.

"What are we going to tell the director?"

"The truth," he said.

The truth was that I'd seen a photograph of this woman in his possession already back then, during the war.

What amazed me was how quickly the sculpture had been made. After all, the wood was real – ancient – which means he had found it in the excavations, which means the sculpture had been created within just those few brief days after he was summoned back, before he showed up at the institute. I knew his friend Kostya Yakushev was talented.

He pulled everyone's leg, but most of all his own. It is one thing to laugh at people's pride, but another thing to laugh at real feelings. You should have seen the director when I told him the whole story. He was silent while I talked, then he removed his pince-nez. His eyes were like a child's.

After that, Soda-Sun was fired.

16. "Welcome, Junk Dealers!"

So in the end we set off on the expedition without him, spent the summer there, discovered much that was interesting, and quickly wrapped up the work. As it happened, I sent everyone back home, and only Pasha Bidenko and I remained at the base camp in the desert.

After we had finished our work and the expedition had departed in a despondent rush, I was faced with one persistent question: why had I stayed?

Everything emptied out. There was nothing left but indentations where the tent poles had been, along with cold stars and an even colder wind that pierced through your soul. That, and the solitary figure of Pasha Bidenko, who was fussing around our beat-up all-terrain vehicle, and also the thin notes coming from a radio – a piece of jazz music that sounded ludicrous over this cemetery of dinosaurs.

It made me think: only a very fine membrane divides our world from the world of monsters.

The batteries died, the radio went mute, and once again, nothing but desert and swirling dust. This is the place where we're digging our own grave as well. We busy ourselves trying to understand humanity, and then these same humans invent a nuclear bomb, which can no longer be wished away.[10] If humanity doesn't succeed in understanding itself, it will end up in only one place – with the fossils. A thousand years from now, a new race will arrive, and they will uncover deposits of bones, and from the looks of our darkened skeletons they will know why these creatures, so unlike dinosaurs, disappeared from the face of the earth.

Well, if the purpose of archeology is to help humanity understand itself, then at least it's worked for one person. Actually, for two: Bidenko and myself. In fact, it's fair to say that not a single one of us remained the same as the person we were before that expedition. I know there were many reasons I began to change my views, and therefore it is hard to identify any one factor that brought about the changes in

---

10. The steppes of Kazakhstan were the site of Soviet nuclear weapons testing from 1949 on. The devasting environmental and human impact of these tests was officially covered up.

every participant of that absurdly truthful, and therefore fantastical expedition. What is the fantastic, if not the truth carried to the point of absurdity?[11]

The expedition was deemed a success. We found a lot, and what we found was worthwhile. There is no way one could characterize this expedition as unsuccessful. Why, then, the withering disappointment felt by every single participant, from the auxiliary workers, who had never seen monster bones before, to the most qualified researchers, whose absolute disdain for all counterfeits and frauds was a fundamental principle? Maybe it was because the expedition had gathered the most talented people, and in science, talent and fervor are almost inseparable. Or maybe it was just the wind.

The wind was debilitating. The sandstorms began almost as soon as we arrived. By following the lead of the previous research group, we discovered new deposits of bones, as well as three "shelves" of dinosaur bones that were well preserved, though rusty from the iron oxide that had seeped into them. It was a rich haul, although not exactly what every participant secretly wished to find. Yet even so, I seriously considered calling it off because of the wind. Then we came upon an ancient abandoned ore mine and the entire expedition basically moved underground. At night, it was rough outside. The cold blew through our tents. The drive to the nearest water source was long and exhausting. The thick reddish-brown dust penetrated every pore, went up your nose, dried out your throat. The constant winds blew so hard that they lifted not only sand, but even small rocks, which could break the glass of our protective goggles. The wind never ceased, day or night. Our clothes, our beds, and our provisions were full of thick sand. If it weren't for our quiet underground haven, it would have been impossible to work at all. But the point is not to describe how this expedition resembled other ones in the usual hardships, but to describe how it did not resemble any other. It was different because of a kind

---

11. Note the author's metaliterary intent here: he is commenting on the genre of "fantastic literature" itself, implying that it is in some ways the most truthful.

of indefinable despondency and the spirit of the clown that seemed to hang over the entire enterprise.

Like it or not, the sad silence and darkness that reigned in those old mines created an atmosphere of stern concentration. It affected everyone, old and young. Bidenko's journal contains the following lines:

"It no longer matters if it is day or night on the surface. Sometimes you pass along sheer, high faces, and your own steps echo and the beam of your headlights is lost; sometimes you can barely squeeze through the narrow passageways; other times you scramble along well shafts that rise up to a different horizon. Here you start to measure time differently, because some of these ore mines go back to prehistoric times. They run along bands of Permian sedimentation partly mineralized with copper, forming so-called copper sandstone and shale. I slipped and fell down one of the miner's drifts, sliding downwards at an angle of about 40 degrees, and landed in a steep well that disappeared deep into the bottomless darkness. Fortunately the well shaft was so narrow that my shoulders jammed against the walls and I was stuck like a cork in a bottle. It took me a while to get out. When I did, the first thing I saw as I climbed back over the edge of the well and turned on my lamp was a notice scrawled in bloody letters on the wall: "WELCOME, JUNK DEALERS!"

17. Why Did I Stay?

That was how our dear friend left us his first message.

By the way, about Valya Medvedeva. Things with her were always complicated. After the incident with the "creativity pills," we dispatched *him* on the expedition, and she went also. At first I didn't even recognize her when she dropped by my place, because I had never seen her fashionably made-up.

"Vladimir Andreyevich," she threatened in her best Commissar's voice, "You either send me on this expedition, or… or…"

"Or one of us dies," I said, maintaining the gangster tone. "Valya, your lipstick – where did all of this come from?"

"From the Wanda."[12] Vladimir Andreyevich, you must understand me," she said in the dramatic voice of an Italian actress, sinking into the armchair.

"Valyusha," I said, "you're a down-to-earth girl. Why the theatrical pathos?"

"I'm not myself anymore." This time it came out in the voice of Sarah Bernhardt.[13]

It was hopeless. I decided to let her go on the expedition.

Only now, when Bidenko found that bloody note, did Valya understand where her precious Polish lipstick had gone.

Everything about that ill-fated expedition was off kilter. Like brown dust, rumors swirled around our expedition, which should have returned to Moscow a long time ago but instead continued to search for who-knows-what with absurd persistence. We never wrote a single report about the latter part of our extended expedition, and our expenditures were written off as part of a cultural program of some sort. The worst that happened is that something managed to seep out into print. Some journalist wrote a column in the "Did You Know?" section of a popular science magazine, in which the sculpture, the skull, and the question of what had served as the prototype of the devil were all discussed. The word "devil" did not escape notice, and another article popped up, playing with the expression "what the devil…?" to make fun of our expedition – and, along the way, to discredit all of archeology. In the end, this commentator posed the question: "Isn't it time for our ministers of finance to take a closer look at how our national funds are being spent?"

One could have answered the commentator quite simply: funding science funds the search for truth. But he probably wouldn't have understood.

---

12. "Wanda" was a famous Moscow store that sold cosmetics, perfumes, and other women's products imported from Poland. It became a symbol of luxury during the 1980s, when such goods were scarce in the Soviet Union.
13. Sarah Bernhardt (1844-1923) was a French actress who became known as "the most famous actress in all the world" for her dramatic roles in early films.

The unseemly press coverage finally forced our return to Moscow. On top of it all, there was the matter of the letter…

When the clown and I had last parted, he gave me a sealed package and made me promise to open it when we found the notorious devil. He was sure we would find it, and not only that, he acted as if he already knew what we would find. Everyone on the expedition knew about the letter, and naturally we were not searching for any devil, we were searching for a way to disprove the whole notion that he could know about the unknown in advance. We all remembered the insulting "creativity pills" hoax, so at this point we were maniacally determined to prove him wrong: there was no such thing as a special way of thinking, and it was not possible for him to guess what exactly we might find in the depths of the earth. We wanted to vindicate ourselves.

Somebody went ahead and opened the letter, thereby violating the rules of the game. It gave him yet another chance to laugh at us. It felt like a slap across the cheek. We received a second slap when we read what was written.

"I will go ahead and assume that this letter will be opened before you find what you are supposed to find," he wrote. "I will assume that one of my female friends will be the one who opens it. Don't blame her – sometimes it is impossible to resist, especially when you are young. They say the same thing happened to Eve. Inside this package is a second one – with the answer."

Indeed, there was a second packet inside. Valya Medvedeva left that very evening. The same evening, I arranged to wrap up our expedition.

He could read people well; more to the point, he understood their weaknesses. But that does not add up to a special way of thinking…

We loaded up quickly and glumly. The campsite emptied out. Only Bidenko and I stayed, along with the all-terrain vehicle, the radio, and the nocturnal emptiness punctuated by prickly stars, which watched over the dinosaur cemeteries without blinking. It was then that I asked myself: why did I stay?

18. With Whom Was He Talking?

I feel as though I was contracted to write this story and got quite carried away with it, until suddenly I lost interest and ran out of steam. I need to finish, but I don't feel like it. It is spring again, and spring is when one feels like avoiding one's duties. Spring is when our desires seem to bifurcate in two directions. We want to think about the future, but we look over our shoulders into the past. We always transfer our unfulfilled desires to a place where we are not. That is why the past seems better than the present, and the future seems more desirable. We either run forward or scramble backwards in our effort to glimpse the merry face of happiness. Reminiscence is a wrenchingly bitter sweetness.

I remember everything. I remember my last conversation with Soda-Sun, and I remember the real reason for why he was fired. The real reason is quite simple. I betrayed him. Nobody knows about it, not even him. I am the only one who knows. I was the only one who could have defended him at the moment that was most crucial, and I did not do so. Nobody can accuse me of having done anything wrong – from any point of view, it seems that I acted correctly. That is, from any point of view other than my own. He taught us a good lesson, that clown, who was interested in science least of all. In fact, he was not interested in any enterprise that could not give an answer to the question: "what does this do for humanity?" In our final conversation, when it became evident that our paths were parting forever, I could have fixed things, if I had not clung to my pathetic need to salvage my dignity, as if dignity in a scientist is not defined precisely as the willingness to examine a new idea, even if it overturns your own.

One sunny morning, some time after the whole episode with the sculpture and the skull, when everything became a mess again and nobody knew what to do about him, I heard his voice in the corridor, coming from behind a half-closed door. I entered the room. He didn't hear me – he was facing the other direction. Sunlight poured in through the open window. In the sweltering heat outside, the grey leaves of the linden tree were completely still, as though in prayer.

He was very agitated, and he seemed to be ranting. But as I listened more closely, I was surprised to find that he spoke quite clearly, as if reading from a text. As I understood it, he was talking about logic. He would ask himself questions and answer them himself. Then I saw a spot of sunlight bobbing on the ceiling, and I realized that he was holding a microphone. I heard the whirring sound of a tape recorder.

"How do we remove the contradiction between a logical answer and an unexpected discovery?" he asked himself. Immediately answering himself, he continued: "Logic is thinking within the boundaries of what has already been discovered. It is a form of thinking in hindsight. It is a way of establishing the connections between known facts. That is why, when we run up against something fundamentally unfamiliar and uncharted, logic has nothing to do with it. Here is the most impeccable logical proposition – and the most untrue: When Copernicus said the Earth revolves around the sun, people said, 'Nonsense. If the Earth is in motion around the sun, why don't all the clouds fly off of it in the other direction?' The logic was impeccable. To overturn this logic, it was necessary to discover the laws of gravity and show that the clouds move with the Earth, as an integrated system, like one object. Therefore, logical conclusions are only relevant at a certain level of knowledge. When it comes to fundamentally new knowledge, logic is not relevant. Virtually all logic comes down to the assertion that 'if this was, then this will be.' Can we adapt such a law to completely unanticipated discoveries, without projecting what we know onto what we don't know, thereby denying the as-yet-unexamined? Fact: sudden, unexpected discoveries happen. Note that they have happened in the past more than once. It follows that they will continue to happen in the future. Fact: the 'coefficient of useful action' generated by these unlooked-for discoveries is enormous. Logically, then, if we can develop a new kind of thinking, one which allows us to anticipate the unknown, the payoff will be enormous."

Sunspots chased each other all over the ceiling. Soda-Sun was imploring people to believe in his greatness.

It was a bright sunny day. It was joyfully hypnotizing. My nose tickled inside, as if I had just had a fizzy drink. That drink could be called "Soda-Sun."

I suddenly realized that all of this sounded like a farewell speech. Or perhaps more like an interview. He was interviewing himself, and the person doing the interviewing was just as smart as he was – except the questions were predictable, whereas the answers were not.

"How would you characterize this new kind of thinking?" he asked himself. "Would you call it knowledge *a priori*, or inspiration from on high?"

"I understand it in the following way," he answered. "Brainstorming, thinking heuristically – from the Greek 'eureka!' How does it work? In fact, it is the end result of a despairing kind of yearning. A yearning is a goal that can't be properly formulated. An unformulated goal is really just a very complicated desire, for which you cannot immediately find the right words. But the need to do so is there. If the need exists, it must have been called forth by some sort of laws that govern our brain. After all, our brain is not just an organ that can generate its own laws; it is also a reflection of the laws that created brains, that guide the way we think. When our psychic need exceeds a certain threshold, the laws that call forth this need suddenly become exposed, like a photograph, and we call this sudden exposure 'an unexpected discovery.' I was happy to find Einstein's confession: 'Discovery is not the result of logical thinking, even if the final product appears in logical form.'"

I was happy to see him this way. He was serious, and his ideas were clearly worth considering.

I moved, and the wooden floor squeaked. He quickly turned around.

"Ahh," he said calmly, "I'm about to finish."

"Hello," I said, coughing lightly.

"If you discard all clownishness, what is your essential interest? In all seriousness?" he spoke into the microphone.

"I am interested in the relationship between creative activity and ordinary thinking," he answered.

He looked at the blindingly white sky outside and said:

"Shakespeare once said that to understand is to forgive. But doesn't it seem more accurate to say that to understand is to simplify?"

He was silent for a moment, then continued:

"…not just in the sense that absolute truth cannot be reached, so our partial truths are only simplifications, but in the sense that the person who simplifies a problem must be more complicated than the problem itself. Otherwise you can simplify and simplify, without understanding your own deceptive schema. Thus, in order for Man to understand himself, he has to become more complicated than his own brain – that is the trick. And how do we do this? We observe the behavior of others and try to understand them. Still, our brains do the observing and simplify what we see into what we can understand. So, yes, we must agree – to understand is to forgive."

I had the eerie feeling that he was waiting for the microphone to answer back.

"Then the creative moment arrives…" he said slowly. "And you can't trace it… the results are so unexpected… Does this not mean that for a moment, our brain becomes more complex than usual?"

A sudden hunch almost choked me. Then I decided: no, it's nonsense.

"Does it not mean that in the moment of inspiration, our brain is both physiologically and energetically more complex that usual?"

I turned off the microphone.

19. "Do You Believe Me?" He Asked

"All I know is that if now we experience moments of creativity as the happiest moments in our lives, when for an instant we step into complete harmony with ourselves *and* with the laws of the universe, then only the absence of a final missing factor prevents us from living in this state of harmony all the time. Yet if the prerequisites are there, then there is also a possibility that we can realize this golden age, when humanity will be able to grasp the essence of what is most uniquely necessary to us. We are moving toward this age… the mass character of creativity is evidence. We need some kind of a final push. Science should provide the push. Poetry should establish the conditions for a felicitous encounter with the new age.

"Can you believe it?" he asked. "A leap in the way we think is just around the corner. People will be able to understand the essence of things without deconstructive analysis. Sheer, direct apprehension. The laws of the universe will imprint themselves directly onto our brains, as onto a photographic plate. Do you believe me?"

20. Stop, I Said

"How am I supposed to believe in this stuff?" I said. "I'm a scientist. You have an attractive hypothesis, nothing more. A fantasy. You can even make it seem logical, although you yourself insist that logic is the connection between proven facts – and are your 'facts' really proven?"

I am saying these things to him, but inside, I feel sick. Deep down, I believe without question in what he proposes. Sure, it's just a hypothesis. Maybe that's why the exact same guess had flashed through my mind as the only possible explanation for moments of creative inspiration.

"So, you don't actually believe in my little theory," he said, and sighed in relief.

Then he began to laugh.

"I can't take this anymore," he said.

"Good for you. Good for you, my friend."

"Do you want me to entertain you with a few more tall tales?"

"Stop," I said. "That's enough."

"I'm just kidding, dear teacher. Clowning around. I made it all up like an old-fashioned yarn. A fantastic tale."

"Liar. Now you really are lying."

"What difference does it make," he said, as his face turned pale and aloof. "Laughter and tears, my dear teacher. There is nothing in this world, dear teacher, that cannot be laughed at. It is easiest of all to laugh at tears. One can even laugh at Shakespearean tragedy. Maybe laughter is the only thing that differentiates us from animals. Only humans laugh."

"Just think what you are saying," I said. "You draw people into the most ridiculous discussions. You know very well that there are some things that cannot be laughed at. *Hamlet*, for instance, unless I don't know the meaning of funny."

That was a mistake – how many had I made by now, and counting?

"Nonsense. You know what funny means," he said calmly. "For instance, take the tragedy *Hamlet*. Prince Hamlet gives the monologue, 'to be or not to be.' Suddenly his pants start to slip down... but he keeps up the monologue, holding up his pants... but they keep falling down. It's even funnier if his pants fall down while he is cursing his mother, and Polonius's corpse lies just behind the wall. But his pants are still slipping..."

"Shut up..."

"Even funnier, if his pants fall off while he's fighting that duel with Laertes..."

I was already wheezing with silly laughter; when I started to imagine the trouser-less duel, tears of laughter came to my eyes. It turns out you can even laugh at *Hamlet*. I stopped chuckling and looked at him. His wide mouth was twisted into a smile, and tears streamed down his cheeks. I felt as though I was looking into a mirror.

"You are a monster!" I said.

"I am a person," he said. "And you just laughed at possibly one of the most important propositions in the history of humanity."

What if he was serious? Afterwards, I went to the director and smoothed everything over. Three and a half hours of conversation – he was forgiven one more time. Let him go off on another expedition. The expedition would be an extremely interesting one. It was then that he came to me and announced that he would not go.

"I'm completely serious," he said. "I will not go with you on the expedition."

I felt tired and disgusted. This was too much, even for me.

"Well then," I said. "You've signed your resignation."

"Yeah... I know," he said. "It's time for me to leave. As it is, I've stayed too long in archeology."

I already felt indifferent, if I can put it that way. I suddenly understood that this was not a joke, and that he really had no place in science. The vague feeling grew deeper. I felt relieved. The relief tasted bitter, like quinine.

"You could have at least warned me earlier. Do you realize how much time I've spent trying to help you?"

"I didn't know, then, that I was planning to leave."

"What changed?"

"I got bored by the expeditions. I started to know in advance what would be found in the excavations."

"I see. Creative inspiration. You guess it all, before even looking beneath the soil. So can you tell me what we ordinary mortals will find there?"

"No way," he said, "Go yourselves and find out. You'll go with my letter. When you find what you will find, open the letter. Otherwise, you won't believe me. That's it… We're parting for the last time."

He laughed again.

"Stop," I said. "Stop."

Whatever. All that was left was to go and prove to him and to myself that we human beings are in fact the pinnacle of evolution, and there is no reason to think otherwise, and he cannot guess what we will find there among the fossils. This way, I can put an end to the crazy ideas that have recently proliferated far too wildly around me, a quiet person.

21. Yes, But The Figure Moved

Now there is only the desert, and me, and Bidenko. We stayed on for another 24 hours. We had some presuppositions of our own. We wanted to check them.

On the day of the main expedition's departure, the wind dropped, so it was finally possible to load the truck decently. We didn't rush the loading, but inside we felt impatient. As soon as the wind died down, all the ardent tension of the last few days seemed somehow overblown, almost sentimental. Everyone felt awkward, and therefore they left with a feeling of relief, as though trying to forget something. The camp boiled with activity, like an anthill. Practical prose, replacing the drunken poetry of the last few days, felt like a gulp of bracing morning air after a night of smoking. The campfires were extinguished, the tents taken down. Pasha Bidenko took me aside by the elbow. "Vladimir Andreyevich," he said. "I've found hell."

"Oh really?" I said. "Along with Beelzebub?"

"No, I haven't found Beelzebub," Bidenko answered. "Do you want me to show you?"

Hell like any other hell. No mystery here. The guy found a realistic hell. And that wasn't the only thing we found. In an abandoned mine shaft we found another *Indricotherium* with human skeletons next to it. It was obvious even without technical analysis that the age of man and beast was the same. It looked as if they gotten into a fight and destroyed each other. We were no longer even surprised. All we could do is try not to think about how this would appear to outsiders, and what our position would be when the entire scientific world called the man versus dinosaur thing by its name – a "hoax." And now Bidenko had discovered hell. Sure, why not discover hell while we're at it?

We descended into the mine. After months of work we were as familiar with this place as a stoker with his boiler-room. Down below, a few people were finishing up work; the last group was heading for the exit. Bidenko and I walked on and on, until we came to the dead-end we knew so well, where the ore vein ended.

That Bidenko did find hell, after all. The dead-end was not a dead-end, but an optical illusion. From our usual vantage point, it certainly looked like a dead-end. And there was no other vantage point, because just beneath our feet was a well that descended all the way down to who-knows-where. Nobody ever went near that well, even though there was a narrow path right along the wall. It turns out that if you move along that path, an archway that has been carefully carved into the rock becomes visible. We crept toward the archway. Steady, methodical Bidenko had actually found hell. I noticed a long time ago that the hardest things to notice are the ones right under your nose.

It even had a river of forgetfulness – the Styx. The only thing missing was the water, and Charon ferrying the dead. Instead, there was the dried-out bed of an enormous river, complete with the breastbones of human skeletons lying on the bottom. Apparently Charon had just flung them overboard. Or maybe the skeletons belonged to those who had tried to flee from this hell and drowned in the Styx. No wonder people forgot everything crossing this river, considering the sulfuric fumes that seeped through every fissure in this basin. Thousands of years ago, these mineral waters must have cured a lot of people of their lives.

We made our way across the riverbed and realized that this is where the real ore mines started; all the rest was just hell's antechamber. I couldn't help but look for a sign: "abandon all hope, ye who enter…," but for some reason there was none.

"They must have kept the *Indricotherium* as guard animals," said Bidenko.

"Who did?"

"I don't know. The devils, I guess."

The strange, fantastic underground world opened one's eyes. Apparently they had mined gold down here, and even more incredibly they had understood how to capture fine gold particles with mercury to form an amalgam. The smell of sulfur rose from hot springs, seeped through cracks and stuck like brimstone to the walls, which were polished smooth by the drafts of millennia. Acrid heat, flashes of light. Strange shadows danced wildly over the glittering crystals. Every movement elicited the appearance and disappearance of grimacing snouts. If you could iron out all the crags and crevices, all that would be left would be shadows, tame shadows, caused by our handheld lanterns. Any schoolchild could explain how the shadows work, and the devils would disappear. Is that all there is to it? A tangled, incoherent world, and suddenly devils materialize, dancing across the walls. Then science arrives, irons out the wrinkles of the universe, and lights the way forward with the steady light of a pocket flashlight. But that's only one side. Now imagine science in the guise of millions of pocket lamps, all illuminating an enormous tunnel leading out into eternity. Is that even science? Maybe it's just a sign of courage. Whereas the bright light, the ironed-out space, in which it is easy to live – one doesn't want to live there. Science that is cautious, science that responds to our anxieties, how dreary this kind of science can be! Thousands of years ago a gloomy wise man thought up a fence that would protect us from the wild horse-beast, whereas a joyful wise man tamed the beast, and jumped onto the saddle. He knew that there is no such thing as dangerous nature, only nature than hasn't been tamed.

We circumvented black shafts, crawled through tunnels and narrow drifts, emerging into chambers in which you could claim the foot of Man had never stepped, were it not for the people who hollowed out these rooms, thousands of years ago. Who were the people who dug out these spaces? Whose unfathomable prosperity was sustained by other people's hellish subterranean labors? It was obvious how stories had arisen about the circles of hell. It didn't take any imagination; all it took was these sketches from nature....

"I don't know who became the prototype for the devil," said Pasha Bidenko, "but when it comes to hell, you couldn't find a better model."

"Wait a minute, Pasha," I said. I wanted to say, now that we've found hell, all we have to do is find the devil, and we can wrap up our report about the expedition.

"Be quiet!" I hissed.

"What is it?"

"Over there... look..."

We had just gone by a deep shaft and now stood at a bend of the tunnel with extremely smooth and even walls.

"What's that, Vladimir Andreyevich?" whispered Pasha.

"I have no idea," I whispered back.

Some kind of figure was visible far ahead of us. It was not a shadow.

"A statue..." Pasha said uncertainly.

"No," I said. "It moved."

"Let's check it out," said Pasha, pointing his light into the distance.

The figure moved abruptly.

I grabbed Pasha and yanked him back. Pasha slipped and grunted. Something like a satisfied guffaw sounded from afar.

"Now what are we going to do?" said Pasha, breathing heavily.

"Let's go back," I said. "We have to think it over."

Trying not to rush, we started back. We didn't dare look over our shoulders. Sometimes it seemed as though someone was running behind us, lightly, as if on tiptoes, and at other times we seemed to hear a multitude of running feet.

"This is nonsense," said Pasha, throwing me a sidelong glance. "Normal echoes. Multiple reverberations. That guffaw – also an echo."

"I know," I said. "But it's still unsettling."

Finally we heard voices and caught up to the groups who were finishing their work. We could hear the business-like rap of their hammers; we saw the flash of cameras capturing a few more images; one group was already slacking off, singing from the same old repertoire of camping songs. Everything was so normal, and therefore so heartwarming. It was impossible to believe in either hell or in devils. Even the behemoths we had excavated and loaded onto trucks seemed like nothing more than instructive models, manufactured by our own brigade. Young men and women, serious graduate students and exhausted doctoral candidates, were busying themselves with the most tranquil of sciences: collecting and preserving the remains of an already disarmed past, so that people would not forget past mistakes, which were always paid for in blood.

Back on the surface, at the camp, it smelled of gasoline and stewed meat. The heavy trucks turned around slowly, transistor radios beeped. This was the most peaceful and cherished of scenes for me – a joyful human caravan, busy with the search for answers. There was nothing devilish in sight.

True, but that figure in the deep underground had moved.

Shots fired. The caravan set off with a pistol salute and cries of "hurrah!" This was the only sporting moment of the expedition –

those were the rules. The last trucks rumbled off, stars spilled out into the sky. Bidenko and I remained on our own.

Except for that figure deep underground, which had moved.

22. That Did Not Help Us

Now we are once again underground, crisscrossing through familiar passageways. We are all alone, if you don't count the figure down there, in hell, which would have looked just like a statue, if it had not moved.

Our freshly charged lamps shone brightly. We had no right to do what we were doing, although it was not risky, at least not according to the handbook of rules. We had not discovered any evidence of a collapse in the mine at any point during our long investigation at this particular site. The mine's galleries had held up for thousands of years, there was no reason to believe they would cave in now. My entire life's experience told me – there is no danger. As far as risk that was not anticipated in the handbook – nobody knew. The only danger was in the fact that we did not take our rifles with us. We didn't want to provoke any unnecessary suspicions. We claimed to have stayed behind in order to finish recording all our data. The only thing Pasha grabbed was a hatchet for each of us. At the last minute, he also took the starting pistol.

Why did we insist on going back? The answer is simple. Although, like all simple answers, it was based on complicated assumptions. The two of us went back into that hell alone, without weapons, without backup, without telling anyone, defying all rules – in short, we went heedlessly – for two opposite reasons. For me, it would be the last adventure of my life, and for Pasha – the first. What does it mean to choose an adventure, to take a risk, without being asked to? A person does it to prove that he is worthy. I am more than seventy years old; Pasha is just over twenty. Between us lies half a century. I will soon be gone; he is just starting. Of all my students, he was the only one in whom I truly believed. Do I need to explain why? I do. He considered the truth to be higher than himself. Half a century – and five thousand years. Only one hundred generations ago, somebody had fled from this hell in order to tell the truth. I am convinced that it was a scholar. Just as I am convinced that the first person to voluntarily descend into this pit was a poet. According to legend, his name was Orpheus. Orpheus's beloved, whom he almost managed to lead out of Hades, could not resist looking back. By the way, this happens to poets to this day. And who among us is not a little bit of a poet? If the ancients could go into hell at a time when devils really existed, then we should be able to do as much, in an age when the devil has been pretty much disavowed by everyone.

Everything around us was so fantastical that I even found myself thinking: what if the devil really exists? Aliens from another world, pursuing their own unknown goals, experiment on humanity, every so often tossing them an idea for, say, an atomic bomb.

I thought of the fantastic because, I'm ashamed to admit, once the rest of the expedition had left, Bidenko and I opened the letter. We opened the letter because we had the right to give ourselves at least a little bit of warning. What if he really did know something about those figures that were dancing about underground?

By opening the letter, we would admit that we were unenlightened bores, whereas he was a visionary genius, capable of directly apprehending essences without first sorting through the possible variants. But this is all blather. The truth is that we just couldn't resist. When we were left alone with the letter, we looked each other in the eyes.

We opened the letter. But it didn't help us.

Here it is.

23. He Looked At Me

It seems to me that I know what you found there. What looks like hell is, of course, an ancient gold mine. However, how did I know that the search for the devil should be carried out in this region? When I was studying Mitus, I noticed that the rebellion in which our poet-bard participated occurred right at the onset of the westward invasion of the Tatar hordes under Ghengis Khan. Then I remembered that the word 'Tatar' meant 'those who come from Tartarus,' which is the Latin word for hell. So perhaps the word 'Tatar' did not designate an ethnic group; rather, it referred to people who came out of the region where Ghengis' hordes moved, a region that the ancients thought of as 'hellish.' I was fixated on this idea because it came to me suddenly, in the form of a clear image.

Nobody knows exactly how an image arises. An image is something different from an observation, a memory, a figment of the imagination, or the coalescence of several details. An image is a concept that springs forth fully formed, and not only is it completely clear, it is also completely convincing. An image can be audio, visual, or verbal, but it is not a hallucination. An artistic image emerges along with its material embodiment – you hear the melody on a piano, you see the courtyard of a place you have never been, you write the page of book that has not yet been written. I can't describe the difference between an image and a figment of the imagination, but you know it when you see it.

When an image appears to you, it is worth pondering. As soon as I had an image of Hell, I thought: nothing in the world is so awful that only the devil could invent it. After all, what does the devil have in his arsenal? Boiling tar and sulfuric gas chambers, hooks to hang people from their ribs, the eternally futile labors of Sisyphus and the eternally unfulfilled thirst of Tantalus. All of this actually existed. There were even worse things – Asian torture by rats and European torture by electric shock. It all existed. Human beings invented all of it. If you coolly and calmly continue this train of thought, it leads inevitably, step by step, down the road to a well-known address, marked by a sign: "Fascism." In the course of the centuries the wording has changed – sometimes the sign reads "Hell," or "Tartarus," but it is always some version of the same thing. Time goes by, the scourge of fascism is forgotten, and eventually children think that mass graves and ovens in which millions of people were gassed alive are fabricated tales. Now imagine that the film reels that captured bulldozers scraping the naked corpses into heaps have decayed completely. What is left one thousand years from now? Legends of hell and torture chambers. By then, nobody will believe that the torturers were biologically indistinguishable from people. They will invent the notion of a devil, not for the first time, and claim that devils come out of hell. Of course, there were never any visitors from hell. There were only ordinary people who lost their human essence. A sclerosis of the soul, which always takes the form of racism – that is, the idea that a human being from a different tribe is not a human being at all.

Enough. It makes you sick to think about it, and it is repulsive to write about.

This is my farewell to you, dear teacher, hence such a long letter. I remember you all the way back to the war, with your gloomy good-naturedness, your willingness to hear new ideas, no matter whose, your ability to give a person an advance based on their humanity, without rushing to collect the profit. Even during wartime, of all the people who happened to see the woman's photograph, you were the only one who didn't interrogate me about who she was, and you were the only person I would have liked to tell. That woman doesn't exist. She is an image. When we were boys, my artist friend Kostya Yakushev and another guy – a physicist named Alyosha Anosov – created that picture out of several hundred photographs of beautiful women. First we put together two negatives and reshot them to get a single picture. Then we reshot that picture with a composite of two more to get a composite of four. And so on in geometric progression, until the composite ceased to change or improve. We ended up with a strange, fantastically beautiful, but somehow ominous, almost lifeless face. Kostya took it with him. First the face started to appear to him everywhere, in the streets and in his sleep. After 24 hours he brought the photo back. You have seen that face. "I touched something on it," he said, "I don't know what, or how it happened. In any case, I retook the picture…" The face had not changed, it was the same woman, but she had somehow come alive. It was then that we understood the essence of art: not a sum of parts, but a leap into some new quality – and we longed for it. We all understood: we will never meet this woman, but we are doomed to keep trying to find her. Also, we realized then how hard it is to experiment on real people.

I am saying farewell, dear teacher. Science is really not for me. If I understand myself correctly, my real calling is art. That is why I am leaving. All I needed was to find a point of departure – a qualitative leap into a different way of thinking. At that point, I figured out simultaneously where we should search for the devil, and how thought will work differently in humans of the future. All talent is essentially the ability to apprehend the truth in a qualitative leap. Leonardo da Vinci was the first normal person of the future – so far ahead of his time that to this day he is considered an enigma.

Do you want to know how I arrived at my idea? All of us sense that people could be better than they are. But what does it mean to be "better"? It means a better fit with the conditions that determine our existence. Our relationship to other people is the fundamental determining condition of our existence, yet our relationships are constantly distorted by lusts and desires. Once I watched as three thousand people listened to an old man, who sat with his back to the audience. Those people were completely different at that moment than I had known them before. They were listening to the old man play Bach on an organ. I remember thinking that if people can be like this now, some day they will be like this all the time. If I have to become a musician, or an artist, or a poet – in short, an organist of some sort – capable of ruffling people's souls until the way they appear in the moment of creative apprehension becomes their hereditary state, then I want to become that instigator. Then I would gladly give up clowning, because clowning is only the beginning. Clowns make people laugh, whereas jesters incite battles. Clowns always let people hang onto to the last thread of their human dignity. The dignity that consists in our capacity for tenderness.

24. Good Luck, Clown, On The Rest Of Your Journey

We had opened the letter, but it didn't help us with anything. There was no clue as to who the "devil" might be. Instead, there was a third envelope. He certainly knew what he was doing with this little game of giving away one thing at a time. We felt lucky enough just to find out that for all his fantasizing, nothing good was predicted for us; the only thing we would find underground was something disgusting. But what would it be? A live fascist, who had lurked down there for five thousand years in order to meet us now? Interesting… what had he been feeding on for all this time? Brrrrr, don't even start fantasizing… Too bad we didn't take the rifles with us.

"Vladimir Andreyevich… there it is," said Bidenko.

 An indistinct figure loomed ahead.

Everything that happened after that was like a bad dream… In fact, it was a nightmare. Only in a nightmare is it possible to fall into a foul cesspool up to your chest, which happened right after I stepped onto something crusty that covered the even ground right before the exit. If it hadn't been for my safety belt and Bidenko's efforts, I would have drowned in that cursed pit. Smeared with some kind of filth, we made our way back to firm ground. When we looked up, a monstrous creature materialized through the dim light right in front of us.

It stood in front of us without moving, although you could hardly call this thing immobile. Sulfuric fumes swirled around it like a veil. A sickly halo rose and fell behind his head, which made its hair stand on end. Did I say "head"? That's not exactly right. It constantly shifted its shape inside the contours of a black silhouette. Its horrible snout doubled, and its hands stretched out and grew longer. You couldn't get a good look at it through the vapors and flickering light, which made its eyes burn like red needles. It was silent.

I fumbled in my pocket for the starting pistol. There is nothing I can defend myself with – this is it, the place where sinners go… I thought, absurdly, maybe this really is an alien…

Paralyzed with fear, I raised my pathetic little pistol – our instincts are stronger than we are.

The monster also raised its arm. It reached forward and lengthened out, just like a tentacle. At the end of the tentacle I could see the enormous muzzle of a gun. There was no escape.

"Lie down!" screamed Pasha, breaking our stupor.

I threw myself face down to the ground just in time – not bad at my age.

A deafening shot rang out. Then nothing but silence and semi-darkness.

Someone snatched me by the ankle. I screamed and lost consciousness.

I woke up in the cold.

The huge black silhouette hovering over me obscured the stars.

"It's me, Vladimir Andreyevich," said Pasha.

I felt my heart resume beating.

"I'm ok," I said. "Thank you, Pasha."

I imagined how he must have dragged me back out through all those circles of hell.

We rested for a while on the sand. Pasha helped me get up, and we made our way back to the truck.

He got the best of us, Soda-Sun.

"When did you figure it out?" I asked Pasha.

"When the lamp broke."

"Me too. Well, let's open the letter. Interesting to see what…"

We opened the last envelope and read it by the light of the truck's headlights.

> A person has to at least occasionally stand up for himself. Because other than one's self, there is nobody else upon whom you can rely. Remember how Alexander Grin put it in one of his adventure novels, 'I am flying, I am rushing along a dark road…'
>
> I am flying, I am rushing, I am searching for the New Man, the one who we all resemble when we listen to a song. Poets are always partly clowns, but serious clowning around is like a

rooster crowing at dawn – it's a signal. Scholars, wish us light for our journey.

By the way, I completely forgot: what did you find there? Don't be upset, dear Vladimir Andreyevich, in you there is less of the devil than in anyone else. It's just that you found the world's first mirror. That's all. Maybe it was crooked.

Soda-Sun.

Good luck, Clown, on the rest of your journey.

First Russian publication: 1961
Translation by Yvonne Howell

THE EXAM

Nuri sat in a tree. Beneath him some kind of spotted beast raged and clawed at the bark. This went on for about ten minutes and it was starting to annoy Nuri. The beast took a running leap and the claws of its splayed paws flashed a centimeter short of his boot. Nuri pulled up his legs, grabbed the trunk, and leaned over.

"Impressive," he said, "but totally out of control."

The beast acknowledged this with a grunt and climbed into the tree. Nuri sighed and gripped the branch more firmly.

"You're not taking the situation into account, that's bad."

He moved down the trunk and poked the beast's snout with his boot heel. The beast flopped onto its back, sprang back up, hissed, and then charged at the aviaplane, as if it had forgotten all about Nuri. Grumbling, it sank its teeth into the plastic covering of a wing and started to tear it apart. The wing shook fiercely. Nuri couldn't stand it. Muttering to himself about how people's nerves can only take so much, he leaped down from the tree, grabbed the beast by the scruff of its neck and the root of its tail, and flung it to the side. The beast landed on all fours, roared, whipped its tail against one flank, and then the other, and jumped again…

Nuri was rummaging in a box under the seat of the aviaplane, looking for a flask, when the voice of the IRN's[1] watchman came on over the PA system:

"What's going on, Nuri? Can't see you and can't hear you."

Nuri rubbed his palm.

"I was sitting at the edge of the forest, just wanting to relax a bit, and then this spotted, whiskered thing comes along…"

"And…?"

"And I remembered the instructions on our agenda sheet and avoided contact. I climbed into a tree. But then he bit into my aviaplane."

"Into a tree!" cried the dispatcher. "Do you need help?"

"I'll make it."

Nuri turned the beast over onto its back and emptied the contents of the flask into its jaws. The beast sputtered and opened its eyes.

"There you go," said Nuri happily, "alive and well. Just a little bit perplexed."

"Can you get home by yourself?" asked the dispatcher.

"Absolutely. I'm flying out right now."

But Nuri was not able to fly at all. The beast had bitten through the plastic, so that the remaining glucose leaked out onto the grass, forming a light blue puddle. Nuri pulled off the torn edges of the covering, applied a bandage, and reconsidered.

He had no glucose in reserve. Maybe, by substituting a sugar solution, he might be able to make it to the Center, but he didn't have any sugar either. Somewhere he had read that if you inject adrenaline, the aviaplane could fly for a while on almost dry muscle, but where was he to find adrenaline?

The beast was already sitting up again, blinking its green eyes.

---

1. Institute for the Restoration of Nature. Most of the earth's originally existing plants and animals were destroyed or became extinct during humanity's earlier period of wanton disregard for Nature. Bio-genetic engineering allowed us to create a secondary nature and interesting new animals, who now roam the grounds of the Institute.

"See what you've done?" Nuri scolded. Then he froze with breathless excitement.

A fat piebald donkey had trotted out of the forest into the field, and on its back, legs dangling down to the grass, sat a cyber. His goldplated body gleamed. An ostrich feather waved out of his straw hat. A blue and red parrot flew over his head screeching:

"Cyber is an idiot! Idiot!"

The cyber unexpectedly lurched, stretching out its mechanical arms to catch the parrot, and fell off the donkey.

"Stupid bird," he said, getting back up. "Really stupid. I don't see anything funny about it."

"Just a second," Nuri's voice still shook. "As soon as I stop laughing, I'll get serious."

"I hereby report that somebody damaged the leopard," stated the cyber, without looking at Nuri. "If everybody feels free to damage animals…"

"Two questions," Nuri interrupted him. "First of all, where did you get the feather? If everybody feels free to snatch a feather, pretty soon the ostrich will be bald. Second of all, what's the leopard got to do with you, and vice versa?"

"I found the feather on the savannah. Secondly, I have a side-job as a ranger. I am responsible for the welfare of animals. I am entrusted with this work because I am kind and invulnerable. I've even been kicked all over, and look at this!" The cyber tried to puff out his chest.

"Look at what?"

"That's the point! Not a single dent."

"So you are invulnerable…" Nuri thought for moment. "Are you also responsible for the welfare of insects?"

"Not included in my orders."

"In that case, bring me some honeycomb. A piece about as big as the palm of your hand. There should be wild bees around here somewhere."

"There are bees, but I'm not in the business of poaching."

"You have to start sometime. And I need honey."

The cyber fell silent and started to think. The donkey munched on some grass nearby. The whiskered beast completely regained consciousness and rubbed its sore snout against the cyber's leg. Nuri sprawled on the grass, looking up at the sky. The air smelled of sap, and a light breeze ruffled the crowns of the trees. Strictly speaking, there was no rush, but he had promised his grandfather he would get home earlier, and he didn't want to be late. Exams were still three days away. He wondered: how were the others getting back?

"I'll get the honey," the cyber said, breaking the silence.

Nuri nodded, chewing on a piece of grass as he watched the cyber disappear into the bushes. His thoughts flowed lazily and seemed unusual in their laziness. The parrot has red pants, and you, Nuri, have a highly developed imagination, as his summer instructor had said, so that you *could* fly like a swallow, too bad there's not enough time for training. The swallows shoot straight up, fold their wings, and then their flight is a free-fall powered by gravity. Sparrows also fly like that. Actually, it is a fairly simple problem, a matter of ballistics and aerodynamics. It's odd the way living things utilize gravity, whereas machines work against it…. For three years he'd been racing against himself, exhausted and exhilarated. Ostensibly this is the normal creative process in any branch of knowledge. And knowledge is the mother of invention…. or is it? What are the formal markers of an inventive imagination? In the Institute there were endless discussions on this topic, but the only aspect of imagination that was ever formalized during work on the Great State Machine was imagination as an object of programming. Actually, "state" was a strange name for that supercomputer, whose main processors consisted of computing systems from other friendly countries, and whose components consisted of all the main computing centers on the planet, with very few exceptions. Today anyone can connect to this machine to get a consultation on any issue, and if necessary, to model any conceivable process. *Any* process? Nuri recalled his attempt to model his condition right before an exam and snickered – the result was too banal. In general, the programs that had to do with emotions all needed corrections, but was it really possible to create a perfect program? Nonsense. He was right to quit. He'd finished the most important work, and the rest of the revisions would require a much lower level of creativity. Can one really think of oneself in these terms when one chooses a new path? "I can work at the highest level?" That means other people work at a lower level, right? So what? Not modest enough? Creativity does not involve the concept of modesty. Isn't that like being shy in a battle? Could Khachaturian really be humble about composing his "Sabre Dance," knowing that nobody had ever written anything like it before? Could Pushkin be modest about his poem "The Prophet," knowing that it would stand as an incomparable work of art? Poor Pushkin, not modest enough… "with me, poetry awakes…" Poetry is the child of silence and concentrated thought. The section of the supercomputer's program devoted to *creating* poetry is empty. There is only information *about* poetry. The act of creation itself could not be formalized, although what contains more logic than that?

"The cyber is in the weeds!" screamed the parrot.

The cyber was indeed emerging from the bushes, holding a piece of honeycomb in its outstretched palm. Bees swarmed over his head, and a giant snake was twisted around his body. The snake's head, with yellow spots for eyes, rested on the cyber's shoulder, and a white flower on a long stem hung from its jaws. At the sight of the snake, the donkey snorted and stomped. The whiskered one quietly disappeared.

"I brought honey," said the cyber.

Nuri sat up and silently observed the snake.

"I unwrapped her from a tree and wrapped her around myself," the cyber felt it necessary to explain. "She fell in love with me for my looks."

"At first sight?"

"Of course. They always fall for looks, and also, I guess, for reaction speed."

"For speed, certainly! Listen, can you fulfill one more request for me?"

"I am obliged to, if it is within my capabilities."

"Then here's the request: Step off to the side, unwrap that snake from yourself and wrap it back around a tree. I am sure that this lies within your capabilities."

The cyber put the honeycomb on the grass and left.

"The cyber is an idiot!" reconfirmed the parrot. The donkey sighed with relief.

Waving off the bees, Nuri threw the honeycomb into a pot, splashed in some water, shook it up and poured the mixture into the fuel tank. Within a minute the wing grew taut and straight. Nuri closed the cover of the saddle, got into it, and fastened the biocontrol bracelets onto his arms.

"All the best!" he said to the parrot. "It was nice to see you, but... gotta go!"

Nuri piloted the machine into the air. The damaged wing did not respond well. Nuri was good at transforming himself into a healthy stork without trouble. But to imagine himself as a stork with an injured wing took a lot of effort. His flight was uneven, and in order to smooth it out, he made a few circles over the field.

"It's only a glider," he whispered. An aviaglider. One could go by foot. Or on horseback.

Nuri bent down. The cyber was trying to convince the donkey of something.

"What is your name, servant?"

"Telesik," the answer floated up from below. "Director Saton's domestic cyber."

Flapping his wings, Nuri gained altitude and with relief settled into his usual gliding flight. The IRN's forest expanse spread out beneath him as far as the eye could see. Occasionally he flew over emerald clearings, and the unusual silence was pierced by the sound of screeching monkeys and birdcalls. On a small panel in front of him there was only one green light, to indicate direction. The aviaglider was designed so that once the pilot plugged into its bio-orientation system, he could feel the feedback with his entire body, making it effortless to diagnose and correct any deviations from the course. The injured wing produced a painful pulling sensation under his scapula. But the adventure in the field had turned out okay, and he could already see the spire of the IRN's main building in the clear distance. Nuri began to relax.

"Hello," he heard close by. Nuri glanced around. A raven hovered, barely moving, about a meter away.

"Hi!" Nuri answered. "Do all the birds around here talk?"

"The smart ones do," said the raven.

"I already ran into a talking parrot. Even parrots talk?"

"Some of them."

"That sounds like progress," said Nuri. "I guess Saton doesn't just restore Nature. He modernizes it. Why are you so tense? Sit down, let's talk."

"I'm a raven," said the raven.

Nuri thought about it. It was worth trying to keep up the conversation. It was not every day that one had the opportunity to talk with a raven.

"Are you married?" he asked.

"Three times. Last time to a white clow," he answered with a slight Japanese accent. "Sepalated. Character diffelences."

"Aha. And how long did you live together?"

"One and a half centulies."

"No way!" Nuri gazed at the bird with respect. "One hundred and fifty years. With a white crow. I wouldn't have been able to stand it." His companion remained silent. Either he was upset, or he was really angry. When Nuri, aiming for the Institute's tower, made a wide flat turn, the crow said sarcastically:

"You call that flying….?" With just a slight movement of his tail, the raven effortlessly executed several loops in front of Nuri.

"Is it really to your credit that you know how to fly?" Nuri was having fun. "But I'll accept your criticism. Without spite. As constructive criticism. So teach me, which feather do you move in order to make those turns?"

"The question is not hald," said the raven. "This is how it's done…" He tried to look underneath himself, fanned out his tail feathers, and dropped like a rock.

"So there," said Nuri. "Don't brag in advance."

The raven hid from sight and did not appear again. Nuri soon landed successfully on the small grass pad of the Institute's airport.

Nuri awoke to the clamor of birds calling and began listening to it. He heard Telesik clomp into the kitchen, the lid of the food processor started to rattle. In the distance, probably from the airport, he could hear garbled voices coming over the speaker.

The door creaked open and a sunbeam fell onto his face. When Nuri opened his eyes, Telesik was standing next him. Telesik clacked his jaw a few times disapprovingly and said, "Get up."

Nuri didn't feel like getting up. The cyber stomped around a bit near his bed and then left to do more housework. The cyber never ceased to be amazed by the human capacity for sleep.

Nuri stepped onto his balcony. Below, in the swimming pool, Granddad was snorting and splashing. He was playing with a dolphin, holding on tight as they raced around near the very bottom of the pool. Nuri followed them with his eyes to the turn, then climbed onto the railing and jumped into the pool, describing a large arc through the air. He swam in the depths along the walls, looking into grottos, scaring out two little crabs with one shell to share between them, and poking at a colony of mussels before, on his last breath, he shot up to the surface like a cork.

Granddad lay on the cool sand of the shore. He sprinkled sand onto his belly and observed Nuri.

"Healthy lad," Granddad summed up his observations. "Sedentary life has not affected you."

"Basically that's true. But my muscle mass hasn't gotten any bigger this year. My physical development has stopped… We should stock this pool with fish, it's empty."

"Won't work, the dolphin will eat them all. Recently a pair of lost mackerel managed to swim in, and you barely saw them before they were gone."

Around the rim of the basin a young wunderkind – accelerated student Alyoshka – hopped on one foot while rolling a hoop in front of him with a stick. He nodded politely to Nuri and reminded him about tomorrow's scheduled tour of the IRN's town center.

"And yesterday, Nuri, you promised to tell me a fairytale!"

"My apologies," sighed Nuri. "Only geniuses can invent fairytales out of the blue. I don't have it in me. I'll try, only later. And don't judge too harshly."

"Don't judge?" Wunderkind thought about this, tracing something with his toe in the sand. "Well, we'll see. Yesterday you were pretty good at deriving the cosine and sine values of the Mathieu functions. I liked the way you did that, although you ended up with a tabular integral…"

"Master!" they heard in the distance. "Master, time for breakfast!"

"I want to change that cyber's voice." Saton got up without touching his hands to the ground, then brushed the sand off of his body. "It has too much bass. With his complexion, a baritone would be more appropriate."

They walked through a small garden. White-winged birches, tangled up in vines, willows and palm trees, sycamores and smooth, thornless, almost black cacti all thrived in this garden.

"Hybrids," Saton remarked absentmindedly. "We're trying to simulate older forms."

While Nuri ate breakfast, Alyoshka waited impatiently. He brought food out to the dolphin and then chased the cat into a poplar tree. Syntax the cat had a bumpy head and hard little meowsers – that's what Grandma called the parts where a cat's whiskers grow. He hissed at Alyoshka, but it was more like a sigh, since he knew the "accelerated" boy would never do him any harm. It's just that Syntax, an inveterate curmudgeon, didn't need anyone's attention, least of all Alyoshka's.

Afterwards the three of them, Alyoshka, Nuri, and the cyber, strolled down a wide street through the residential base of the Institute for the Restoration of Nature.

They went by the parking area for on-call flyers. Nuri spoke with the mechanical surgeons, who had transplanted a new muscle into the wing of his aviaglider. Then they all continued on to the hotel. Outside, at little tables that had been carried onto the lawn, people who seemed oddly familiar sat in shorts and sandals eating grapes spilling in purple bunches from baskets centered on each table. Two spotted puppies chased around nearby. A jolly giant with a bandage wrapped around his head – Nuri immediately recognized him from portraits of the Yogi-Commando who first set foot on the fiery surface of Venus – squinted with one eye. With the other eye he peered through a large glass of ruby-colored wine. Spying Alyoshka, he put down the glass and said dramatically:

"Take pity on an old man! Once upon a time I grew the most incredible vegetables. In the middle of the night an overly ripe watermelon exploded, and as you see, a shard of it hit me in the face." He shook the wine bottle. "I'm treating my wound… Here, we'll drink this up. Come to our table, Nuri."

"Leave them alone, Rakhmatulla," his companion interrupted. He had a long, immobile face and his voice seemed to emanate from the space around him. "These folks have their own agenda. Let them continue on. You'd be better off noticing the fancy cyber that just showed up. Look at how much sunlight reflects off his rounded belly. I'm going to collect it."

The companion stretched out his hands and held between his palms a blindingly white ball of sunshine, about the size of a soccer ball.

"The sun!" said Alyoshka.

"Here, do you want me to give it to you? No? Well, then, I'll let it go."

He tossed the blinding sphere lightly upwards, and the small sun shot up towards the big sun and dissolved in its rays. Alyoshka and Nuri stared openly at the famous magician they were seeing for the first time in real life, not on a screen.

"Give him a rainbow, Ivan," said Rakhmatulla.

The magician snapped his fingers and pulled a black box out of the air, divided it in half, and spread the two parts out as wide as he could. A rainbow hung over the basket, the air smelled as if it were charged with freshness, and tiny droplets of rain moistened the grapes. Ivan admired the rainbow along with everyone else, heaved a sigh, and then wound the rainbow around his finger, slipped the coil off, and placed it back into the box, which he handed to Alyoshka. The wunderkind took the box with trembling hands and whispered:

"Thank you very much. I will occasionally let her out in the evenings."

"Just make sure she doesn't burn out," said the third member of their party, a fat black man with thick lips. Everybody knew him. This was the town doctor, Akanius. He was the only person in town who never had anything to do: his patients were the completely healthy employees of the Institute for the Restoration of Nature.

When they resumed their walk down the main street, Nuri said:

"I shouldn't have flown in. If people like Rakhmatulla and Ivan Ivanov are here, then there's no reason for me to be here."

"Ivan Ivanov is a very smart person." The cyber stroked his belly with the soft paws of his mechanical hands. He glanced at the black box and added "And he is kind, too."

The reached the stadium where soccer players trained. The stadium only had one side, so the entire field eventually merged into a meadow at the far end. At the edge of the meadow a large moose stood grazing. The players didn't pay any attention to her, and she didn't pay any attention to them, either.

Alyoshka wandered off towards the goal posts and suddenly squatted down: not far away little ugly ducklings were nipping the grass. One of them came right up to Alyoshka, took a grass stem in her beak, and pulled. The grass didn't break. The duckling gathered her strength, orange feet set wide apart, while the accelerated child braced himself in empathy. Finally the fledgling managed to break off the piece of grass.

"She bit it off," the cyber whispered. "An unproductive waste of energy. She won't eat that grass anyway."

They had seen enough and moved on. A milk cart drawn by two zebras rushed by; on it they glimpsed "IRN. Milk Cans." To avoid the risk of getting run over, the cyber jumped to the shoulder of the road and continued to stare. The cart bore a handwritten sign:

"Monday is a voluntary workday to sort robin and nightingale eggs. Only domestic cybers *with* suction cups allowed."

Telesik flexed his four-fingered hand thoughtfully. Doctor Akanius emerged from the door of the corner drugstore holding a pipette. A twelve-year old boy turned up out of nowhere. He was dragging along a puppy on a leash. The boy's entire expression reflected a kind of militant independence and did not bode well for the puppy. He was naked above the waist and barefoot, but what really did Nuri in was the boy's pants. They were so impeccably ironed that they had a light sheen.

Alyoshka focused on the puppy; the boy focused on Alyoshka. Then the boy looked Nuri in the eyes and said:

"The dog is the embodiment of good qualities, walking loyalty, a clump of humanity and love. In short, I will trade the dog for that bracelet."

Nuri listened to this surprising boy's bombastic speech and sighed. It was perfectly clear to him that Alyoshka would not leave without the puppy, but his own coded bracelet…how could he give that up?

"You won't catch *me* empty-handed," said the boy. "Give me the bracelet device, and take the dog. Otherwise, we'll just take this pup back to the lab and see what its insides look like…."

He addressed the last few words to Alyoshka, and made a cruel face.

Alyoshka slumped to the grass and started rocking back and forth.

The boy snickered.

"As you like," he said, and jerked the leash.

"What do you think you're doing?" said the cyber. "He may be a wunderkind, but he's only five years old. What do you expect from a five-year old?" The cyber pulled off the wunderkind's shirt, which was wet with tears, and helped him blow his nose.

The boy gave a fake sigh. "You don't feel sorry for animals, but you're sorry for your little ward, you stamp-collector."

Nuri shuddered. Nobody had ever called him a "stamp-collector" before, but sure enough, that time had come. He was going to have to do what it would take to pacify both this little puppy-peddler *and* the distraught wunderkind. He took his bracelet off. The boy dropped the leash, grabbed the bracelet, and laughed.

"That's right! A few more puppies and I'm done for the day!" He wiggled his ears, turned on his heel and disappeared, exactly as if he had dematerialized, leaving only a ripple in the air.

The fat man with the pipette had stood aside and observed with obvious pleasure while Nuri bargained.

"Nuri, for me you are nothing more than a potential patient. But you can understand the kid. For him, you are the Designer-in-Chief, and your bracelet is going to occupy a place of honor in our Museum of Heroes. It's not every day that the Designer-in-Chief of our Great State Machine comes to visit. And in general, these kinds of opportunities to add to the museum won't happen again. I myself didn't expect to see so many celebrities in one place."

"But the way he did it... the means... "

"What about the means?" The doctor crossed his eyes and slapped Telesik's resonant belly a couple of times. "Does a little joke offend you so badly?"

"I'm just a stamp-collector, that's all."

The puppy sat on the porch. He was starting to perk up, although he still seemed to feel a bit subdued. Alyoshka petted him. Members of the family gave their two cents' worth.

"No, it's not a poodle," said Grandma, and she was right, as always. "Stupid of you both, but of course he can live with us."

Grandpa touched the puppy's disproportionately large paws and stiff little whiskers, but didn't say anything about the leonine features of this "puppy."

Syntax the cat lay on his back on the couch with his belly facing up. He disdain for everyone was so thorough that he even allowed himself to purr a bit, which, as Grandma pointed out, hadn't been heard for years. Granddad tried to push him a bit to the edge of the sofa. Syntax stopped purring but didn't even open an eye, although his head now hung off the sofa. Finally he slid to the floor on his side and remained there without moving. It was only when Grandma started to lightly make fun of him that he jumped up and snarled at everyone. His tail twitched.

"S-s-s-atton," the cat hissed. "Pssst!"

"Hey, what's that? He's learned to talk?" the cyber asked nobody in particular.

"He's always been able to swear, even as a kitten," answered Grandma. "But no matter how hard Alyoshka tried, he's never wanted to talk. Too lazy."

The cat got up and made straight for the garden, shaking his paws. However, he did return for lunch.

Two identical sculptures decorated the entrance to the Institute: a mongoose named "Beauty" reclining on a golden dolphin. Beauty gazed serenely at all the visitors. The best people on the planet strolled on the Institute's lawns, conversing. Rakhmatulla sat with his face turned toward the sun, in a pose of deep concentration. He had not taken a breath in twenty minutes and could not answer any questions. He was wearing a Cosmonaut's Belt around his bare torso – only three other people had ever earned the highest honor of the Belt. Ivan Ivanov stood next to him, holding a little devil in his hands. The imp was about the size of a kitten. It blinked its eyes sleepily, then lay its head with tiny corkscrew horns on Ivan's shoulder and yawned sweetly.

"Is it a real one?" asked Nuri.

"More than real. You can test it out."

"Holiest of holies! Perish, unclean spirit!" said Nuri, making the sign of the cross over the little devil. There was no reaction from the imp except a light waft of sulphuric anhydride.

"A bit of hell gas," said Ivan apologetically.

The imp snuggled more comfortably in his hands and fell asleep again.

The majestic Hogart Brown approached, wrapped in an orange toga. His violet-tinted eyes watered. The great spelunker, cave expert, and humorist never wore his prescribed sunglasses. On the other hand, he always wore brightly colored clothes and an enormous emerald jewel hung from his right earlobe. Hogart spent most of his life underground, so when he came to the surface he relished in the colors of the sky, the forest, and the water. Soon it would be time for another descent into the kingdom of darkness and silence. His best jokes, of one or two lines, were composed in the gloom of the caves, where he and others like him risked their lives. Hogart insisted that he had no sense of humor at all, and therefore he tried out all his jokes on himself: if even he managed to smile, then anybody else would laugh hysterically.

"A little devil, that's nice..." Hogart said seriously. "But I wonder, why hold today's celebration of heroes in the Institute for the Restoration of Nature? I received the summons and was surprised. Naturally, I came. On a double-humped camel. But there are not many of us here."

"Plenty of people wanted to come," said Nuri. "But today is Exam Day, with exams in every restoration center. One hundred centers, ten people in each. But why hold exams in the Institutes for Restoration, after all? I think it's because the demands on us are too contradictory."

"Demands...?"

"Well, *you* have nothing to fear. Right, Beauty?"

Beauty opened her jaws, showing a firm pink tongue, and turned the other way.

"Doctor Nuri Metti, your presence is requested in the office of the director of the Institute for the Restoration of Nature!" blared the loudspeaker over the entrance.

"Looks like you're the first," said Ivanov. "I don't know if that's good or bad. I'm a little bit worried." The imp stirred in his arms, opened one eye and yelled after Nuri: "Break a leg!"[2]

"Go to the devil," muttered Nuri, opening the door to the elevator. He had just enough time to see the little devil vanish, prompting Ivan Ivanov to wave his empty hands and shout:

"Nuri, what have you done? I worked so hard to domesticate him…"

The ascent was fast, at least one and a half g-forces, so that Nuri's head began to spin. At the top, from a broad platform surrounding the building, the turquoise bay looked like a careless smudge on the side of the ocean. Beyond the smudge one could clearly see a line of green mountains, bending around the bay in a gigantic arc. From this altitude, nearly a kilometer above sea level, the entire territory of the Maritime Branch of the IRN was visible.

The director's office was enormous and almost completely empty. A green square in the middle of the room attracted Nuri's attention. Inside the square was a miniature jungle with trees that barely reached to Nuri's waist. A white sphere hung over the jungle, and opposite it, Saton sat at a large old-fashioned desk. Saton glanced at the armchair next to his desk, indicating that Nuri take a seat.

A tiny deer stepped out of the jungle onto a miniature meadow. It was actually a real deer, graceful and perfectly proportioned. It froze and tilted up its head, crowned with tiny branching antlers. You could see the muscles rippling under its brown velvet haunches. The deer stamped its leg – a sharply cloven hoof flashed in the light – and started to walk around. Saton picked him up and placed him on top of the desk, offering him a tiny cube of salt on his palm. The deer sniffed at the crystal and began to lick at it with great concentration.

Nuri watched this tiny miracle with bated breath.

---

2. The proper Russian response to the expression for "good luck" is "go to the devil," the traditional "rude" response which precludes the Devil coming to spoil the "good" luck.

"Dwarf deer," said Saton sadly. "The last one like it was killed in the last century. We managed to resurrect them, but there are not even two hundred of them in the entire herd, and the demand is so high! A deer is fairly simple, though – make a small one out of a big one. It's harder with predators…" Saton hooked a finger under the deer's belly and lowered it to the floor. The deer disappeared into the jungle's undergrowth. "Or maybe you are against predators?" Saton looked towards the corner of the room, where a cyber held a muzzled leopard on a leash.

A raven flew in through the window and landed on the desk. Nuri winked at him: "Hello."

The raven did not answer. It cocked its head to the side and calmly studied its reflection in the polished desktop. A few feathers bristled out of his crown, revealing the blue-black, wrinkled skin underneath.

Then Alyoshka, the boy in the shiny pants, and Doctor Akanius quietly entered the office and sat around the desk. Saton pulled a piece of paper out of his drawer and announced ceremoniously: "The commission has gathered. Sociologists from the toddler group could not be here and will participate virtually." The sphere above the desk grew bright and then disappeared. In its place arose a three-dimensional image of two naked children holding onto a low railing, which surrounded a small pen.

"Here are the facts: Nuri Metti. Twenty-seven years old. Born in the third Martian colony. Has worked on Earth for eight years. Ph.D. in mathematics. Last assignment – chief designer of the Great State Machine. Bachelor. Application submitted two years ago. That's it. Please feel free to ask for information."

"I testify that for all intents and purposes, comrade Netti is perfectly healthy. I have a question: What is your secondary specialization?" asked Doctor Akanius.

"Fauna Mechanic."

The sociologists in the toddler group exchanged glances. The puppy-seller wrinkled his nose.

"A hard-to-fill profession," he said. "Of course, children's establishments nowadays are almost guaranteed to have live stock on hand. However, adults snap up mechanical beasts by the thousands. Puppies and kittens that don't shed and don't grow, little caged birds with programmed songs, cybermockingbirds and synthetic storks that clack under roof rafters. Are you the one that made all this stuff?"

"Well, it wasn't just me…"

"I don't see what's so bad about it," said Alyoshka. "As you know, the Earth Council does not limit IRN in time or material resources. But it will still take about ten years for us to restore the forests and waters here on this continent. As far as fauna goes, it's probably impossible to ever restore it completely, the way it was. It's easier to create a new species of animal, as, for instance, you know we cultivated multiple spotted *cheburashkas* – everyone's favorite little cartoon creature. We are able to control the direction of mutations, the manipulation of stem cells, the process of selection. But there just isn't enough original material… so for the time being, why not let the cybermockingbirds sing?"

"Fine," said the boy in the shiny pants, "but I want to know, Nuri: what is your moral profile?"

"Objection!" chorused the toddlers. "What kind of moral profile does a bachelor have? We'd rather see if he can tell us a good story."

This whole unexpected discussion among the various members of the commission put Nuri in a state of pleasant stupefication. On top of it, the raven still sat there, looking as if the entire outcome depended on his vote alone. Nevertheless, Nuri had to come up with a story. He'd prepared, but he hadn't thought up a fairytale in advance. He began to improvise, and this is what came of it.

A fairytale.

"It's awful to live without a name!" thought the small, shaggy one. "But that's hardly the worst problem, when our meadow is overgrown with prickly thistles."

The grey shaggy one ran over on his short little legs to admire a scarlet-purple flower. He guessed that the flower would smell of sultry heat; and if the sun itself does have a scent, then it would indeed smell like a thistle. Still, the shaggy grey one wanted to smell the flower, but he was too short to do so. He wanted to try to taste the thistle as well, but prickles got in the way. So the shaggy grey one ran off to do his errands, leaving a green trail in the dewy morning grass.

One day he arrived as usual early in the morning and saw a large golden dragonfly on the flower.

"Who are you?" asked the beautiful dragonfly.

"Who am I? I don't know," the grey and shaggy one bitterly answered.

"But everybody is somebody," said the dragonfly. "Look, you run to this place every morning at dawn to find the key to happiness. Do you want me to call you a dawn-key?"

"Yes," said the runner, "I like that name."

"Hmmm, well…" commented Saton, after a long pause.

"Not a word about cybers," said Telesik. "Although I'll grant you that a golden dragonfly is nevertheless a cyber-dragonfly."

"Not exactly a fount of creativity, is he…" commented one of the sociologists, scratching his stomach.

"What do you mean?" said the other one. "A fairytale is beyond even our limits. Just try and make one up. I, for one, could not even start…"

"I like it!" Alyoshka asserted decisively, and the sociologists respectfully stopped talking. "In general, I like Nuri Metti as a person. Justification: he is active, kind, and brave. These are qualities we need. He has many good qualities…"

"For instance… humor," hinted the raven.

"Yes, that too."

"He beat up the leopard. He subdued that primordial animal's powerful instinct to bite. Here's proof," said the cyber, adjusting the bandage around the leopard's meowsers. The leopard purred in bass tones.

"The IRN dispatcher affirms that Nuri didn't want to do it, he was forced…" Alyoshka hastened to add.

"I thought," Nuri interrupted the wunderkind, "that we were talking about my knowledge."

"Knowledge! Who is impressed by knowledge nowadays?" shiny pants asked. "Character is the most important thing. Individuality, preserved even under the most extreme conditions. Uniqueness – along with the ability to bow to the collective interest. Personally, I'd give you an A, because you impressed me with the way you bargained with me over that bracelet. None of that wimpy "ahh, come little boy, let the puppy go," stuff, which I can't stand."

"We have been analyzing the actions of Nuri Metti since the day he got his summons," said one of the sociologists. "We compared them to the recordings in his coded bracelet. He always stayed true to himself. He is who he is. He is genuine."

Rakhmatulla came out of his state of nirvana.

"People," he said, casting his glance over all of them. "I have returned to reality, and it is beautiful. I will read aloud what Nuri has deserved; indeed what all of us deserve. Listen."

He took from Nuri's hands a wooden tablet and read:

"In the name of the future. Diploma. The examination commission of the Maritime Branch of the Institute for the Restoration of Nature, acknowledging its responsibility towards humanity, hereby certifies Nuri Metti to perform the duties of preschool teacher on the planet Earth."

First published in Russian: 1979
Translation by Yvonne Howell

VLADIMIR SAVCHENKO
1980

MIXED UP[1]

1

Entering into the antenna is both a shock and a delight. The joy of a traveler returning home multiplied by the speed of the return, by the speed of light. And I am not just coming home, but into my body!

Until now I had tuned myself to thinking that in radio-wave form I am the same as I am in corporeal form: a rational being with consciousness, memory, and purposeful behavior, the same Maxim Kolotilin, thirty-two earth-years old. This was really just a self-deception to help me do my job. In reality, it was like I was riding a rubber band: the further I flew, the more strongly I felt myself pulled back.

---

1. The first published version of this story appeared in Ukrainian in the magazine *Nauka i suspil'stvo* [*Science and Society*] 9, 10 1980, under the title "*Zelenyi kolir holosu*" [The Voice's Green Color]. The second installment of the story ends with the note "Translated from the Russian by Oleksandr Teslenko." It is possible, given Savchenko's penchant for playing with language, that this translator is some sort of "literary mystification," particularly since the same Teslenko is evocative of Tesla, a name connected closely to engineering and electricity.

And now, after four months of radio-flight, I am returning into myself. It's no big deal that I will once again become tiny: one meter, ninety centimeters tall (one seven millionth of the diameter of the Earth), weighing ninety-two kilograms, subject to gravity and all the vagaries of the elements. On the other hand, I will hear, smell, and feel my world. I will breathe! I will walk on the Earth. I will eat all different kinds of food… Stop, Max, don't be in a hurry to indulge your cravings. Help the machine.

For them, for the earthly ones, with their slow ion processes, the entrance is an instantaneous process. But this is a fragment of time saturated with complex work for both me and the automatic receiver, programmed to redistribute my biocurrents and biopotentials through electrodes implanted in my body, each to its proper place, in a well-defined sequence.

But now for me everything has become slow, weighty: ordinary. I am lying facedown on the platform in the chamber, I feel the beats of my heart... Oh, how it is now pounding hurriedly! I feel the pulses in my temples and in my wrists that lie alongside my body. Here I am: I have a muscular body with a somewhat slouching spine (this is inherited from my ancestors: peasants and slaves who leaned over plows, over lathes), dark red hair, an elongated bony face, sharp nose, thin lips, a prominent forehead set off by a receding hairline; for someone of my height the shoulders could be a little wider. And in general, for a star-pilot, my appearance could be a bit more classical; but this one suits me, I'm used to it. The way you get used to worn-out shoes that feel good on your feet.

Someone is lightly touching my spine near the small of my back, my neck, my shoulders: they are taking out the now useless electrodes. Who is it, Patrick Yanovich or Yulia? It's probably her. Patrick works more slowly.

With fingers light as a dream
He touched my eyes.
My prophetic eyes opened

Like a frightened mother eagle's.
He touched my ears:
And noise and ringing filled them...[2]

And that's what will happen now. After the "all clear" tap I will sit up, see everyone in the semi-darkness of the chamber, get situated, stand up. There will be embraces, handshakes, many exclamations of "well, how was it?" My body obeys me: arms, fingers, legs… I do a few test contractions of my muscles. My face as well: lips, cheeks, tongue, eyelids… they work.

But further up things are worse. In my head, in my brain something is off. Especially in the frontal and the temporal lobes. Something feels heavy, empty, like I have a bad hangover. Did something did not turn out right?

I raise my head slightly from the breathing-channel hollow in the platform. And right away… some sort of semi-darkness, a calm silence… an incomprehensible roaring with wavering flashes of light comes crashing down on me. Where am I? What's happening, a fire or something? It doesn't look that way, I feel no warmth. Unless it's in the figurative sense: they won't leave me alone, they're slapping me on the back, someone hugs me. Wait, I can't deal with this right now! I have to get my bearings.

I sit down, propping my head in my hands: it's like someone else is controlling me. I get to my feet, but I can't stand, I lose my balance. They don't let me fall, they catch me… does this mean that they are here? I recognize the arm muscles: Boryunia, my partner and stand-in: Boris Geraklovich, son of Hercules, descendant of Ossetian princes and my best friend. He's a full-blooded type, an overly informal lover of life.

What the hell is this: they're here, but I don't see anyone, don't hear anyone! I perceive a fiery extravaganza, a grating sound, a roaring,

2. Lines from Pushkin's famous poem "Prorok" [The Prophet, 1826], in which a six-winged seraph violently transforms the poetic speaker into a being with "all-wise" eyes, all-hearing ears, a serpent's tongue, and glowing coal for a heart. This prophet is then given the task of "burning men's hearts" with God's word.

voices of the jungle. Have I not reentered my body completely? That's nonsense, the machine wouldn't have switched off... and this isn't my first time out.

Something in my head is off... but what? If the assignment of biopotentials had seriously failed, I'd be dead already. This means the failure is not serious, but a trivial omission in allocating my sight and hearing. All right, I will try to fix it myself. Once again I lie facedown in the hollow, I cover my ears. Silence, darkness: zero start. Concentration: all of me is under my skull, with thought-volition I shine light from within on my brain, on the bones of my face, on my eyes, on my ears, from my cerebellum, from my hypothalamus. Well?! *See, hear, see, hear...* the world is right there, on the other side of a thin partition, close by! *See, hear...* good job, guys, they understand, they aren't disturbing me... *see, hear, see, hear!*

The pain and emptiness in my head abate. A light clarity emerges. This means that everything in my head has fallen into place (but what on earth just happened?). I get up, open my eyes: once again the optical pandemonium, roaring, and a blizzard of howls. So what is this?!

This time I easily remain standing. At least I have my feeling of balance back, that's something. But in every other sense I am incommunicado.

"Let me get dressed."

Even my voice is not mine. I have a pleasant baritone, but this is some sort of deep-seated voice, like from a barrel. And these flashes in my eyes. Someone thrusts a cellophane-wrapped package into my hands. My pajamas are in it. No, I'm not in the jungle... I sit down, I get dressed.

(They are probably interrupting each other, asking me questions. They can't help asking: "What's wrong? How do you feel? Can you walk?" and the like. But why, why can't I perceive anything?! Where are you, world that I was in such a hurry to get back to?)

"I can walk. Take me to my room." (That voice!)

They lead me there. Boryunia, son of Hercules, leads me, I can tell by his arms: the left one holds me by my shoulders, the right supports my elbow. And these flashes, these flares, these roars… what are they? It would be better to see nothing than to see like this. Hercules' son's pulse is also in a hurry: boy-oh-boy, my poor psychonaut!

My room, which serves as both a pre-launch room and an office, is on this floor.

We make it there, whew! I feel for the armchair, I sit down.

"And now leave me alone." (The flashes, the noise: their reactions?) "Please! I have to get my bearings. Then I'll call you myself."

They seem to have done what I asked, they're gone. Silence, darkness… zero perception. At least that part lines up.

So much for being "back home."

2

Here I'm like a little animal in its burrow. I don't need eyes or ears. I know without them where everything is. To the left of the armchair, at the distance of an outstretched hand, is a wide windowsill (I stretch out my hand: there it is. What is it like outside? If I completed the flight precisely on schedule, it should be the middle of the night, two in the morning; but was my timing really that accurate?). In front of me is the desk (there it is!), to the right, along the wall, are bookshelves, microfilms, magnetic cassettes, record cases; above them (I have a habit of piling everything on top) a stereo, a tape recorder, an Epsilon electric typewriter, a portable computer: all I need for work, thought, and relaxation. On the opposite wall are watercolors that I did myself: nothing special, done for my own enjoyment. The left one is Camilla, the middle one is a pine forest by the Volga, and the right one is the sunrise as seen from my room. Under the watercolors there is a wide sofa, with bed sheets in a drawer under the headboard. To the right is the door into the entranceway (the one they brought me in through), along with the bathroom and all that stuff. (Should I take a bath, splash around, lounge? Wait, now is not the time to hurry with joys of the flesh; get your bearings first.)

The one thing that I do not have in my room and never will is a television. The first attempts to read "radio-essences" for subsequent transmission used television raster scanning: it seemed a tried and true way of doing things, and, more importantly, it was ours, earthly. I drew the lot to be the third one to undergo reading. But the first two, Patersen and Gumenyuk, were killed, and the experiment was terminated. Ever since then, I can't stand televisions.

My room is on the twelfth floor. During the day it has a wonderful view of the wide curve of the upper Volga with its banks of yellow sand and orange-burgundy clay, of its barges and white liners, as well as of the meadows and pine forests beyond it, the concrete bridge with eight arches, the Institute campus; you can also see the blue sky with dipping swallows, with processions of clouds marching off to the horizon... all that I missed and all that I was in a hurry to get back to.

I am a psychonaut, a star-pilot without a starship. We participate in a program of exchange flights (more accurately: exchange psy-transportation of intelligent life-forms) with the crystalloids of Proxima Centauri and the silicon-based humanoids of Barnard's fast-flying[3] Star. We are still in the beginning stages. Humankind is participating in the program at kind of the lowest trainee level.

It's just what it sounds like: there are star-pilots, but no starships. Starships did not work out. Human extrapolations are very linear. The first sources of light were powered by chemical batteries: aha, this means that the power plants illuminating the cities of the future will be enormous galvanic batteries! And so it goes in all things, scorning the well-known law of transition from quantity to quality. Even apart from the technical difficulties that simply could not be overcome (we didn't find materials suitable for the nuclear energies and temperatures, the super-penetrative emissions of Deep Space), would it really be worth it? Dragging your protoplasm, your microclimate, food, and bodily wastes across the parsecs into what you know to be an alien world?

---

3. Kolotilin is referencing the fact that Barnard's star (about 6 light years from Earth, in the constellation Ophiuchus, near 66 Ophiuchi) has the largest known proper motion (the apparent motion of a star among other seemingly fixed stars) of any star that can be observed from Earth.

An alternate way was always there, humankind from the very beginning had penetrated along it a great deal further into the Universe than by means of mechanical transposition: radio signals, radio technology. But for broadcasting information very far away, this method does have a flaw compared to sending physical bodies: dissipation. A cobblestone billions of kilometers from where it was launched will remain the same, while a radio or light beam, no matter how narrowly it is focused, will dilate and blur. If only we could come up with some kind of non-dissipation or auto-compression technique for the beam!

It's probable that if we had really looked, if we had poured as many resources and as much effort into it as we had put into the insoluble problem of starships, we would have found the method ourselves. But everyone was stuck on the idea of an interstellar taxi (with a tip jar above the meter) and galactic trading posts, where our guys would get cheated by beetle-eyed creatures from other worlds offering fish fur, yet they would still maintain that human conceptions of morality, justice, good, and evil are universally valid throughout the Cosmos.

In a word, to be blunt, we had our noses rubbed in it. The rub was information-laden millimeter-band "radio-packets." When the "radio-packets" began to broadcast video-information about the aliens, with a thoroughness and a level of detail that ruled out any thought of a hoax, there was plenty to watch on television screens and plenty to listen to on VHF receivers. At first they sent video-information about themselves, which was the most accessible, but then moved on to codified information in general. This was work on a grand scale! In those five days all other matters on Earth fell to the wayside; hundreds of millions of television viewers and, more importantly, hundreds of thousands of scientists observed, correlated, decoded, and compared results. The richest day was the third, when a multi-channel dialogue began between Earthlings and the "radio-packets."

Five beings from the trinary star system of Alpha Centauri[4] had flown here as "radio-essences" to verify the intelligent origin of electromagnetic emissions from the Solar System. As later became apparent, there was no sense in trying to determine from which of the three stars – from which planets – they'd originated: all the planets there had long ago been assimilated, transformed into hives of crystal beings, who flow around those three heavenly bodies – the sources of their lush electromagnetic life – as meteor showers, rings, discs, and spheres. Those five beings were unable to become incarnate in our material forms for the simple reason that we lacked the appropriate technology. Even so, once they'd verified that Earth's radio emissions did contain a component of intelligence, they made themselves right at home, retransmitting themselves along the ring of communications satellites, reflecting themselves from the antennae of lunar and Martian radio telescopes, and gallivanting around the Solar system, so as to enlighten us and answer all our questions (questions that in fact were precisely formulated only after they arrived).

Solving the problem of just what information you need to broadcast so that the carrying radio signal doesn't dissipate turned out to be simple: you have to broadcast *yourself*. You have to broadcast the whole of your make-up, as expressed in biocurrents and psy-potentials, your individual distinctiveness, your motivation, your life activity, the depths of your understanding of the world – all that makes man an intelligent being. On Earth, as the result of an elevated psy-charge (and not of a hearty diet, since cows and tigers eat a great deal more) people walk on two extremities, have hands free for complex work, and a head elevated for wide-ranging observations and reasoned understanding of the world. In space this quality (in conjunction with an electromagnetic boost, of course) allows them to remain intact over a much greater distance than radio-packets, which carry "dead" information.

The "crystalloids-in-essence" expressed their unbiased opinion that humans had matured to only the most minimal degree required to

---

4. Alpha Centauri is a binary star system with components A and B. A third star, Proxima Centauri or Alpha Centauri C may or may not be gravitationally associated with Alpha Centauri AB.

apply the method of psy-transmission, and would submit to the process only with difficulty. Some would manage it, some would not. There are still other means of interstellar, even intergalactic, communication exchange between intelligent beings, but they'd require such a reconstruction of our psyche, our conceptions of the world, even of our way of life, that… in a word, it was still too early to talk with us about them.

This happened twelve years ago.

They called us madmen, suicides, condemned men. To be honest, that's how it was in the beginning. The point is that they couldn't use experimental dogs or monkeys: only creatures with intelligence, consciousness and free will can be "read." You must not only not fear the transition into radio-wave form, you must want it, must long for it, must invest the whole of your soul – with no exaggeration – into the process. You must also take a risk. The crystalloids gave us the idea, the information-transfer method, and the confidence that such a thing was possible. For the rest we had to pay: there were sacrifices in our search for a reading mode, there were sacrifices in finding the optimal methodology for storing half-alive bodies, and in returning into these bodies, in retransmission, in dissipation there were sacrifices, sacrifices, sacrifices…

Then again, aviation, back in its day, began no better than this.

So, four months ago I launched from the Institute's vortical antenna towards the median, a line that traces the shortest possible route from Earth to the chain of retransmitters linking Barnard's Star and the Alpha Centauri trinary star system. It was from this very route that the crystalloids' radio-packets "turned off" to get to us. Now the route, made with us in mind, jackknifes at an angle towards the Sun, and soon it will be just a stone's throw of one and a half light years from Earth to the intersection leading to two other worlds.

Four retransmitters with twinned vortical antennae are already on their way to this intersection, moving along the median from Earth. One looks back, to the Sun, the other forward. The interval between them is a month's flight at light speed.

My task was to reach the first retransmitter, get replenished and gather my strength, and radiate myself forward to the second. Then, after getting replenished the same way there, I would manually switch over to the opposite transmission and radiate myself back towards the Sun. If I had not been successful in this, the third retransmitter would have done it automatically, and then I would have spent half a year in space.

Before me Boris Geraklovich had done the same trick with the closest retransmitter.

This was my sixth working radio flight, and in all the preceding ones everything had been normal. My body, in a state of minimal metabolic function, of lethargic depression (just sort of being an idiot, as Boryunia says) was located on the platform in the chamber, slowly breathing and drooling into the opening below the face; instruments controlled, and, if necessary, stimulated my heart, kidney, and lung activity, along with the blood flow to all my tissues. Everything was like usual. So what happened?

Wait, maybe some transitional process was delayed, and everything is done now? Can I come back from the zero-point of "quiet and dark?" Well, let's give it a try.

I extend my left hand to the desk lamp (it stands where it always stood), I fumble for the button. I press it, and then jump from the sharp bang just beside me. There's no light. Did the lamp break?

But what are these sounds that have sprung up: dim ones, hissing, with sudden clicks? Did someone come in here?

"Who's there?! I asked you not to..."

Flashes of rosy light, alternating in time with the words. And the voice is the same, like from a barrel, deep-chested. And no answer. What the hell! I get up, find the light switch on the wall, and turn on the overhead light.

Boom! It's like a cannon went off overhead. And still there is no light. This is getting to be monotonous. The clicks, the noises, the murmurs all around are stronger, more distinct. Interesting. I close my eyes, the sounds die away. I open them – with bangs, as if someone uncorked two bottles of champagne right under my nose – the sounds are stronger. And no light.

Once I guess the truth, my skin goes cold. I clap my hands firmly: once, twice, a third time. Now I perceive bursts of yellowish-green light: flash, flash, flash. My hands go limp, my legs go weak.

I turn off the overhead light: let's have some *quiet*. I find the armchair. I sit down. So that's how it is. Well isn't this great. A fine way to fly home. I'm back.

"… he touched my eyes, and noise and ringing filled *them*." It's not the way Pushkin wrote it.

During entry into my body, the paths of the optic nerve (from the eyes to the analytical region of the brain) and the cochlear nerve (from the ears to the temporal lobes) got mixed up, but why, how?! And now I *see sound* and *hear light*.

3

Identical bluish flashes in front of me and to the right, lasting a half-second each, with pauses of the same length. Aha, it's the telephone. Someone couldn't take it any longer. I fumble for the handset on the table and raise it to my ear. Now some uneven shimmering flashes have started up: just try and figure out whose voice it is and who's talking! Oh, well: let them listen to me.

"Hello, if this is not Patrick Yanovich, give him the phone." (Rapid flashes of elevated brightness. It's probably him on the phone? Well, let's assume so.) "Don't say anything, I won't understand anyway. Just listen…"

I inform them of what has happened to me. And that in all other respects I am all right, and require no assistance. I don't understand how it all happened. I ask them to stop by in the morning with everything they can find on learning to read Braille. Reading with your fingers. And let them assign someone (the word in my mind is "caregiver") who will communicate with me via Braille and will help me make contact with the world. And now I intend to rest. That's all! I hang up the phone. There are no more flashes: they understood.

It's a cheerful little life that lies ahead for me. I see, I hear, but I am more blind than a person who has no eyes and I am more deaf than a person who has lost his hearing. I need to make a pile of everything that I know (no more than anyone else, unfortunately) and all that might come in handy in *decoding* what I will "hear" now with my eyes and "see" with my ears. That I lived to see the day! My realization of the sheer mockery of this situation so burns me that I sit and curse for a full minute, cursing the way my ancestors – workers and peasants – cursed in high latitudes and in bad weather. In the room there is a crimson flickering, as if it's lit by a bonfire.

OK. My eyes perceive signals as before – in the range of electromagnetic oscillations between 0.76 and 0.4 microns – as do my ears (air vibrations from approximately 30,000 to 20,000 hertz). I will see lower-pitched sounds in the red part of the spectrum, higher-pitched sounds in the blue part. Loud sounds, of course, will be bright, quiet sounds dim… Bats catch midges on the wing with the help of ultrasound target location. This will not work for me, as the shortest sound waves that I can sense are about a centimeter in length: I would not even be able to make out something as small as a fly. (Just the same I should acquire some sort of device that buzzes or squeaks, a "flashlight." Although… would I be able to "illuminate" things with it? Ears don't provide images. Maybe I would at least not bump into posts?)

What was once light is now electromagnetic oscillations. Bright light will sound loud, dim light, accordingly, will rustle quietly. Red light will give a low tone, violet will be the highest… Wait, not all of this is so simple; in the eye we have the phenomenon of adaption. It follows that brightness will be loud at first, and then will get increasingly quiet. But what are these clicks I hear while "looking at" the stationary objects in the room that are illuminated by still light? This is from another capability of the eyes: the pupils, while viewing, move not smoothly, but in hops. They pause on contrasts, on distinctive places, and then skip to something new. That's your click. (I stage an experiment: I concentrate a stationary gaze… at nothing. The sounds die down to a whisper. I move my eyes around freely: right away there is a click. So that's all correct.)

But what good does all this physics do me? I'll be analyzing my perceptions: aha, the red light means a low-pitched sound. The light is getting brighter: the source of the sound is getting closer... And only once I end up under the wheels will I understand that it was an automobile.

The fact of the matter is that the normal ability to distinguish objects has a billion-year service record of *instinctual* reactions to all stimuli, of unconditioned reflexes, fixed and unequivocal. The world is really not "optical" and "aural," it is integrated. But certain reactions of a certain frequency and force (and from them reflexes, and then organs) developed in protein-based flesh in response to its manifestations. For other manifestations, again depending on frequency and force, there is a different specificity of reactions and abilities to distinguish. This specificity is in us; it is something like our agreement to regard the world just as we do.

But now a certain person has appeared with his own special point of... view? hearing? of the world: me. And now what?

The feeling of deprivation, of existential defeat, is gradually abating. It's being crowded out by a sharp sensation of the novelty of the situation. It is interesting, after all: for thirty-two years I saw the world like everyone else, and now I will perceive it in a new way. Maybe I will be able to observe something that I did not notice before, that was not noticed by other normal people. Your view of the world is not in your eyes, but in what lies behind them: in the analytical regions of the brain. And, to take it even further: in deep reasoning, in understanding the essence of a thing. In ancient Indian philosophy, in the Upanishads, there is a thesis: "You cannot see your seeing from within; you cannot hear your hearing from within."

But now I *must* find a way to do this.

Some new murmurs and noises are getting louder to the left, coming from the window. Daybreak? I extinguish the lamp, I open the window wide (not without difficulty), and I breathe in the cold, harsh air. Now it is September, the time of golden fall, of the farewell feast of nature's colors. What will it sound like to me? Over there is a faraway, low-pitched sound, building up like music; in conjunction with the movement of my eyes emerges something like the plucking of the strings of a double-bass: the crimson dawn? Or are there light, white clouds today? And that drawn-out rustling sound if I direct my eyes to the right: is that not the right bank of the Volga – all covered with dark fir trees with red trunks, with yellow birches and aspens – the side lit first by the rising sun? And this deafening triumphant roar that overwhelms all other sounds, is it the bright morning sun itself? Is this all that I have left? My God!

I feel my face quivering.

4

"Now D."

Three pins touch the index finger of my right hand: two above, one below and to the right.

"Press the button several times, let them vibrate. Now E?"

Two pins along a diagonal.

"F?"

Two pins above, one below and to the left.

I am assimilating the alphabet of the blind, the system of Louis Braille, a boy who went blind at the age of three, and later became a musician and teacher. My hand rests in a cradle, my fingers in hollows; from below, electromagnets hit the pads of my fingers with pins in various combinations, from one to six: they go completely through the letters, numbers, punctuation marks, even mathematical symbols and musical notation. And they are more simple than the usual tracings, by the way. I would have died never knowing about this. Thanks, Monsieur Braille, my dear colleague!

"Now dial in some simple little phrase… like, say: "Sally sells sea shells by the sea shore." Don't go too fast."

"One more time! Again... Say that phrase." (Wavering greyish-green flashes with intervals of darkness.) "Don't overarticulate, say it normally. Just one more time... Did you know that your voice has a green color? Now type out that phrase. Give me the piece of paper. Thank you!"

I feel the piece of paper in my left hand. I hold it at a normal distance in front of my unseeing eyes and move them back and forth. Aha, there it is, the typed phrase: the even high-pitched hiss becomes irregular, tripping. So this, it seems, is "Sally sells sea shells by the sea shore?" Well screw you, Lord-God-and-differential-calculus, dammit! Be calm, Bob – or what's your name? Max? Easy does it, we'll get it. The main thing is to make it so that a one-to-one correspondence develops, new reflex arcs. For this to take place, I have to perceive visual and aural "images" along with what I touch.

"Now dial in your name, pronounce it, and type it out."

From the other side of the wall... no, more like from the other side of the mine collapse through which a thin little ray of information has begun to bore in my direction: at the teletype is Yulia, Yulia Vasilyevna, the boss's lab assistant and head deputy. What is she like? To be honest, I can't bring up an image of her, or I don't remember her well. And it's not because we never saw one another, since we did so fairly often. I simply didn't pay much attention to her: she was always in someone else's shadow, close at hand, diligent, and nothing about her appearance jumped out at you. I think that she has blondish (or brownish?) hair, with short bangs above a steep little forehead, a thin face, a sharp chin, and early wrinkles that she feels no need to conceal; I think that she is not even thirty yet. Yes, she also has nice, derisive lips: she often twists them to the right or to the left in a sort of self-directed incredulous smile, a sneer at herself. She has a thin, upturned nose, her eyes are... grey? No, I don't remember. Her voice, as far as I remember, is quiet and pure, but without those overtones that so penetrate a man's soul, overtones of femininity. She is very petite, and put together more or less normally.

Now it seems very important to me to recall, to at least see in my mind, what she is like. Because Yulia Vasilyevna is present in my room as these liquid, inexplicably soft sounds (this when I move my eyes from left to right or down to up and back again), and as a green-colored voice… and also as a barely perceptible smell of some sort of cosmetic product, either perfume or lipstick. In fact, when I felt her name under my fingers, I was not certain that it was definitely her; I only knew that it was not Patrick and not Geraklych.

"You know what, Yulia, you really need to fall in love with me right away. Then I will hear the sparkle of your eyes and the flushing of your cheeks… as some sort of rippling sound? Or a purring sound? I will see the intimate visual modulations of your voice, the sunflecks of your laughter… What do you say?"

No answer on the teletype. Just a sort of hissing from her side, with a touch of buzzing. What is that? Maybe I made her blush; she's an old maid, after all. I can feel the tension.

"Fine, let's do the next phrase. Maybe, 'Anna und Marta baden' in Cyrillic…"

5

We've consulted with many biologists and neurophysiologists. It's a unique case, no one will venture to explain exactly what has happened to you…

We'll find out during the autopsy, huh!

Stop it, Boris, you should be ashamed of yourself!

"It's fine, Patrick Yanovich, he can joke, let him."

Lip movements convey sounds. Those of the person on the left are more distinct; those of the one on the right are smeared. Their voices form visual sunflecks: greenish-yellow to the left (Patrick's little tenor), reddish-orange to the right. But this is all seasoning, the accompaniment to the talking, not the thing itself. The talking I receive with my fingers. Mind you, I can already use two blind-reading devices fluently, with both hands at once. But from the other side, from *their* side, the talking flows freely: they've replaced the teletype with an adapter that transforms words into discrete signals, into impulses for the electromagnetic pins. They have it good!

I am receiving Patrick Yanovich with my right hand; with the left – closer to my heart – I receive Boryunia, who just now put in his two cents about my autopsy, and I guess that this isn't all he wants to say. I understand him. He is flatly disinclined to regard me as unfortunate, as crippled, to pity me and imagine things from my perspective. I returned alive, and in this I am more than lucky. He and I are the last of our psychonaut team, and we know how much this really means.

I personally find Wu Chun's hypothesis the most convincing, Patrick semaphores in yellow and green flashes. The pins tap into my fingers. *You should remember him, he taught you all acupuncture.* (Of course I remember him, but I didn't think that that dried up little old man was still alive.) *He thinks that the problem is the length of your radioflight. The body cannot remain that long without its psyche, without that excess of life that shapes our complexity and our rational behavior. To put a finer point on it, the body can do fine without the psyche, but the brain cannot: it begins to manifest a simplification of structures... a smoothing, a diffusion, a dedifferentiation, as Chun says. In you... more specifically, in your body, towards the end of the storage period the connections of your eyes with your visual analyzers and your ears with the auditory areas of the cortex in the temporal lobes of your brain probably broke off...*

It's simple liquefaction of the brain, issues Boris into my left fingers, after which I recognize, without the pins, his "Ha-ha-ha" in explosive scarlet flashes.

And when you returned and entered your body, the pressure of your psy-potential caused the connections in your brain to come out all wrong, Patrick concludes. *It's most likely that your visual channels took the shortest routes to the nearest analyzers, and they outflanked your aural channels, which took form in the occipital region, and connected up with the thalami optici. We played the situation out on a perceptron model of the brain: this kind of reorganization of structures is possible in the process of switching fields.*

So that's it. That, it seems, is how it happened. And I can even guess why: because of my impatience, because of the pressure of my desire to see my native world as soon as possible. And then I further reinforced this reorganization with my *see! hear!* Yep.

"But did you play out a reverse reorganization on the perceptron?"

We did. It is possible. On the perceptron anything is possible, but you, of course, are not a perceptron…

Patrick Yanovich falls silent: no light, no sound, no touch. And what could he really say? The devil himself wouldn't understand the mess in my brain. From the retina alone a million nerve fibers run into the depths of the brain… but how many of them are there now, where have they gone, and how? No surgical intervention will help. It's a miracle that I am still alive and can still understand anything.

It's dark, quiet: the zero start of perception. Sounds appear only when I move my eyes. They're somewhat complex, here higher in tone, there lower, louder, weaker, with all sort of overtones. I am "seeing" them: the excitation signals from the eyes, transcribed for the language of the ears. I move my eyes to the opposite side: the reverse sequence of noises. Now more quickly: the same sounds, but sharper, higher… This, too, can be learned. So do that, correlate these impressions with the images you have in your memory. Patrick Yanovich: our trainer and boss, massive, with a big head and a wide brow transitioning to a bald spot ringed by light blond hair; the hard stare of his dark blue eyes, a straight, broad nose above drawn-in lips; a high voice, his words very clearly enunciated (this is why the flashes from him are separated by pauses of darkness more sharply than those from Boris… there is a correspondence, there is!)

But I recognized him only because he shook my right hand with his left. His right arm is paralyzed and withering, a souvenir of the first readings and radio-flights.

I did not recognize my friend and enemy Boryunia so much as I sensed him: he's here. Right away I pictured his face with gunmetal-blue cheeks, full lips and a thick, craggy nose, his scheming and cheerful eyes and his thatch of red, tightly-curled hair (the kind that, as I once noted to him, it would be more decent to grow somewhere besides one's head). I know him not only from the outside, but from the inside as well: we switched bodies. I was in his body on the Moon, and he was in mine here. A sensational experiment. I felt his presence, was instantly renewed.

"But why didn't the ones from Barnard's Star and Proxima not warn us about these possibilities? With all of their experience…!"

My dear boy, that's the thing: in their radio-flights and exchanges they probably didn't run into problems like these. The Barnardians are silicon-based, their matter exchange processes are slowed down, their structures are invariable. Just think about how long they live, a few years is nothing to them! But the Proximids are altogether crystalloid, for them moving from corporeal existence to electromagnetic and back is like turning on and programming an electronic machine. They don't experience dedifferentiation.

Only people like you experience it… And again "Ha-ha-ha" in scarlet flashes.

"Of course, you wouldn't have liquefaction of the brain after a flight, since you have to have a brain for that!"

Oh, well said, dear man! And even before the noises and the visual fluctuations, I guess that Geraklych is in a state of childish glee and wants to hug me. This is what happens. I struggle free.

"Take your hairy hands off of me! What manners!"

Boris didn't have anything similar happen to him, because his radio-flight didn't last as long, Patrick elaborates civilly. *And if this hadn't happened to you, then it certainly would have happened to him during his next flight. And it would've been even worse.*

I ponder this for a minute: can there be an *even worse* situation? Of course there can. A complete inability to communicate. Descent into idiocy. Autolysis of the body. So it really could be worse… Looks like I saved you, Boryunchik.

"What will happen now, Patrick Yanovich?"

We will immerse the bodies of those on long radio-flights in maximally chilled suspended animation, in order to retard all processes to the utmost. We didn't think of this before; not I, not you… none of us.

Yep, this is how it always goes: no one ever makes preparations until it's too late… At first, we practiced short radio-flights, for minutes, hours, a day at most, and the body had to be kept in reception readiness, at an almost normal level of vital activity. This methodology remained on the books. A lot of people at the Institute are probably throwing up their hands: how did we not think this through?

"And me… what about me?"

The question probably had a note of dramatic strain in it (I have no control over this, there is no feedback), because there followed a pause of darkness-silence.

You… well, the first thing is to dictate a report of your flight. Do your duty, so to say, to the last. Get situated in your new state. I'm not going to take it on myself to give you advice, but… in your place I would try to be as useful as possible to humanity, even as a unique clinical case. Neurophysiologists are going to fight for the opportunity to study you, to experiment with you, because you are now the exception that will help them understand the rules. The rules of information processing in the brain – until now they have been impenetrable.

"Well thanks a lot! And you're just going to hand me over to them to be torn apart?"

Well… you do as you wish. As far as we're concerned, we'll do everything we can to maximally restore your ability to communicate.

No, I'm the one who will do it! I have an idea. You are going to kiss my hairy hands! Boris comforts me in reddish-orange.

One last thing: Camilla is here. Do you want us to let her see you?

"Does she know?"

No more than everyone else.

"But what does everyone else know?"

The official statement is: M. A. Kolotilin, psychonaut and doctor of physics has completed the longest radio-flight in the history of humanity, along the median line and with independent course corrections. His return was completed within satisfactory parameters. The psychonaut is under observation.

Of course, if I am alive, that alone is satisfactory. Like getting a C.

"No, don't let Camilla up yet… since I am 'under observation.'"

They get up: booming noise from their movements, from changes in illumination. They leave. I feel very tired, either from the method of communication, or from what I have learned. "Abandon all hope…"

It's dark, quiet, and lonely. Very lonely.

6

English, in school and later at the Institute, was not my easiest subject. It really made no sense to me, especially that horrible sound "th." I barely passed my exams. This was how things stood until some articles about me appeared in British and American scientific journals. Not just about me, of course, but also about Boris and about the now dead Olaf Patersen, Vanya Ptakh, Arjun, Gumenyuk, about our entire team of psychonauts. But here and there was a paragraph, or even two, about me. And that's where my commitment to "Inglish," and my understanding of it, finally came from! I just had to read, to verify whether they had distorted either my inimitable likeness or some tiny fact. Personal interest is a big deal.

Now I felt the same attitude erupt in me towards neurophysiology, psychophysiology, psychocybernetics, psybionics, and theories of perception – towards that entire knot of sciences attempt to explain why we see as we do, hear as we do, etc. The photoelement glides along the lines of text, and the pins fluently convey the words and symbols to my fingers. I dictate the parts that particularly interest me onto a tape recorder so that I can later see them in light. It's like reading a detective novel, staying up into the dead of night.

Unfortunately, this detective novel is not yet finished. The structure of the eye and the ear is understood. The arrangement of nerve paths from them to the brain are more or less known, where they branch and converge, where they intersect… in short, we know all that, in Boryunia's precise expression, can be found out through dissection. But as concerns the intercommunication of the *living* eyes and ears and the *living* brain – orientation, recognition of images, deciphering sounds, searching for and isolating the information one needs, all the foundations of rational, intelligent behavior – oh, here things are bad! "Despite the fact that the process by which specific objects are found by their visual images is still not understood (!), it should be assumed that..." "What happens to acoustic information as it makes its way from the ear to the brain? The answer to this question can generate only disappointment."

This is how the more conscientious authors write. The others, in their scholastic aplomb, are simply silent on the unanswered questions, as if they don't exist. And what can you say: how can you ask a student to know something if you yourself admit that you don't know a damn thing about the given problem?

They conduct experiments on rabbits, frogs, cats ("Why does a cat need frequency-modulating detector neurons in its cerebral cortex? We do not know." P. Lindsey, D. Norman. "Nor do I." M. Kolotilin), less often on monkeys. For the most part they all boil down to destroying or removing some part of these poor creatures (a region of the brain, nerves, some component of the ear or the eye), and in this alone they bring to mind – may Mighty Science forgive me – the anecdotal experiment that proves the cockroach hears with its legs: if one taps on a table, then the control cockroach runs away, but the test cockroach, with its legs ripped off, calmly stays in place.

I will not bring my "ailment" to the doctors. Sure, they can provide me with the minimum preventative care or operate according to equipment safety standards. But there's just no hope for me in seeking a cure from them.

But just the same, reading these "detective novels" has gotten me in a good mood. What did the job was one particular little chapter – as intoxicating as a car chase after gangsters with guns blazing – called "Temporary Encoding in Neurons." Here is what it talks about. We perceive sounds with a frequency of up to twenty thousand vibrations per second (whereas bats can perceive much higher vibrations). But the fibers of the auditory nerves – the so called "hair cells" – cannot send vibrations of this frequency: they are limited to hundreds of nerve impulses per second, and they still have to keep a reserve of frequency to transmit intensity (the stronger the sound, the faster the impulses). So how do they transmit high-frequency notes? It's very simple: a dozen or so neurons divide up the work amongst themselves. One nerve fiber transmits the first high-frequency vibration, and then runs out of steam for a few milliseconds; but the next vibration gives rise to an impulse in the neighboring neuron, the third in the next one down… and so it goes, until the first nerves recharge and once again switch on to work. But if the sound is not only of a high frequency, but is also intense, then more neurons switch on to transmit it: everything is accounted for.

Let them suspect me of bad taste, but I savored this little chapter with the delight one would usually reserve for a great work of art. Somehow everything became clear at once.

This is the reason why this kind of research is difficult, because the brain, a very responsive and sensitive hypercomplex system, does not tolerate rude intrusions. And it is a more *honest* system than all the sense organs. The world is integrated, and all of its manifestations that we perceive as distinct in quality actually differ quantitatively (the simplest example: "red" light and "blue" light are distinguished only by the length of the light wave), though this extends across an enormous range of values. But the brain transforms even the quantitative coloration of our impressions back into something whole, something universal: into impulses, impulses, impulses, racing along our neurons. Thanks to this we can isolate, from the motley variety of life, *essence*, meaning, the point.

But if this is so, then what should I trust more: the world as others perceive it, or the world as I myself perceive it?

The brain is a living homeostat,[5] inexhaustible in its striving for the balance that life (impressions, experiences, the influences of the environment, bodily processes, problems) is constantly pulling it out of. But the usual impressions/problems/processes pull the brain out of

---

5. Designed and constructed by the English psychiatrist and cybernetics pioneer William Ross Ashby, the homeostat was built to maintain homeostasis when subjected to various environmental changes. Its construction is described in Ashby's 1952 monograph *Design for a Brain*. Ashby is a favorite thinker of Savchenko's, and his work is referenced frequently throughout *Self-Discovery*.

sync by just a little, and balance can be restored by the usual reactions: having something to eat, exercising bodily functions, blushing or turning pale, saying "come by tomorrow," and so on.

My breakdown of balance is far more severe. To restore it, a fundamental reconstruction of how the brain works must take place. Such a reconstruction is probably already underway inside me. How? Some sort of new interpretation of all these bursts of impulses?

I still have one advantage over the "not mixed up," and generally over all those frantic scientists experimenting on cats; namely, I have flown as a "radio-essence," and while doing so I perceived the world not at all in the usual way.

7

"…Reading is a conscious, willed process. I comprehend the essence of my essences, the wholeness of my nature, the continuity of my existence. At the same time, I, so to speak, survey and weigh, appraise the differential distinctions of my personality with an inner glance. I appraise the distinctiveness of my health and life force, my manhood (and it exists, Yulia, in addition to my irresistible exterior), the distinctiveness of my intellect, the depths of my memory, and, finally, the distinctiveness of my character. These essences, I have to say, are distributed predominantly in the upper part of my body, for I, as you know, am high-minded…"

This is me, following Patrick's order, fulfilling my duty to the last, dictating my report. Even when it was just an ordinary task, these dictations always seemed boring to me, translating into words that which is more meaningful and deeper than any words, and now I'm not at all in the right mood for this. My thoughts drift away.

"But this does not happen to everyone. Some have characters centered in the stomach, concerned only with matter transfer, with the working of their internal organs. Other's hearts are entirely in their boots. Of course, we won't exchange those kind of people with the Barnardians or with the Proximids…"

You're getting side-tracked… I perceived the yellowish-green phrase even though my fingers at that moment were not touching the pins of the blind reader. These were maybe not the exact words: *don't get side-tracked* or even *stop being silly*, but the meaning is right, you have my word. I can already do a little.

"No I'm not, Yulia, why do you say that! The question of exchange-partner personality equivalence is important. It has been insufficiently studied, and here we could run into something unexpected. Did you know that we and our stand-ins place different, sometimes even opposite content in certain identically designated personality features? Let's take morality…"

Max, you're impossible! I've just turned on the tape recorder.

(The mores of the Barnardinians is a subject that shocks not only our women…)

It's not that I'm completely impossible, kind Yulia Vasilevna, and it's not that I'm a vulgar jerk: it's just that right now I have to excite emotions in people. Negative emotions, positive emotions, any emotions at all. Then I understand them better. The information collected by the senses cannot be boiled down to what we see and hear, otherwise how is it that we feel it when someone directs their gaze at us?

"Fine, I'll continue the report… So, self-control, a renunciation of all that is earthly; I allow (and then aid) the machine to read, in the correct order, my psy-charges, to imbue them with energy of super-high-frequently oscillations, and to transmit them to the vortical antenna array. In this way I launched in the form of a "radio-packet," eight hundred meters in diameter, with a duration of two seconds (or, and this is really the same thing, a length of six hundred thousand kilometers), a carrying frequency of twenty gigahertz, my own energy output being 5.5 megajoules. This is serious energy, the amount we consume in the form of food calories over ten years. The rotational period of my energy vortex, naturally, was also two seconds: the antenna formed it this way. You saw how this happens, Yulia, a pillar of radiant ionized air pierces through the whole of the atmosphere above the Institute, and then nothing…"

I've seen it, I know, don't get side-tracked, semaphored my assistant in green light.

"Um-hm... I should say that I did not even for a split second feel separate from the material world. I had simply moved from one state to another, and then, in an electromagnetic state, I sensed outer space far more closely, more palpably. It's probably how a fish senses the water.

"My basic concern during the flight was to compress my vortex, not to allow it to diffuse. As for the other worries, well... we are probably still at the beginning of our evolution in the Universe, we exist in space on the same level as mollusks in the ancient seas or worms in the soil; my interference interaction with the surrounding radio emissions had the character of tangential contacts, of the touch of something diffuse, sometimes of warmth or cold, sometimes of fear or pain, nothing higher than that. The Sun, the Earth, and later even Jupiter *warmed* me with their radio waves, like three stars; I even got a little replenishment from them. But soon they were left far behind.

"This energy diffusion – and only a small fraction of my vortex reached the first retransmitter – gave rise to a feeling of weakness, fatigue, and then even hunger, as well as fear that I would be lost in the emptiness. Only the pings of the radio-impulse beacon from the retransmitter, which grew stronger and stronger, increased my buoyancy and hope. And when I reached the receiving antenna, and then the power plant, I experienced a wild joy: I satiated my "hunger," increased my energy and distinctiveness. And I flew forward as a mighty vortex!

"No, of course it was not all just animal sensations. There was the feeling of my own enormity and impetuosity, commensurate with the scales and movements of the real world, the Galaxy, the feeling of confluence with space-time, with the mighty and calm stream of matter. Besides that, I recalled – somehow at a remove – my former station, a petty corporeality, with a false isolation from the environment (on which one wholly depends), but rich in the sensations and complexities of relationships. I recalled how I had been transformed, where I was rushing to, my objectives… not in words, but in essences, through a readiness to do the thing. And of course there was a feeling of triumph when I *myself* consciously switched over the second retransmitter and set off on the way home. Now I could recognize the surrounding "radio-landscape"… On the whole, Yulia, the Galaxy in radio emissions looks not at all like it does in the visible spectrum."

How much time did you spend in space?

"How much time? It's difficult to say. When radio-flight becomes available to the masses, it will be possible to compare volumes of accomplishments and sensations, to establish an account of one's individual time. But in the meantime, let's say that I lived there the same amount of time that I was not here."

I get up from the chair.

"That's all, Camilla… I mean Yulia, please forgive me! That's enough for today. Fit me out for a walk. Let's go to the woods."

(Another awkward moment: I really put my foot in it. That means that the fact that Camilla is here waiting for a meeting is stuck in my subconscious, stuck like a nail. And I have been putting it off for two weeks. Are you scared, psychonaut?)

We psychonauts are still monsters of myth for the surrounding populace, even for much of the Institute staff; they stare, they run over for a look, they fish for reasons to have a conversation, they ask for autographs. Well, how much more attention would a star-pilot *without* a starship attract? So as to avoid this kind of attention, we resort to simple tricks. So this time, with Yulia Vasilna's help, I put on a life vest that alters my head-turning figure, a reddish wig of the same color as the moustache and beard that have grown out over the past four months, and filtered glasses in gold-plated frames. I stick a pipe with no tobacco in my teeth… *I* wouldn't even have recognized myself, let alone anyone else! We take the elevator down, come out of the Institute, and set off along the embankment to the woods.

"Yulia, stop me a half-meter before I hit one of the columns. But not any sooner than that!"

Now is the beginning of October. The air is filled with the slightly bitter smell of fallen leaves. It's a sunny day (I can feel the right side of my face being warmed) and quiet, so for me dark and very noisy. Only the cars flying past along the embankment "illuminate" themselves as if they have headlights in front and in back.

I'm shuffling my feet, shuffling them like mad, with my whole sole: this gives off a greyish-yellow light. Its flashes light diffuse lines, flickering surfaces from below (the barrier wall, the bases of columns?). I've walked along this embankment thousands of times, but now I'm not sure about anything. Twice Yulia stops me just before I touch a concrete column. I commit the picture of swelling light-noise to memory, and after that I go around them on my own.

To the right, where the Volga is, there is a noise; if I cross my eyes, it is far-off and reverberating, like that of a jet plane hurtling away over the horizon. I raise my eyes, and the noise transitions into high, crackling sounds, into the plucking of strings, the pizzicato of the deep blue fall sky. But if I move my eyes to the right, there the Sun starts to yell deafeningly, like a trumpet.

To the left – away from the buildings, the trees, the columns, the fences – there is an intermittent, varying noise. It's easiest for me to recognize trees during a light gust of wind; I perceive the appearance of the leaves like their rustling, and the rustling itself like the crown of a tree with the sun shining through its changing outline.

This was probably why I recognized my favorite grove the moment we entered it: it became lighter and noisier. The flashes from my footsteps, though I was no longer shuffling, became far brighter, as my shoes were pushing around heaps of dry leaves. Soon afterwards I recognized not only the trunks of the birches, approaching with a high-pitched – "white" – hiss, but also those of the maples (with a slightly lower, somehow grumbling, tone), and even their differently ringing crowns.

"Is this a stump here?"

Yes.

"Whew!" I sat down. My heart was pounding, my back was wet, my knees were shaking: it was as if I had been spinning in the centrifuge at maximum acceleration. Boy, that was hard work! But it's fine, like studying a foreign language: at first every syllable is difficult, your throat protests against the unfamiliar pronunciation, the mind against its lack of calibration with the phonemes and the writing system, against the discrepancy between the colossus of efforts and the paucity of results. But in your memory the new information is accumulating all the time, being generalized, being strengthened, and then you're off. That's how it is here. I will probably never see the Sun, the sky, human faces, will never hear waves splashing or birds singing, but I *will* recognize the images of everything, I *will* orient myself in my environment, both natural and civilized. Necessity will force me, and life will teach me.

"Yulia, please read me some poetry. Something canonical or really well known, appropriate to the setting. With feeling."

In my youth there was a pastime, among the boys and girls I went to school with, of reciting poems without words, by means of "ta-ta-ta," with the requisite intonation and rhythm, to see who could guess it first. So let's try it now.

Yulia Vasilyevna probably loved poetry, too, and the task was not a burden to her. As far as I could tell, she stood leaning against a golden-headed birch that rustled steadily, and she looked towards the Volga, and recited as if to herself. Pushkin, Blok, Yesenin, Tyutchev… I recognized "The woods let fall their scarlet clothes…"[6] at the second stanza, "There is the archetypal fall…"[7] at the third line. It turned out that our tastes in poetry coincide.

And this was remarkable: the moment I would recognize the poem, first in rhythm with the greenish-yellow flashes of Yulia's voice, coinciding with them, then outpacing them and guessing ahead of them, *the voice of memory* would ring out in me. It's not a man's voice, not a woman's; it's not tinted in overtones, but almost colorless; yet at the same time it precisely conveys all of the hues of feeling and thought

---

6. An 1826 poem by Pushkin.
7. An 1857 poem by Fedor Tiutchev.

that the poet poured into the line. And the combinations of the flashes with the voice of memory expressed the sensitive poetic thought, the essence of the thing, even more clearly and richly than if it had been just a voice, even a good actor's voice. In listening, I actually fell into a kind of trance.

And after that my ability to perceive Yulia's speaking through her flashes was much more accurate!

We also lit a fire, and it had a musical sound. Then we walked down to the Volga, to a place where a spring of pure water flowed into it, and the bubbling of the stream looked something like a fire.

8

For me that walk was the discovery of the world. To put it more carefully, the world opened, just a tiny bit, new sides of itself to me, opened in a way that promised much, that tantalized. And I had regarded it as lost!

That evening, having returned to my room, I decided to test something that I had dreaded even thinking about: how would music sound-appear?

Music… It has always been a big part of my life, no less so than books. It's strange for a person of non-lyrical disposition, for a scientist and engineer, but that's how it is. Among the arts I place music exactly where mathematics stands among the sciences: music, after all, is just as merciless to phoniness as mathematics is to error.

Our family was not particularly well-off, and so I was not taught to play the piano or the violin. But if they gave diplomas to listeners, I would certainly have graduated with distinction. And my record collection contained the very best recordings of the best works.

Only now I could not pick out a record.

Even before, I liked to listen in the dark. Arrange the speakers, place the record, lower the tone-arm onto the edge of the record, and right away I am surrounded by all colors of flame: here like a bright wildfire, there like a dim smolder. My eyes (or the visual regions of my brain?) had apparently been starved for clear-cut images, and so now they were springing up. Semitransparent, with shifting outlines, permeating one another – waves? snakes? tall grass in the wind? fantastic animals? I've seen something like this in the paintings of Čiurlionis: now it's like I'm watching an abstract film based on his work.

But what composition is it, whose? It's clearly a symphony.

I could not figure it out. I took it off so as not to strain myself, not to expend my attention to no purpose: first, I need to learn to recognize the music. I put on another record.

Fleeting, sporadically glimpsed flashes, bright at first, slowly fading: yellow, turquoise, sky-blue, dark blue… and all in very clean colors. Repeating scarlet inclusions… the accompaniment? Piano? The rhythm is a waltz. It's a Chopin waltz, I don't have any others performed on the piano. Seems more like a minor key than a major… After this I picked through melodies in my memory, and found it, and it all fit together: opus 69, No. 2, C minor![8]

And as soon as it fit together, the melody sounding in my mind superimposed itself over the rhythmically shifting flashes in the same *effect of enriched perception* that happened while I was hearing-seeing Yulia's verses. There were no flashes, no sounds, no room, no piano music, but my soul trembled and exulted at the understanding of a stranger's soul, at the understanding of thoughts and feelings that could be expressed only in this way – not through words or any other means.

I recognized Beethoven's *Egmont* overture without guessing and without picking through melodies to fit the flashes, but by experiencing the feelings that only it can express. The burning Čiurlionis-esque visions loomed like hanging cliffs, like blue waves breaking in the sea, groaning under the blows of a storm; and the notes that sprang up in my memory flowed together with them… not the notes of a symphonic orchestra, no, the very musical essence of the thing. And the power, audacity, and stormy joyfulness overwhelmed me.

The next record was also Beethoven. The Seventh Symphony burned like heat lightning on the horizon. I recognized it by the second

---

8. Either Savchenko or Kolotilin has made a slight mistake: Chopin's 69/2 is in B-minor. 64/2 is in C#-minor

part – an allegretto in the form of a funeral march – my very favorite, I recognized it by the feelings of pensive sorrow and wrathful grief that the music summoned, the grief of a strong person.

But what's on that first record, the one I put aside? I put it on again. Iridescent violet flecks: that's the violin section. Fluctuating Čiurlionis-esque landscapes approach, yellowish, with green contours… a bassoon solo, French horn, tuba? A lift-off of luminous spray, bright, like a noiseless explosion: the *tutti* of the whole orchestra. The spray falls back and darkens, the uproar of colors and vividness forms a calm, march-like rhythm. A pause of darkness: this is the end of the movement, the needle is sliding along a chink of light. The second movement, semi-transparent flickers in a different rhythm. It's a symphony, not a piano concerto, but which one, whose? So far it isn't summoning any particular emotions. Or maybe I am wasting all my time on trying to guess the instruments? Why should I care about them?

Another pause of darkness. The third movement: hasty flickers across the blue part of the spectrum: flutes, violins, violas. Ripples of water driven by the wind, the circling of swallows above a bluff… once again I'm not getting it, not grasping it. A pause of darkness before the final movement.

And suddenly – what is this?! – it's like a blindfold has been ripped from my eyes. Trees along the bank of a narrow river: willows, alders, aspens, and further up the hillside oaks, birches, maples. And the wind rinses them in snow-storm gusts, ringingly tousles their leaves, bends their branches and tops. At times it swoops down in free, measured gusts, at other times dismisses them, and stirs the flowers, tousles the grass to the right and left of me, rocks the little rope bridge up ahead… Where is this, what is this? I was in this place. I came down this steep slope to the river, I saw-felt this entire windswept landscape. Then I had the feeling that you get when you hear-understand music (though there was no music). But it was stronger, more dramatic, and gave me a lump in the throat. Where was this?!

The main thing is the wind, the frantic, symphonic gusts, the bending of branches, the trembling of leaves that are ready to tear loose and fly away. And the clouds in the clear sky, and the procession of three-hundred-year-old oaks on the ridge in a circle of fresh underbrush (I also saw them later in a very old photograph: a century younger and without the underbrush by their stout trunks). The wind fills the sails of the clouds, tousles my hair; I cross the rickety little bridge, go uphill along a clay path among grass and flowers… and a lump rises in my throat from the view and from understanding everything. Why?! The path splits: the right way goes towards gloomy barns and oaks beyond them, but I have to go to the left. At the fork in the path leaves quiver, the wind carries them off in bunches and whole branches, a young birch is springily bending and straightening out. And looking at it makes the lump heavier, tears well up in my eyes. "In the field there stood a little birch…"

That's what it is. I am hearing/seeing Tchaikovsky's Fourth Symphony, the finale.[9]

It was a year and a month ago. I was on my way to Moscow, and got off in Klin. I scorned the tourist service, and set off on foot to the other side of the town – a very ordinary one, with the standard houses and dusty streets – to Tchaikovsky's house. A local showed me the way straight to it: a little bridge over the Sestra river. And as soon as I, moving away from the five-story apartment buildings, came off the bridge onto the left bank and saw the neighborhood, the finale of the Fourth began to resound in my head.

Yes, it's probably the wind that was at fault, precisely repeating in its gusts the finale's vorticose, snow-storm opening. And it was not important that he was strolling not in a field, but above the Sestra river, and that the little birch stood on a hill. It was not important that Petr Ilyich, as I knew, had written the Fourth way before he settled in Klin, in the house to which the path led, not even here at all, but in Italy… this was all wrong and beside the point. What was right was the wind, the oaks, life-size and in the photograph (in the composer's bedroom), the violin modulations of ripples on the river's expanse, the

---

9. The Russian folk song "In the field there stood a little birch…" is incorporated into Tchai-kovsky's Fourth Symphony.

lump in the throat, the tears of understanding, and the fact that the little birch at the fork in the path appeared at the very moment when, in the symphony, silencing the riot of the orchestra, its simple melody appears. "In the field there stood a little birch…"

Because that music *lived* there, lived in its primary essence. And I was going to its creator, who, having died an age ago, also lived, more soundly and more fully than many thriving today.

The record ended. I sat in the darkness-silence, recovering. So this is how it is. Then, in Klin, the view awoke sounds, music in me, and now music has awoken visual memory. The reflex arc has closed the circuit through something with a deep-seated significance, as the cat-rippers would explain, and the idiocy of rigorous science lies in the fact that they would still be right. But I am also right in my intuitive search, and right specifically in that I am not a cat, but *homo sapiens*. Yes, we see like animals, hear like animals (many of them far exceed us in the sharpness of their hearing and vision), but, as we are people, we grasp something that is inaccessible to the beasts, something that is beyond that which we see and hear: thought. The meaning of existence. This is why I in my mixed-up state can better perceive that which holds great meaning: poetry and music.

It's probable that, with some more practice, this is also how I will perceive what people say – by the thoughts it contains and by the deep emotions in it. That is also how I will perceive people's artistic creations, and in nature all that is harmonious, majestic, and significant.

And that which is petty, stupid, empty and low in people and in the world will remain for me incomprehensible noise and visual trash. And good riddance. I hear that which is seen and see that which is heard, but I perceive not sounds and not light, but *that which lies beyond them*. So am I poorer or richer for it?

Before going to sleep, I put on, for the sake of experiment, a record with songs. The third song was my favorite, "We are High-Flying

People."[10] And I perceived immediately what I had not understood, not felt before – that the singer doesn't care at all about flying, about high ideals, but is preoccupied only with loudly and correctly stretching the notes, and that it is an aging, unwell man singing, preoccupied with his little personal troubles.

I broke the record on my knee.

9

Flash-rings in the morning. I pick up the phone:
"Yes?"
Why haven't they let me see you yet? What happened?
I recognize Camilla's voice from the first word she pronounces, even though it's through the telephone. I also recognize the vain resentment in it.
"It wasn't allowed. Now it's fine, come on in."
I wait impatiently and uneasily. But it's not the right kind of impatience, not like you would have for a meeting with the one you love; it's as if I want something to be over and behind me as soon as possible. What am I saying? Maybe we shouldn't be meeting yet?

Before, she would always tear into my room without ringing the doorbell or any advance notice, and would throw her arms around my neck. I put a stop to this after the experiment in which Geraklych and I switched psyches over the Earth-Moon distance. He himself contritely admitted to me that he had been unable to control himself when she appeared suddenly (there was a "window" in her filming schedule), threw herself on his neck – in my body – and kissed him passionately. "Go ahead, hit me!" I did not hit him: what can you do? It's not difficult to understand him and justify his actions, but I myself was not a little wounded.

(How deeply this is ingrained in us! What actually happened? You couldn't even say that Camilla cheated on me. Just the same I felt insulted, humiliated: she didn't understand that I wasn't me, and

---

10. A 1947 song (music by B. Mokrousov, lyrics by A. Fatyanov) celebrating Soviet aviation.

it turns out she loves just my body! Camilla did not learn about any of this; at most she felt a chink in our relationship.)

She is offended now as well. She rushed here as soon as she heard the statement about me, abandoned filming (no small sacrifice for a young actress), and I, you see, "am not taking visitors." I really did not want to appear before her helpless, deaf and dumb, inferior. And now I am tightly wound, like a student before a test. This might seem ridiculous to a third party, but I even take care to recall and review her face: a twenty-three-year-old brunette, a wide face and forehead (or maybe it only seems this way to me because she is short and looks at me with a frown?), big, dark eyes, spectacularly pale skin with a purity and smoothness that highlights a birthmark on her right cheek; her dark chestnut hair usually gathered in a braid; a melodious soprano voice (how fine it will look in light!), an easy nonchalance in her pronunciation of difficult words… All this I've learned by rote over years of interaction. But how will I perceive her face now? her fine figure, her well-rounded arms, the shine of her eyes, her mood? It would be good if my memory of her would superimpose itself over my new perceptions in an enriched understanding of her feelings, of her soul. Because this *is* a test. And not just for me.

There is a movement from the door, like a racing flame. Sounds from the lines of her body and clothing: something between noise and intimate music. And then there is something that requires not sight, not hearing, not even words: a head on my chest, warm hands around my neck, the smell of perfume and something intrinsic to her alone. I swoop her up in my arms, bury my face in her hair, her cheek, her hot lips. And my final sensible thought is: "Maybe we shouldn't?"

Why were they studying you for so long this time? Did something happen? They're saying all kinds of strange things about you in town. But everything's fine with you, isn't it?

We are lying on the couch, her head is on my arm. I perceive not so much the warm yellow flashes of her voice, but meaning of her questions.

"Well, what do you think? How do you find me?"

She raises herself up on an elbow, looks – movements, sounds, apprehension.

Normal. Completely. It's just your eyes are blank, floating around. Are you tired?

"It's because I'm blind. And besides that, I'm deaf…" I tell her everything.

The silence-darkness of motionlessness… she has frozen up next to me. Confusion, fear, stupefaction, and – oh, God! – aversion, disgust towards me, a cripple. I have no interest in analyzing how I perceive this, but I do perceive it. Right away she checks herself, is angry at herself over these feelings:

My poor little dear… and nothing can be done?

"Nothing, of course. What can you do?"

It's horrible! (A line from many plays.) *Listen… but could this be passed on to children?*

"It's possible."

No, I don't want to recall or retell her behavior, which, the further it went, the more it smelled of some well-practiced game. Her initial flash of alienation and aversion towards me was the sincere one. A famous psychonaut was one thing, a worthy match for an up-and-coming star of the screen, but an invalid with a unique deformity who could now only lick envelopes was another. And then children… well there's no way to hide it, the future mother's holy care. She doesn't need me, no matter how you look at it.

And I now don't need her either. I was surprised myself at the feeling of relief and calm once Camilla had left. A woman I had been so afraid to lose…

There are perceptions that enrich; there are also those that weaken, that strip away illusions. But in any case what you gain is clarity.

10

Listen, it's still good that your eyes and ears got mixed up, and not your eyes with your tongue, say, your sight with your sense of taste. And wouldn't it have been even worse if it had been your hearing with your sense of smell… oh! Imagine what sort of miasma you'd have to sniff up, what sort of filth you'd have cram yourself with, and still be hungry, ha! Listen, please get mixed up like that next time, in the interests of science, OK?

I am finishing the dinner that was brought to me. Food in tubes, just pieces of bread and some milk in a glass. Now, it seems, I can switch over to normal food, but at first my perception of what I was eating in the new interpretation was so nauseating that it made me want to throw up. Sight and hearing are informator-senses, but taste is the Great Consumer. So Boryunia is right, I really am lucky.

I am eating, and he is strolling unhurriedly and somehow very weightily from the window to the closet and back. I perceive him in the form of multiple roundish sounds, building in proportion as he approaches the window: something like a wave rolling onto a pebbly beach. Geraklych is in an excellent mood; I generally have never seen him in a bad mood, but today he simply strutting out of satisfaction and friendly feelings towards me. He has appeared in order to do me some great good, only so far it is unclear just what kind. Boris's voice flames in rainbow modulations.

A complicated relationship connects us. They choose people with great excessiveness to be psychonauts, people with an excellent charge of life energy, and Boris Geraklovich has this. As for the rest… I am a scientist, an author of papers and inventions, and he is an all-around athlete, of the highest class, to be fair. But when we switched bodies, even though it was only for twenty-four hours, an intimate, sensitive, preverbal mutual understanding arose between us; such an understanding probably occurs only between monozygotic twins or between a mother and child, flesh of her flesh. And such an understanding – of words, and movements, and silence, all the way up to one's physical state – is of no use between strangers. This is bad, indecent. Leonid Leonov has a phrase about two old friends who "knew one another closely to the point of hatred."[11] That is something like what we have: we are estranged from one another by our independence of actions and judgments, even by how we egg each other on, but just the same we are connected.

It's all because of your impatience, Boris switches to a homiletic tone. *I understand very well how it all happened: quickly, quickly, home quickly into my body! If you could've, you'd've been in an even bigger rush, and you basically would have jumped into your body like you were pulling on your flight suit while half asleep. Picture it: your arms are legs, you have to walk on them, your shoulders are your pelvis… But it's best not to say anything about what, heh, what sort of remarkable place your intelligent head would end up at. Ha-ha-ha-ha!*

He lowers himself to the couch and snorts in pleasure, tearing up. The room fills with a yellowish-raspberry bonfire and a rhythmic quaking. That's what he is like, Boryunia, the simple soul. He can never hold himself back, he is the first to laugh at his own jokes; and when other people start to laugh as well, then it's not clear what they are laughing at. But it is noteworthy that here, too, he is right: everything happened precisely because of my impatience.

Tell me, please, how do I look in your new perception? Still interesting and handsome?

"Even better: intelligent. So hurry up and get mixed up yourself.

Oh, well said, dear man! and he sidles over to hug me.

"Go away! I'd rather you cleaned up in here. What did you come here for?"

To turn you back into a person. To reduce you to the common denominator. For a start I will… you.

"What will you do?" I put my fingers on the pins of the automatic reader.

Calibrate you!

---

11. A slightly inexact quotation from Leonov's 1932 novel *Skutarevsky*.

He draws the thick curtains: the sunny noon beyond the window falls silent, the murmur from the objects in the room dwindles; he places a hefty device on the table, turns it on.

What do you see?

"Red. Is that the ZG you have there?"

That's the one. You just figure everything out, don't you! Now I will slowly increase the frequency, and you tell me when it changes to orange.

It would be hard not to figure it out: it's the ZG-10, an audio-frequency generator. Boryunia is using it to find the border frequencies of the sounds that I perceive in a given color. All very proper.

"You're already there."

One thousand one hundred hertz. Let's go on.

The transition from yellow to green was marked at two-and-a-half kilohertz, from green to blue at four. And beyond ten kilohertz there was an impression of violet and a gradual transition into darkness.

Let's go on to the next step. What do you hear?

"A-flat in the first octave."

Whoa, now that's some musical literacy for you! I suddenly feel like calling you "sir." This one?

"C-natural second, minor…" He is showing me plates of specific colors; I'm starting to feel playful. "Listen, Borya, stop this nonsense."

What do you mean, stop? I've organized a volunteer laboratory. First we will create an "auditory inverter" that transforms sounds into flashes according to our calibration. You will see them, and hear sounds. You will hear my voice! Then we will figure out the visual inverter. The idea is still not clear, but we will think of something. Seeing with your ears, heh, it's more complicated than with your eyes, but you will be able to do it on the same level as a cheap television.

"No, well… go ahead and do that for the glory of science; I'm not against it. But what you will do is hook those invertors up to yourself, so that you can see and hear as I do. Why is it, I'd like to know, that you want to force on me your way of perceiving reality only because there are many of you and one of me?"

A second's worth of stupefaction with a hint of violet.

Now would you look at that! Nope, I will not in my life meet another person like you. So you want everyone to get mixed up so they'll be able to communicate normally with you? Listen, maybe you're not Maxim Kolotilin, but Napoleon Bonaparte? Tell the truth, I won't give you away.

"It would be useful for you! As far as communicating with me, you and I are communicating without invertors, and even without the teletype."

But that's just you and I! Listen, old boy, don't jerk me around. Let's continue. What do you hear now?

"I'm not going to get calibrated. Keep playing without me."

Well, then… sorry, but I have to do this… Boris dials a number, and (I almost hear it) speaks into the receiver in a schoolboy's voice: *Patrick Yanovich, he doesn't wish to be calibrated! It would probably be better if you talked with him yourself. I don't have the strength or the words.*

11

The next scene: the same characters as before and Patrick. Now I also feel a little like a schoolboy. We have pulled the boss away from his work, he is impatient and angry.

I already mentioned that I don't like televisions, that I don't watch them. But during trips, when I am put in a hotel room with the obligatory TV, I sometimes amuse myself by turning it on its side or even upside-down. It's pleasant to watch someone bash out some jazz while sitting on the ceiling, or actors, standing on the wall, explaining complicated dramatic relationships: "Die, you miserable wretch!" and the "miserable wretch" does not fall, but just the opposite, she seems to stand up… But here's the remarkable thing: in those instances when they show *real* drama, or when realness manifests itself in the actors' performances, in inspired production, then you stop noticing the television's incorrect positioning. Apparently, the nature of true art, like the nature of physical laws, is such that it operates independent of any coordinate system.

Something similar happened this time as well: I ceased to noticed the chromatic peculiarities of Patrick Yanovich's speech, of Boris's replies, the shades of noise of their gestures, and saw just the meaning. Thought clashed with thought.

Why do you not want to calibrate your perceptions for the invertors? People are burning with impatience to help you!

"Because it is silly, Patrick. I am grateful, of course, for the burning and for the impatience, but this is just wrong. I *see*, I *hear*, I have the same sense organs, at least in their exterior parts, as all of you. And the impressions that result from them inside me… that is my personal business!

Your personal business, right! (Hand movement.) *Well, then please be so kind as to lay these two matches cross-wise.*

I couldn't even see them, the matches: they were too small.

There you have it: "The other one fell silent and walked back and forth in front of him. He could raise no better objection!"[12] That's Boryunia, who was a good student in grade school and remembers his Pushkin.

"Well… I can't yet do that. But I will learn in time."

In time… Listen, my dear man, let's be frank. You know what complex work we are doing, how grueling everyone's work is, how much is still unstudied and how many hidden dangers still remain. And if your comrades – at Boris's initiative and with my consent – want to spend their time and energy on this work, then it is because, in the first place, we want to help you, and, in the second place, we do not want to lose you. We will find you some sort of radio-flight consulting position, and you, your experience and knowledge, your exceptional abilities will remain in our field. But for this to happen, it goes without saying that we will need a satisfactory means of communicating and getting oriented. For a start, they will whip you up visual and auditory invertors… well, in the form of some sort of complex earphones and glasses, an inversion unit in your side pocket, batteries in your breast pocket. It will be cumbersome, of course, but the good thing is that everything will be normal. And then the neurologists and psychocyberneticians will get started on you, and maybe they'll come up with something better before you know it. And you will be a person. But otherwise, where are we going to put you?

---

12. From Pushkin's "Dvizhenie" [Movement] [1825], a poem that uses Zeno's first Argument and Galileo's heliocentrism to consider the problem of physical motion.

"Hold on, Patrick Yanovich… hold on with these works of mercy and the practical side of the matter. (I was annoyed at being treated like an invalid who had to be stuck someplace.) First let's consider this wonderful idea of inversion as a method of combating this 'mixed-up' condition. Like scientists. So, let's say we create a device that transforms sounds into visual images (you will not manage with just flashes for conveying complex information, quasi-representations on some sort of mosaic screens will be required; you've made it too simple there) and directs them into the eyes. The eyes, after all, are our most informative organ…" The thought was just forming in my mind, I was talking in fragments. "We will test this on a person whose sight is fine, but whose other senses are a disaster – no hearing, smell, or sense of touch. So, his auditory perceptions are directed to his eyes. We make another inverter that transforms smells into visual signals and images. Then another one for touch. We could make another one as well, for taste impressions, we will also translate them into the visual. Everything goes into the eyes! And what's more, the world around is full of infrareds and ultraviolets, radio-signals and other sorts of infra- and supersonic signals that communicate something just their own about reality; we will transform these as well and feed them into the eyes. What would a person with such a fully visual perception of the objective world see?

He wouldn't see a thing!

"Worse, Boryunchik: he would see 'white noise.' A polychromatic fog. Now mentally play out an inversion like this based on hearing or touch, and you will get the same thing: 'white noise.' You have to understand that the world is not like this. We do not perceive it as such, because our sense organs… well, they're like radio receivers or something, each tuned to a different bandwidth. Change the tuning, and you receive the wrong thing. Why would I fool myself with reverse inverting? If you were to give me back normal vision and hearing, I would have a great deal of mistrust in what I would see and hear!"

Well, what do you know! I could not tell who that reply belonged to – they were both shocked.

"Patrick Yanovich, you yourself said that what has happened to me is possible only for protein-based bodies, that this kind of thing could not happen with the silicon-based beings and the crystalloids, and could not…"

It's not going to happen to us, either, we are going to be cooling the bodies.

"There you have it. It emerges that, your intentions to invert me and stick me in a pensioner's consulting role will ruin a one-of-a-kind potential, something unique across three worlds, something that, just the same, needs to be studied in full. They also have the same arrangement: they see with their eyes, hear with their ears, and are content…"

Ha-ha-ha-ha! Boryunia has gone up in flames like a gas tank. *So you wish everyone would get mixed up. Both here, and on Proxima, and on Barnard's Star! That's what it is, Patrick Yanovich, he proposed that I put the invertors on myself.*

Patrick did not laugh, but I could sense that he also did not understand me. He even doubted whether the changes in my mind were limited to my analyzers. Does one really have to become "mixed up" in order to understand what I am trying to explain?

So we did not agree on anything. The boss suddenly realized that he had to attend an experiment, said that we would talk about it further, that there was no rush, and left, a talented, narrow-minded man. Boryunia stole out after him. *I'll leave the equipment here, my dear man, heh-hm!*

I found no words… Oh, words are not what is important, but rather what I decide and what I will do. And I already know what this will be. But first I have to get a good night's sleep.

12

In my sleep I was looking at myself in the mirror, running an electric razor along my cheeks. I saw my hands with slender, strong fingers, well-defined veins, sparse, light hair. Then I saw Camilla, Vitka Strizhevich, a friend from my university days; I saw leaves on the asphalt, fire-red and yellow maple leaves, rusty-yellow elm leaves, a newspaper kiosk that's not far from the Institute, a section of brick wall with a drain pipe, a street with pedestrians and shining cars, and something else, and something else. When I woke up, my pillow was wet; I had been crying while I slept. People are weak in their sleep.

Oh, well, let this, too, inform my new perception of the world; my sense of sight that I lamented in my sleep is something we inherited from the animals, something that seemed like the only possible way of seeing.

It's quiet outside the window, which means that it's dark. The Institute has emptied out. To "light" the room I put a record on the player, and perceived not only the dim outlines of objects (give me time, Patrick Yanovich, and I will lay those matches cross-wise!), but also Čiurlionis-esque images, this time fairly concrete. A sea in a storm heaves with huge waves, reeling, all the way to the grey-blue horizon, great white-maned waves fly onto the shore, ring cannon blows against the cliffs, fling up to the sky exulting fireworks of sea-spray.

Ta-dim, ta-dam-ta-dam-da-dum!

There it is: I pulled out Beethoven's Ninth symphony, the very beginning. I have not been to the places where he lived, but that is it.

I don't take long getting packed: inflatable gardbrace and breast plate, wig, glasses, briefcase with the bare necessities. Yes, I cannot forget the plastic bag and shoelace! Now a note: "Patrick Yanovich, Boris, Yulia, everyone! I earnestly ask you not to look for me. If it becomes necessary, I'll find my own way back. So long, my love to you all!"

I take the elevator down in light blue silence. The lobby. To the right the night watchman, covered by a newspaper, drowses in a leather armchair. Here they only look at who is coming in, and even then not all the time… That's the help for you!

And now I am free. For everyone it's an autumn evening, like in "dark is the little night,"[13] but for me it is light: the wind whistles[14] in the naked branches, stripping the last leaves from the trees, and to the

---

13. The opening words of a 1911 poem by Esenin.
14. A half-line from Lermontov's "Parus" [The Sail, 1832]

right splashes the Volga. I am walking along the embankment to the grove. The streetlights drench me in a shower of noise. Approaching passersby are perceptible from below, from their hasty steps. They're probably thinking: what a weirdo, it's not enough for him that it's the middle of the night, he's also put on dark glasses!

The streetlights and asphalt have ended. My feet hew a gleaming path through the rustling leaves. And if I lean my head back, the stars above sing out something of their own, something cosmic, with the voices of violins. There, where they ring out as an entire orchestra, is the Milky Way.

I am using words that describe what I perceive through "sound" and "light" – so far I have no others. But in reality everything is both this way and not this way. It is already different, my perception, and in it memories of my former days, my knowledge, and my recollections of radio-flights have been superimposed over my "mixed up" senses. Now I perceive the world with a fullness of which I previously had no notion.

I came out of the woods at the spring. Ringing, it illuminates (this will have to do!) the clay bluff, the waves that obliquely rebound onto the sand. I get undressed, pack my clothes together with the briefcase in the plastic bag. I tie it up with one end of the shoelace, the other end, with a big loop, goes over my shoulder. Well?

Whew, the water is cold in October, it burns my skin! It's no big deal, psychonaut, you've overcome worse. I swim. On this side they could catch me quickly. But about thirty kilometers down along the other bank there is a wharf. I'll get there by morning, get on one of the last steamships, and then on a barge, and on down through the Motherland.

I'll start somewhere with the simplest activity I can find: I will roll something round, drag something flat. It will probably look a little strange at first. "Listen, are you kin to Maxim Kolotilin, the famous psychonaut? You look like him." "That's me, I'm him." And the guys will go *ha-ha-ha!* like Boris. It's the most reliable way of disappearing… And I will return to the Institute "normal" in my ability to communicate and orient myself, no worse than anyone else (I will try to be even better), but having kept *everything* in me.

Because, with this effect that we have unfortunately named being "mixed up," we are opening a new chapter in the history of human knowledge, of our perception of the world. In it the former "sight/hearing/smelling/feeling/tasting" will be just one of many.

And this will not be just a human sense. They, too, the ones from Barnard's Star and the trinary system of Proxima Centauri, will rush to adopt this experiment for themselves.

A shining wind rambles above the water, above the bright banks. The waves illuminate my hands as they thrust forward fathom by fathom. The stars sing with delicate voices. The Volga flows, the Earth flies in space… Come on, pull harder, so you can warm up!

"Ta-dim… ta-dam-ta-dim! We'll win the next round!"

First published in Russian: 1980
Translation by Kevin Reese

JUBILEE-200

I sat down in the shade of the sycamore, which according to legend was planted by Academician Sosnora himself, and began to watch the kids.

The kids squealed and frolicked along the shore of the pond, while their teachers trotted after them, convinced that any minute one of the little ones might fall into the cold water and catch pneumonia.

I could easily guess the genetic lines of every youngster just by looking at them.

More than a century ago, a male named Stark with a light-colored, shorthair coat, homozygous for that allele, left his mark on several generations to come. The dominant phenotype still appears in the kids, who have no idea who their great-grandfather was. Just think of the receding chins and drooping mustaches of the Habsburgs – these traits continued for six hundred years or more, as is obvious in their portraits, no matter how hard the artists tried to ameliorate them.

We subdue nature, and nature finds ways around us, in order not to be subdued.

The Experiment seemed modest on the face of it, but beneath the surface, it was pompous and full of human vanity: let's put ourselves in God's place, figure out how to humanize chimps, and call upon radiation genetics to flip every switch towards biological advancement.

We the omnipotent will take a herd of chimpanzees, mobilize the mechanism that directs mutations, drive out of the blind-alley of evolutionary progress, pick up tremendous speed and then take a look – will nature allow us to create our own brothers in Reason?

Those who planned the Experiment, who secured the financing and housing, convinced academic and funding organizations that this experiment was vital for the human race – they themselves understood that they would not live to see the results. That is, they understood in the abstract, but in fact nobody believes in their own mortality, and every one of them felt that perhaps a miracle would happen, and within just thirty years there would be a mutant who could communicate in words and learn the multiplication tables.

Naturally, everything turned out as they'd planned, but nothing turned out as they'd hoped.

Once, I searched the library for a journal from two hundred years ago, and there I found a lively article about how they combed the zoos and sanctuaries for the brightest, most advanced chimpanzees and brought them together to breed in places that had been specially set up for them – kind of a cross between a zoo, a genetics research institute, and a dormitory for idiots.

At first, enthusiasm made up for the lack of financing and equipment. Not everyone in the world was convinced that this experiment should take precedence over other issues occupying humanity. But at the helm of the institute stood Sosnora, who used part of the premises for an ancillary project: treating cows to exponentially increase their milk production. Therefore, with the help of those witless creatures who still graze near the pond today, he proved the profitability of the enterprise. He himself died ten years later.

The next director gradually expanded the operation. He added exceptionally gifted new chimps to the herd so that the existing genetic pool would not become so isolated as to give rise to a new species, incapable of interbreeding with wild stock.

Throughout various crises and conflicts, the institute never closed. There was something unreal about the entire principle of the institute's activity. It was science with pretensions to godhood.

Directors came and went, researchers received salaries, made discoveries, defended dissertations, retired; in general, their activities resembled those of their colleagues in related scientific institutes.

In the course of things, genetic concepts and methods changed, new theories arose, or obsolete theories were resurrected. Neo-Lamarckism was suddenly in vogue, followed by the triumph of post-Darwinism, only to be finally replaced by super-Mendelianism.[1]

Every one of these theoretical turns reflected in some way on the politics of dealing with the herd of chimpanzees. The most promising specimens fell into disfavor and were sent off to zoos or medical institutes, and the greatest accomplishments were suddenly viewed as setbacks, only to be viewed again as grand discoveries a few years later.

The ascents, falls, defeats, and changes in theory hit the chimpanzees the hardest. Having created a new race of rational beings out of monkeys, human beings then denied humanity to the creatures they were in the process of humanizing.

Not all that long ago there was a case in which a female named Sienna-4 was written off to a zoo to perish there, despite the fact that she possessed remarkable mathematical abilities. The reason was simple: her boss – a very nice, talented, but wayward man – got into an irrevocable dispute with his department chair and left the Experiment. And this man was the only one who Sienna-4 had trusted or liked.

Therefore, as a participant in the Experiment and one of many who contributed to it, I harbor a deep personal objection to what is going on here. In the course of two hundred years of directed

---

1. Jean-Baptiste Lamarcke (1744-1829), Charles Darwin (1809-1882) and Gregor Mendel (1822-1884) are the seminal nineteenth century founders of modern notions of evolution and genetics.

mutations, continuous tests and operations, experimental medications, and changes in habitat, no stable outcomes have been reached. Moreover, as the results accumulate, the gap between homo-chimps and experimenters grows ever wider. Oddly enough, Man – who thought up the Experiment, expended two hundred years and a heap of resources on it, employing hundreds of minds that might have been far better used to advance other fields of knowledge – Man is mentally unprepared to accept a repudiation of his own exceptionalism. For people, homo-chimps are still nothing more than chimps. They may be objects of research, but not partners in Reason…

My rather depressing thoughts were interrupted by shouts from one of our behaviorists, whom we'd nicknamed Formula.

"John!" she yelled, running through the corridor, "where are you?"

When she saw me, she asked, "Have you seen John?" But she didn't wait for my answer and kept running. She couldn't stand me.

John is an old homo-chimp, and a real creep from an anatomical point of view: nearly bald, with a bulging forehead and a conniving mind. For some reason, he's the one all the Experiment people trust. The meager vocabulary by which he communicates strikes them as the epitome of their accomplishments. Whenever some kind of delegation or important guests visit, they always bring out John, and John presents himself as a parody of man, even putting on boxer shorts and a red shirt. He pretends to engage in elementary conversation, but he comes off as a parrot in the company of monkeys.

I started to wonder why Formula needed John so badly on such a crazy day. I went to the window and saw her standing next to an old flower bed calling, "John, where are you? I need you!"

Naturally, John, who was snoozing somewhere nearby, climbed out of the bushes lazily, scratching his enormous belly, which had grown fat on handouts.

"Johnny!" Formula was overjoyed. "Come welcome the new girl. You know how to do it best. Please!"

"Whaddaya give me for it?"

"Johnny, you know I have never let you down…"

"Okey-dokey," said Johnny, and started to walk behind Formula, stooping more than necessary, so that his fingers touched the ground in front of him. This time he was wearing blue trousers and a white cap worn backwards, so that everyone could admire his frontal lobes.

I decided to follow them.

They walked out to the landing platform. A huge guy from park services hung around the transport helicopter, holding a young female chimpanzee on a leash. She was frightened to death by the flight and the unfamiliar circumstances.

As soon as he saw the pretty female, the pride of genetic science turned into a rutting chimp. He liked the girl a lot. Hopes that he might bed this young thing stirred in Johnny's brain. He started to ape around, pursing his lips and hooting, hopping and beating his chest with his fists, as if he were a gorilla. Naturally, the young female became even more terrified.

She really *was* very pretty. Her mind still slept; then again, nobody had any intention of inspiring her with Reason. She was only here to prolong the species, to bring a new stream of genes into the pool.

"Johnny, don't scare her," Formula begged. "Explain to her that she will live in very nice conditions. Tell her to calm down."

It's amazing how naïve some of our researchers are. Having created a race of humanoid chimps, they somehow imagine that an ordinary chimpanzee also has primitive speech and can converse with someone like John. On the other hand, John, who never knew the language of his wild forbears – a primitive but all-encompassing language of gestures and breaths – needed to uphold his reputation. Nothing worked. The girl bared her teeth and tried to hide behind the huge guy with the leash, figuring that an ordinary person was still better than an animal of unknown species in a white cap.

I could see that the situation was reaching a crisis point, so I started to approach the girl, convinced that I would be able to calm down this poor creature. And everything would have worked out, if not for that damned Formula.

"Stop!" she screamed. "John, restrain that hooligan! Where is the fire hose?" John frowned and tried to look like a defender of humanity, although inside he was terrified of me and knew what I would do to him if he even dared touch me.

I met the trusting glance of the female chimpanzee and returned it with a smile. I knew that from that moment on, she would be my loyal servant. That's all I needed. I snorted quietly to calm her down, and let her know with a grimace that she had nothing to be afraid of. Then, over Formula's shrieks and the alarmed movements of the confused park services guy, I jumped into the nearest tree and swung up from a lower branch onto a higher one, all the while feeling the ecstatic gaze of the girl on my back. I swung on a well-worn path through the trees all the way back to sleeping quarters.

Several homo-chimps were relaxing on their cots; some were reading, some were watching video clips. Barry, a natural-born carpenter, was fixing a stool. We'd hammered the chairs together in the work training shop.

"What happened?" asked Gitta, an elderly, wise homo-chimp blessed with remarkable intuition.

"Damn that Formula," I said. "They brought in a lovely young creature. Formula called Johnny, and that old goat…"

"Don't even go on, I get it," Barry interrupted. He put aside his hammer. "You know, today they dragged me in for testing again."

"Let me guess, you thought about bananas."

"Yeah, and oranges, too," laughed Barry. "They were disappointed."

"Oh, this is hard," said Gitta. "I'm especially afraid for our youth. Sooner or later they're going to catch us."

"What alternatives do we have, though?" I asked. "Admit everything? Become the objects of a media sensation, while remaining third-class beings, talking macaques?

"If only everything would go off without a hitch today," said Barry.

"Dr. Vamp asked me about you today," said a young homo-chimp named Third. "He wanted to know if I respect you."

"And what did you answer?"

"Oh, you know, 'I speak bad, I am stupid-stupid homo-chimp,' I said, 'Leader is strong.'"

I grabbed a banana from Third – I suddenly realized how hungry I was.

"Is the girl pretty?" asked Second.

"None of your business," I cut him off. "In the forest you'll find even prettier ones."

"The conference is starting," said Barry. "We have to listen in."

"They are discussing where to put the guests and arrange the banquet," remarked Gitta.

"Maybe we should go anyway?" Barry inquired.

"I'll go by myself," I said, and climbed out the window. I used the grapevine to get up to the roof and then crawled along the roof to the conference rooms. All of our routes have been tried and proven by generations of homo-chimps. We still fall short of humans in intellectual power, but we never forgot how to climb trees, jump, and – most importantly – how to hide our thoughts and actions. The laws of the forest are stronger than the laws of the city, and two hundred years is not long enough for our blood and muscles to have forgotten about the past. I don't know which one of us was the first to make it undetected to the windows of the conference room, but the homo-chimp who first understood that his mind had advanced to the point where he had to hide from humans what they themselves had created – he was a genius.

People surrounded us with instruments that elicit fear and distrust. People imagined that any flight of thought or flair of emotions would immediately be recorded on their self-recorders and bio-phones. They made a big mistake – they tried to remake us in their image. But nature turned out to be stronger. We understood this once we discovered that by trusting their instruments, people judged us wrongly. This great discovery was made before my appearance into the world.

From that time on, while subjected to instruments and cruel experiments, in which we were forced to eat, sleep, think, work, and procreate under their eyes, under their control – in all this time we have learned stealth. We are not second-rate people, we are a new race: homo-chimps!

I got to the room in which the conference was taking place, right on time. They had just turned to a discussion of my own humble personage. Formula had the floor.

"He's becoming unbearable," she spat. "And he is starting to have a bad influence on the other subjects."

Ahh, I thought, how hard they try to avoid the word "animals."

"Can you be more specific?" asked Dr. Vamp.

If you select the most positive "subjects" out of the human lot, then undoubtedly Dr. Vamp belongs to their ranks. Perhaps this is because he oversees the infirmary and occasionally takes a stand against the excessively cruel experiments. His job is only to heal, and he has a good touch.

"Today we received a new female," said Formula.

The sweet image of the girl, pressed in fright against the leg of the giant from park services, once again rose before my eyes.

"I asked John to help me."

"John does not seem particularly trustworthy to me," commented Batya, the institute's director.

"Why, he's a very developed creature," said Formula, "and he often helps us. The female was very scared. We probably would have been able to handle her just between the two of us, but then Leader jumped out of the bushes and threw himself at her. I think he wanted to fight over the little thing."

Formula was close to tears. For God's sake, I thought, what kind of monster does she take me for?

Then Skripnik, head of the physical plant, unexpectedly came to Formula's defense.

"He's becoming a wild beast," said fat Skripnik. "Yesterday he got into the storage pantry and took half of our supplies. I don't know how we are going to put on the banquet now."

I smiled inwardly. Gitta and I had carried out that raid on the pantry with two of our youth. At least at first, we are going to need cans of condensed milk and other tinned goods. But we had to make it look like an act of vandalism, so as not to raise suspicion.

"It's time to give him to a zoo," said Formula. "Even if he is a mutant, he's a regressive one. An ordinary monkey. A danger to the entire experiment.

"What do you think, Doctor?" asked the director.

"I have to refrain from drawing any conclusions," said the Doctor. "According to my observations, Leader is a healthy individual and carries authority in the tribe."

"Exactly – in the *tribe*. But we're trying to create a *society!*" exclaimed Formula.

"What do you think?" This time the director turned to the chief of the experimental assessment laboratory, my main enemy, the one we had learned to lead by the nose by driving all real thoughts from our minds and thinking only about food.

"Level of intelligence is below average…" The assessment guru delved into his notes, extracting them from his pockets and laying them out on the table, whereby he mixed up my data with the data on other homo-chimps, eventually confusing things so badly that the director asked him to stop. Then he asked the opinion of the other specialists present. Everyone agreed. I am a troublemaker, I have a bad influence on the youth, and they should get rid of me.

On the one hand, hearing all of this was really gratifying, because it meant that I had successfully deceived everyone. On the other hand, it's insulting to the sensibilities of any rational being to hear that they want to send you to a zoo.

"To sum things up," said the director, "we will prepare Leader for departure. This should be done in strict secrecy. We will call the zoo in Sukhumi,[2] since they have demand there. I think it will be best to do it today, late at night. Now, on to other matters. When is the flight with our guests due to arrive?

---

2. Sukhumi is a city on the coast of the Black Sea, in western Georgia.

"Five-thirty in the afternoon," said Skripnik. "The flyer is very large; we'll park it on the reserve field."

I knew about this flyer. It would arrive from Australia. The rest of the guests would fly in on smaller flyers. We needed the big one.

Well, that's it. I could go now. I had found out two very important things.

First of all, there was no time to lose. If we didn't carry out our plan this evening, then in the middle of the night these treacherous people would smuggle me off to a zoo. Secondly, the flyer we needed would be sitting on the reserve field from five-thirty on. What a stroke of luck! The field is surrounded by forest, so our approach to the flyer will be hidden by foliage.

I dropped back down into the garden.

I glanced at the pond, the playground, and our nice rooms with a touch of sadness. I'll never see this world again, the world in which I grew up and became conscious of myself and my duty to my race.

Well, what of it? Everything comes to an end, as they say. Even fairytales have an ending.

They were waiting for me in the bedroom.

"We're all set," I said. "The flyer lands at five-thirty. It will be parked on the reserve field."

This news was greeted with cries of joy.

I decided not to say anything about the decision to send me to the zoo. Ill-wishers – and there are several of them even in our small group – would call me an egoist who is only trying to save his own skin.

We watched the guests begin to arrive. Since it was already going on evening, and the jubilee celebration was not to take place until tomorrow, the guests were not yet supposed to meet any homo-chimps. Only that idiot Johnny, of course, sashayed around with the new arrivals, had his picture taken with them, and uttered banalities, which astounded them the way a parrot astounds us with "Polly want a cracker!"

Even before darkness fell, we carried part of our supplies from our forest hiding places closer to the flyer. We had no intention of turning into wild animals once we reached the Big Forest, on the shores of the Congo. We gathered together educational microfilms for the kids, recording devices, and all kinds of other equipment and instruments – in short, we were launching the great migration of a small nation. A nation that was tired of serving as another's guinea pig. A nation that had found its leader in me.

In the evening, they turned on the lights in the garden. The news guests gathered under the apple trees. Skripnik set out appetizers on long tables. Before bedtime a children's choir came out to sing "A little fir tree grew in the forest." The guests were charmed.

I checked to see whether all the necessary locks were broken.

It got dark. Everything was ready.

It's a good thing they didn't think of leaving someone to guard the big flyer.

I liked the flyer. It was really huge. I had never flown on a flyer like this before, none of us had. But we knew how automatic controls work. We would fly low, and people would only realize what had happened once we were already over Africa.

The moon was waning, so we could move freely, almost without hiding. In this respect, at least, people simply can't compete with us.

It grew quiet. The only sounds were voices and songs coming from the windows of the hotel and cottages that had been turned over to the guests. All the better, let them make merry. Tomorrow they will be faced with a big disappointment. There won't be anyone to demonstrate to them.

"Listen," I asked wise Gitta, "are we going to take Johnny with us, or leave him here?"

"What do *you* think?"

"I would leave him here as a consolation prize."

"I agree. Especially since he won't be happy with us. He is used to comfort, and we are about to give up our comforts."

Third brought the children. The mothers accompanied their kids, who were sleepy and fussy.

We quickly loaded them into the flyer. How wonderful that people are so self-confident, it didn't even occur to them to leave a guard, or to lock anything up.

Gitta counted all the homo-chimps.

"Sixty-four 'subjects'," she said with a smile. She did a good imitation of Formula.

"All on board?" asked Barry. He was already climbing into the cockpit. He will be my co-pilot.

"Wait!" I said. "We forgot *her*!"

"Who?" Gitta did not understand.

"The girl they brought in this morning. We can't leave her here with Johnny!"

"In the forest you'll find even prettier ones," Third tried to taunt me with my own words.

I growled at him so ferociously that he quickly disappeared into the flyer, and I have a feeling that he won't speak again until we get to Africa.

"Don't do something stupid," said Gitta. "You'll arouse the entire institute."

"No," I said firmly. "Everyone get settled. I'll be back in a minute."

I tore off towards the quarantine room.

Unfortunately, this door was actually locked. I crept up to the window. The window was shockproof, there's no way I would get in there.

The girl's beautiful big eyes stared at me from the other side of the window. She understood that I had come for her. She pressed her lips against the glass, as if urging me to come in. Stupid, dear, irrational being.

In two jumps I landed on the roof. It took two minutes to unscrew the ventilator grid. I rushed; I could imagine how nervous the rest of my people must be. Without me, there could be a rebellion – to some degree, only my iron will held the entire group together in obedience.

Finally the grid flies off.

Someone is already coming down the road.

I had to lie down, pressing myself against the roof.

I smelled Johnny. Of all things! I almost laughed. A romantic tryst! A rival in the darkness!

I could hear that idiot knocking on the glass, calling to the girl. I was seized with horrible jealousy. But what should I do? Start a fight with him? A risky idea flew into my head.

"What are you doing prowling around here?!" I asked in a deep bass voice, imitating the director. "Go back to bed immediately! Otherwise I will send you to the zoo!"

My play-acting worked. Johnnie chickened out and took off with rapid footsteps, abandoning the field of battle…

Now I had to work even faster. Someone might hear me. I especially hated the watch-robot, who, it's true, was usually not deployed until after midnight. We had wanted to break it, but clearly our natural inattention won out – and we forgot.

I squeezed through the ventilator hatch – it was pretty tight.

I hooted softly, calling the girl. She understood. I felt her long tender fingers grab my arm.

I pulled her up and helped her scramble out onto the roof.

She followed behind me trustfully.

What happiness! With every look and movement, she seemed to say: "You are my chosen one."

"You'll be speaking in no time," I thought.

Back at the flyer, panic had set in. I had disappeared, leaving no orders. Gitta was barely restraining the warriors within the flyer. Barry threw himself at me with reproaches. I handed off the lady and quickly moved through to the pilot's seat.

"Attention!" I said. "Everyone take a seat. Mothers, hold onto your children. We are in a hurry. The forests of Africa await us. Freedom awaits us!"

I threw a final farewell glance at the institute. A few windows were still lit up. The dark mass of the old building, constructed in the style of the twentieth century, rose above the trees.

I ran my hand over the console, turning the automatic system on in my mind's eye. The dashboard lights lit up.

I punched in the code – I knew how to do this. Direction…. A map of the Northern hemisphere glowed. I located the Congo.[3] I moved the indicator arrow to the exact point of our destination. I hit the start button. The flyer began its rapid ascent.

The little ones in the back chirped and squealed.

The institute disappeared into darkness.

The lights on the ground grew dimmer. We flew through sparse clouds. The machine turned, sticking to its designated route.

I looked at the map in front of me. The thin green line – our route – started to grow and bend towards the south. I fell into contemplation.

Suddenly I felt someone's touch.

I turned. My beloved stood next to me. She wanted to be with me.

I smiled at her.

"We are safe," I said to Barry, who was in the other seat. "They won't catch us now."

"They can still launch a machine from one of the aerodromes along our way."

"Doubtful," I said. "They still haven't even caught on. And when they do catch on, they won't figure out where we have gone."

Right at that moment, the contact screen blinked on ominously.

My first impulse was to hide from the video eye of the screen. I ducked.

Barry gasped.

Then I realized that there is no use hiding. Better to confront the danger face to face.

The director of the institute appeared on the screen. Batya looked serious.

---

3. The area known as the Congo lies in Central Africa, and is bisected by the equator. Bulychev wrote this story in 1985, during the long period of Mobutu's reign over the country then known as Zaire. Despite his corrupt and dictatorial rule, Mobutu was supported by the U.S. as a staunch anti-communist ally. This feature of Cold War politics does not seem at all germane to Bulychev's story, which properly invokes the Congo as the natural habitat of several great ape species (all of them now endangered): the common chimpanzee, bonobo, western gorilla and eastern gorilla.

"Leader," he said. "I know you're there."

"I am here," I said, straightening up. "You can kill us, but you can't stop us."

"Leader," Batya said, "maybe you would prefer to continue this conversation without any witnesses? If so, tell Barry to leave."

"I'm going to stay," said faithful Barry, "I'm not afraid."

"The director is right," I said. "Please step out. You have a loose monkey tongue."

Barry was offended. He slowly crawled out of his seat, grumbling something under his breath. The girl grew timid and looked at me, then at the director, who did not notice her. He knew that she was not able to understand anything anyway. Unlike many of the others, the director knew us all by face.

I extended my arm – the pilot's cabin was small – to close the door.

"What do you have to say?" I asked. "What is your ultimatum?"

"It's not an ultimatum," said the director, "just information."

"Good." I felt desperately afraid. The whole world was against me – three billion people.

"Leader, it's been several years now since we realized that our instruments do not give us an objective picture of your condition. We did not immediately understand, nor did we easily understand, that our Experiment had in fact succeeded. It succeeded even beyond what we had expected. Two hundred years of experimental research had inculcated certain fixed behaviors into the experimenters. We became rigid. But when we realized that we had driven you, our younger brothers – to whom we had given reason and consciousness, without asking! – towards a total impasse, we had to hide the fact of our realization…

"How long have you known all this?"

"A long time."

"Why did you hide it?"

"Because we couldn't come to any kind of consensus, because we didn't know how to continue the Experiment, because we had to hand over responsibility to those who had grown up before our eyes… It's complicated. Maybe someday you and I, Leader, will sit down over a cup of tea and talk about this problem.

It struck me that for the first time in 200 years, someone had addressed a chimpanzee using the formal *vy* instead of *ty*.

"I'm sorry," I said firmly, squeezing the hand of the girl, "but we will not return. The experiments are over."

"I am certainly not arguing with you," answered the director. "Although to tell the truth, I am very sorry to part with you. You and I have lived together for twelve years. You were still a boy when I arrived at the institute."

"I remember," I said. "But I'm not coming back."

"Fly, fly, nobody is stopping you. You should know that in the luggage compartment of the flyer there is a good stock of food. You didn't take very much, and before you leave the flyer, the children will need to be well fed.

"You mean, you knew!" I suddenly understood that this was a real blow. It was a blow to my pride, to my vanity, to my secret…

"Don't be upset," said the director. "It doesn't diminish your accomplishment. You did as much as the whole institute put together. I say this sincerely."

I knew that he was sincere. We, homo-chimps, have a much better sense of intuition than humans. There is a lot we can still teach people.

The director guessed my thoughts.

"I hope that you will be able to teach us a lot. That's another reason we had to part. To leave each other in time. You found the way out that we couldn't find."

"So today's meeting with the resolution to send me to the zoo…"

"…Was partly staged. We have known for a while that you listen in at our meetings."

"And Formula?" I wouldn't be able to stand it if she…

"Dr. Pimenova was not in the know," the director smiled. "She would never have agreed to let you go to a tropical forest, where you can't boil your drinking water!"

"Never mind," I said with relief, "she still has her beloved Johnny."

The door behind me opened. I turned to see the alarmed faces of Gitta and Barry.

"Everything is in order," I said. "The flight will continue."

I reached out to switch off our connection, only to find that it had already gone blank.

"That was the director?" asked Gitta, "What did he want?"

"He wanted us to return," I said. "But I refused. The flight will continue."

Barry's face looked ecstatic. I had conquered the director himself!

Gitta frowned. She didn't believe me. But she would keep it to herself.

I stroked the girl's head.

"No, I won't teach her language," I think. That conversation with the director has to remain a secret. The President of the Republic of Homo-Chimps must always be beyond reproach.

First published in Russian: 1985
Translation: Yvonne Howell

ARKADY AND BORIS STRUGATSKY
1988

THOSE BURDENED BY EVIL

EXCERPT

The builders had left the building live-in-ready in the late fall: the rains had already gotten icy, and from time to time little snow pellets sprinkled down. It was somewhat strange and possibly even unique in its ornate and awkward-to-describe architecture. It was made wholly of red brick and stretched along Balkan Street for more than two blocks. The roof was flat, as if intended as a landing-place for the airships of the future, the façade lavishly decorated with pits and whorls of complex form, right-angled tunnels hanging above mountainous archways. And for what purpose, it would be interesting to know, did they carve narrow niches into the façade all the way to the fifth floor? Could they really be meant for the long, gaunt statues of unspecified heroes or martyrs of the past? And why did the architect need to erect towers at the corners of the astonishing building, just like you would see on a fortress, rounded, and of various heights?

The scaffolding had long ago been dismantled and taken away, the window-glass was clean and transparent, the brand-new doors in the entrances could not provoke any censure, and the stone steps that led up to them were clean, but the entire expanse from these steps all the way to the asphalt of the road was nothing but mud mixed with construction trash. There one could see wet, frayed sheets of plywood with frightful, protruding nails and broken bricks, cracked cinderblocks with rusted rebar, water-pipes twisted into spirals by some unknown force, sections of steam radiators forgotten by all, and buckets of some sort, smashed flat. Between the eleventh and twelfth entrances abided, listing to one side, some kind of tracked machine, and the wet wind kept slamming its half-open door.

The building was live-in ready, but there was no sign at all of inhabitants. It was empty in the stairwells, empty, dark, and quiet, and it smelled of paint and disuse, and the elevator cabs, lifted all the way to the roof, were frozen and lifeless. All the doors of all the entrances seemed firmly and dependably locked, and this was probably actually the case, though it was possible to get into the building. And people went into it. And they probably came out, as well. At any rate, on the stone steps of the thirteenth entrance, leading into the south corner tower, dirty footprints could be seen. On the long, painted handle of the front door a criminologist could find fingerprints with no effort. The dust on the vestibule's cement floor had here and there rolled up into a multitude of little balls, as if someone, having come in from the street, had energetically shaken out his rain-soaked hat.

And someone had forgotten, or thrown aside because it was useless, or forgotten in a panic, an ancient, half-opened little suitcase on the stairwell landing of the fourth floor, and lolling out of the little suitcase was a waffle-weave towel of doubtful freshness. On the landing of the eighth floor, in the corner, by the door of apartment number five-sixteen, two spent shell casings gleamed faintly: it is possible that they had also been forgotten here by someone, but most likely they were lying where a firearm's extractor had thrown them out. It should be noted that the door of apartment five-sixteen was firmly locked and had not opened since these areas had been abandoned by the foreman of the finishing crew. Or, let's say, by the foreman of the cleaning crew.

In the building only a single solitary apartment was open. For some reason, it lacked a number, but, if one were to count according to the logic of the layout, it would be apartment five-twenty-seven, intended to be a three-room apartment on the twelfth (last) floor of the south corner tower.

In one of the rooms of this apartment the window looked out onto Labor Avenue. The room itself was covered in cheap, unassuming wallpaper, twisted electrical wires stuck from the center of the ceiling, the parquet floor, though passably smooth, was still in some need of a sanding, and in the corner farthest from the window stood, forgotten by the builders, a wooden fold-out bed, thickly caked in mortar and oil paint.

In this room people were talking. Two of them.

One stood by the window and was looking down at the muddy expanses under the grey, drizzling sky. He was immensely tall, and on him was a black chlamys that completely concealed his frame. Its lower fringe fell freely on the floor, but in the shoulders it rose steeply upward and to either side like a Caucasian burka,[1] but so energetically and steeply, with such dreary defiance, that one was no longer thinking about a burka – there are no such burkas in this world! – but about powerful wings hidden under the black material. Then again, of course, he could not have any wings there, and, probably, he didn't, but simply some sort of clothing of an unusual and unfamiliar cut. And this clothing was no more strange or unfamiliar than the material itself, with moiré shadows looming over it: on the uncanny chlamys not a single fold could be guessed at, not a single wrinkle, so that it seemed at times this was not clothing at all, but a gloomy spot in space where there was nothing, not even light.

---

1. The "burka" is not the Muslim religious garment "burqa," but a traditional garment worn by men in the Caucasus mountains. Made from felt or karakul, it has high, squared-off shoulders meant to give the wearer an imposing silhouette.

And on the head of the one standing by the window there was, doubtless, a wig, white, maybe even powdered, with a short braid almost to the shoulders, tightly plaited with black string.

"How sad!" he pronounced, as if through clenched teeth. "You look, and it seems as though everything here has changed, but in actuality, everything has remained as before…"

His companion did not answer right away. Apparently completely unafraid of getting dirty, he was sitting on the fold-out bed, having crossed his short legs that did not reach the floor, and was quickly leafing through a plump, beat-up notebook, now and then snatching up and replacing the little pages that fell out. A little, pudgy, somewhat dirty man of indeterminate age, in a grey, shabby little suit: tapered pants, drooping socks, also grey, and half-boots, grey as well from long use, never having known brush, shoe polish, or even a rag. And a grey, contorted little tie with its knot, as the English say, under his right ear.

The little man was probably hot, his plump face was red and covered in small beads of sweat, his moist, whitish hair, through which his skin shone pink, clung to his skull. The little man had taken off his hat and jacket, and they sprawled in the corner in a disorderly, soaked-through pile together with a bulging, scratched-up briefcase from the days of the first NEP.[2] A completely ordinary little man, no match for the one who towered like a black boulder before the window.

"But how *you* have changed, Potter!" he shouted back, finally. "You are positively impossible to recognize! And no one *will* recognize you…"

The one who stood by the window snorted. His little braid jerked. The wings of his black chlamys stirred.

"That is not what I am talking about," he said. "You do not understand."

It was as if the grey little man did not hear him. He would leaf through his notebook and then leaf through it again. It was an unusual notebook: now one, now another little page would suddenly light

---

2. The New Economic Policy, a short-lived (1921-28) Soviet-era experiment with free enterprise.

up from within with a clear red light, and sometimes even a distinct trimming of fire would flare up along the edges, and it seemed even that a little puff of smoke would leap up, but then these tricks would suddenly cease, after which would come relief that, this time, the little man's fat, dirty fingers had remained whole.

"And you cannot understand," continued the one who stood by the window. "You have been idling here all this time, and you can no longer see what is in front of you… I, on the other hand, am looking at it with a fresh eye. And I see: some fundamental essentialities have remained unwavering. For example, now as before, they do not even know why they exist in the world. As if this is some sort of secret behind the Seventeen Locks!.."

"Behind the Seven Seals," the grey little man corrected him absently.

"Yes. Of course. Behind the Seven Seals… Now have a look at them: walking straight through the mud, clinging to each other like sick men… And they are drunk!"

"Oh, yes, that happens here," pronounced the grey little man, distracted from his activity. He marked his place in the notebook with a dirty finger and began to look at the back of the one standing by the window, into the smooth, black expanse under his braid. "It's been happening less lately, but it still happens just the same. You will get used to it, Hephaestus, I promise you. Don't be moody. You didn't used to be moody!"

The one who stood by the window slowly turned and looked at his grey companion, and his companion, as always, instantly averted his eyes, and backing away, scowled, as if a scorching heat had puffed into his face.

For the countenance of the one who stood by the window was such that no one would succeed in becoming used to it. It was lean like an ascetic's, cut along the cheeks by vertical wrinkles, as if by scars on either side of a lipless mouth, itself narrow as a scar and deformed either by chronic palsy or cruel suffering, but possibly simply by a deep dissatisfaction with the general condition of things. Still worse was the color of the emaciated countenance: greenish, unalive, suggesting, it must be said, not decay but rather verdigris, disordered oxides on old bronze that has gone long uncleaned. And his nose, disfigured by some sort of lupus-like skin disease, looked like a discarded bronze casting that had been carelessly welded to the statue's countenance.

But most terrifying of all were the gleaming black eyes below the high, eyebrowless forehead. They were huge and bulging, like apples, their whites riddled by bloody veins. Always, in all circumstances, they burned with one and the same expression: equal measurees of loathing and fierce, rabid aggression. The eyes' gaze acted like a cruel blow that brings on ringing, half-swooning silence.

"It is not moodiness," pronounced the one standing by the window. "Even before, I hated drunks, all those devourers of toadstools, of poppy, of hemp… Maybe that is what I should have started with, but there would have been no time for it, after all! And now, I see, it is already too late… You surely noticed: yesterday's client presented himself drunk! To me! Here!"

"But they are frightened!" said the little grey man reproachfully. "Try to understand them, Weaver, they are afraid of you! Even I am sometimes afraid of you…"

"Fine, fine, we have already talked about that… I have already heard all that from you: that man is intelligent does not always mean an intelligent man… Homo sapiens means the possibility of thinking, but not always the ability to think… and so on. I do not occupy myself with self-solace, and do not advise you to do so… Here is the thing: let me have an assistant here. I require an assistant. A young, educated, well-raised person. I require a person who can meet the client, can help him put upon his coat…"

"Put on," pronounced the little grey man very quietly, but the one who stood by the window heard him.

"What?"

"You should say 'put on his coat'."

"And what did I say?"

"You said, 'put upon'."

"And what should I say?"

"You should say 'put on'."

"I do not sense any difference," the one who stood by the window said imperiously.

"And just the same a difference exists."

"Fine. All the more reason. That is what I am saying: I need an educated person who knows the local dialect to perfection."

"The young people these days, Ironsmith, know their own language poorly."

"And just the same, it is precisely a a young person I require. It will be uncomfortable for me to command an old person, and I intend precisely to command."

"Here no one does anything for free," hinted the little grey man with a cynical smirk. Neither the old nor the young. Neither the well raised nor the louts. Neither the educated nor the ignoramuses… Except maybe some enthusiastic drunk, but even he will be in expectation the whole time that they will bring him a little something. Out of respect."

"Well, so be it. No one is going to force him to work for free… How talkative you are, though. Do you have anyone in mind?"

"You're lucky, Khnum, I have in mind a suitable individual. Forty years old, a PhD in mathematical physics, so well-bred that he can use knife and fork, practically doesn't drink. And as concerns his life essences, pictured separate from the body…"

"Spare me! Spare me your deals! You would do better to tell me what he will ask. His price!"

"I don't know very much about that, Ilmarinen. I guarantee, however, that his request will amuse you. Whether you will be able to fulfill it is another matter!"

"Even so?"

"Precisely so."

"And do you believe that this lies beyond the bounds of my abilities?"

"And do you still believe that you can do anything in the world?"

The bloody-black apple glanced at the little grey man from over the left wing, and the little man again shrank and lowered his eyes.

"Tame your foul tongue, slave!"

A baleful silence fell, and only after several long seconds did the untamed little grey man mutter:

"Well why do you have to be so pompous, my Ptah? Just call me Ahasuerus Lukich."

"What sort of nonsense is this?" the one who stood by the window pronounced with loathing. "Why.. Ahasuerus?"

First published in Russian: 1988
Translation by Kevin Reese

DOORINDA

(EXCERPT)

That's when police captain Chernishev realized: this was exactly how the onset of schizophrenia would feel. "Comrades, you're getting this wrong," he said with confidence. "This can't be. Your mystery hand has most likely come from here—"

He pointed at the black drapes that blocked out the light from the window (the window was too close to the theater stage and the light was unwelcome).

Director Berman drew the drapes. The window frame, the sill, the panes – everything was covered with ancient dust and grime. "This window hasn't been opened in a hundred years. Even if you wanted to, you couldn't, particularly from the outside," the director said.

"So you also think this devilish hand emerged from the cabinet?" asked Chernishev, hoping for a definitive no.

"Sounds demented," the director said, "but it's true."

The whole story was pretty crazy.

The incident happened during the *Romeo and Juliet* performance. The director's wife was playing Juliet. Well, the passing years are hard on anyone, so to fit the wife to the part, they'd fabricated this luxurious mane of a wig for her. (As a matter of fact, it had been a while since anyone had seen her onstage in her own hair.) And so there she was, the aging Juliet, standing in the wings and waiting for the prompt. Right in front of her was a three-step staircase that led to the stage. Next to the stairs was a steel cabinet, which was always locked. Past the cabinet was the above-mentioned draped window, followed by a wall with a set of hooks, then a door to the service stairs, another wall, and a passage backstage. Nowhere to hide, in other words.

Our Juliet stood and chatted with her girlfriend from younger days, who back then used to show more promise than Juliet, but was now playing Juliet's nanny. (Consorting with a director does marvels in the theater world.) It was almost time for Juliet to flounce onto the stage like the fourteen year-old she portrayed. Already she had advanced her varicose-veined leg onto the first step, underlit by a dim little bulb – and then all hell broke loose. The cabinet's door opened and a pitch-black hand reached out, clutched the wig, yanked it off Juliet's head, together with all the hairpins, and vanished back into the cabinet.

Naturally, Juliet shuddered, while the nanny flung herself at the cabinet door. It would not budge. Realizing that it was high time to be onstage, but quite impossible to be there with a wretched little ponytail on her head instead of a luxurious wig, Juliet proceeded to thrash around, knocked down a hanging rack of medieval capes, and finally collapsed onto the floor.

A furious director's assistant descended upon the scene, abandoning his console as well as the utterly lost and confused actors on stage. He needed to know why the hell Juliet was late. Seeing her without a wig, he froze, then burst into hysterical laughter.

That was it. A scandal. Curtains down.

And now captain Chernishev was supposed to figure out all this hocus pocus and find the culprit. And it's not like he could expect help from anywhere else.

The theater collective, as usual, was made up of three cliques. Fans of the director's wife comprised the first one. The second, more numerous, represented her mortal enemies. The third clique was composed of those who were above this rat race and worshipped pure art. Naturally, when the sleuthing captain reasonably asked if the Juliet-wife suspected anyone, he was treated to a long list of enemies of both sexes. And then it all broke into chaos and mayhem right before his very eyes. The actors and actresses accused each other of all possible sins, the cliques took to fisticuffs, and the director begged for a Valium. In the middle of the scramble a costume designer ran in from upstairs and broke the news that the wig had been found on the fourth floor. Adorning a fire extinguisher.

Everybody set off to see the wig.

Left on the scene were: Berman the director, Chernishev the detective, and the theater's electrician, the owner of the keys to the cabinet. The cabinet held his stuff, some spotlights, and other valuable sundries. The electrician unlocked the cabinet (with effort, since the lock was hardly ever used). The doors squeaked open.

They saw shelves filled with gadgets. Not enough room to hide even a cat. Reach in there with your arm, and the arm would hit the back wall of the cabinet. As for the pitch-black hand, there was no trace of it.

Chernishev looked at the director suspiciously: what if these people were simply making a fool out of *him*, an officer of the law? The director pointed his index finger at his own temple and twisted it back and forth, like a screwdriver. Juliet checked the cabinet's integrity.

"You know what?" said Chernishev firmly, "this is ordinary hooliganism. You know how many hooliganism cases I have?"

No one answered.

"If you insist, I'll open a case. If you insist."

Juliet sobbed. Now that the wig had been found, there was nothing wrong with having a good cry.

"Where's the exit?" Chernishev asked.

They saw him out.

Once outside the temple of dramatic arts, Chernishev was pleased to see the burbling of normal human life, devoid of anything mystical. He headed down the street with a bounce in his step, and he even smiled at some funny-looking kid. He was leaving the schizophrenia behind.

About two weeks prior to the aforementioned events, the director's wife was lying on a couch at home and growing a grudge. Right above her head, the upstairs neighbors seemed to be rolling logs and barrels and stacking freight containers. Once the grudge reached critical mass, she got up and, still in her housecoat, went to straighten the neighbors out.

A woman in her thirties, also in a housecoat, opened the door. She held a sponge, and a boy of five or so years old poked his head from behind her back. He had a toy truck on a string.

The woman, whose name was Ksenya, would've been pretty, if only she'd been able to dedicate to her looks even a quarter of the attention and resources commandeered to the same cause by the director's wife. Now, however, Ksenya was in a state of cold war with all her family members except her son; so it's no wonder her face and appearance were paying the price. Her haircut was at least a year old. Her nail polish was peeling. Crow's feet had shown up around her eyes, the kind one could easily beat back with fancy imported creams and massage, if only the poor wretch had the time to scout the stores for creams – not to mention perform those daily massages.

As for Ksenya's son, he was the cutest kid ever, with his huge, dark-brown eyes and blond curls. A complete angel. One look at such a charming child, and even a professional hitman would have softened up. But a dramatic actress – not so much. Who knows how she managed it, but the director's wife hated children.

The director's wife said that the child needed attending, that lately he'd been running roughshod over everyone, and that she would complain. She pointed out that her stressful job required – demanded, in fact – that she, indispensable as she was for the arts, rest completely and comprehensively when at home. Remember, by the way, the director's wife concluded, how the child had flooded the bathroom, not a month ago?

Ksenya nodded, sighed, and agreed with everything. She apologized about five hundred times. At long last the director's wife ran out of steam.

"See now, Mishka," Ksenya told her son when she finally managed to close her door, "I told you, didn't I, not to roll your truck around. Now we've made the lady upset."

Mishka felt at fault, and so he hugged his mom and hid his face in her tummy.

"You know what?" Ksenya said, "I'd like to go take the garbage out. But you have to sit quietly and watch TV. Okay?"

"Okay. And after that?" asked Mishka.

"After that we'll have supper, and you'll go to bed. And I'll do the ironing."

In order not to lose time, Ksenya put a kettle on the stove, turned the iron on, pulled a coat over her housecoat and ran downstairs with the garbage pail.

Upon returning, she discovered that she hadn't taken her keys. It wouldn't have been a problem if another adult had been in the apartment. Her husband, however, had moved in with his new wife-to-be, and her mother-in-law hadn't come near them for two weeks now. On top of that, Ksenya and her mother had fallen out over the impending divorce, and had left town to live with her other daughter.

As for Mishka, he was absolutely forbidden to come to the door if the doorbell rang, or to enter into conversations with strangers. That's because just recently some thieves had taken advantage of a child's innocence to break in – and *that* incident had made news all over town.

Anyhow, Ksenya stood by her door, completely at a loss. The situation was both stupid and intractable. Suddenly, noises came from below: wheezing, some unintelligible but ferocious voices, and dull thumps. Then a man ran up the stairs.

He was rather short – just about as tall as Ksenya herself, but astonishingly broad-shouldered, stocky, and red-haired, besides. His skipper's beard was most impressive, a tad darker than his hair and bristling out every which way. He wore a blue beret with a red pompon and a roomy blue blouse along with blue pants tucked into humongous laced boots.

Halting, he asked the petrified Ksenya, "Hanging out?"

Naturally, she did not answer.

"You hanging out here, or what? I'm asking you," he urged impatiently.

"I'm locked out," she said plaintively, while trying to put some distance between the man and herself.

"Stepped out without a key, huh? You silly woman," the red-head concluded. "Hold on, let me see—"

He took a bunch of shiny metal objects out of his pocket, and Ksenya realized that she was facing a hardened criminal. She heard footsteps down below – undoubtedly the police were chasing the red-head. She should have screamed, but – as often happens under such circumstances – her voice was altogether gone.

The redhead inserted something long into the key hole, jiggled it, and the door unlocked. Then with sudden nimbleness he pushed Ksenya inside, jumped in after her, and slammed the door shut.

Ksenya dashed into the corner of the entryway and froze. She had to do something, she thought, scream, call for help, protect her son. But it would be useless, wouldn't it: one squeak, and the redhead would take her down.

He, meanwhile, stood by the door, put his hands on his hips, and began to hum a tune.

"All right then," he said. "Ma'am… look. I reckon I've broken your lock. But that's okay, I'll fix it. It'll be better than new." He went about messing with the lock. Once he opened it up, he pulled out of his pocket another strange object – a snuffbox made of something golden, semi-translucent, and very pretty. Inside lay three rainbow-colored wafers. The red-head took them out, regarded them, wiggled his nose, returned two out of the three to the snuffbox, shoved the third one into the lock, and followed it up with a screwdriver.

"Excuse me—" Ksenya addressed him timidly.

"Not to worry. I told you, it's going to be better than new." He listened to the noises coming from the stairwell, and chuckled. "Boatswain Gangrene's word is golden."

Gangrene? The criminal sound of the name stupefied Ksenya.

The redhead closed up the lock and turned to her. "Don't think ill of me, ma'am." He opened the door, and went out, shutting it.

Finally recovering her courage, Ksenya yanked at the door and found herself face-to-face with a group of men. They were dressed even more strangely than boatswain Gangrene. Above their blue blouses and pants they wore countless belts, criss-crossing their backs, hips and thighs, and snugly attached to these were all manner of terrifying things: Japanese nunchakus, knives sheathed and unsheathed, tubes with handles and other thingamabobs – these had to be firearms – and many other god-awful devices.

"I'll kill the red-headed bastard," exclaimed the leader of the crazy gang. "Feed him to the sharks!"

"A female!" another cried out, and all the cutthroats instantly fixed their eyes on Ksenya.

"My lady," the leader said chivalrously, "Would you be so kind as to… a certain gentleman has advanced up these stairs… red-haired and of a firm build. It's quite likely that you, madam, may have seen this… this scoundrel, may an anchor get stuck up his—"

"—his stern," interrupted the cutthroat who was first to notice Ksenya.

"Yes, yes, his stern," agreed the leader. "Have you seen him, madam?"

"I did," said Ksenya, utterly confused. The boatswain had just left her apartment. He *had* to have fallen right into the bandits' arms. So where was he? She had to assume that he had somehow flitted like a bird up to the top floor and was cowering there now…and of course, a trap door to the attic was there…and to the roof…

"Madam," the leader reminded her reproachfully. "The clock is ticking and we are waiting—"

Silently, Ksenya pointed up the stairs.

"We've just been there!"

This puzzled her so much that she couldn't even shrug, and just stood there like a statue. The bandits got nothing more out of her.

"He escaped," stated the leader. "Virgin Mary, what a man won't do to save his most eminent adornment!"

The gang guffawed and tumbled down the stairs.

Ksenya backed into her apartment and quickly locked the door. All of this was terrifying and inexplicable, but at least she was still in one piece, and what's more important, she'd managed to get back into her apartment. Then she remembered about the kettle and the iron…

There was no fire yet. The kettle was boiling, but hadn't boiled dry. Not that long ago, she had completely forgotten about a boiling kettle, so its spout had come unsoldered and fallen onto the stove with a clang, which then had drawn Ksenya back to the kitchen. She'd had to buy a new kettle and she was nearly broke. Her husband had done the part where he dumped her quite promptly, but had yet to begin the part where he paid child support.

Despite all that, as she was making supper for her son, Ksenya more or less recovered her senses, and by fairy tale time she was back to her usual self. A fairy tale at Mishka's bedtime was a must. Without it, Mishka refused to go to bed, period.

☆

It all began when Mishka had intuited the sadistic nature of a children's tale called "Little Doughball." Namely the fact that in the end, despite all his resourcefulness, the Doughball nonetheless died in pain, devoured with gusto by a cunning fox. This realization had made Mishka cry inconsolably, so his mother's solution to the problem had been to come up with a different, happy ending for the fairy tale.

Yes, she'd headed down the path of least resistance.

"Don't cry, Mishka," she said, "Give me the book. Here is the fox, here is the Doughball. And here are some bushes. Do you know who's hiding in the bushes?"

"W-h-o-o-o?" wept Mishka.

"A fairy. A beautiful fairy with a magic wand. When she saw that the cunning fox was about to eat the Doughball, she came out of the bushes, struck the fox with the wand and put a spell on it. The fox froze and the Doughball jumped out and rolled off on his way."

They say that no initiative goes unpunished: Mishka liked the new ending very much, and the Doughball's story turned into a series, sprouting new adventures each evening. Little Doughball had close calls with the evil witch Baba Yaga, the hateful wizard Kashchei the Immortal, the villainous Karabas-Barabas and other unsavory characters, and each time the beautiful fairy would spring out of the bushes and strike foes left and right with her magic wand.

As Mishka got older, his mother, being a romantic at heart, began to feed him Celtic myths, medieval legends, and generally all sorts of fictions involving fairies.

"…and then the prince touched the doors with a branch of lilac," She would say. "Who gave him this branch?"

"The lilac fairy," Mishka would whisper, his eyes glittering.

"That's right. He touched the branch to the doors – and they opened all by themselves. So he started walking… and came to a throne hall. There, everyone was asleep: a king and a queen on their thrones, dames and knights, valets and maids, and cooks and cooks' apprentices. Only the evil fairy Karabas was awake. She sat in a corner with her spinning wheel, and around her swarmed huge rats. But the prince did not fear rats.”

“And where was the lilac fairy?”

“She was nearby. She wanted the prince to free Sleeping Beauty all by himself. Well, if the evil Karabas turned out stronger than the Prince, the lilac fairy would have lent a hand, of course.”

The only problem was, even this tale was one she’d already told and retold about fifteen times. And she was wondering where to find another plot with fairies in it. Unbeknownst to her, the plot had already emerged, weaved itself into her life story, and set up its traps. One extra step – and she was going to fall into the first of them…

In the mornings, Mishka traveled to his preschool like a child of privilege, in a company car. That’s because the neighbor’s daughter Angelica went to the same preschool as Mishka, and the neighbor was a man of importance and had a personal chauffeur. After preschool, though, there were no cars. Ksenya picked Mishka up.

It was the morning after the lock incident. “Ksenya, sweetie, can you do us a favor,” said the neighbor’s wife when she collected Mishka. “Can you pick Angelica up tonight? My husband won’t have time, I’m afraid. He’s got a business meeting. And it’s across town for me.”

“Of course, not a problem,” Ksenya said.

“And have her stay with you for the evening, all right?”

“Yes, of course, no worries. I’ll take care of everything.”

Mishka rode off, and Ksenya was alone in the apartment. She had about twenty minutes to wash dishes, brush her hair, and get dressed. She looked out the window. It was raining. She had no desire whatsoever to go outside. Still, there she was, standing in front of her door with her purse and umbrella. Because life hadn’t been kind to her lately, instead of the nice things associated with rain – the fresh air, for example – she was already envisioning all the unpleasant things that come with it: rain splatters on her hose, wet feet, catching a cold.

Schlepping through puddles to the transit stop, pushing through wet bodies in the trolleybus…. Ugh. If only she could open this door – and teleport right to her work, to her warm, dry office.

As she was exiting her apartment, her inner vision produced an almost one-to-one image of the office: four desks aligned pair-wise, a china rose on a windowsill, and Ms. Yeremeyeva, who was always first to come in. Only Yeremeyeva for some reason was wearing a denim dress, which was fashionable, yes, but an odd choice for a fifty-year-old, to put it mildly.

Ksenya stepped over the threshold and instead of a stairwell, she saw in front of her a room with four desks, a china rose, and Yeremeyeva in denim.

"Ksenya, is that you?" Yeremeyeva was surprised. "This early?"

Stunned by the fact that an apparition could talk, Ksenya backed up, shut the door and for about a minute couldn't collect her wits. She'd had enough sleep, so there seemed to be no reason to have hallucinations… She opened the door once again, praying for a stairwell – and there it was, the stairwell.

Naturally, Ksenya went on to soak her feet through and get rain splatters all over her hose – what else? But the most peculiar thing yet was still waiting for her at the office. When she entered, Yeremeyeva looked at her with great suspicion.

"Hello, Galina Petrovna," said Ksenya to her coworkers. "Alex, hey. Alla Grigoryevna—"

"We've already greeted each other today," said Yeremeyeva. "Are you in your right mind, deary? Have you got enough sleep?"

"What are you talking about, Alla Grigoryevna?" said Ksenya, going cold inside.

"Have you had an adventurous night with someone?" Turning to her coworkers, Yeremeeva said, "Half an hour ago the door opens and in comes our lovely Ksenya. I say hello and she looks at me like I am some kind of poltergeist and shuts the door on me – can you imagine?"

"Ksenya," Galina Petrovna gasped, "what is going on with you, sweetheart?"

Alex, the youngest, only snorted.

"I… did—" Ksenya began. Then she noticed that Alla Grigoryevna really was wearing denim.

Fortunately, a phone rang and the workday began. They were the purchasing department of a large trust, so they were kept rather busy, and in under half an hour everyone – except Ksenya – forgot about her strange comings and goings.

She, however, kept mulling it over. There was nothing unnatural in a woman coming to work early. Perhaps she had spent the night at a friend's. Being almost a divorcee, she had a right to stay overnight anywhere she pleased… Let's say she had rushed to work. She had wanted a quiet moment there all by herself. And let's say she saw Yeremeyeva and bolted, instinctively. Ah, when she was young, it used to be so cool to say to her girl friends: "I was so drunk I don't remember that!" Even though the girls hadn't really known what it was like to be drunk.

Presently Ksenya reconstructed her "teleportation." How she'd been unwilling to go outside and how her mind traveled to a warm office where soft house-shoes waited for her, and where a shawl so huge you could wrap your whole body in it was kept on a hook behind a cabinet, just in case. It was that and a china rose on a sill she'd had in front of her mind's eye when she'd opened her door…

And then of course that boatswain Gangrene, on the run from a gang of cutthroats, had tampered with the door. And, as a matter of fact, he had installed some kind of a thingamajig in the lock. The big question: was there a link between today's teleportation adventure and yesterday's mischief by the boatswain?

Ksenya was burning with impatience to go home and find the answer. But she had to pick up the kids first, entertain them before supper, and then again after supper. At last, having tucked Mishka in, she was left alone with her front door.

Which place should she visualize in her experiment? She chose her mother-in-law's apartment. Since she'd lived there once, she knew the place well. She summoned an image of a futon, a cocktail table in front of it, two ugly armchairs – your standard relaxation corner, which her mother-in-law for some reason deemed sacred. Maybe she was just keeping up with everybody else, thinking a proper apartment simply had to have this impractical monstrosity of furniture?

With trepidation, Ksenya pushed on the door –

"Is that you?" said the mother-in-law. She was in the armchair, knitting, and Ksenya was standing in a doorway to the bedroom. "How did you get here?"

Climbing out of the armchair was not so easy for the mother-in-law, while Ksenya could shut her door in a flash. That's why she took her time to watch how the astounded mother-in-law groped for the armrests, as a ball of yarn dropped off her lap.

Back home, Ksenya figured out why she had been standing in the bedroom doorway just now: it had been her most customary vantage point. She went to the kitchen, brewed herself a cup of strong tea and leaned on the windowsill, deep in thought. Fate had handed her something inexplicable. It seemed random and had nothing to do with her virtues and achievements, yet the strange gift gave her power. Yes, power. Up until now, everyone had ordered her around: her parents, neighbors, husband, mother-in-law… She'd been enduring it, seeking solace in adult versions of the same fairy tales she'd been feeding to her Mishka.

You had to give her credit, though: she didn't think up anything unlawful. Even settling scores wasn't on her mind, at first. She just wanted to stay out of the rain and overcrowded trolleys. That's all.

The next morning, that dream came true. Well, not without a small glitch.

In the office, Alex marveled, "You must be a fast runner. How did you keep your coat and your umbrella dry?"

"A friend gave me a ride," Ksenya said.

☆

Little by little, as she experimented with the door, she figured out the rules by which the boatswain's contraption operated. She could visualize any place and then open her door – and she would enter that place through whatever portal was available, be it a window or even a fridge door. Also, she could return only to her own apartment. Once, when she saw an endless line to a visiting exhibition of the French impressionists and decided to sneak in at night and have the place all to herself, she accidentally set off the alarm. She had to flee. She was certain the security guards banged on the door that she had fled through, though she heard no banging.

Soon the contraption delivered another surprise. Ksenya was kind of sweet on Alex, her co-worker. If one's husband had moved out, was it so wrong to attempt to take care of one's personal life? Naturally, it wouldn't have even occurred to her to show Alex that she was interested, if not for the door. One time, very much disbelieving that it would work, she visualized Alex's pleasant face (she had never been inside his home), and found herself in his bathroom, of all places. He was taking a shower and had his hair all lathered up, so luckily, his eyes were closed.

"Babe, is that you?" Alex asked through the foam.

Ksenya closed the door. That's how she learned the contraption could work off a single detail.

At first, she had fun with her new role of ghost, and didn't think of any other uses for the door. Don't we all use things in our own way? Let's say you gave a rock to a housewife, a construction worker, an artist, and a thug. A housewife would use it to weigh down the lid of her pickling barrel; a construction worker would use it in a foundation; an artist would whisk it off to his rock garden, and a thug… oh, no, let's not give a rock to a thug.

Anyhow, being a ghost was quite all right by our fairy tale-loving, drudgery-enduring Ksenya. She really had very little time to experiment anyway. It was the fault of the bad weather that she had to extend the uses of the door.

One day Mishka returned from preschool with a runny nose. Later in the night the malaise worsened. He developed a fever – and not a single pill of aspirin could be found in the apartment. Ksenya cursed herself: what a failure! Her husband, who'd scolded her for poor homemaking, had been right. Maybe that's why he'd dumped her in the first place. Now she needed aspirin and hot compresses – at one thirty in the morning.

At first it didn't occur to her to use the door, and when she remembered it she was in such a rush that she wasn't about to stop to congratulate herself.

She entered a dark pharmacy. She didn't know where the light switch might be, so she had to go back for a candle. Then she snatched the aspirin from a display case. The hot compresses were past their expiration date. She had to search all over. Before she left, she put the money for the medicines in the display case from which she had taken the aspirin.

A few days later there was another hurdle. Suddenly, plain old cream of wheat had turned into a rarity in the grocery stores. It's not that Mishka was that fond of cream of wheat, but it was the item his mother cooked best, compared to some others, like cream of rice,[1] for example.

Ksenya rationally concluded that stashes of cream of wheat were squirreled away in every grocery store. She visualized shelves with bags and boxes of it – and opened the door.

It appeared that the storeroom she entered did not belong to a grocery store. Rather, it was some kind of cellar. There were shelves made of splintery boards, and a potato bin in a corner. In search of cream of wheat, Ksenya went through every box and chest – and oh my God, the foodstuffs she discovered! Choice but inexpensive sausages, buckwheat, canned delicacies; at first Ksenya stubbornly insisted that cream of wheat was all she needed, but when she ran into canned pineapple juice, she gave in to pure rage.

---

1. In the hierarchy of breakfast cereals during Soviet times, buckwheat was considered the most nutritious and hard to acquire. Cream of wheat was the next most favored, for its pleasing taste and texture. The cans of cod liver Ksenya grabs are a Russian delicacy that was much sought after in times of (artificial) scarcity.

Her Mishka had never once tasted pineapple juice in his life, and he didn't even know what a pineapple was. Moreover, if Ksenya ever tried to feed him as prescribed by all these child development manuals, she would have no money left to put clothes on his back. That's on the one hand. And on the other – where the heck did people even get all this yummy stuff?

Her child rightfully deserved to eat fruits and vitamins, just as the neighbor's girl Angelica did. Moreover, he was recovering from a serious cold, so fruits and vitamins were absolutely essential. Feeling no reservations whatsoever, she grabbed two jars of pineapple juice, some cans of cod liver and a couple of other delicacies, and once again left the money on the shelf, fair and square.

Never mind cream of wheat.

The convalescent Mishka demanded attention, and Ksenya used up her sick days doting on him – and visiting the door. But those visits just couldn't go on unnoticed forever. Sooner or later Mishka would find out, and frankly she was getting tired of keeping it a secret. Besides, she was terrified by the thought of him learning about the door from someone other than her.

"Mom, fairy tale time," Mishka said, pointing at the clock.

"You want one about a fairy?"

"Yes, again."

"All right. But after that – sleepy time. Okay?"

"Okay."

She stroked his curly hair and thought she better give him a haircut once he got well – his hair had grown so long that he already looked like a girl.

"Once upon a time, there was a fairy who lived in a faraway country," she began. "When she was little, her mother noticed that she was lonely. 'What would you like to have?' the fairy's mother asked. The fairy wouldn't answer. 'Do you want candy? Tangerines? A kitten?

A puppy?' The fairy kept mum. Then the fairy's mother got it. 'I know what you want,' she said. 'You want a baby brother to play with.'

"At once the little fairy cheered up and said, 'Yes, please, bring me a baby brother right away!'

"But you do know, Mishka, how hard it is to find a good baby brother. The fairy's mother thought and thought about it, and she got an idea. She called up her loyal servants, the white swans, and told them, 'Fly to the Kingdom Beyond the Seven Seas. Their king and queen have three sons. Take the youngest and bring him here. He'll be a baby brother to my daughter.'

The white swans flew on, found the king's palace, and stole his youngest prince. They brought the baby prince to the little fairy, and the children went on to grow up as brother and sister. Once, the fairy had a birthday party. Every guest brought a present. One old fairy gave her a magic mirror, another gave her an invisibility hat, and the third one said, 'I will give you a new name.' 'What is it?' asked the birthday fairy. The old one said, 'From this day on you will be mistress of all doors in the world. You will be able to enter the door to your bedroom and exit into Bluebeard's castle, a hundred miles away. And so they will call you the fairy Doorinda…'"

First published in Russian: 1990
Translation by Julia M. Sidorova

SERGEI LUKYANENKO
1992

MY DAD'S AN ANTIBIOTIC

Half asleep, I heard the quiet rumble of a flyer touching down. The thin, fading song of the plasma engines, the rustle of the wind straying around those smooth surfaces. The window to the garden was open, and our landing pad was right by the house. For a long time, dad had been threatening to haul off the ceramic slabs that made up that five-meter circle and move them further away, into the garden. But he probably had no intention of doing that. Because if he needed to land without any noise, he could just shut off the power. That's a no-no – it's too dangerous and complicated, but dad pays no attention to little things like that.

And that's because my dad is an antibiotic.

My eyes still closed, I sat up in bed, fumbling on the table for my folded clothes. Then I changed my mind and shuffled to the door in my pajamas. My feet tangled in the carpet's long, warm nap, but I deliberately tried to keep them in contact with the floor. I really liked that chunky, soft carpet; you could turn somersaults, jump and do whatever else on it without risking a broken neck.

The thudding outside the window was from the flyer's landing skids. The dull red light of the brake exhaust seeped through my eyelids.

Keeping my eyes tightly shut, I opened the door, and began going down the stairs. If dad had done a loud landing, that meant he wanted me to know he was back. But I wanted to show that I knew it too.

One step, another step. The unpainted wooden steps were pleasantly cooling to my feet. Not with the dead dampness of metal, not with the uncaring, icy chill of stone, but with the living, affectionate coolness of wood. A real house, if you ask me, has to be made of wood. Otherwise, it's not a house but a fortress. Just a shelter from bad weather.

One step, another step… I came down off the last tread and stood on the smooth parquet of the hallway. It's fun to use the flooring to figure out where you are. One step, another step. I ran face-first into something hard and smooth, like steel. Slippery and supple, like fish scales. Warm, like human skin.

"Sleep-walking?"

My father's hand ruffled my hair. I peered into the darkness, trying to make out anything at all. Of course dad had come in without turning on any of the lights.

"Put the light on," I said huffily, trying to duck my father's hand.

Yellow-orange lights began burning in the hallway corners. The darkness cowered, escaping into the broad rectangles of the windows.

Dad looked at me, smiling. He was still wearing the assault force's protective suit, and the pitch-black bioplastic that fit his body so snugly was beginning to brighten. It was adapting to its new circumstances.

"Did you come straight from the cosmodrome?" I asked, eyeing him admiringly. How annoying that it was night and none of the guys in my class would have seen him.

The suit seemed thin, probably because the muscles stood out so sharply under the chameleon cloth. But that was just an illusion. Bioplastic can take 500-degree temperatures and deflect a burst from a large-caliber machine gun. It's flexible on one side. I don't know how that's done, but if you touch the outside, it's hard. It might as well be made of metal. And then, when you put it on (dad let me do that sometimes), it's soft and stretchy.

"We landed an hour ago," dad said distractedly, still ruffling my hair. "We handed our weapons in and headed for home."

"Is everything OK?"

Dad winked at me, looked around furtively.

"Everything's better than OK. The disease has been eliminated."

That was what he always said. But still, he couldn't manage a smile. Even his suit was restless, with the sensors scattered across the fabric twinkling and the indicator panel on his left wrist glimmering in a multicolored pattern that meant nothing to me. The color of the suit was by now impossible to distinguish from the pale-blue wallpaper. If dad stepped over to the wall, he'd drop out of sight.

"Pop," I whispered, feeling the sleepiness slipping away, "was it rough?"

He gave a silent nod. And frowned. And that was absolutely for real.

"Quick march, now, back to bed! It's two in the morning."

That was probably the voice he used to give orders out there, on the diseased planets. And no one dared argue.

"Yes, sir!" I replied in the same crisp tone. But I still had one last thing to ask him: "Pop, did you see?"

"No. But never mind. Now you'll be able to gab with your friend again. The planet will be back online by morning."

I nodded and went upstairs. In the doorway, I turned and saw my dad standing on the threshold, stripping off the flexible, light-blue armor. Leaning over the railing, I watched the taut coils of muscles rippling across his back. I could never be that ripped; I don't have the patience. Dad noticed me and waved me away.

"Go to bed, Alik. I won't show you your present until the morning."

That's cool, I like presents. Dad had been giving them to me since I was just a little kid and didn't know what he did for a living.

☆

When mom left us, I was five years old. I remember her kissing me; I was standing by the door with no idea what was going on. Then she left. For good. She said I could go and spend time with her whenever, but I never did. Because I had found out what she and dad had been fighting about, and I was ticked. It turned out that mom didn't like dad serving in the Assault Force Corps.

Once I accidentally heard them fighting. Mom was saying something to dad, quietly, wearily, the way people talk when they're trying to persuade themselves rather than the other person.

"Don't you see what you've become, Boris? You're not even a robot. They have their Three Laws, but you don't have any. You do what you're told, and never think about the consequences."

"I'm defending Earth."

"I don't know... It's one thing when your corps is fighting the Pilgrim Saboteurs. It's something else altogether when the assault forces are pacifying the colonies."

"I have no right to think about that. Earth decides. It diagnoses the disease, it prescribes the cure. And I'm just an antibiotic."

"An antibiotic? That's true. They lash out indiscriminately too, at the person as well as the disease."

They were silent. Then mom said, "I'm sorry, Boris, but I can't love... an antibiotic."

"Good enough," dad said calmly. "But Alka stays with me."

Mom was quiet then, and a month later dad and I were on our own. To be honest, I didn't feel it at first. Even before, mom had been away a lot. She's a journalist and travels all over Earth. Dad was home a lot more, although once or twice a month he left for several days at a time. And when he came home, he'd bring me presents, amazing things that nobody sells in any store.

Once he brought me a Singing Crystal. It was a little pyramid less than a centimeter across and made of transparent blue stone, and what it did was play – quietly but never silent, not even for a second – an eerie, never-ending melody. The sound changed when it was raining and was louder in sunlight. When you moved it closer to metal, its tone changed. Wrapped tightly in cotton batting and hidden in the farthest corner of the closet, it sings its eternal song to this very day.

And there were the Lota mirrors, and those little sculptures from Rethe – people molded of soft pink plastic that grew up, got old, were sometimes all smiles and sometimes sullen.

But the best present ever was the pistol.

That time dad had been away almost a week. I had been going to school and playing with my friend Mishka (a.k.a. Chingachgook). His parents drove the two of us to the next town for the start of the Laughter Festival. Mishka even slept over at my house several times. But still, it was kind of boring. And dad probably realized that. When he came back, he didn't even launch into the usual stories. Instead, he rummaged a while in his pack and held out a hefty metal object to me. I clutched it for a second without the slightest idea of what this was all about. It wasn't until my hand got tired and I nearly dropped the thing that it came to me: this weapon wasn't a toy. They would never have made a toy too heavy for anyone but a grown-up to hold.

"It doesn't shoot," said dad, guessing what I was going to ask. "I broke the beam generator."

I nodded, trying to aim it. The pistol trembled in my grasp.

"Where's it from, pop?" I asked hesitantly.

Dad smiled.

"You remember what my job is?"

Sure I did. "An antibiotic," I replied.

"That's right. This time around we were curing a disease called cosmic piracy."

My breath caught in my throat. "Real pirates?"

"All too real."

It wasn't just the unusual presents that made me like my dad's work, of course. I also liked that he was so strong, stronger than anyone we knew. He could get a flyer off the ground single-handed, could walk right across the garden on his hands. Every morning, in all kinds of weather, winter and summer, he would spend two hours training in the garden. I was used to it, but first-time visitors who saw my father glumly doing two-finger pull-ups with his left hand or shattering big thick planks set in special stands all over the garden – they were blown away. And when they noticed that he was moving about and throwing those punches with his eyes closed, a lot of them got rattled. When that happened, my father would laugh and say that his work was ninety-nine percent fitness training. After all that, the question would come: What is your job? Dad would give a cheerful shrug and say "I'm an antibiotic." The guest would digest that for a second and then, understanding, would blurt out, "The Assault Force Corps!"

The first thing I did when I woke up was look out the window, sort of checking that I hadn't dreamed it and my dad really was back. But everything was as it should be, with a swift shadow flickering through the trees. Dad was training, cutting himself no slack for having been up half the night. There was a dull thumping. Those wooden targets were having a bad time of it.

I went over to the videophone, a little matte-white panel on the wall. With unspoken hope, I punched in the number – a long one, a whole five digits. The planet code. The city code. The videophone number…

The screen lit up, pale blue, then the text appeared: *The Communications Service apologizes. The connection with the planet Tuan is down for technical reasons.*

Just what I needed, an apology… And so glib! Of course if a planet is in its third day of rampaging rebellion, and the insurgents' heavy tanks have been firing on the relay stations at close range, that could be called a technical reason. Just like a person's death could be mislabeled as "the process of decay winning out over the process of synthesis."

After pushing a few more keys, I left the room. Now the computer would continue redialing on its own every fifteen minutes. Arnis and I had an arrangement only to make manual calls to each other, but today was special. So I didn't think he'd be peeved.

The present was waiting for me in the kitchen. On the little table by the window, where I like to have breakfast. Next to the coffeepot and the sliced raisin bread.

First I poured some coffee. Nibbled on a piece of raisin bread. And only then did I pick up the broad metallic bracelet lying on a box of fruit jellies.

As bracelets go, though, this one was strange. It didn't look like any kind of accessory and even less like some tricky gadget from an assault force kit. It was just a flattened tube of gray metal. A very heavy tube, weighing almost as much as the pistol. There were no buttons or indicators, not even a latch. But no… there was a button, just one. Large, oval, made of the same metal as the rest of the bracelet. It was pressed in, almost flush with the smooth surface. I tried to dig it out with my nail, but couldn't.

I didn't get it, this present. As I finished off my coffee, I put my fingers in the middle of that heavy ring and spun it. It rotated a bit unevenly, as if it had mercury inside or lead ball bearings were rolling around in there. Which was perfectly possible… But how did you put it on? The opening was so narrow that even my hand wouldn't slide through.

Dad came in, dressed only in swim trunks and slick with sweat. He pulled a bottle of cola from the fridge and casually suggested: "Want to take a run to the lake? We'll have a nice brisk dip."

What am I, nuts? Ten kilometers through the woods. After a cross-country sprint like that, anybody would pass on a nice brisk dip in favor of spending the rest of the day sprawled under the nearest tree.

"No. I'm not an antibiotic."

Finishing his cola (just three good mouthfuls for my dad), he smiled. Now he was just razzing me.

"Oh, all right. We'll take the flyer."

I perked up, then shook my head again.

"Dad, I can't. I have to find out how Arnis is."

My father gave an understanding nod. The assault force knew very well what friendship was all about. That's why dad never griped when he was paying the videophone bill.

"The connection will be back up in a couple of hours. We drove by the relay stations and they were in good shape. The antennas are intact, and it's no problem to switch out the equipment."

I gave my father another admiring look. To talk so calmly about it! As if they'd been tooling around in the family car, not driving the assault force's ceramic-clad combat vehicles. Amazing! The planet Tuan orbiting a star called Behlt. Almost forty light-years from Earth. And my dad had been there. Saving people. Treating a disease called Rebellion.

"What's this, pop?" I asked, holding up the bracelet.

"It's the rebels' ID tag."

Explaining the value of a present is an art in itself, no less so than picking out a good one. My dad could do both. Now I was looking at the metallic ring with a lot more respect.

"What's the button for?"

"That's like a signal." Dad had taken the bracelet from me, and was spinning it with two fingers. "We never did make complete sense of it, but as far as we can figure, the bracelet contains a powerful single-use transmitter. The button's supposed to be pushed when the situation's critical, after the wearer has been wounded or captured. It signals 'I'm out' – get it? You can only push the button once."

I got that too. The bracelet's owner had already sent his signal…

"Did you take it off a rebel?"

Dad nodded.

"And how do I put it on?"

"The usual way. Push your hand through, and it'll expand. The metal gives in one direction, like my jumpsuit."

I was all ready to put it on when something dawned on me.

"Dad… how do I take it off? Because it won't expand the other way."

"Of course it won't. It'll have to be cut off. You take a cutting tool, push it under the bracelet and turn it on. The same on the other side. And then there'll be two halves and a smell of burning in the air."

Dad was silent, and I felt, almost physically felt, the tension in him. Whenever dad made a mistake, I would notice it straightway. We understood each other very well.

"All right, then, I'm out of here." He made a vague gesture.

"To the lake?"

Dad nodded, and I was left alone. Holding that heavy bracelet. I looked at it, simply unable to bring myself to push my hand into that stiff metallic ring. The answer was in the bracelet…

How could anyone get it off a rebel's arm without cutting it? Without ruining a once-in-a-lifetime present?

Very simple. All you'd have to do is…

I shook my head. No.

No!

That couldn't be. It was a whole lot simpler than that. A direct hit. Blown to bits by plasma fire. Leaving only his ID tag on the heat-blackened ground.

In a hurry, afraid I'd change my mind, I put the bracelet on. It was unexpectedly warm, as if it was still preserving that spurt of flame. And it wasn't all that heavy. It would be no big deal to wear it for a couple of days.

We lived on the outskirts of Irkutsk. It was a hundred kilometers or so to town, meaning that at night we could see the gleaming needles of its tower blocks on the horizon. But if there's one thing I've never, ever, wanted to do, it's to live in a building like that. A kilometer of concrete, glass and metal, stretching aimlessly upward. Like there's not enough room on the ground…

And I'm not the only one who thinks so. If I were, every megalopolis like Irkutsk wouldn't be surrounded by commuter belts two hundred kilometers across.

Comfortable, upscale, single-family homes and multistory villas mixed in with scraps of forest and the occasional mirror of a lake.

I was walking down the path to Mishka's house. It was an easy walk, maybe too easy. Even if two kids like us ran back and forth to each other's houses ten times a day, they would never wear out anything like this.

The path had been laid by robots following the template of a perfect forest trail that was stored in their memory crystals. And it had come out just as it should.

Behind every bend, behind every unpredictable curve there was something absolutely unexpected to look at. In an ancient stand of pines, there'd be a scenic little marsh circled by all kinds of willows. Or hiding behind an enormous oak would be a little clearing covered with lush green grass. Where the stony bed of a fast-flowing stream cut across the path, a tiny wooden bridge was there to arch smoothly over it.

You could walk along that path forever and never get bored. A fifteen-minute trip shrank down to an instant.

Mishka's house looked more like a medieval fortress. It was a square building of gray stone with small turrets on the corners. Mishka's parents had probably come up with that. They were archeologists and had never met an antiquity they didn't like.

Mishka was waiting for me in the doorway. I hadn't called him, hadn't set up my visit in advance. But it wasn't at all strange for him to be waiting there.

The thing is, he's a sniffer.

Of course there are prettier words to use, but that doesn't change what it is. Mishka smells odors an order of magnitude better than any dog can, let alone a person.

His parents had done a special course of treatment to be sure that Mishka would be born the way he was. But if you ask me, he doesn't appreciate it much. He told me one time that smelling hundreds of odors together is very unpleasant. Like listening to the din of a whole lot of tunes being played at once. I don't know. I would have liked to be a sniffer myself, so I could guess when my friends were coming from a good hundred meters away, just by scenting their odor on the air.

Mishka waved at me.

"Your dad's back," he asked, but it wasn't a question.

I nodded. Sometimes, when Mishka's in a good mood, he likes to show off.

"Yes. Is it strong?"

"Sure. Something charred, tank fuel and explosives. Very strong smells…" Mishka hesitated for a split second. Then he added: "Sweat too. The smell of tiredness."

I shrugged. You got that right, Sherlock.

"Want to go for a swim?"

"At the lake?"

"No, that's too far. In Tolka's pool."

Our buddy Tolik Yartsev – he was seven – had the biggest swimming pool in the neighborhood. Fifty meters long and twenty meters wide is no laughing matter.

"Let's go."

Then Mishka saw the bracelet on my arm.

"So what's that, Alka?"

"A present from dad."

"What's that, Alka?"

He repeated the question as though he hadn't heard what I'd said.

"A present. It's the ID tag of the rebels on Tuan."

"That's where your dad's been?"

Mishka looked at the bracelet with a fear I didn't understand. I'd never seen him like that before.

"What's with you?"

"I don't like it."

An unexpected thought shot through me.

"Mishka, what can you tell me about this contraption? Sniff it! You know you can."

He nodded with the slightest hesitation, as if he'd been trying, and failing, to find a reason to say no.

"Disinfectant," he said after a moment. "It's been processed very carefully. There's nothing left. And a trace of ozone."

"Correct," I confirmed. "The rebel who lugged it around was burned up with a plasma gun."

"Toss the nasty thing, Alik," Mishka said quietly. "I don't like it."

"Not a chance. Dad brought me this bracelet from an assault operation."

Mishka turned away. And in a hollow voice, he said: "I'm not going anywhere, Alka. See you tomorrow."

Just what I needed, a know-it-all. Brimming with scorn, I watched him go. Mishka was jealous of me, that was all. And no wonder. My dad's an antibiotic.

I went to swim at Tolik's on my own. There, my pride unruffled itself a little. The kid listened to my every word with bated breath and a half-hour later was scampering around with a bunch of other little tykes, playing assault forces. After I had climbed out of the pool and was lazily drying myself with a thin, pink towel, I could hear all the "You're dead! Take that bracelet off!" coming from behind their house, a modern heap of huge plastic spheres.

I couldn't help smirking. For the next couple of days this new game, with its loud yelling and deafening "blaster" fire, would give the neighbors no peace. And that was all my doing… Maybe I should have told Tolik that the assault forces do their fighting quietly and stealthily, like Indians?

When I got home, the videophone computer was still redialing. The connection with Tuan hadn't come back up.

I found my dad in the library, sitting in his favorite deep armchair and leafing unhurriedly through a book with the brainy title of *No Peace Among the Stars*. The cover showed a starship breaking apart for no visible reason. When I bent my head a little, the picture shuddered and changed, shifting the illustration into another phase. Now the starship was in one piece, but a dark-blue ray was drilling into its side, somewhere between the main reactor and the crew quarters. Dad carried on reading, acting like he hadn't noticed me. I turned around and quietly left the library. If dad was into one of his old outer-space blockbusters, that was a sure sign he was in a bad mood. Even an antibiotic can probably be sad now and then.

Back in my room, I scrambled up onto the bed and spent a minute wondering what to do. Lying on the the table was a copy of *The Saga of Fire and Water*, an ancient book about war that I had mooched from Mishka's archeologist dad but hadn't gotten around to finishing. Its worn paper pages had been laminated and its cover was completely gone, but that only made it a more interesting read. It was showing me a side of the Second World War I hadn't expected to see. Not that I've ever been much of a history buff…

There was something else to keep me busy, though – the undone math problems that had been sitting on the computer for three days. It wasn't the best idea to put that off, because the teacher could be checking them any time now.

But instead of picking up the book or sitting down at my school computer, I said: "Turn on the TV. News about the uprising on Tuan over the past six hours."

The soft light of the TV screen lit up on the wall. The frames started flickering by one after another, too fast to register. The television was sifting through thirty-plus twenty-four-hour programs, fishing out all the reports that mentioned Tuan. The search was over in a few seconds.

"Twenty-six broadcasts, total run-time eight hours, thirty-one minutes," the blasé mechanical voice told me.

"Begin with the first," I ordered, making myself comfortable.

The logo of the entertainment channel and the title card of the Victor Show flashed on the screen. An artificially young-looking man gave a jaunty wave and said: "Hi! What's got you all so deep in thought, like insurgents waiting for the Assault Force to drop by?"

And, obedient to the unseen director, thunderous laughter rolled through the studio.

"Deselect," I ordered, feeling a disgust even I couldn't understand.

Then there was the solemn tone that introduced the government channel, and a huge hall came up on the screen. A man was speaking into a microphone.

"Events on Tuan have brought home to us the need to maintain the financing…"

"Switch."

The screen filled with a dense blackness. And slowly, smoothly, a coppery yellow bell surfaced from the gloom, accompanied by a long, full-bodied pealing. It was the news program "I Witness."

"Stay."

The bell dissolved, morphing into a human eye. The pupil grew larger, became transparent, giving way to the outlines of armored vehicles, of people carrying weapons. Then the familiar voice of Grigory Nevsyan, the broadcast journalist everyone knew, came up.

"We are on Tuan, the first planet in the Behlt system. The tragedy that has played out on this quiet, peaceful world must surely have touched us all…"

I lay there, listening. About the extremists who had tried to seize power on Tuan. About the residents being suckered into the rebellion. About the members of the Assault Force who had risked their lives to restore order.

"Some are calling the use of assault weapons a crime. But isn't it twice as criminal to drag teenagers, children, into your political games?" Nevsyan was asking. "There were twelve- and thirteen-year-old boys fighting on the rebels' side. They were issued weapons and ordered not to give themselves up."

Now I was mad: how low was that? Kids of my age – that meant Arnis could have been one of them. He could have been ordered not to surrender…

"Not one of the rebels… I'll say that again: not one… was taken prisoner. Once cornered, they kept firing until they ran out of ammunition and then blew themselves up with grenades. Now here's a thought, and it's a no-brainer: that kind of fanaticism can only be achieved through hypnotic suggestion."

"Off," I commanded, rolling onto my back. I lay there, looking at the ceiling. Time to order some soothing music with a smooth drop in volume and a seamless transition into the rustle of falling rain. And when morning came, something lively and feisty to wake me up…

The videophone summoned me with a cheep and announced respectfully: "Call accepted. Contact in twenty seconds."

I jumped up. Rushed to the screen. Stood in front of the camera's round, bluish lens. Contact in twenty seconds.

Station antennas hundreds and maybe even thousands of kilometers away were preparing to hurl my call upward, into space, as a coded signal compressed into milliseconds. Somewhere high above the planet, parked in a geostationary orbit, the automatic relay stations would take over, transferring the message via modulated laser beam to the interstellar transmitter, a sphere two kilometers across moving in an independent near-solar orbit. And from there, translated into the language of gravitational pulses and packaged together with thousands of other messages, the signal would take off, into the cosmos. In deep space, near Behlt, the local station antennas would pick it up. And then it would all go in reverse order.

The screen was glowing with a calming emerald light. "*Wait*," it said. But I didn't need any convincing; I'd already waited all day. Now I'd stay in front of that screen through the night if I had to.

The screen came to life. The picture was out of focus for a second, then adjusted. I saw a wood-veneer wall and in front of it, a woman with a tired face. Arnis' mother. She was wearing a severe dark suit, and I suddenly realized that the subjective time on our planets was in sync. So, then, it wasn't likely that I'd dragged her out of bed. But still, I was horribly uncomfortable.

"Hello," I said awkwardly. "Good evening."

Her name had suddenly slipped my mind altogether. And the harder I tried to remember it, the more firmly I forgot it.

The woman on the screen stared at my face for several seconds. Either the videophone image was still too fuzzy or she simply didn't recognize me. We had seen each other two or three times at most, and then only on a video recording.

"Hello," she said, without a hint of surprise. "You're Alik, Arnis' friend."

"Yes," I gladly confirmed. And for some reason, I added: "We were at sports camp together last summer."

She nodded. And carried on looking at me in silence. With a look that was off-kilter somehow. Indifferent.

"Is Arnis asleep?" I asked uncertainly. "Can he pick up?"

Her voice lost even more of its color.

"Arnis isn't here, Alik."

I got it. I got it straightaway, perhaps because, despite what my rational mind had been telling me, this is what I'd been afraid of. But still I asked again, stubbornly refusing to believe.

"Is he asleep? Or out somewhere?"

"Arnis isn't here anymore," she repeated, adding only one word. A crucial word. Arnis isn't here *anymore*.

I heard my own voice: "It's not true!" Then I was shouting, not understanding what I was saying, "It's not true! It's not true!"

And that was when she cried.

It always scared me when grown-ups cried in front of children. It's not normal, it's unnatural. I would start feeling like I'd done something bad, would start saying all sorts of dumb things – how I was going to be better, stuff like that, even though I hadn't done anything wrong.

But this time I didn't give a rip about all that. Arnis, my friend, my truest friend in all the universe, the one I'd spent two months with in Florida and would never see again, was dead. Killed. People don't die of colds in a war.

"Tell me. Tell me what happened," I begged her. "I have to know, I need to know."

And why exactly did I have to? Because Arnis was my friend? Or because my dad was an antibiotic that had taken too long to cure a disease?

"He was with the insurgents," she said quietly. So quietly that the idiotic videophone automatically regulated the sound, making her whisper so loud it was almost deafening.

She was talking, and crying all the while. And I listened. Hearing how Arnis had left the house and she hadn't been there in time to stop him. How he had called home, proud as could be, to announce that they'd given him a real military machine gun. And how she found out that the insurgents had been issued not only machine guns but also devices that would automatically self-destruct after the wearer was dead. And that Arnis, thank God, hadn't been given one of those devices, so she'd be able to bury him. His face was peaceful, though. He had felt no pain. The neutron ray had killed him instantly. And he had almost no visible wounds, just a little red spot on his chest... where the ray had hit... and his hand... with a laser...

She was talking, probably unaware right now that I was from Earth. From the great planet that had sent the antibiotic assault forces. The ones who had destroyed the insurgents, and the little boys who just couldn't wait to play with real machine guns.

We'd enjoyed playing war in Florida too.

Of course she didn't remember who my father was. So she could look me in the eye. But I couldn't look at her the same way. And when she stopped talking but kept on crying, turning away from the videophone camera's unpitying eye, I reached out to the keypad and cut the connection.

It was dark and quiet in my room now. There was only a branch swaying in the wind and stroking the window with a soft rustling sound.

"Lights!" I roared. "All the lights!"

The lights blazed, every single one in the room. The matte dome lights on the ceiling, and the crystal chandelier, and the night-lights with their dark orange glass, and the table lamp on its thin, flexible stem.

The light was blinding. It cut the silence that hung in the room to shreds. And the silence came back to life, sidled over to me, crawled into my ears. Even the branch outside the window had stopped swaying.

"Music! Loud! News program! Educational program! Loud! Cycle through the radio programs! Loud!"

The silence exploded, vanished, turned into nothingness. Modern rock blasting in surround-sound, one radio program following another every three seconds. On the TV screens, lessons in the subtleties of Italian, instructions on how to grow orchids, the latest news…

"Stay with the news!" I yelled, in a pointless shouting match with the racket. "Everything else off, stay with the news!"

The din stopped. The familiar name of the planet had already disappeared from the news screen. Now they were showing us smoking ruins. Little human figures in glossy fireproof suits were meandering among mounds of concrete.

"… of enormous force. Not only the morgue but also the attached hospital complex have been destroyed. A spokesperson for the security forces has refused to rule out the possibility that a terrorist raid was responsible for that. It was this morgue that only twenty-four hours earlier had taken delivery of a group of insurgent fatalities that, contrary to their usual practice, had not blown themselves up but had died fighting."

The title card for the news on the hour flashed onto the screen.

"Turn off," I ordered, without thinking. And I looked at the bracelet.

It was a very good idea, a device that explodes after the combatant's death. With a brief, two- or three-minute lag, so that whoever had killed him would have time to approach the body. A device like that could be made to look like a bracelet, but one that was impossible to remove. Could be equipped with a pulse monitor and a payload of powerful explosives, or, even better, a plasma charge with a magnetic trigger.

And it would need a delay too, for when a group was fighting together so an immediate explosion wasn't wanted. For example, a button that could be depressed to postpone the blast for twenty-four hours. Even an explosion like that could do a lot of damage to an enemy who didn't know the secret. It would be best, of course, if the stupid enemy got the bracelet off and took it as a souvenir. But if he gave it to his son, that wouldn't be such a bad thing either.

I tugged on the bracelet with all my might. But the tube that had given so easily when I'd shoved my hand through wasn't budging now.

I tried to pry it open with a screwdriver, to widen it and tear it off that way. But that was useless too. That bracelet had been made by some smart, savvy engineers. They were probably the only ones who knew how to release it.

In a mindless frenzy, I started tearing at the bracelet with my teeth. And I smelled a light, pleasant odor.

What had I been thinking? Mishka could never have picked up the odor of ozone hours after a shot had been fired. Ozone, the triatomic molecule of oxygen, is one of the most unstable compounds ever. But it's given off by working electronic devices and by magnetic booby traps with a plasma charge.

Death had latched onto my arm. A fearsome, fiery death that was determined never to release its prey. But suddenly, that no longer frightened me.

This was not my death. It had been intended for Arnis. Dad had brought it to me, even though he hadn't known what he was doing. An unthinkable coincidence had become valid simply because it was unthinkable.

Slowly, like a sleepwalker, I walked to the door. The carpet's soft pile… the chill of the wooden steps…

I pushed open the door of dad's bedroom. And entered the room where the weary antibiotic was peacefully sleeping.

Settling into an armchair at the head of dad's bed, I still didn't know what I was going to do. Wake dad up; doze with my head resting on the cold bracelet; or sit for a minute and then go into the forest, as far away from the house as I could. Whatever I did, it would make no difference.

But dad woke up anyway.

Jumping nimbly out of bed, he turned on the light with an imperceptible movement. He relaxed a little when he saw me, then was immediately tense again. He asked his question with a shake of the head.

"Pa, this bracelet's a bomb on a timer," I said, almost calmly. "I won't waste time explaining. But that's for sure. It will explode twenty-four hours after its first owner died… give or take. Do you remember when you killed him?"

I've never seen my dad go so pale so fast. An instant later he was standing next to me and was trying to yank the bracelet from my arm.

I howled. I was in a lot of pain and a little annoyed that my clever dad was doing something so clueless.

"Dad, you won't get it off. It was sized for a boy. Do you remember if he had a mole on his left cheek, pop?"

Dad glanced at his watch. And went over to the videophone. I figured he was going to call someone. But instead he punched through the wood-veneer panel to the left of the screen. And reached into the small opening and pulled out a pistol with a long, mirror-bright barrel ridged with heat-dissipating channels.

That was when I got scared. A member of the assault forces who kept a functioning weapon at home faced being kicked out of the Corps and having to pay a whopping fine. And if the weapon was fired, there'd be prison time.

"Pop," I whispered, staring at the pistol. "Dad…"

Dad grabbed me, slung me over his shoulder. And bolted to the door. He didn't say anything, probably because there was no more time for talking. Then we sprinted through the garden.

He jumped into the flyer cabin and started keying in the distress-call program on the console. He had flung me onto the rear seat, and a second later threw the pistol back there too and the first aid kit.

"Take a double dose of painkiller," he ordered.

Frightened as I was, I almost laughed. A painkiller just before a plasma charge exploded? That's like bringing a penknife to an elephant hunt.

Still, I found two tiny, bright-scarlet ampules. Crushing them in my fist, I clenched my fingers, feeling the icy cold of the medicine oozing through my skin. My head spun a little.

Dad was running the flyer at its top speed. The air wailed as the cabin's transparent canopy split it apart. Did he really think that someone, somewhere could help us? Would have time to help us?

The flyer braked, hung in the air. The shriek of the high-powered motor transitioned to a soft roar. We were hovering in the night sky, two people in a miniscule husk of metal and plastic.

"We're above the lake," dad said, adding a clarification that meant nothing to me: "Can't be done above the forest. A bunch of animals would die, and the animals haven't done anything wrong."

He pressed something on the console, keying in commands I didn't know. The safety routine chirped – it wasn't pleased – and the cabin canopy rolled slowly back. With a kilometer between us and the ground!

The cool night breeze slid over us. There was a faint smell of water. And of ozone, that damned ozone – not from the bracelet, of course, but from the running engines.

Dad clambered into the rear seat. The flyer rocked a little, and I saw down below the dim glistening of a smooth expanse of water.

"Hand," dad commanded. And I obediently laid my hand on the cabin's outer ledge. Dad sat next to me, pressing me against the seat back with his whole body. When he took me by the hand, my fingers sank into his broad palm. It was very cold. And hard, like the fabric of his protective jumpsuit.

"Don't be scared," dad said. "And you'd better not look. Turn away."

My breath caught in my throat. My body went limp. I realized that I wouldn't be able move now. I wouldn't even be able to turn away.

Dad picked up his pistol. For a second longer I felt his fingers. And then a blinding white light flashed in the darkness.

I'd never known real pain before. All the pain I'd had to that point was just a preparation for this – the one, the only, the real, the unbearable. A hurting that no human being should ever know.

Dad smacked me across the face, driving the cry back into my lungs. And roared, his voice cracking: "Hang tough! Save your strength! Hang tough!"

I couldn't even close my eyes; the pain was forcing the lids to stay open and my body to contort in a tortured spasm. I saw my hand in my dad's. And a ridiculous, pathetic stump where my wrist should have been. And the silvery bracelet slipping off that stump and plunging into the lake.

Five seconds passed, no more. The cabin was beginning to close and dad was pressing 03 on the console, setting a priority flight to the nearest medical center. Then the flash came from below, a piercing, hot, orange light. An instant later, something jolted the flyer. And I watched a towering fountain woven from steam and spray falling back into the reddish-orange mirror of the lake.

Dad was right, as always. Something like that couldn't be done over the forest. It would have been too hard on the squirrels. And the animals hadn't done anything wrong...

They say that the more people love animals, the more they love people. Probably so, up to a certain point. But after that, it's the straight-up opposite.

I came to on an operating table. I was stripped and had sensors attached by suction cups all over my body. People kept coming up to the table, one after another. Dad was there as well, dressed in a white surgical robe and muttering something. The doctors were talking back and forth too as they leaned over my hand.

"It's amazing for a cutting tool to leave such an even wound. There's almost no blood, as if it was done with a laser…"

"Nonsense. Where are you going to find a military laser on Earth?"

Someone noticed that I had opened my eyes. He leaned down until we were nose to nose and said calmingly: "Don't be scared, pal. Your hand's going to be fine. We'll put it back. Just be more careful with tools in future."

And, turning aside, he added: "Nurse! An analgesic cube… and an antibiotic. Best get the Octamycin, 500,000 units."

I burst out laughing. The pain was as bad as ever. It was still gnawing at my arm with its blunt, red-hot fangs. But I laughed anyway, twisting away from the mask with its mind-numbing anesthetic smell. And all the while I was whispering, whispering, whispering.

"An antibiotic… an antibiotic… an antibiotic…"

First published in Russian: 1992
Translation by Liv Bliss

A SPECIAL THANKS

The significant costs of translating, editing and producing the first print run of this book were met by a successful Kickstarter campaign held in January 2015. The following generous souls (and many others who chose to make anonymous or smaller donations) made the vital financial commitments that helped bring this book to life.

A V Tony SCHWAN
Aaron Willis
Abhilash Sarhadi
Adam Hagger
Alexander Burchenko
Alexandra Israel
Aliece Cosby
Amanda Lerner
Amanda Rose
André De Smet
Andrew Blossom
Andrew G. Grant
Andrew Hatchell
Andrew Janco
Andrew Thomson
Anita Byczkowska
Anna Rose Hancock
Anne Freeman
Anne O. Fisher
Annie Platoff
Anonymous
Anonymous
Anonymous Reader
Ansar "Morte" Ashraf
Arielle Saiber
Bengt Henrik Sørensen
Benjamin Hausman

Bob and Ginger Clough
Boris Karl
Brendan M.
Brent & Elizaveta Simpson
Brenton Clifford
Brian Hargrove
Brian St. Clair
Bridget O'Brien
Bruce Clarke
Caleb Pimmel
Carol-Lynn RÃ¶ssel
Cary Meriwether
Chad J. Bowser
Chi-Chi Bello
Christine Aicardi
Christine Watson
Christopher E. R. Richardson
Christopher Goodgame
Christopher Ilyas Shaikh
Christopher M. Rose
Clyde B Alexander
Cory Slep
Craig Smuda
Dale & Mary Frances Stafford
Daniel and Sarah Singleton
Daniel Domer
Darren James Longhorn

Dave Constant
Dave Haylett
David and Carolyn Meisel
David M. Curry
David M. Poole
David Moskowitz
Dennis and Elizabeth Blair
Dennis Roussey
Diane Wakim
Dominic Doneux
Donald A. Thumim, Ph.D.
Donald Laursen
Donald McCarty
Dr. Brett Young
Dr. Madhury Ray
Dusty Jepkema
Effie K. Ambler
Elias Puustinen
Elise Roberts
Elizabeth Brock
Emily Finke
Eric
Eric Doud
Eric Schulzetenberg
Erica Pelta Feldman
Erin Sackmann
Esther Haines
Felipe Burattini
Gary R. Basham
Gerald D. Jones
Giovanna Dessy
Grant McLaughlin
Greg
Gregory Engel
Helen Richardson
Helen Treasure
Henry L.
Holly C. Gaffney
Hugh Charles O'Connell
James Corker
James Holbrook
James W. Wood
James Young

Jane Robin Shaw
Janet Miller Anderson
Janet Whatmough
Jayson Shenk
JD Talasek
Jeanne McIntosh Branson
Jeffrey J. Hanson
Jennifer L Edwards
Jennifer L. Guernsey
Jennifer Roberge
Jeremy M. Gottwig
Jeremy W. Frutkin
Jesse Toldness
Jewel
Jim McHugh
Jim Richardson
Joan Bridgwood
John Carter McKnight
John Hiller
John Lunney
John R. Cross
John Shahan
Jon S.
Jonathan D Abolins
Jonathan Waterlow & Andy
    Willimott
Jordan K. Voellinger
Joseph Schlegel
Joseph William Bishop
Josh Bird
Juli Mallett
K. JoAnn Clendenen
Katherine Bowers
Kathleen Evans
Kathleen Macfie
kaz
Kern D. Lunde
Kirk Gee
Kitty Ang Shi Yee
Krista Hanson
Kurt Phillips
Lara P.
Larissa Bainbridge

Laura A Burns
Lisa McLendon
Lucian
M. T. Anderson
Madeline S Francis
Madelyn Carey
Maria and Don Essig
Marion L. Kiker
Mark & Lynn Gwynn
Matt Smith
Matthew Derby
Matthew Hipple
Matthew Pattemore
Michael Brown
Michael E. Taylor
Michelle O'Brien
Mike "Moke" Quijano
Mike C.
Mike Lynch
Millie Kim
Miri Mogilevsky
Natasha Kalina
Neala Schleuning
Ng Jun Siang
Nina Allan
Noah Donner-Klein
Oleg Krapilsky
Paige Westmoreland
Patrick B. Ludwig
Patrick H. DeVito
Patrick J. Pelham
Paul Andolina
Paul M Selker
Paul Morisset
Peter Merrill
Peter Moody
Peter Morley
Peter R Brooks
Phil Siddle
Piotr i Bożena Imach
Pls do not include name
Ralph Kreisl
Rebecca D. Flowers

Renata Breytman Kersus
Richard Leitao
Richard Rossi
Rob McArthur
Robert Cole
Robert J. Young
Robert Phillips
Robert R Narmore Jr
Robin L. Bayless
Romney Maron Manassa
Ryland Aziz
S. Bennett
Sage Deranek-Williams
Samantha N.
Sandy Newman
Sarah Paris
Scott Russell Griffith
Shannon Donnally Spasova
Sharon Altmann
Sidney A. Fein
Stacia Street
Stanford Maxwell Brown
Stefanie Dooley
Stella Sick
Stephanie Elko
Stephanie Trinity Turner
Stephen P. Suelzle
Steve and Liz Boulay
Steve Burnett
Steve Dean
Steven Dengler of
    Dracogen.com
Steven Rodger McSwan
Stuart James
Tamara Vardomskaya
Tania Jane Louise Campbell
Taradash
Tatyana Rodzinek
Ted Buter
Terry W. Brandsma
Thom Serrani
Thomas Mikkelsen
Thomas Negovan

Tiffany and Anthony Stanley
Timothy Hay
Timothy Youngs
Tjaart de Beer
Tom & Becki Lee
Tom Harrington
Treve Hodsman
Tsvetelina Yordanova
Ugo Corti

Vinton Eberly
Visalachy Sittampalam
William B. Spencer
William Benton Whisenhunt
William Squibb
Yuriy Kudelin
Zack Moxley

ALSO THANKS TO

Artyom Ancharov
Artur Artenyan
Nikita Babichev
Irina Belichenko
Robert Chandler
Ekaterina Drugal
Fantlab.ru
FTM Agency
Taisia and Alan Yefremov
Vladimir Gusev
Nikita Kazantsev
Yana Kisileva
Andrei Konstantinov
Maxim Korzavchikov
Pavel Krasnov
Olga Tideman
Sergei Lukyanenko
Andrey Malyshkin

Mikhail Manakov
Zinaida Medvedeva
Maria Ordynskaya
Sergei Paltsun
Eugene Permyakov
Nina Polosukhina
Franz Rottensteiner
Grigory Ryzhakov
Victoria Savchenko
Matthias Schwartz
Galina Shepkina
Andrey Skorobogatov
Kira Soshinskaya
Ilya Sukhanov
Dalia Truskinovskaya
Dmitry Tsvetkov
Words Without Borders
Aigul Yangalina
Victor Yurovsky

To order additional copies of *Red Star Tales*, or any of the other
fine Russophile fiction published by Russian Life Books,
visit our website at store.russianlife.com,
call us at 800-639-4301 (802-223-4955).

Russian Life Books
PO Box 567
Montpelier, VT 05601

www.ingramcontent.com/pod-product-compliance
Lightning Source LLC
Chambersburg PA
CBHW031607180726
48284CB00005B/1435